Home is the Prisoner
The Little Lie

Two Novels by
Jean Potts

Introduction by J. F. Norris

Stark House Press • Eureka California

HOME IS THE PRISONER

Published by Stark House Press
1315 H Street
Eureka, CA 95501, USA
griffinskye3@sbcglobal.net
www.starkhousepress.com

ISBN-13: 978-1-944520-90-8

Book design by Mark Shepard, shepgraphics.com
Cover Art by James Heimer
Proofreading by Bill Kelly

First Stark House Press Edition: February 2020

HOME IS THE PRISONER

Jim Singley has served his time. Accused of killing his business partner, he left a lot of bad feelings in Athena—but now he's back. Back to a wife who hates him, a son who has been raised to despise him, and a town full of folks who wish he were dead. But Jim has some unfinished business. There is his former partner's wife, Audrey, now married to someone else. And her daughter, Cleo, the only one who spoke up for him at the trial, corroborating his defense when no one else would. There's Matt, his only real friend, harboring a long-kept secret. And Wayne, the son who has been raised to hate, ready to explode with unanswered questions. Athena is a town that can never forgive, but Jim won't leave until he's confronted them all.

THE LITTLE LIE

Everyone knows that Dee and Chad will eventually get married. They're such a perfect couple. So when boarder Mr. Fly overhears them having an argument that results in Chad's moving out, he assumes that they will soon make up. But Dee knows that it's over. She just can't stand the public humiliation. So she lies about it. Just a little lie. She tells everyone that Chad has moved to the city to pursue a new job. Then she tells everyone he's headed for California, where she will no doubt soon join him. She even convinces herself that it's all true. Still, when the plane that Chad is supposedly on crashes, and someone with his last name is listed as a passenger, Dee breathes a sigh of relief. Her secret is now safe. But is it...?

Deadly Flights of Fancy
By J. F. Norris

In this latest reissue of Jean Potts work Stark House has paired up an interesting duo of her novels that complement each other by exploring two polar opposites, and feature two recurring motifs found in Pott's fiction. In *Home Is the Prisoner* (1960) we have a male protagonist stirring up the past, uncovering lies, exposing secrets in an attempt to clear his name for a murder that he was sent to prison for. Like many detective novels the pursuit of truth is the primary motivator here and yet no one seems to be interested in being truthful other than Jim Singley. Our protagonist in *The Little Lie* is female, making for a nice contrast in point of view from the first novel. The motivator in this case, as the title suggests, is deceit. Dee Morris is living in a world of her own design, comfortable with fibbing in order to protect her sheltered microcosm, ignorant and uncaring of the consequences her lies will have on the people in her life.

In each case we have characters attempting to preserve their place in the world. Jim is mindful of his family and the need to regain trust and love (especially from his son Wayne) by revealing the truth of his tarnished and violent past. Dee, self-involved to an almost pathologic degree, tells lie after lie in order to protect herself and herself alone in a dangerously imagined alternate reality.

Jean Potts is often lumped in with other woman crime fiction writers of her era like Margaret Millar and Charlotte Armstrong, who shared with Potts a fascination for the dark underbelly of American suburbia. But I would dare to suggest that Potts belongs in a class by herself for she is the bridge between the domestic suspense, the specialty of those other women writers, and the noir crime fiction of her male colleagues. While *Home Is the Prisoner* is ostensibly constructed like a detective novel, Potts is not solely concerned with ex-con Jim's transformation into an amateur sleuth eager to solve the crime he never committed. Potts uses the solving of the murder mystery as a framework for plumbing the emotional depths of her characters. The word "hate" appears on almost every page. When characters dare to speak of their emotions nothing is held back, arguments explode. For much of the book emotions are at a fever pitch. In one key moment Potts describes Elroy's torrent of rage as "snarling" in "a climax of invective." Along the way we also get some interesting commentary on juvenile delinquency, mental illness and its hereditary taint, random gun violence, and whispers of police corruption, making the novel seem extremely topical and resonant for our troubled 21st century America.

Potts has a talent for penetrating character sketches deftly drawn with a few choice words and clever turns of phrase. Her innovative descriptions often exhibit a theatrical flair. Like a true theater artist she also knows that costuming adds to character as in this passage:

"...she had a good deal of elegance in spite of the shabbiness of her clothes. A kind of ostentatious shabbiness; as if she were going out of her way to prove that she was Poor but Proud. Today she wore a navy blue suit, very neat, very shiny and a hat that looked vaguely familiar to [Mack]. A hand me down from Marge? Probably. It was a hat whose spirit had been broken. The little knot of once perky flowers in front was wilted now and the bit of velvet ribbon drooped forlornly. But beneath it Velma's fine featured face was still innately elegant. A maximum of distinction, a minimum of warmth."

Those last eight words are what I like to call the Potts punch. Like a sudden left jab in boxing match Jean Potts will give you a dainty description and then go in for the kill with a few perfectly chosen words. That paragraph artfully sums up Velma Carson, Jim's ex-wife in *Home Is the Prisoner*, giving the reader an indelible and innovative image. We know who we are dealing with for the rest of the scene and for the rest of the book.

Similar to the first Stark house volume of Potts work (*Go Lovely, Rose / The Evil Wish*) in which the power of the imagination possesses the characters and leads them to their inevitable fates, *The Little Lie* presents another example of a Potts woman who has been imprisoned by her thoughts and perverse imaginings. In Dee Morris Potts has created one of her most unnerving and deeply disturbed characters. The story hits all the right notes, focuses on the lives of women and their husbands (or in the case of Dee, her intended husband) with the perceptive plot gimmick, a seemingly innocuous lie, serving as the catalyst for all that follows.

Even the slightest interference will only add to the snowballing trouble. The elderly schoolteacher Mr. Fly is a well-intentioned interloper who only wants the best for everyone. His habit of eavesdropping (another favorite plot device of Jean Potts) and gossip leads to a deadly confrontation between Dee and her sister-in-law Erna. Mr. Fly appears to be some sort of male version of Dolly Levi trying to spread happiness wherever he goes, but only succeeds in augmenting trouble and bringing about ruin instead. In dealing with his intrusions Dee only becomes more desperate. Desperation makes her intractable. Her every action is about self-preservation. If people won't stop talking and gossiping then she will have to take matters into her own hands and permanently silence them.

While sitting in a tea shop Mr. Fly, like many of Potts characters, indulges in some flights of fancy. He dreams of his Good Samaritan work and how it will affect the people whose lives he envisions he is improving. He fantasizes Dee and Chad, the couple he wants to reunite, talking about him in a moment of deluded grandeur: "If it hadn't been for him we might never have gotten together again. He was only here the one winter, a quiet sort of men, a rolling stone, but we owe him more than tongue can tell." Sipping his tea and drifting off into his own fantasy world, Mr. Fly is no more different than Dee Morris. If only he had the brains to see what damage his interfering will bring about.

Jean Potts began her work as a writer in college on the Nebraska Wesleyan University newspaper. Even at this early stage she was intrigued by mystery novels and is noted for having interviewed in 1935 bestselling mystery writer of the 1940s Mignon Eberhart. When she moved to New York to pursue life as a freelance writer she began writing stories aimed for women readers in magazines like *McCall's* and *Redbook* but even those were tinged with dark motives that would become the hallmark of her crime novels. One of her last published stories, "In the Absence of Proof" (Ellery Queen Mystery Magazine, July 1985), has some resonant key components that recall both *Home Is the Prisoner* and *The Little Lie*.

It is a compact tale, almost a novel in miniature, that includes the discovery of a stabbed body, a quick murder investigation and arrest, a trial and verdict. An ironic coda involves the fate of the main suspect who is acquitted of the murder that the victim's sister is certain he committed. The story is dominated by the presence of the spinster sister who just like Jim Singley is relentless in her refusal to accept that justice was served at the hands of a jury. While evidence is required by law and none was provided to ensure a guilty verdict gut instinct and judge of human character are the guiding forces that lead the spinster to condemn the man in her imagination. She longs for a personal retribution never expecting the final outcome that Justice with a capital J serves up for the very guilty murderer. No escape is possible for the truly guilty in a Potts story or novel.

In this present volume from Stark House you will find two novels that offer up more examples of the trenchant observations that exemplify Jean Potts' work not only as crime fiction at its finest, but as timeless literature that still resonates with powerful truths for a twentieth century audience.

—October 2019
Chicago, Illinois

....

John (J. F.) Norris is the creator of the blog *Pretty Sinister Books*, a celebration of forgotten crime, supernatural, and adventure fiction. Over the past ten years he has contributed essays to an Edgar nominated nonfiction anthology, various internet sites and small press publishers devoted to reprinting the books he enjoys. He lives in Chicago surrounded by shelves filled with hundreds of books still waiting to be read.

Home is the Prisoner
By Jean Potts

ONE

The thing of it was—as Ernie Brewer was to spend many happy hours explaining afterwards—he didn't take it in right away. Well, sure, he noticed this guy getting off the bus when it pulled up in front of the hotel. Right on time for once, right on the dot of three. Ernie ran the hotel, which also served as the bus station, so naturally he noticed whoever arrived in or departed from Athena. There weren't any passengers waiting to catch the bus this afternoon, and there wasn't but the one guy getting off. Just an ordinary guy in a new, bargain-basement suit. He stood with his back to Ernie for a minute, getting the kinks out of his legs, with his zip bag (like the clothes, new and cheap looking) on the sidewalk beside him.

The bus driver didn't linger; with a casual wave at Ernie and a clashing of gears, he was off. *And* the two prolonged toots on his horn that seldom failed to throw Ernie's little dog into a nervous fit. She had been curled up, sound asleep, on her stool back of the desk. At the first toot she started up with a shriek of alarm. At the second she dived headlong to the floor, sending the magazine rack spinning. So it happened that Ernie was hunkered down straightening out the magazines and didn't see the guy come into the hotel. Didn't even know he was there till he heard his voice.

"Hey there, Ernie. You open for business?"

And the thing of it was, Ernie still didn't take it in. Not till he straightened up and found himself looking right into the eyes of Jim Singley.

"For the Lord's sake!" he whispered. "Jim Singley! Where'd *you* come from?" Which was a fool thing to say; having said it, Ernie swallowed audibly. Because he'd always liked Jim well enough, always got along with him okay. So why rub it in, where Jim had come from? To cover up the tactless question, Ernie asked a couple more: "How the hell are you? How you been?"—which didn't sound so good either, once they were out—and extended his hand. He didn't really intend to go that far, but he was rattled. After a minute's hesitation, Jim shook hands with him.

"Have you got a room for me?" he asked. "Or are you all filled up?" Giving Ernie an out, in case he wanted it; the Athena Hotel had never in its history been all filled up, and they both knew it.

Again Ernie swallowed. The Mrs. was going to have plenty to say about this. "Sure I got a room for you. How long you planning to be around?"

"It all depends. Let's say a week to start with." He took out a wallet, also new. "Here. I'll pay you in advance."

They got that settled, and then Ernie bustled around from behind the desk with his bunch of keys and led the way upstairs. And he didn't mind admitting it afterwards, he had a very peculiar feeling going up that staircase with his back to Jim Singley, Jim just two steps behind him, so close he could hear him breathing. Yes sir, a very peculiar feeling.

He didn't waste any time getting to the top, and once there he headed for the handiest door, unlocked it, and stood aside (with a secret, shaky sigh, as if he had escaped something by the skin of his teeth) to let Jim go in first.

"Bathroom's two doors down," he said. "Make yourself at home."

Jim put his bag down on the chair and crossed over to the window. The hotel was on a side street, but you could see half of Main Street from up here: quiet in the thin, early-spring sun, nobody in sight but a few loafers in front of the pool hall and the beauty parlor girl in her green uniform sashaying back to her shop with a container of coffee from The Snackery. You could see the garage from up here, the garage that used to have a big sign, "Singley & Fleming. Sales. Service & Repairs." Changed hands now, of course. And the apartment above it, where the Flemings used to live—it wasn't an apartment anymore. It had been made over into real estate offices. Jim must be noticing that. But he didn't let on.

"It hasn't changed much," he said. "Well. This ought to be a pretty good time for me to catch Mack in his office. He's still in the same place, isn't he?"

"Sure. He's Judge McVey now, you know. But sure, he's still in the same place." At the thought of Mack, Ernie felt an easing up on the strings of curiosity that had started tightening in him the minute he recognized Jim Singley. Of course. Mack was what brought him back to Athena. He hadn't turned his back on Jim; with Mack it was once a friend, always a friend; he had handled whatever business had to be handled for Jim and like as not now he was going to help him get back on his feet. "I guess Mack's expecting you, isn't he?" He waited, but Jim didn't answer, and Ernie's tongue went rattling on of its own accord. "I mean, it won't be the surprise to him it was to me. I don't mind telling you, I like to fell off the perch when I looked up and saw you there."

Still no comment from Jim. He always did have a way of looking at you—level; right straight in the eye. Ernie heard himself floundering. "I mean, nobody figured on you ever coming back here ..."

"I guess not," said Jim. He smiled. Not very much, though; it occurred to Ernie that smiling didn't come as easy to him as is used to. "But I've got a little unfinished business to tend to. So here I am."

Unfinished business. The phrase was like a ball of quicksilver dropped into Ernie's mind, splattering off in all directions. Family business?

There was Jim's wife—ex-wife, that is—so bound and determined to root Jim out of her life that she'd insisted on taking her maiden name back, not only that, she'd even had the boy's name changed; she wouldn't touch a penny of Jim's money, not if she and the boy both starved. You take the average woman, she'd have left town, but not Velma Singley. Velma Carson, that is. The damage was done, she said grimly. The boy was old enough to realize. He knew what his father was, and if they went to the ends of the earth, they still couldn't run away from it. You had to hand it to her; she had real grit, to stay here and face it out. Whether you believed—as she did—the worst, the very worst, of Jim or not.

Was this unfinished business of his something to do with her? Or with the others who had spoken against him? For it turned out that they had quarreled before, the two partners. Singley & Fleming. Never got to the point of an out-and-out fist fight, but all the same. A little bad blood there. Arguments. Sharp words. And naturally, always somebody to hear and remember. Friends, Jim must have thought of them, until one by one they took the stand to get in their two cents' worth of truth, the whole truth, nothing but the truth.

Or—the quick-silver ball in Ernie's mind rolled again, deliriously— could it be something to do with Herb Fleming's widow? All the talk, the never-quite-proved, never-quite-disproved stories that still cropped up now and then, even though she had remarried …

My good Lord, thought Ernie, and look who she married! The man, the very man who had testified the strongest against Jim, claimed he'd heard Jim making threats not more than an hour before it happened. And then up and married the widow so quick it wasn't hardly decent. No sir, thought Ernie with zest, I wouldn't want to be in *his* shoes, now that Jim's home again. I wouldn't, and that's a fact.

They went back downstairs together. Except that this time, giddy though he was with the wine of conjecture, Ernie took the precaution of letting Jim go first.

He waited only until Jim was out the door, headed for Mack's office in the court house. (Which was not on Main Street, either; Ernie still had a monopoly on the juiciest piece of news to hit town in years.) Then he called out, "Hey, Hazel!" The swinging door between dining room and kitchen opened, and Hazel, who doubled as chambermaid and waitress, poked her frowzy head out. "Mind the desk, will you? I've got to leave for a while."

The next minute he was off for Main Street, with his little dog trotting at his heels and the news ticking in his chest like a time bomb ready to explode.

TWO

For six years Mack had been bracing himself against this moment, sometimes with foreboding, sometimes with assurance, sometimes with morbid eagerness. Depending—as he himself was wryly aware—upon such variables as the weather and the state of his digestion.

Well, here it was, and here was he, totally unprepared for what he felt as he rose from behind his desk (rather ponderously; Mack was a tall, heavy, balding man) and stretched out both his hands to Jim Singley. Because what he felt was the simple, pure pleasure of seeing an old friend again. Fresh as a fountain springing up, unclouded from the sludge of doubt and guilt and dread.

"Jim!" he said, while they thumped each other's arms. "Jim, my God, I'm glad to see you! Why didn't you write to me? I didn't know whether you were coming back here or what the hell you were going to do. Jim! How are you?"

"I figured I'd surprise you," said Jim, and at once the fountain lost some of its sparkle. But he was smiling, almost the way he used to; his gaunt face was lit up with what seemed to be a reflection of Mack's own original uncomplicated joy. "You look great, Mack. Excuse me, I mean Your Honor. How's it feel to be a judge?"

Did he notice that Mack's eyes shifted away from his? Maybe not. He was going on, asking about Marge and the kids.

"Fine, they're fine. Well, Bill was in a car accident two, three weeks ago. Smashed up his ribs bad enough to keep him home from college the rest of this term. A lousy break, but he can make it up in the fall. He's doing fine down there at the University. And Sally's finishing up high school this year." He was smiling fatuously. Knew it, and didn't even care. "You won't know her, Jim. She's blossomed out like a—Well, here. Here's a picture of her. Isn't she a good-looking kid?"

Jim took the silver-framed photograph that was thrust upon him, and obliged with an appreciative whistle. "So that's little old Sally! She must have so many boy friends you stumble over them every time you turn around."

"They've thinned out lately. She hasn't got time nowadays for anybody but—but Wayne."

He hadn't meant to mention Jim's son quite yet, in quite this way. Embarrassed, he replaced the photograph on his desk; when he turned back Jim's head was bent over the package of cigarettes he was opening. At last he said, "Yes. I keep thinking of him as a little kid, but of course he's grown up too. Is he—how is Wayne?"

"He's a fine boy, Jim. Handsome. Bright. A fine boy." He was aware of the forced note that had crept into his voice; Wayne Singley—or Wayne Carson, since the divorce—left him lukewarm, if not downright cold. For one thing, Velma's lady friends, including Marge, were always going into transports about what a model son Wayne was, how well-mannered, what a credit to his mother, they only wished *their* sons were as thoughtful et cetera, et cetera. Of course it wasn't fair to blame the kid for that. But somehow it made you suspect him; Mack was ashamed to remember with what keen relish he had snapped up the one or two bits of gossip that had come his way, rumors that Wayne might not be quite such a paragon of virtue, after all. Nothing really serious; the kind of stories you were apt to hear about any boy in town. And unfounded, as far as Mack could discover. He had firmly, regretfully, resisted the temptation to believe them.

No. He might as well face it, the only thing he had against Wayne was that Sally got stars in her eyes at the mere mention of his name. The good old classic pattern of fatherly jealousy.

"He's a fine boy," he repeated. And now that they were on the subject, he might as well mention Velma and get it over with. "You've got to give Velma credit, she's done a good job on Wayne."

"I'm glad to hear it," said Jim. "I'd like to see Wayne, if he—"

"That I don't know. If Velma has anything to say about it, you won't get near him. She's just as bitter as she ever was."

"Can't blame her, I guess," said Jim impersonally, and it struck Mack once more how little he really knew about this friend of his. In spite of their closeness (and in spite of the bit of secret information he possessed, and wished to God he didn't), Mack was still as much in the dark as everybody else about what had actually happened between Jim and Herb Fleming six years ago. The one solid fact was that Herb had wound up dead. Manslaughter, the jury finally decided; death brought about, without premeditation or intent, in the course of a sudden, violent quarrel. But juries could be wrong, and a good proportion of Athena's citizens maintained that this one had been wrong. If so, Jim was not an unlucky killer by accident, but a cold-blooded murderer. The double motive, doubly persuasive: Herb was not only a dishonest business partner, he also had a wife ...

And there again Mack, who of all people ought to know, did not know. Probably never would know, either. Jim showed no signs of having turned into a blabbermouth. And you simply did not ask a man if he was a murderer, a liar, and an adulterer.

"What I do blame her for," Jim was going on, "is the money. Okay, in her book I'm a bastard. But there wasn't anything wrong with my money. Nobody ever said I didn't make it fair and square. She can starve herself to death if she wants to, but Wayne—I meant for him to have that money, Mack. It's his. She's got no right to cheat him out of it."

"I agree," said Mack. He himself had handled the investing of Jim's money in his absence. By no means a fortune, but a comfortable little sum that Jim had kept separate from the assets of Singley & Fleming. If you could call them assets; the firm had wound up bankrupt. "But try and tell her that. According to her, everything connected with you is contaminated. Everything except Wayne, that is, and it wouldn't surprise me if she's found some way of getting around that. She's probably convinced herself it was a virgin birth."

"Yeah." Jim sighed. "She'd like it that way, in more ways than one."

"So there it is. I don't want to be discouraging, but I don't see any way you can force money on somebody that won't take it. Velma won't. And it stands to reason Wayne won't either. After all, she's had six years to work on him, and she hasn't wasted a minute. If that's your reason for coming back here, to try to help Wayne financially—" He paused, but Jim passed up the chance to confirm or deny. "—then I'd advise you to forget it. Incidentally, they're not starving, you know. She has her job at the bank, and the house her father left her. She makes out, one way or another. She's sending Wayne to business school—"

"Business school!" Jim broke in scornfully. "You know where a diploma from the Athena Business School is going to get him. Nowhere. He could be going to the University, along with your Bill, or anywhere else he wants to go." He paused and rubbed the side of his face helplessly. "I don't know what he wants anymore. He always used to say he was going to be an engineer. But I don't know anything about him anymore. I don't know him at all."

A series of little pictures flashed across Mack's mental eye: Wayne as a baby, riding on Jim's shoulders; later on, trotting at his heels like a miniature shadow; last and sharpest of all, in the garage, Jim saying, "Wayne here, he's my helper," and the twelve-year-old face lifted, radiant with love and pride ...

"Maybe he'd like to see you," Mack offered. "No harm in trying, I suppose. Only Velma mustn't get wind of it. I can sound Wayne out, if you want me to."

"Thanks. I better try it my own way. You've done enough for me already."

Again Mack could not keep his eyes from shifting, or his ears from searching anxiously for the hidden significance that might be lurking beneath Jim's words. Were they just a shade too guileless? Maybe, maybe. Could Jim know his guilty secret? Yes; just possibly, from Herb, in that final, fatal quarrel. Or Jim might have divined it. He had had six years to turn everything over in his mind: everything that had been said (or not said), every tell-tale glance and gesture and intonation. Could his purpose in coming back be to settle a score long overdue and by this time swollen to fantastic proportions? Nonsense...

"I've done nothing for you," he said curtly.

But Jim persisted. "No? It was you got me the lawyer. And it was you stuck by me, Mack, when it would have been a damn sight easier not to. I haven't forgotten that. It could have hurt you plenty, just when your name was up for judge—"

"Cut it out," said Mack. He was sweating. "Listen, do you have a place to stay? We've got plenty of room, and you know you're welcome as the flowers of May."

"Not to Marge, I bet." Jim laughed, without rancor. "She's too good a friend of Velma's to give me house room. Or at least she used to be. No, I've got a room at the hotel. It'll do me fine for the present. Till I decide— I guess it's going to take me a little while to get back in the habit of making plans." The halting words trailed off into silence. Six years of it, thought Mack, six years, only somehow Jim had stood it, and that god-awful suit, and now he had come back to—nothing. No wife, no son, a sweetheart—if Audrey Fleming had ever been that to him—long ago married to someone else. And a "friend" who could not meet his eyes.

Mack cleared his throat. "We'll figure it out. No need to rush into anything. Meantime, how about a round of golf tomorrow, if the weather stays good?"

"Sure," said Jim. "I mean, if it won't hurt your reputation—Okay, okay. Sure. I'm probably as lousy a golfer as you by this time." He stood up. "I'll be on my way now. A few things I want to tend to. A few people I want to see." Now it would come. Audrey Fleming's name. (Did he know she had married again?) But it was Audrey's daughter that Jim asked for. "Is Cleo Fleming still around?"

She was, Mack told him. "She's teaching school out in the country this year. The East Ridge District. Matter of fact, Bill ought to be turning up any minute for the car keys, he drives out and brings her back to town every Friday afternoon. Oh, I tell you, Jim, it's l'amour l'amour and nothing else but around our house these days. Close the doors and it comes in the windows."

"I'd like to see Cleo. Only I don't know exactly how to go about it—"

"Audrey's married again," said Mack abruptly. "I don't know whether you heard or not."

"I heard. Velma wrote me." (She would, thought Mack. Trust her not to keep a morsel like that to herself. Probably the only letter she ever wrote him.) "That's why I'm wondering about the best way to get hold of Cleo. I haven't forgotten what she did for me, either."

Yes. There was irony for you: Herb Fleming's daughter had done for

Jim what his best friend could have done, should have done, and hadn't. When he closed his eyes Mack could still see that scrawny, pigtailed thirteen-year-old telling her story, visibly swaying the jury toward their verdict of manslaughter. They had to believe Cleo's report of the quarrel she had overheard because it corroborated Jim's version. It was inconceivable that the dead man's child would lie in favor of his murderer.

"Of course you want to see Cleo," said Mack. "I'll tell you, why don't you borrow my car and drive out after her this afternoon? It won't kill Bill if you take over his chore this once. He can keep her out a couple of extra hours tonight to make up for it. Come on, I'll show you where the car's parked."

They crossed the court house yard together, and after watching Jim drive off Mack walked slowly, heavily back. The familiar dialogue ground on and on in his head: I would have told my story if Cleo hadn't told hers. *How do you know you would have?* Well, of course I would have. No matter if it lost me the judgeship, I would have spoken up if it had been necessary. *But it wasn't necessary, so how can you be sure?* Cleo's word carried more weight than mine would have, anyway. They would have discounted mine, just because I was a good friend of Jim's. *Friend, did you say?* Certainly that's what I said. Friend. I did everything else I could for him, didn't I? I would have done that too, if it had been necessary. *Exactly. It wasn't necessary. So how can you be sure?*

He was inside now, climbing the flight of stairs, turning down the corridor to the door with its austere gold lettering: District Judge W. F. McVey. He had an extraordinary impulse to drive his fist through the glass panel, smash title and name into a million unmendable splinters.

THREE

"The thing of it is," said Ernie Brewer, "I figured you'd want to know about him being back here. No telling what he's come back *for*, of course." He paused and peered, bright-eyed, at the proprietor of Hild's Hardware Store. Ernie had thriftily saved the choicest audience for last. His news was beginning to lose its first sharp kick through simple repetition; it needed recharging. And here was the place and the fellow. Elroy Hild. Ernie wouldn't want to be in his shoes, and that was a fact.

"No," echoed Elroy. "No telling." He had a perilous impulse to laugh. Because he knew exactly what Jim Singley had come back for, only—Ernie was right, all unwittingly, he would never in his life speak a truer word—there was no telling. It wouldn't do to laugh, either; Ernie couldn't be expected to see the joke. No telling. No laughing. No ...

Elroy took a deep breath and said, in very much his usual precise way, "In all probability he's come back to straighten out his financial affairs. Whatever they may be. I've always understood Judge McVey was looking after things for him, so in all probability that's what he's come back for."

"Sure. That's most likely it. Business matters," said Ernie forlornly. Then he brightened. "They say, though, that it affects different people different ways, a stretch in prison. I was reading an article about it just the other day. It affects them different ways. Changes them entirely sometimes. Depends on how long they've been in, of course, and whether or not they figure they had it coming."

"Jim Singley had it coming, all right."

"Well, now. Some say yes, some say no. Judge McVey always stuck up for him. And Cleo, she claimed he was telling the truth. But there was plenty of others—Why, sure, come to think of it, wasn't you a witness yourself? For the prosecution? Why, sure. Slipped my mind there for a minute, it's been so long ago. But it was you told about the dust-up they had right here in this—"

"Right here in this store," said Elroy grimly. "Certainly I was a witness for the prosecution. It was the only course open to me, as a civic-minded citizen. Whether or not it was premeditated murder is a matter between Jim Singley and his God, if he has any, which seems doubtful. I only know what I heard and saw. He showed every sign of being beside himself with rage when he came in here after Herb Fleming. I gathered that he had discovered some discrepancy in the partnership books. He uttered threats. To the best of my recollection, his exact words were, 'I'll get you for this if it's the last thing I ever do.' They left together, and an hour later Herb Fleming was dead. It's not for me to draw conclusions. But I certainly would have felt that I was shirking my duty if I had refrained from testifying."

Again Elroy drew a deep breath. It was the truth, every word of it; Jim himself had never denied it. And it was only the half of what Elroy could have told if he had wanted to. Would have told, if he had not realized ...

"Well, sure," said Ernie heartily. "Only thing to do. And I don't know that I hold with everything it said in that article I was telling you about. I just can't see Jim turning into the kind of a guy that would harbor a grudge, no matter how long they kept him locked up. He'd get mad and blow up, sure. But he never did *stay* mad at anybody. Why, I bet you, sore as he was at Herb Fleming, by next morning he'd have cooled off and made it up if—if—"

"If he hadn't already killed Herb," Elroy finished for him. And this time he did permit himself a short, dry laugh. Not just at the way Ernie had tangled himself up; he saw now the direction of Ernie's verbal ramblings.

"I suppose it's possible," he said carefully. "Maybe that's what he's come back for, to get even with me because I testified against him. If so—"

"I didn't say any such a thing," Ernie protested. "Why, he could have any number of other reasons. There's his boy, he always thought a lot of Wayne, and there's his wife, used to be his wife. How do we know but what— Even if she did turn against him. She wouldn't be the first woman in the world to change her mind. Not that I think Velma Carson's apt to. And then his financial affairs. Why, he could have any number of other reasons. Any number!"

(But Elroy knew, he *knew*; and a feeling of sudden, wild unreality rushed over him. The enormity of it, that he should be standing here socializing, with Jim Singley back in town! Like Nero fiddling while Rome burned. He gripped the counter between himself and Ernie. Solid, reassuring. But nothing he looked at or listened to stayed steady. Ernie's face, and behind him the neatly arranged shelves of paint and varnish; the drawers of nails and bolts and screws, each with its proper label—everything seemed to pulse and flicker. Ernie's voice, too, came at him in waves, one moment amplified out of all proportion, the next barely audible. He held tight to the counter and willed himself not to cave in, please God, at least not in front of Ernie.)

He just managed it. In the nick of time Ernie's voice boomed out: "Well, I've got to be getting along ..." And then from the door, remote but clear, "I never thought he'd come back here. Never in the world."

"No," said Elroy. "Neither did I."

Never? He used to have nightmares at first. He would wake up sweating and shivering, terror pounding his chest. But only at first. Time restored his sense of balance. With each passing year of his orderly, prosperous life, his happy life, the menace of Jim Singley faded and dissolved into absurdity. Come back? Of course not. Nothing to come back for.

It can't be, Elroy whispered to himself. He can't do this to me. I won't let him, I'll ...

He stumbled to the back of the store, where his desk was, and sat down there. Rigid. Not caving in even now that Ernie was gone. He gulped in the familiar, metallic smell of the store. Reality. Hold on to it. His store was real; and his beautiful, modern, happy home was real; and he himself, Elroy Hild, hardware merchant, respected citizen, devoted husband. His share of reality, the product of his own painstaking efforts. No one could destroy what he had built up. No one could take away from him what he had earned for himself.

But there was the other terrible bit of reality: Jim Singley had come back. Against all logic, against all justice.

He kept remembering snatches of Ernie's conversation: "No telling what he's come back *for* ..." "It affects them different ways ..." "I just can't see Jim turning into the kind of a guy that would harbor a grudge ..."

Elroy knew, he *knew*. He sat at his desk and stared desolation full in the face.

FOUR

Friday at four o'clock. That magical hour of the school week when—with the prospect of release so near at hand, two and a half whole lovely days of not being Teacher—Cleo found it possible to love practically everything about being Teacher. Even her pupils.

She stood on the schoolhouse steps in the half-raw, half-balmy April air, watching them straggle off down the road. "Night, Teacher!" they cried, in voices shrill and tender. (After all, the release was for them too.) The Roszynskis shambled along. All five of them had the same awkward gait. The Siegel boys followed an erratic and quarrelsome course, throwing clods at each other and, when they considered themselves out of earshot, shouting obscenities. The beginners loitered, their mittens on strings flapping, their caps crooked, their jackets hanging open. They played endless complicated games, dragging sticks in the puddles along the road. Cleo had to call to them: "Hurry up, Francis! Leona and Stanley are way ahead of you! You mustn't play along the way!"

They turned abstracted faces with half-open mouths toward her, loped obediently for a few paces, dropped back into their leisurely meandering.

Ah, how she loved them on Friday at four o'clock!

Her eyes strayed beyond to the ridge a mile away where, any minute now, she would catch her first sight of Bill's car bucketing along the rough country road, a chariot come to carry her home. Her bag stood, packed and ready, just inside the cloakroom door. She had only to snatch it up, her coat, her purse, the blessed key that would lock the door behind her. Let the usual after-school chores go—the sweeping up, the blackboard washing, the dusting of chalk-filled erasers. It could all wait till (ages hence) Monday morning.

There. Her chariot of deliverance lurched over the ridge, good old Bill, he was always on time, all kinds of weather, how she loved him too on Friday at four o'clock. She dashed inside, scrambled into her coat. One last look around ... Damn, she had forgotten to close the windows, and the north one always stuck. Worse than usual, of course, when she was in a hurry. She struggled and coaxed and tugged, and still the perverse thing would not budge. As if, knowing that Bill was practically here, and that it would have to give in to *him*, it was spitefully making the most of these few minutes. Well, if it thought she was going to give up— While she grappled, she kept track of the sound of the car. Loud and louder. Now it had pulled up in the school yard, and Bill would either honk the horn or yell for her.

But what she heard next was footsteps. He was coming in, then—not at his usual pounding rush—still, coming in. The window must have heard, too. When she gave it one last infuriated shove, it slid down meek as Jesus. "Hi," she began, over her shoulder.

Then she turned all the way round, and saw Jim Singley.

"Hello, Cleo," he said, and started down the aisle between the desks toward her, holding out his hand, his murderer's hand.

What jolted her most was her own lack of astonishment. She had always known, then, that some day it was going to happen? Had been waiting for it, all along? Yes; only not like this, not in an empty schoolroom, with the smell of chalk and Penmanship paper and Roszynskis mingling in the forlorn, dusky air; and, for sound effect, the absolute living end of all banal conversations. Because it seemed that she had asked, "Where's Bill?" and he was explaining about Bill's father and the car, as if it mattered to either of them, only having asked she must at least pretend to listen.

Her eyes shifted from his hand—so unsuspectingly stretched out, so vulnerable to the rebuff that she *might* be capable of—and took in the rest of him. He was not so tall as she remembered. But broad-shouldered and strongly built, with an ease and assurance of movement that even the ill-fitting suit did not hide. (It seemed strange to see him in a regular suit, instead of shapeless, grease-stained coveralls. He had been the "Services & Repairs" part of Singley & Fleming; Daddy was "Sales," so he was usually out somewhere demonstrating or sales-talking when she ran into the garage after school. But Jim was always there, always good for a dime for ice cream. "Young lady," he used to call her, and it didn't make him nervous to have her watch him at work.) She saw it with a pang of triumph: they hadn't been able to grind the sure, smooth way of moving out of him, he still held his head up. But it had cost him dearly to preserve that much of himself. His was no longer the pleasant, uncomplicated face she remembered—on the bony side, with deep-set hazel eyes and stubbly hair. There was wariness in it now, secrecy; it was set in lines of bitter endurance. A lonesome face.

He killed Daddy, she told herself; and, in the same breath, he thinks of you (with every right) as his friend, he's probably come out here to *thank* you! Out of the swarm of childhood memories, the welter of push-pull impulses, those were the only two things she knew for sure about him. Her story, impressive to the jury, must have been doubly so to the man who had killed Daddy. On purpose or not on purpose—she did not know, any more than she knew why he had come back. Here he was, and she was going to have to face in her own mind what she had been dodging all this time. Because the one thing Jim knew for sure about her was the story she had told at the trial.

He had paused in the aisle, but quite close; he was trying to smile in the old way. She still might have withstood the pressure—even the inner pressure that was making such a terrible ache in her throat—except that he called her "young lady." "How are you, young lady?" he said, and she couldn't stand it, she put her hands over her face and broke into a storm of weeping.

To the consternation of both of them. Jim stood helplessly by, repeating that she mustn't cry, while somehow or other she rushed past him up the aisle to the recitation bench and collapsed there, bellowing and heaving. Once she had let go, her own consternation melted into something like voluptuous pleasure, and she wouldn't have stopped, even if she could have. Jim did not interrupt. No coos of comfort from him; no soothing pats. After a while she heard him go out to the cloakroom and come back. "Here," he said, "you want a drink of water?" and he held the glass for her while she gulped. It seemed to sober her up. She blew her nose and said haughtily, "I'm all right now. Thank you."

"I should have had better sense than to barge in on you." He stared at the maze of long division problems on the blackboard. "Only I figured—I wanted to see you."

What was there to say to that? Nothing safe. He added awkwardly, "You look fine. All grown up," and she realized—with alarm—how badly out of practice he was at making small talk. Dear old safe silly small talk.

"I guess I don't look so fine right now," she said. She took out her compact and peered at her drowned-looking face.

"You've turned out real pretty," he said politely. And then, still staring at the long division, "How's your mother?"

They were in the same fix, and it was awful: she had no small talk either. She heard herself blurting out, "She's married again. She married Elroy Hild." The old feeling of outrage swelled in her, unreasonable and bewildering. As if for God's sake it were a piece of treachery, black infamy, for Mother to have married Elroy Hild.

Jim nodded. "I heard."

"Well, why not?" she cried. "What else was she going to do, I'd like to know? She had me to raise, and no folks of her own, no way of making a living. I'd like to know what else—"

"I'm not blaming her," said Jim. In the gathering dusk he turned and looked at her, very straight. "What have you got against Elroy?"

"I've got nothing against him! I get along with him fine! He's been wonderful to me. Just wonderful." But Jim watched and waited. "What difference would it make, anyway, whether I liked him or didn't? After all, it's Mother's business who she marries. Nobody else's."

"That's right," said Jim. "Is he good to her, too?"

"Yes, he is! He certainly is. And always has been, from the very beginning, when she had that breakdown after Daddy—He can't do *enough* for her. One of the nicest houses in town, every modern convenience you can think of, all the money she wants for clothes ..." Only Mother (though she pretended) wasn't really much interested in the array of gleaming, purring, whirling household gadgets; she seldom went anywhere to wear the expensive clothes; sometimes she seemed to Cleo like a lost creature, wandering through her own fine house as if she didn't belong there. Most of all on Monday mornings, when Bill came to take Cleo back out to the country; she roomed and boarded, during the week, at the farm closest to the school house. On Monday mornings Mother lingered in the doorway, not waving goodbye, just hanging on till the last possible minute, hanging on with her abandoned-child's eyes. Crazy. You'd think she was being left behind forever, instead of for only five days. Crazy, but all the same haunting. Like a good many other things about Mother.

"He must be doing all right with that hardware store of his," said Jim. "Well. Good for Elroy Hild."

"Good for Mother, too. And for me. He wanted to send me east to college, only I decided—I changed my mind." (Why? To save her life she couldn't explain that sudden about-face of a decision. For she had yearned to get away; and Mother, never mind the look in her eyes, had said of course she must go, it was wonderfully generous of Elroy. Which it was. Only something smug about the way he made the offer, something avid about the way he waited for her to accept, had turned her into a solid chunk of rejection. Instead, she had settled for a term at Normal School.)

The silence stretched out. Jim seemed busy with thoughts of his own. Finally he said, "You're a funny kid. The hours I've spent—that's one thing I had plenty of, time—trying to figure you out—"

At once, as if he had turned on a faucet, chatter poured out of her. "And got nowhere, of course. Because, haven't you heard, nobody can figure Cleo out. But nobody. I baffle all the best minds." With a tinkling-glass laugh, she sprang up and fastened her coat. "It's been too too divine, but I really would like to get into town. My public, you know. Do you mind?"

It worked. It gained her a little time against being questioned, and against the even more unthinkable embarrassment of being thanked. Looking rather dazed, as who wouldn't, he stood up too and said sure, of course they must get going.

But it was only a temporary postponement. It struck her when, having locked the schoolhouse door, she paused and watched him going down the steps to the car, carrying her bag: Jim Singley was a very *purposeful* man. If he set out to thank a person, that person was eventually going to get thanked. And if his purpose happened to be something quite different? She shivered slightly. The warmth of the April day, shifty at best, had all but dissolved; against the immense, transparent sky, deepening into evening, Jim's figure was silhouetted, dark and self-contained and unswerving.

The drive into town was on the whole a silent one. Jim, poor man, was no doubt leery of setting off another spate of chatter or tears; Cleo could not keep her imagination from circling and hovering, like a distracted hen, over what was almost surely impending—the moment of meeting between Jim and Mother. Because Mother would be watching for her, either from the window or the porch, she always came flying down the walk to the car—each Friday it was as if she had not really believed that Cleo was coming back—all a-tremble with pent-up joy and relief. If the sight of Jim-instead-of-Bill could throw Cleo into an unprecedented fit, what would it do to Mother? All her protective instincts rose in a flurry of anxiety for the woman she called "Mother" but thought of, more often than not, as her child, her own special problem child, at once charming and erratic, so easy to hurt, so hard to understand ...

Because Mother, for all her dependence, was not communicative. Or maybe just not articulate. Anyway, there was a lot of uncharted territory in her geography, great areas that Cleo knew absolutely nothing about. Had not *wanted* to know about. Jim Singley, for instance. They had both steered clear of him—Cleo out of a rich hash of emotions that included adolescent squeamishness, wrenched loyalties, shame and shock, not to mention her own privately owned nightmare. And Mother out of—what? Cleo discovered in herself a sudden, engulfing curiosity. It broke over her like a wave, carrying, as a wave carries shell fragments, seaweed and sand, its load of remembered gossip and prying, lip-licking questions.

Not that the questioners had gotten much out of Cleo; very little to get. Jim Singley had simply been part of the fabric of her childhood, like the garage and school and roller-skating and Daddy, who was sometimes fun and sometimes a bore. Depending—she supposed now, though it had not been clear to her then—on how many drinks he had had. Fun when he came bounding in for supper, all high spirits and infectious laughter and roughhouse games with her. A bore when, sodden and stumbling of foot and tongue, he had to be helped up the stairs to the apartment above the garage by Jim and put to bed. She had accepted Daddy—as she had accepted Jim—without question or fuss. Just one of the facts of her life. What an unobservant, insensitive lump she must have been, never to catch an inkling of the adult high-tension wires all around her! For they had surely been there, whether or not there was anything "between" Mother and Jim, as the saying went. There was Daddy's death to prove it.

And every turn of the wheels was taking them closer to town, to Mother and who knew what. She had to ask it: "Does Mother know you're back?"

"No," said Jim, without shifting his eyes from the road.

"Well, then, I'm not sure—I don't know how she's going to take it—"

"Neither do I," said Jim. "We'll find out, soon enough."

There was no arguing about it. His mind was made up: he was going to see Mother, if not today then tomorrow. Just as, eventually, he was going to bring Cleo face to face with what she had managed to dodge, out there in the schoolhouse. Purposeful, she thought. And patient.

"Which way do we go?" asked Jim. They had crossed the bridge now. There was Athena sprawling in front of them. To the right, Cleo told him; Elroy's house was across from the Presbyterian church. A "nice" location, and the house itself—ranch style, pale green, with picture windows—had a substantial, well-groomed look. If anybody was interested. Cleo was not; all she could see was Mother, fussing around in her tulip bed. It seemed to her that the car was all at once wobbling, and for a minute she thought they might be going to hit the big elm beside the walk. But when she glanced sideways, Jim's face was as impassive as ever. No sign that he was aware of that slight, flyaway figure. Which by now was racing across the lawn toward them. The failing light intensified the impression Mother so often gave of girlishness, the leggy, touchingly awkward kind of girlishness. She had on a full skirt (just the wrong length), and her sweater was buttoned crooked. Her odd little face—all eyes at the moment, and eyes only for Cleo—flickered between tears and laughter. When Cleo jumped out of the car to hug her, she half-sobbed, "You're late, I got so worried—"

Then Jim said, "Hello, Audrey," and she stiffened and sucked in her breath as if someone had hit her. She stepped away from Cleo, turned her back to her. Waited rigidly while he came toward her across the spongy lawn. When at last she raised her two hands, Cleo could not tell whether it was to ward him off or to welcome him. Maybe he couldn't tell, either. He paused.

"Audrey," he said. "Audrey."

It was so quiet that Cleo could hear the faint whisper of wind in the elm tree, barely leafed out, above her. After that the footsteps on the sidewalk; Elroy always walked to and from the hardware store. His constitutional, he called it. The footsteps approached at a brisk, regular pace, broke off suddenly for a moment, and then came on, no longer regular.

But neither Mother nor Jim seemed to notice. They stood like statues, absorbed in whatever it was between them, all unprepared for Elroy's voice. It screeched across the silence like a fingernail on a blackboard—high-pitched, quivering; so unlike Elroy's usual measured tones that Cleo herself was jolted. His face, too, was quivering and unfamiliar.

"You get out of here, Jim Singley! You get off my place! Haven't you done enough damage in this town, without coming back and—Get out! Get out of here, you murdering bastard!"

Tidy, almost prim-looking, the smooth surface of his straw-colored hair undisturbed even by this transport of rage, Elroy advanced upon the enemy. His fists were clenched. Cleo fully expected him to hit Jim, who turned a startled, unprotected face toward him. But Elroy stopped just short of striking the blow.

Maybe because Mother let out a scream. Not loud, but violent; a sort of whispered scream. Then she turned and fled up the walk to the house. Cleo caught a glimpse of her face as she passed. It was alive with terror.

"All right," said Jim calmly. "Keep your shirt on, Mr. Hild." There was an absent-minded contempt in the way he stepped around Elroy and headed back to the car. He set Cleo's bag out on the sidewalk, got in, and settled himself behind the wheel. "Be seeing you," he said, before he drove away.

Cleo, sprinting up the walk bent on looking after Mother, had no doubt of it.

FIVE

Velma Carson (who had made such a point of eradicating the Singley from her name that it was now indelibly inscribed there) and Marge McVey were best friends and had been from their high school days. In spite of everything, as they sometimes said. "Everything" being a handy way of referring to the fact—so distressing to Marge, who was both loyal and peaceable—that her husband had sided with Jim Singley instead of against him, he simply refused to believe what was plain as the nose on your face. Not that the McVeys ever really quarreled over the Singley affair. But to Marge her husband was the final authority on every subject from slipcovers to religion; it was very hard on her to disagree with him about the Singleys. She had been surprised to find she could hold out.

Velma herself had been surprised. At the strength of her own influence over Marge. She had always been the leader, of course, and had known it. But in a crisis of loyalties like this, she would have picked Mack as the winner without a moment's hesitation. And would have picked wrong. It was very gratifying. (Naturally, she didn't put it quite like that to Marge. "I can't tell you how much I appreciate it," she often said to Marge. "It wasn't easy for you, and don't think I don't know it. I wouldn't have blamed you if you'd gone along with Mack instead of me. It would have hurt, but I'd have understood perfectly. Only you didn't do it. You're a true friend, Marge, truer than I deserve." Marge usually cried on these occasions. Her round, powder-puff face would crumple up into tears of pride and admiring protest: "Oh no, Velma, I'm only glad I had the strength. You *do* deserve it, Velma, you're the bravest person I've ever known.")

So of course, on the Saturday after Jim Singley came back to Athena, Marge telephoned Velma. "I didn't know whether you'd heard or not, but—"

Velma let a small, brave silence fall before she answered. Yes, she had heard.

"Now dear, you don't have to be polite with me. I mean, if you'd rather be alone, just say so. I don't want to intrude. But if you want me to come over, I'd be only too glad. Sometimes it helps just to have someone to talk to."

It was a tempting choice of roles. The wronged wife—once more wronged, another wound to lick now—suffering in lonely silence. Or the same wronged wife, unable to bear this new indignity alone, accepting gratefully such crumbs of comfort as her friend could offer. In the end the prospect of an ultra-exclusive, ultra-sympathetic audience won out. "Oh please, Marge, could you come? I've been hoping you'd call. You're the only person I can *face*."

In a way, it was true. Last night, when word of Jim's arrival reached her (through Ernie Brewer's wife, who didn't want Velma to think it was any of *her* doing that Jim was staying at the hotel, if she had *her* way he'd be run out of town) her reaction was one of instant, genuine drawing back. She had shrunk away from the avid curiosity that showed through Mrs. Brewer's veneer of concern. She had wanted to hide, from all the Mrs. Brewers, from all of Athena, even from her son Wayne. Only that was impossible, and she knew it. There was Wayne at the supper table, sullenly avoiding her eyes: "Sure I heard it. I know he's back. Everybody in town knows it. So what?" The sullenness was not aimed at her. Of course not. Wayne was devoted to her. The sullenness was because he too wanted to hide, and was not old enough to understand that it couldn't be done.

As Velma did. All too well. Sometimes—today, for instance—she even caught a glimmer of what happened to that original, pure impulse to hide when it was balked. What happened was that you turned it inside out, and there, like a cozy fur lining, was the impulse to dramatize the very part of yourself you had wanted to hide and couldn't.

Velma closed her eyes to the glimmer. The basic truth was still there, unchanged and undeniable: Jim had wronged her; he had ruined her life by committing not only murder but adultery, and even that was not enough for him, he must top it all off by returning to the scene of his crime.

"What I can't understand is why." Marge said it almost as soon as she came in the door, her eyes brimming with tears of indignation and sympathy. "What *possessed* him to come back here? You'd think he'd never want to set foot in Athena again, and yet the first thing he does ... I just can't understand it!" Agitation made her seem more than ever like a plump, pretty baby, peering out round-eyed at a mystifying world. Still simmering, she slipped out of her coat and followed Velma into the living room. It was large and shabby, like the rest of the house, which Velma had inherited from her father. Luckily; if she had had to pay rent out of her bank clerk's salary, she would have found it even harder to make ends meet; and there were three extra bedrooms upstairs, which she rented out to high school teachers during the winter. Even so, she barely managed.

Velma herself did not speak until they were settled—Marge in the worn leather rocker, Velma in the straight-backed "occasional" chair with the wobbly arm. Then she said, in a strained, remote voice, "He told Ernie Brewer he had some 'unfinished business' here. I suppose Mack knows, if anybody does."

Marge flushed, as Velma had known she would. "Oh dear, I do wish— Of course Mack told me he had seen Jim, that's how I heard he was back. But it's so hard to get anything out of Mack. He didn't seem to want to talk about it. I wouldn't even have known he lent Jim the car if Bill hadn't made such a fuss about it. Fuss, did I say? Well! He practically blew his top. The idea of letting Jim go out to that schoolhouse, and Cleo alone out there ..." Like a puppy eager for praise, Marge offered this small trophy. At least her son was on the right side, even if her husband wasn't.

But Velma was not impressed. "I don't see why that should worry him. Jim certainly isn't going to do Cleo any harm. After all, it's thanks to her he got off as easy as he did. She must be his favorite character. Outside of her mother, of course." (And now the strain in Velma's voice was real, not calculated. She still could not mention Audrey Fleming, or even think of her, without this strangled feeling, this cruel pressure in her throat.)

"Audrey? Well, but now that she's married—"

"That didn't stop him before," said Velma.

Marge caught her breath at the lurid vision: another fatal triangle, with Elroy Hild replacing Herb Fleming at the one corner; Jim, mad with jealousy, bent on revenge. "Oh Velma, you don't suppose—"

"I wish I did. I wish it were as simple as that." She looked down at her hands and unclenched them. He had found out about his precious Audrey, all right. Herb Fleming barely settled in his grave, Jim in his prison cell, before she found herself another sucker. "No, Marge. Infatuations don't last six years. His 'unfinished business' isn't with Audrey or Elroy Hild." She paused, and again the suffering was real. "It's Wayne he's after. He can't even let me have Wayne to myself!"

"But he must know what Wayne thinks of him! Why, Wayne's devoted to you! Jim can't get anywhere with *him*."

"I know that. But he can try. He can make Wayne—and me—miserable, just by being here, just by never letting anybody forget that he's Wayne's father. He'll say I taught Wayne to hate him. I taught him! He did it himself. But that won't stop him. And he can offer Wayne—money. It must still be there in the bank, I've never touched a penny of it ..."

"No, and neither will Wayne," said Marge staunchly. "He can't be bribed."

"But maybe he *should* be! Maybe I've been wrong all this time, letting my own selfish pride cheat Wayne out of his rights." She got up and began to pace the floor, clasping her arms tight against her body. Against her tall, still-elegant body. (She was aware of that, though the suffering remained real and sharp; aware of her ash-blond hair, her regular features, her graceful carriage, and of the figure of noble grief she was presenting to Marge.) "Of course he wants the things all the other boys have—a car of his own, money for clothes, a college education. Real college, not this half-baked business school I can afford for him. Why shouldn't he want them? Why shouldn't he have them, except for me?"

"Velma," said Marge solemnly, "you mustn't talk like that. There are things in this world that are worth more than any amount of money. It wouldn't make any difference if Jim was a millionaire, he still couldn't give Wayne what you have. He hasn't got it to give. The standards, the set of values, the—the character ..." Awed by the profundities into which she had floundered, Marge broke off and repeated lamely, "You mustn't talk like that. You simply mustn't."

Velma let her voice drop to a wistful murmur. "It's just that I get so tired. I can't help thinking sometimes how easy it would be to let go, stop fighting ... But of course I'm not going to stop. Not with Wayne practically raised. I *have* done a good job on him, haven't I?"

"You've done a wonderful job. There isn't a finer boy in town than

Wayne. So nice and quiet. I only wish Bill had his manners. If Jim would just leave the two of you alone! Has he tried to see you? Called you or anything?"

"Not yet." But of course he was only biding his time, keeping her waiting in the hope of wearing her down, or—nothing was beyond him—cold-bloodedly plotting which moment, which method, would humiliate her most. He might even be waiting till Monday morning, when he could walk into the bank and force her into a public encounter. For she knew that he would never forgive her for turning his son against him. Her own defection was of little consequence (damn him, damn him; "I didn't expect you to stand by me," he had said) but Wayne's struck him to the heart. And he blamed her for it. Never himself. Oh no, none of it was Jim's fault. All he had done was murder Herb Fleming because he wanted Herb's wife ...

Marge, poor simple-hearted Marge, with her stricken eyes and incoherent babble of comfort, brought her back to her chosen role. She produced a wan, brave smile and (always thinking of others) said that Marge had listened to enough of her troubles, now they would have a nice cup of tea and talk about something pleasant.

"What you ought to have," said Marge, "is a slug of brandy. If I had you over at my house, believe me, I'd pour it down you. There are times when it's the only thing, I don't care what you say." It was a familiar little bone of contention between them: there was never a drop of liquor in Velma's house. Even if she could have afforded it, she said, she did not believe in exposing an impressionable youngster like Wayne to temptation. He wasn't like Marge's youngsters; he didn't have a father.

Over the cup of tea, Marge said, "Look, Velma, why *don't* you come home with me? Stay for supper and the evening. I hate to think of leaving you here by yourself with nothing to do but jitter. Wayne won't be here, he and Sally and the other kids always eat together Saturday nights."

Velma was grateful but firm. Marge mustn't worry about her; really, she was all right. She couldn't resist one little sting: "I wouldn't want to embarrass Mack. I know how he feels about me." And, when that had taken effect, she finished, in character. "No, Marge, bless you for all your help, but this is something I have to face alone."

Lonely in the doorway, she watched Marge trot off down the walk to the convertible Mack had given her for Christmas. Lonely, lonely—but with no one now to see and pity—she turned back to the bleak living room, where the shadows of late afternoon were already gathering. She did not turn on the light. Wayne would be home soon, from the creamery where he worked on Saturdays; he would find her sitting in the barn-like dusk. Devoted as he was, he would announce that he was breaking his date with Sally McVey to stay home with her; of course she would protest; but Wayne would not listen, he would insist …

He was late tonight. Late and later. She made several trips to the bay window to watch for him. She carried the tea cups out to the kitchen, which was also large and bare-looking, and rinsed them out at the sink. At last she gave in and turned on the table lamp. The glass-domed clock on the bookcase struck seven. But lots of times it was fast, not a reliable clock at all; a wedding present from Marge. It was one of the few things she had brought with her from the house where she and Jim had lived. Jim.

Why didn't he call her, if he was going to? Why didn't Wayne come home?

The peal of the telephone jerked her, quaking and unstrung, to her feet. She did not recognize Wayne's voice at first. Maybe because she had been primed for the other voice. Or maybe—yes, that was it, Wayne didn't sound right. Queer and husky. Not like himself.

"I can't hear you," she said. "What's the matter? What's wrong?"

"Nothing." He cleared his throat. "Everything's great. The greatest. Just wanted to tell you. I'll be late. I have to work late."

But the creamery never stayed open after five thirty. And surely she heard radio music in the background? "Wayne," she said sharply. "Are you all right? Where are you?"

"At the—Oh. At The Snackery. Getting a snack at The Snackery." He gave a blurred laugh and said something else that she didn't catch. Then he hung up.

It took several minutes for understanding to creep through her and settle into an icy lump of certainty. Wayne was drunk. Her model son, so devoted to her, so nice and quiet, never a moment's worry, not like the other roughneck kids. *Drunk!* As she fumbled the phone into its cradle, she said the word aloud, and instantly another certainty leaped to her mind. This was Jim's doing. His idea of fun—to urge liquor on an inexperienced teen-aged boy; watch the effect; and listen, snickering, to that mumbled telephone call. Ah, how he must have enjoyed that!

Her coat was in the hall closet, her worn purse was on the shelf. She did not bother with a hat. It was six blocks to Main Street, and she made it in record time. Once she was there, the impetus that had sent her half-running along the quiet evening streets slackened. What was her goal? The Snackery? Wayne, who never lied, might very well have lied to her about where he was tonight. Probably had. The Snackery did not seem a likely spot. Though of course she could look there first. She paused in front of the post office, thinking over the other possibilities. The pool hall. The hamburger and beer joint out beyond the railroad tracks …

Then she saw Jim. By himself. He was across the street from her walking toward the hotel. Hands in his pockets, head up, smooth-moving as a cat. She turned and followed him. She waited outside, watching. For once the hotel desk was deserted; Ernie Brewer must be either helping out in the kitchen or eating his own supper. She let Jim get partway up the stairs before she pushed open the door and walked in. As she crossed to the stairs, Ernie came tearing out of the dining room. "Hey, Jim," he began; then he saw Velma and stopped in his tracks. She swept past him without a word or glance, and caught up with Jim on the top step.

"Where's Wayne? What have you done to him?"

Ernie's voice had already alerted him. He was turned toward her, with his hand on the stair rail, and in the yellow haze of the hall light she saw, with bitter satisfaction, the lines in his face and the sprinkle of gray in his hair. He was staring at her incredulously.

"Wayne," she insisted, in the same tense but low-pitched voice—for Ernie must be listening with all his might; any minute now he would turn off the radio in the dining room. "Don't lie to me. I know you got him drunk—"

"What? Have you gone crazy? I haven't even seen Wayne." He spoke no more loudly than she. But the familiar edge of irritability was there. The Oh-God-here-we-go-again look in his eye. They might have been picking up a conversation where they had dropped it six years ago.

"Oh no, of course not! Where did you leave him? Where is he?"

"I have no idea," said Jim, evenly. "Where does he usually go to get drunk?"

He wanted her to scream, of course; nothing would make him happier than to goad her into a fishwife scene. Therefore she remained calm. "Wayne isn't that kind of a boy. He has never had a drink before in his life."

"High time, then." He moved toward the door of his room. "He's almost twenty. Wouldn't be normal if he didn't try it out pretty soon. If you don't know where he is, how do you know he's drunk?"

"Because he—"

At that moment the door to Jim's room opened, and everything came to a dead stop. Wayne was standing there. His face (a blond face, with regular features, like Velma's) had a swollen, mottled look. His eyes were blank.

"Mother?" He sounded dim and helpless. "Mother, what are you—"

She turned on Jim, in furious triumph. "You didn't know where he was! No idea. Hadn't even seen him. And all the time—Well, of course you didn't fool me with your lies. I knew right away it was your doing."

Jim took—or pretended to take—no notice of her. His eyes were fixed on Wayne. Finally he said, "Hello, Wayne." He started to put his hand out, then changed his mind and let it drop back.

"I was waiting for you," said Wayne. "Mr. Brewer said you weren't here but like as not you hadn't locked your door, so I—"

"Please, Wayne." Velma used her "disciplining" voice. Kind but firm. "Don't try to cover up for him. I understand exactly how it happened. I know who's responsible for—for the state you're in. I know you're not to blame."

"Shut up," said Jim savagely. (And that was good; that would show Wayne what a brute he was.) "Wayne's got a right to talk to me if he wants to, without interference from you."

Oh, he was playing right into her hands; he didn't know her son as she did. "Certainly he has," she said. She looked coolly into Wayne's fuddled, pleading eyes. "I have no intention of interfering with anything Wayne wants to do. He's perfectly free to stay here and let me go home alone. I realize I should have stayed there in the first place. No matter how worried I was. I hope you'll forgive me, Wayne, for—well, I guess for worrying about you."

She started down the stairs, ignoring the cry that burst out of him: "Mother! Wait. Mother—" She did not stop until he plunged after her and caught her arm. "Mother, you can't leave like this. You must let me—"

"Of course, dear. I must let you make your own choice." She gave him a cool smile and disengaged her arm. Kindly but firmly. She went on down the stairs without looking back—though for a terrible moment he hesitated, and she had to force her feet not to stop moving, her eyes not to shift from straight ahead. Then came the rush of his footsteps behind her, and as she walked briskly through the lobby he was there at her heels.

She could not resist one backward glance when she reached the door. Jim was still standing at the head of the stairs, watching.

SIX

"Still asleep," reported Elroy. He closed the door of Mother's bedroom behind him with elaborate care and tiptoed down the hall and into the living room. There was wall to wall carpeting, but Elroy tiptoed anyway. "That's the best thing for her. Rest. 'Sleep that knits up the ravell'd sleeve of care,'" he added.

As Cleo had known he would. She rattled the Sunday paper and said, "I expect so," in an aggressively normal tone. Elroy's sickness-in-the-house voice irritated her beyond all reason. But then so did a lot of other things about him, by no means least his faculty for making her feel ashamed of her own irritation. For there was no mistaking the marks of genuine anxiety: his eyes were red from lack of sleep, his face pale and drawn with worry. And how unfailingly kind and gentle he was with Mother, how pathetically pleased when either he or Cleo managed to draw from her the faintest smile or the tiniest flash of animation.

He loves her, thought Cleo ... As much as I do? Is that why he gets on my nerves?

She said, to reassure them both, "Of course it's the best thing for her. That's why the doctor left those capsules for her, to make her sleep." And to put an end to the terrible, tearless weeping of Friday night. For Cleo had rushed into the house to find Mother crumpled on the floor beside the couch, sobbing uncontrollably. Past all human comfort. A shot of something to calm her down, the doctor said. (It was Elroy who thought of calling him; Cleo had been witless with alarm.) Quiet. Rest. Capsules to calm her down. Calmed down, as a matter of fact, into apathy. "A couple more days of rest, and she'll be all right again. It was just the shock."

Eagerly, gratefully, Elroy agreed with her. Yes, of course. The wonders of modern science. Wonderful. "She's so delicate. High-strung. She can't take as much as the rest of us."

"All right. You don't need to rub it in. It was my fault. I shouldn't have let him bring me home, without warning her."

"No, no," protested Elroy. "I didn't mean it that way. I shouldn't have done what I did, either. Only it got me, just the sight of him ... I'll tell you the truth, Cleo, I doubt if it would have made any difference, anyway." He sat down and stared at his neat, polished shoes. He was a very tidy man. Somehow the tidiness made him seem even more forlorn. "It would still have been a shock, seeing him again. What it did, it brought it all back to her. Too much for her then. And too much for her now. He's got a lot to answer for, Jim Singley has. If this throws her into another nervous breakdown, like the one she had before—"

"It won't," insisted Cleo. "She's better already. Much better. There's no comparison between then and now." Of course there wasn't. Then there had been the violent ruin of her whole life—her husband suddenly dead, his name dishonored (and hers too, in an underground way), a half-grown daughter to raise, and no money to do it with—enough, surely, to shatter a woman of far more stamina than Mother. But now, encircled as she was with security, what had she to fear, now, from Jim Singley or anyone else? It was quite natural that his reappearance should unnerve her temporarily; after all, Cleo herself had burst into tears when she saw him. He did "bring it all back." But Mother had been more than unnerved. She had been terror-stricken. Why?

"No," said Elroy. "No comparison. She's got us to take care of her. It's up to us to see that he doesn't get a chance to do her any more damage. We just won't let him see her again, that's all."

Very simple. Like the defense plan Elroy had mapped out yesterday: Cleo was to take time off from teaching to stay with Mother during the day, while Elroy was at the hardware store. He had arranged it all with the director of her school board, who was a friend of his; they had found a substitute teacher with no trouble. Evenings, Elroy would take over. Between them they would form a round-the-clock guard. Very simple. Still, they eyed each other nervously. An odd alliance, Cleo couldn't help thinking: herself and this tidy, straw-haired, irritating man, pitted against Jim and his unswerving purpose.

"Why would he *want* to see her?" she burst out, and immediately wished she hadn't. This was dangerous ground. She would prefer not to explore it. Definitely not in company with Elroy.

But it was too late. He was clearing his throat in that way of his. Prim, and at the same time portentous. "I don't know if you were old enough to hear any of the talk at the time—"

"Certainly I was old enough," she snapped. "I know what they were saying, under their breath, about Mother and Jim. You don't think for a minute I believed it, do you?"

Elroy surprised her by looking her in the eye. "I don't know. I don't even know what to believe, myself. What difference does it make?" He paused, making a visible effort to control the sudden vehemence in his voice. "It doesn't make any difference. I do know this. If there was anything between them, it was because he took advantage of her, caught her at a weak moment and pulled her into it. Against her will. She's not bad by nature. I don't care what anybody says, Audrey's not a bad woman, and she never was!"

"But you think maybe that's why he's come back, to try to—" Cleo swallowed.

"He's not going to get a chance to try anything. He ruined her life once. I won't let him do it again. You saw how she ran away from him, the other night. She wants no part of him, anybody can see that. And if he won't get out of town, I'll get *her* out of town. Why not? We can take a trip somewhere, anywhere she likes, as soon as she feels up to it. Do us both good. There's nothing like a change of scene to restore a person's perspective."

The prospect alone was apparently enough to restore Elroy's perspective. His eyes brightened; Cleo could practically see the contented bustle (road maps, points of interest) starting up in his mind. The melodrama of a moment ago was suddenly incredible. She had very likely imagined it.

The church bell began to ring, breaking into Elroy's pleasant reverie and recalling him to his duties. He was an usher or something. Anyway, a conscientious church-goer. It was wonderful, he said, what an hour of quiet, worshipful contemplation could do for a person's soul. Good for business, too. He sprang up, smoothed his hair, which was already smooth as glass, and straightened his tie, which might possibly have been one millimeter off center. "I'll pick up some ice cream for dinner," he said. "Pineapple. That's Audrey's favorite. Maybe we can coax her appetite back to normal. Good nourishing food. And rest. That's the best thing for her."

There was nothing wrong with Elroy except his personality, Cleo thought, watching through the picture window as he crossed the street and—with the dignified tread that befitted a leading citizen, Athena's God-fearing hardware merchant—ascended the church steps. A man of sterling virtues, she thought, all of them tiresome.

There. Did she hear Mother stirring? She hurried down the hall and gently opened the door. "Hi, Beautiful," she said. "Have a good sleep?"

The "Beautiful" was a sad overstatement these days. It was a shock to discover that Mother's charm was almost entirely a matter of animation. Without the flicker of constantly varying moods, her features showed up irregular and all out of proportion—too much forehead and eyes, not enough chin, a rather muddy skin and a fantastically frail-looking neck. There was nothing, now, to account for the impression of near-beauty that Mother quite often achieved. Since Friday night she had been so blank-eyed and listless and unresponsive; as if shock (or maybe just the drugs) had sealed off all her senses.

But today—Cleo, turning from the window where she had raised the blinds to let in the sunshine, saw it with a surge of joy—yes, today there was life in her face again. She was sitting up in bed, unbraiding her hair, and when Cleo cried, "Oh Mud, you're better!" she made a mocking face and said, "Certainly not. I'm in terrible shape. What day is it?"

"Sunday. Eleven o'clock. Time for breakfast."

"Sunday!" Mother paused with the hairbrush in midair. "Yes. It feels like Sunday. Poor old Saturday, it got lost in the shuffle." She gave Cleo a curious, nervous glance. "What did I do, sleep it away?"

And she waited for Cleo's answer. "Practically. The doctor gave you a shot. And capsules. Turned you into a zombie. Now about breakfast—"

Not in bed, Mother declared; except for her wobbly legs and her two enormous heads, there was nothing wrong with her. So Cleo helped settle her on the living room couch (how small she looked, like a quaint child in her sprigged peignoir) and fixed her a breakfast tray. Good, nourishing food. Coax her appetite back to normal. She didn't really eat her poached egg. But she pretended to, and that was progress. Be thankful for small favors, Cleo told herself. And don't push her. If she wants to talk about Jim, she will.

Only there was one thing that had to be said, and Cleo blurted it out:

"You mustn't worry, Mother, there's nothing for you to be scared of. You've got Elroy and me to take care of you, we're not going to let anybody hurt you. You know that. I'm going to stay home with you this week, and—" She blundered to a stop, for Mother's face went suddenly gray and pinched and her eyelids shuddered down. "Don't you want me to, Mud?"

"Yes. Oh yes," gasped Mother, and her eyes opened again, those fabulous eyes that, like water, could change from gray to green to blue to almost black. They were luminous now with tears. Cleo rushed across to her, and they clung together, whispering incoherent comfort to each other.

"Cleo, Cleo ..." She put her hands up to Cleo's face and drew back a little, murmuring, as if to herself, "You look so much like your father. Like seeing a ghost ..." But she did not sound frightened, only wondering and tender. After all, she must be used to this particular ghost by now; people were always saying how much Cleo looked like Daddy. The same light brown, wavy hair and high color, the same general expression of candor and good humor. Which had looked fine on Daddy; for herself Cleo would have liked hollow cheeks and a touch of decadence.

"You *are* like him, too," Mother went on, in the same musing tone. "The best part of him. The way he used to be, before he started drinking so much. He didn't at first, you know." Cleo didn't know; she couldn't remember that better, happier time. But even with the drinking, Daddy had remained basically likable—a gregarious, good-hearted, boyish sort of man. Everybody's friend. Cleo remembered the phrase from Daddy's obituary in the local paper. "Herb Fleming was everybody's friend." Everybody's except his partner's. And perhaps his wife's. Even Cleo, oblivious to the adult world, had sometimes been aware of a strain of savage anger, usually buried, but now and then erupting to the surface. She had heard some of the middle-of-the-night quarrels. Dimly, through veils of sleep and confusion. She had known that, when Daddy was really drunk, Mother was afraid of him.

She could think of nothing to say, and Mother seemed to expect nothing from her. She was intent on her own compulsion to explain: "He never meant to be a crook. He shouldn't have taken that money out of the business. I know. That was wrong. It didn't belong to him, it belonged to the business. But he didn't mean to steal it. He would have put it back. He wasn't dishonest, Cleo, he wasn't a bad man. It was just—circumstances. Everybody liked him, you know how sociable he was, and he fell in with that drinking, gambling crowd ..."

Not bad by nature. Pulled into it against his will. As Elroy had said, in defense of Mother herself.

"And I was the wrong wife for him." Mother let her hands drop into her lap. Small hands, but not well kept, the nails rough from work in the garden. She looked past Cleo and said desolately, "It's true. I ought to have known when I married him. I didn't fit in, like the other wives. Parties and clubs and all that. I don't know, I never seemed to fit in. He would have been all right, except for me."

"Don't, Mother. It's past now, anyway."

"But don't you see, Cleo, time's not like that." She leaned forward tensely. "Past. Present. Future. In three separate compartments. That's not the way it *is*. It's all run together, the past makes the present, and so you can't ever—"

And then the telephone rang, and the frail, rare thread of intimacy snapped. It was Bill, of course; characteristically picking the wrong moment to call, and sounding uncommonly casual. On account of last night, which hadn't been a howling success. Not quite a quarrel; what Bill called an intellectual discussion. It went back to Friday night; he was still furious with his father for lending Jim Singley the car, and he said Cleo had a thing about her mother and probably Jim too, which stood to reason, all that business of the trial and Cleo's testimony had been a traumatic experience ... Oh, Bill had a tag for everything. As Cleo had caustically pointed out, it was wonderful what one course in elementary psychology could do for you. She had been very crisp about the trial and her part in it. "I simply told what I heard. I was in the kitchen getting supper, because Mother wasn't home that night, she was taking care of a sick neighbor, and I heard them quarreling in the living room. My father and Jim. They quarreled about money. The door was shut, so I didn't see. I just heard. And at the trial I told what I heard, and the jury decided it was manslaughter, not murder, because my father started the fight, he hit Jim first. Period. No traumas. No psychological fancywork ..."

"So I'll pick you up about four?" Bill was saying breezily into the phone. "We can go out to Louie's or someplace. Sally and Wayne are coming along."

"They are? I thought she was through with him forever." For that was another thing about last night. Wayne had broken his date with Sally— no explanation, he just didn't show—so they had had Sally on their hands, a Sally whose mood teetered wildly between the high tragedy of unrequited love and the fury of a woman scorned. Just to add to the merriment.

"That was last night. All is now forgiven. I saw Wayne this morning. Tell you about it when I see you." There was a smug note in Bill's voice now. He had insisted on reading into Wayne's behavior a dark significance, had made some kind of sinister connection between the broken date and the fact that Wayne's father was back in town. Wherever he looked last night, Bill saw traumatic experiences.

"The suspense is terrible," said Cleo drily. "I'm all aflutter. I've got to go now. See you at four."

Having thus disposed of Bill (he was nice, only such a lug sometimes), she turned back to Mother. But of course the thread that had snapped was beyond repair; Mother's unfinished sentence was doomed to dangle in space forever.

Besides, Elroy was coming in the door, his soul refreshed, the carton of pineapple ice cream tucked under his arm. He stopped short at sight of Mother. "Audrey darling! What are you doing out of bed?"

"She's much better," said Cleo defensively. Which was ridiculous; what was wrong, for Pete's sake, with Mother's being out of bed? "So much better that she wanted to get up and have her breakfast out here. Any objection?"

"Objection!" cried Elroy. "Why, nothing could please me more! A sight for sore eyes!" He bustled across to the couch and deposited a kiss on Mother's cheek. There sat the breakfast tray, with the damned uneaten egg leering at everybody. "We just don't want her getting up too soon, is all. Mustn't overdo it. Mustn't try to rush old Mother Nature. Good nourishing food and rest, that's what it's going to take. Plenty of both." He tapped his package jovially. "We've got a surprise here that's going to tempt her appetite. Oh, don't you worry, we'll get the roses back in her cheeks! Right now, darling, are you sure you wouldn't be more comfortable in bed? You look a little tired."

And all at once Mother did look tired. So pale; and with her hair twisted up on top so that it looked more than ever too much of a burden for her fragile neck. Some of the blankness had crept back into her eyes.

"Maybe I had better go back to bed for a while," she said. "I am a little tired." Docile as a doll, she let Elroy pick her up (and sure enough, he said "Upsy-daisy" in the process) and carry her down the hall to the bedroom.

Cleo, as she took the ice cream carton and the tray to the kitchen, was suddenly engulfed by sorrow, a vast wave of obscure sorrow. Mother's unfinished sentence seemed to echo back to her from the white enamel, the Formica counter tops, the inlaid linoleum. "The past makes the present, so you can't ever—" Can't ever? Can't ever?

Can't ever escape, thought Cleo. That was what Mother would have said, if the phone hadn't rung. You can't ever escape.

SEVEN

Psycho, thought Wayne, I must be some kind of a psycho, only what do they call it when you're not just a plain split personality, you're *splintered?* Fractured. That was good, that "fractured." I fracture me.

"Finish your dinner, dear," said Mother. "You've hardly touched your meat."

"I've had all I want." The plate of wan, bedraggled pot roast stared back at him in mute reproach. He closed his eyes and swallowed. Oh God, one splinter of him groaned. One of the silent splinters. While simultaneously one of the yak-yak splinters added politely, "Thank you."

The yak-yak, model-son splinter. Such a well-mannered boy. So good to his mother, such a comfort to her, such a credit to her, poor woman, the visible justification for all her self-sacrifice. Never gave her a moment's worry. Helped her with the dishes. Went to church with her every Sunday morning.

Every goddam Sunday morning, including this one, when he was so hung-over that he felt tall and improbable, like a giraffe, and the simple process of putting one foot in front of the other became a perilous project. (But of course that was why he had done it. She hadn't expected him to, after his performance last night. Again he closed his eyes; he was pretty sure he had been sick last night, in front of her, maybe right on the street. God knows what else. So it was absolutely compulsory for him to go to church with her this morning. To prove something or other. To show off. To punish himself. Cruel and unusual punishment.)

But even that wasn't enough for her. Oh no. You could knock yourself out going to church with her and saying you were sorry and—just barely, just barely, oh God, that pot roast—keeping your stomach under control; and it still wasn't enough for her. Nothing ever was or ever would be. You could never make it up to her.

It was like the time he ran away. Years ago, not very long after ... Not very long after. He hitched-hiked way out to the western part of the state, only of course the last guy that picked him up had to be one of those nosey, do-gooder types and Wayne didn't have the sense to keep his mouth shut and ... Well. They came after him. Mother and the minister. The minister got on that man-to-man, frank-and-earnest kick they all get on at the drop of a hat; Wayne knew it was phoney even then, and dug in his heels. It was Mother that took the fight out of him. "Wayne, Wayne, you're all I've got." Her face, and her hands reaching for him. One of the rare occasions when she permitted herself such an unguarded, vulnerable gesture; he melted against her.

Was that what he wanted, for her to *gush* over him? No. No. Only in those days it was still so strong in his mind, the way it used to be before … Before. The lost golden warmth of a world with Dad in it. Time-less summer afternoons on the river, fishing; tramping the autumn-brown hills hunting rabbits or pheasant; wood smoke and pipe smoke and hot charred wienies on a sharpened stick and the oily, metallic garage smell and Dad's hands—loose-knuckled, criss-crossed with in-grained grime—his hands that could fix anything; his slow, kindling smile. His Dad …

He knew better now. His Dad. Yeah. And Santa Claus. And the fairy godmother with three magic wishes.

So anyway, that was the end of his running away. He trotted back home with her like a good little boy, and until last night he had gone on being her good little boy. As far as she knew. What she didn't know, of course, wouldn't hurt her. (And that was still another splinter, the part of him that got a mean, sly satisfaction out of deluding her. She thought today's was the first hang-over, ha ha, ho ho. She had never heard one word about the other times, or about that crazy deal last fall down in Spring City, when the only thing that kept them out of jail—girls and all—was that Jug Wohler's father was the sheriff. She didn't know. Ha ha, ho ho.)

She knew about last night, though. And he could never make it up to her. Well. He could never make it up to himself, either. It was too igno-minious, the way he had trotted off at her heels. She hadn't even reached for him this time. (Yes, but her face had been the same as when he ran away, and maybe she hadn't said it in words, but it was what she meant: "Wayne, Wayne, you're all I've got.")

No excuse. He wasn't a kid any more. If he had any guts he would have let her go. Would have stayed and said his say. *You leave us alone,* he had intended to say, *you've done Mother all the damage you're going to. I don't know what your idea is in coming back here, but if you think ei-ther one of us …* He couldn't say it sober? He had to get stoned first? Right. No guts.

But she wouldn't even give him credit for getting drunk on his own. He was her good little boy, her precious, innocent model son, and it was-n't his fault, he had been lured up there and plied with liquor into sid-ing against her.

He looked across the dining room table at her face—so composed, so impervious to argument, so committed to suffering—and he gave an-other inward groan. Try and talk her out of it. Just try.

"More tea?" she asked, and poised the teapot over his cup. Rubbing it in again. Couldn't she let up on it for a minute? The tomato juice, dear. And the black coffee, dear. And maybe an aspirin, dear. *He* knew he had a hang-over, and *she* knew he had a hang-over, so could they please kindly drop the subject, just leave it lay for a moment of silence ...

He shoved back his chair violently and got to his feet; the sudden motion set about a million wires jangling in his head. "I don't want anything! Let me alone, will you! That's all I ask. Just let me alone. Just *listen* to me—"

"Sh, dear. No need to shout." She glanced toward the ceiling, beyond which the high school English teacher might very well be listening. A familiar gesture; he couldn't even yell when he felt like it in the privacy of his own home on account of the everlasting roomers. Calmly she went about stacking the dishes, and calmly she spoke. "I've listened to you, Wayne. I know it wasn't your fault. I understand perfectly. I know it's not going to happen again. We'll simply forget it and say no more about it. Why don't you go upstairs and take a little rest while I do the dishes?"

Why not? Sure. Why stop now? Make her a martyr all the way and be done with it. "I'll do the dishes," he said through clenched teeth. He snatched up his cup and saucer and carried them, rattling like castanets, to the kitchen.

She followed him without a word. The stack of dishes in her hands made not the slightest clatter. Silence. That withering forbearance of hers.

"Mother—"

"You'll be here for supper, won't you?" she said smoothly and pleasantly. "You remember I told you, I've asked the Rices over."

"No, you didn't tell me!" But she had, a day or two ago. He remembered it now. He glared at her. "You know perfectly well I've got a date with Sally. You heard what I said to Bill, when we met him on the way to church. You know perfectly well I've already called her. Why didn't you—"

"Sh, Wayne. Please. It's nothing to get excited about. I didn't realize what you and Bill were saying. I guess I had my mind on—other things. I thought I told you, just the other day, the Rices always look forward so to seeing you. But it's all right. Really. I'll try to explain to them." Patiently she bent over the sink full of dirty dishes.

"I'll *do* them. I told you I'd wash the—Mother, I can't break another date with Sally. Not after last night. I've already called her!" (Yes, and it had been almost embarrassingly easy, making it up with Sally. Owing to his being such a hell of a fellow in her book. He regarded, with detachment, this particular facet of the many-splintered thing known as Wayne Sing—Wayne Carson. A bright kid like Sally, wouldn't you think she'd get the picture? She was younger than he, that was all, just enough younger to be flattered when he started calling her for dates. Those three little years made all the difference, they gave him an edge over the high school punks she used to run around with. So all right, they had their fathers' cars to drive, and money to spend on her. Wayne had those three little years that made him one of the older guys and therefore madly exciting. That was all it was. She'd get the picture soon enough, don't worry. When she went away to college … A heaviness closed in on his chest. He wasn't kidding himself. Next year, when she went away to college, it would be So long Wayne, nice to have known you. Oh well. There were always other babes, like the ones in Spring City. Meanwhile, if she was flattered, so was he. Because she was a "nice" girl, her father was Judge McVey, and his father was in jail, and … Yes. But also because she was Sally. Just simply because she was Sally.)

"Of course you can't break your date with Sally," said Mother. Her back was still turned to him, eloquently uncomplaining. "She's such a nice little thing. I'm so glad you've made it up with her."

Such a rage filled him, such a fury of frustration, that he had to grip the edge of the table to keep from—from what? From grabbing her, shaking the *hell* out of her, choking her, anything to crack her everlasting glassy calm. "You're not either glad!" She turned quickly toward him, and he saw, with savage satisfaction, the quiver of shock and fear in her face. "Why don't you say so? Nice little thing! You can't stand her. You hate her, why don't you say so? Yes, and me too, you hate me too—"

"Wayne," she whispered. "Son. You can't mean that. How can you say it?" Again her face quivered, only now that it might really happen he was terrified by the possibility of her composure cracking, he knew he could not bear it. Soapsuds dripped from her hands. My mother, he thought, I almost hit my mother. Appalled, he stared into her eyes, and all the million wires in his head jangled, all the splinters of himself grated against each other.

He cried out, "Damn him, damn him, why did he have to come back here?"

"To turn you against me." She said it with pouncing, cold assurance. (Crack? Not she. Never fear.) "He won't be satisfied until he's done that to me too. He wants to destroy you, because you're all I have, the one thing I have left to live for. He doesn't care anything about you. He never did. Oh yes, yes, I know. He took you hunting, he took you fishing, he had you down at that garage, 'helping' him, handing him things, trotting at his heels. All for himself, all for his own pleasure. You never really meant anything to him. Did he stop to think about you when he murdered that woman's husband?" She took a long breath. Her eyes were glittering. "And now, after the way I've worked to bring you up, to give you a decent home—Oh, I know it hasn't been easy for you, having to skimp along, doing without some of the things the other boys have. But I've done my best, Wayne. I've done the best I could."

"Mother, I *know*."

"He offered you money. Didn't he? Didn't he?"

The same old deadlock. She was never going to let up on him till she got it out of him, the lie she coveted. *Yes, Mother, yes, you're right, you're always right. He fed me the drinks, he offered me money, he tried to turn me against you. You're the good team, and he's the bad team, and don't mind me, I'm just the football you kick around between you ...*

She was not going to get it out of him. He had groveled enough. Trailing after her last night, wagging his unaccomplished mission behind him. And today, hanging his head, blubbering his apologies, giving her the I-was-naughty-I'll-never-do-it-again bit. Yes, and—obscurely, the thing he resented most of all—letting himself be goaded into almost hitting her. But this he would not give her, this particular lie. Never mind that he lied to her quite often, about where he had been and what he had done. This was different. Here he drew the line.

"He offered me nothing. How many times do I have to tell you?" (Keep your voice down. Don't yell. Don't let her pressure you into blowing up again.) "He didn't know I was up there in his room. We didn't even talk to each other. It's the truth, I don't care whether you believe it or not."

She did not. She stood motionless, inflexible. Impervious to the truth. And into his mind there flashed the treacherous idea: Maybe it was that way with *him*. Maybe her version of what he had done was as off the beam as her version of last night. It made him panicky. He drew back from it. Tried to draw back from it; it had the giddying, visceral pull of a great height.

A false idea, of course. Mother hadn't dreamed up her version all on her own. Wayne remembered the overheard phrases: Narrow squeak. Skin of his teeth. He could thank his lucky stars for the Fleming kid's story, the only thing that saved him.

And Cleo, of course, had been covering up for her mother.

"It's the truth," he said again, very loud, and fled upstairs. In the hall he nearly collided with the English teacher, who occupied the room across from his and who always washed her hair on Sunday afternoons. Cerise chenille robe. Medusa head swarming with wet black snakes. Naked face shining with soap and curiosity. (How much of last night's goings on had she overheard? How much of today's?) Giggle. "Whoops! My, aren't *we* in a hurry!"

He hated her too. Everybody, everybody. Most of all himself, every solitary separate splinter of himself. No guts. Contemptible. There was even one loathsome splinter left over from childhood that wouldn't shut up, wouldn't stop whimpering for the lost world that never was, the world with Dad in it.

He slammed viciously into his room and leaned against the door, trying to keep from shaking to pieces. He had a wild, helpless feeling of impending violence, a foreknowledge that he might do something terrible to somebody. He didn't know what, he didn't know who ...

Damn him, he thought, damn him, why did he have to come back here?

EIGHT

It made Cleo nervous, the way he kept watching her. Get right down to it, Wayne always made her a little nervous. Usually it didn't matter; he seemed as leery of her as she was of him, and—even before he took up with Sally and all this double dating set in—they had evolved a routine of avoiding each other without ever being obvious about it. It worked fine. Usually.

Not tonight. It took two to make their little routine work, and Wayne wasn't pulling his weight tonight. Not only that, he was making it practically impossible for her to pull hers. At first it was just the watching, but now here she was, trapped into dancing with him again. If you cared to use the term loosely; their dancing was all shuffle and jerk and trample ... There, she had landed, but good, on *his* foot for once.

"Give up?" she asked maliciously.

"Okay," he said, and before she knew what was going on he had steered her out the side door of Louie's, out into the fresh, starry night. The door slapped shut behind them, abruptly muting the blare of juke box music. Louie's was on the edge of town, just past the railroad tracks; beyond the cars parked up close to the low stucco building she could see, to the right, the twinkle of a few lights on Main Street, and to the left, shadowy fence posts and a pasture. In the sinister light from the neon sign Wayne's face took on a faint, unhealthy green cast.

"Well!" she said, and then, "Let go of me!" because when she tried to pull free and reach for the door she discovered just how tight a grip he had on her arm.

It got even tighter. She stumbled against a trash basket that stood beside the door; cans and empty beer bottles clattered. Wayne seemed to be grinning at her. "What's the matter? What are you scared of?"

"Nothing. I just don't—"

"Scared I'll make a pass at you? You needn't be. I wouldn't dream of it."

"Thanks," she said. Her heart sank. Just as she suspected. Nothing so simple, nothing so manageable, as a pass. "I think you're irresistible too."

"Pretty sharp, aren't you? But then you always were." He really was grinning now. "I just want to talk to you a minute. A sharpie like you, that shouldn't scare you."

"It doesn't," she lied. "Why should it?"

"Come on, then. We can sit in the car."

She clutched, feebly, at the only straw in sight. "What about Bill? And Sally? They'll wonder what's happened to us. You don't want to get Sally sore at you again ..."

"She won't be," he said. "Neither will Bill. If they are we'll talk them out of it." Not bragging. Just stating the facts. It was nothing against Bill and Sally that they could be talked out of things, that they were uncomplicated and trusting, not sharpies. Different from Cleo and Wayne.

But she was in no mood to acknowledge any bond, however slight, between herself and Wayne. "You don't have to *drag* me," she said bitterly.

"I'm not," he said, and went right on doing it. He didn't loosen his grip on her until they reached Bill's car, and then only after he had shoved her into the front seat and slid in after her.

The neon sign still tinged his face with greenish pallor. She was suddenly aware that he was trembling.

"You look seasick," she said.

He glanced at her absently. "Yeah. So do you. Look, Cleo, I—" He took a tight hold on the steering wheel and swallowed convulsively.

He's as scared as I am, she thought. It made her feel much surer of herself. He wanted to talk to her, did he? So let him talk. The floor was his. She manufactured a yawn and patted it away, with an apologetic smile. She waited.

He stared straight ahead of him and began. Sharp and rapid. Like a machine gun. "Well. It's about him. My father. You saw him the other day and you—" The machine gun jammed.

"So did you," she pointed out. "Or would have, if you hadn't been blind drunk."

"Skip it, will you?"

"All right. Only you'd better watch yourself. You and your model boy bit. They're not going to buy it forever. It beats me, how you've gotten away with it this long." Though she had to admit to herself that for the past few months Wayne's model boy bit had been for real. Maybe that Spring City episode cured him. Too close for comfort. Or maybe, more likely, it was Sally. "If Sally's father ever gets wind of some of your—"

"Skip it, I said." He looked at her wildly. "You saw him. He went right out there to the school house, the first thing. Almost the first thing. As soon as he'd talked to Judge McVey."

Well. If *that* was all Wayne had on his mind, her little ride into town with his father ... She felt so sure of herself, now, that she spoke quite kindly. "Look, Wayne, you're taking this too big. No kidding. I know it's been a shock to you, his turning up again—"

"Wasn't it to you? Did you know he was coming back?"

"Of course not. Why should I? But it's not the same with me. I don't feel about him the way you do. You and your mother. I don't—hate him."

"No, and never did. Did you? Matter of fact, you must have had a real thing for him when you were a kid, judging from the way you—"

She broke in nervously. "For your father? Don't be silly. I was madly in love with the music teacher. What was his name? It slips my mind at the moment." So much for the wishful thinking, the false security, of a moment ago. Of course he hadn't dragged her out here for a harmless little chat about his father's return and nothing more; he was bent on going all the way back. Unless she could stall him. "What was his name?" she repeated. "It's right on the tip of my tongue." It certainly was. Mr. Rohman. And his image was sharp in her mind: the lock of lank black hair that fell over Mr. Rohman's forehead, pallid as Hamlet's, and the eyes, the voice that used to melt her adolescent bones.

"Rohman," said Wayne. "Okay. So Mr. Rohman was the one you were mad for. So that wasn't why you did it." He kept his hands clamped on the steering wheel, but his gaze was turned on her now. Boring into her. Relentless. Like a pin impaling an insect.

"Did what?" she whispered.

"You know. The trial, Cleo. Is that what he came back for? To thank you?" She wet her lips, but no words came. And she could not pull free from his fanatic, challenging stare. "That was a very convincing story you told at the trial, Cleo. Very, very convincing."

Could he know? How could he possibly know? She managed another dry whisper: "The truth."

"The truth, the whole truth, nothing but the truth," he said. "That's where you were so clever. That's why you were so convincing. The truth, and nothing but the truth." He leaned toward her; the strange fixed grin was back on his face. "But the whole truth? Oh no. Not the whole truth. Not by a long shot."

"No?" she said tremulously, and she put her hand up to her mouth, to hold back a giggle. Because it was so absolutely hilarious … "Not the whole truth?"

"Of course not. Just so much and no more."

"You're crazy," she said serenely. She leaned back, weak with relief. And yet the spell was not broken. They continued to stare into each other's seasick faces, and it was like a slow, insistent pull, from the safe depths of her mind to the surface. So that against her will she remembered. The first lie (of which Wayne had no inkling; she needn't have worried for a minute) and all that it had led to …

It was the sort of lie, the first one, that was frequently necessary when you were thirteen years old, on account of the things that were always happening to you. Things that couldn't be explained satisfactorily, so there was no use trying.

What had happened on that particular evening was that her heart broke at glee club practice. "Altos!" cried Mr. Rohman in a voice rich with suffering. He tapped with his baton on the music stand, tossed back his lock of black hair, and fixed his divine burning eyes on Cleo, who had been pouring forth what she felt was a flood of pure melody. "Cleo. Would it be possible for you to curb your enthusiasm just a little? Ever so slightly?"

Everyone looked at her. Everyone snickered. And her heart broke, she literally felt the jagged pieces of it gouging her under her sweater, and when—an eternity later—she reached sanctuary she was surprised to find that she was weeping not blood, as she had expected, but ordinary tears.

Sanctuary in those days was a secret cubbyhole on the roof, above the garage and the apartment, a perfect spot for transports of grief or joy. No one could see her there; she huddled in the corner, pressed up against the rough brick of the ledge, with nothing but sky above her. A winter sky, already dark at six o'clock, and pricked with the cold glitter of stars. There was the smell of tar and wet wool, from the tears she shed into her coat sleeve. After quite a long while the storm of sobs subsided, and she began to feel chilly and empty. In fact, hungry—and that was when memory smote her and she sprang up, guiltily aware of the responsibilities she had forgotten. Supper. Beef stew. Daddy. She was supposed to come straight home from glee club practice and fix supper for Daddy because Mother was taking care of old Mrs. Johnson ... Oh oh.

She scuttled down the narrow stairway to the apartment, her mind already busy with glib answers, in case there were questions. Where were you? Why didn't you? How could you? Unless she was lucky, and it wasn't as late as it felt. Daddy might not even be home yet; or he might be stretched out on the living room couch, he sometimes fell asleep before supper. She paused at the apartment door. Not a sound. So she probably was lucky. Still, she would play it safe; there was a hall down the middle of the apartment, with living room and kitchen off one side and bedrooms off the other. She would nip into her bedroom first, and out of her wraps, then across the hall and into the kitchen and—always with luck—there she would be, conscientiously peeling potatoes when and if the questions began.

It worked like a charm. Still no sound from the living room, though there was a line of light under the door. So let him sleep; all the better to wake him at the proper moment with the news that supper was ready, thanks to good girl Cleo, so dependable, so reliable. When she heard the footsteps—coming up the stairs from the garage, down the hall into the living room—she was not upset, she merely revised her theory. Daddy had not been sleeping, then. He was just coming up from the garage. She finished peeling the last potato and dropped it into the stew before she opened the living room door.

It must have been Jim Singley, not Daddy, she had heard coming up the stairs. Because Daddy was sprawled out on the floor (drunk?) and Jim Singley was bending over him. He looked up at Cleo. His face was completely blank, no expression whatever. In her mind the scene was still vivid as a dream: the cozy, lamplit room; papers scattered on the coffee table beside the whiskey bottle; one of the big upholstered chairs pulled askew and an ashtray knocked over on the rug, with Daddy's out-flung hand (the signet ring, the fine golden hairs) seeming to point at it accusingly. And beside Daddy the crouching figure of Jim Singley, shapeless in his coveralls, with his unearthly blank face lifted toward her. "Cleo?" he said. "I didn't know you were home."

The lie slid out of her, glib and automatic. "Oh yes. I was in the kitchen fixing supper."

"Then you heard. You must have heard us fighting."

Her head bobbed up and down, confirming the already irrevocable lie. "Is Daddy—"

"He's hurt," said Jim. "I didn't know he was hurt so bad. We have to get the doctor." He straightened up jerkily and went over to the telephone. Now she could see Daddy's legs in their dark gray trousers, his white shirt front and sky-rocket tie, his fair head tipped to one side and beside it the door stop. The famous, infamous door stop. Weapon of death, the newspapers called it while the trial was going on; and people in Athena still argued about it. Some said that Jim was telling the truth: Daddy simply, accidentally, hit his head on it when he went down. But there were others who believed that Jim had grabbed it up and slugged Daddy with it, either in the course of the fight or—even more blood-curdling—afterwards, mercilessly finishing off the man he had already knocked senseless. It was an old-fashioned kind of door stop, a brick covered with a bit of ingrain carpet ...

They stood and waited for the doctor. Once Jim said, "Poor kid, you must have been scared. I guess that's why you stayed out there in the kitchen, you were too scared to come in." Again her head bobbed up and down in mute confirmation. By then, of course, she really was scared— of Daddy because he didn't move; of Jim because his face was still so strange and blank; of the lie she had told and couldn't possibly take back now. And even so, she had only the dimmest glimmer of what she had let herself in for, with that harmless-sounding, little fib. How deeply it would entangle her in more and more fabrications; how often, finding herself in another tight corner, she was to fall back on the one Jim had already given her: "I can't remember, I was so scared." It did not occur to her to mistrust Jim; he provided her with the only guide posts she had.

For a moment, just before the doctor got there, the blank look left his face, and he said with sudden urgency, "Listen, Cleo. We must keep your mother out of this. If the doctor, or anybody, asks you anything, don't mention her. She had nothing to do with it. We must look out for your mother. You see that, don't you? Promise. You must promise." She promised—Why not? Why should it even cross her mind to mention Mother?—and she kept her promise. Which was easy enough; she had nothing to tell them about Mother. Or about any of the rest of it, if the truth were known. Only she had said she was there in the kitchen, and so ...

The doctor said, "God almighty, Jim, he's not hurt. He's dead." He got himself up on to his feet again, wheezing; the gold watch chain looped across his solid stomach gleamed in the light from the floor lamp. "Dead?" whispered Jim, and he rubbed his hand along the side of his face helplessly. Then they waited for the sheriff. The doctor kept relighting his cigar. He and Jim talked, in awkward snatches; they seemed to have forgotten that Cleo was there. You had a fight, you say? You knocked him down? "He hit me first," Jim said. "He'd had a few, and I was sore as hell about the money, so when I called him a crook he took a swing at me, and then I let him have it—" And slammed out of here, down to the garage? But then you came back? "I sort of cooled off," Jim said. "And I'd left the papers up here, the accounts that showed what he'd been up to. I figured I'd come up and get them and maybe, well, I'd said some pretty rough things to Herb, I guess rougher than 1 needed to, and—"

They made a great deal of that return trip of Jim's, at the trial. They hashed and rehashed it, trying to turn it into a murderer's efforts to remove evidence, or rearrange it to his own advantage, only to be surprised in the act by his victim's young daughter.

But all that came later; Cleo, listening to the low, strained voices of Jim and the doctor, had no suspicion of the sort of thing that lay ahead. What she felt was not so much sorrow (for she had not really taken it in yet, that Daddy was dead) as a bewildered, devastating kind of loneliness. She began to snivel, and then they remembered she was there. The doctor patted her and called her honey. So did the sheriff, when he came charging in a few minutes later. There must have been other people too; Cleo had a confused recollection of a sudden swarm of faces in the living room, eyes peering in from the hall, voices everywhere. One voice kept asking, "Where's the Mrs.? That's what I'd like to know. Where's the Mrs.?" A hush; a moving aside; Mother ran into the room, she had a purple scarf around her head, and her eyes were as dark as the scarf, before she fainted against the doctor's gold-chained stomach. And out in the kitchen the stew burned to a cinder.

Six years ago. Past. Over and done with.

But Wayne still sat there watching her; waiting; slowly, insistently pulling it out of her—To the surface of her mind, maybe. But no further. Not all the way out. He could make her remember. He could not make her talk. Never.

"You were covering up for your mother," he said. "Weren't you? That's why you didn't tell the whole truth. To keep her name out of it."

"Shut up!" she cried. Too much vehemence. Too much protesting. The expression on his face told her so, and yet she plunged on. "It's not true! My mother had nothing to do with it. She wasn't even there."

"Maybe not. But she had something to do with it, all right. She had plenty to do with it. They fought about her. Didn't they? Didn't they? Sure they did, only you never told that part of it, you let him get away with murder just so you could cover up for—"

"Stop it! No, no, it's not true. Stop it!" Her heart beat so thickly that she felt choked. She shrank away from him, his crazy eyes, his crazy pale-green face. "Leave me *alone*."

"Not till you tell me. You've got to, Cleo, I'll make you tell me the truth, so help me, if I have to drag it out of you ..."

He reached for her, and pure panic saved her; without it she could never have twisted free. Her elbow struck the door handle, she felt it give, and the next instant she was out of the car, scrambling in the gravel, almost falling but not quite, she was on her feet, running headlong for Louie's side door. Wayne was close behind her.

All at once someone was coming toward her, too, from around the corner. "Jim!" she panted in a voice ragged with relief, and she all but fell on his neck. "Jim, don't let him, he's trying to make me tell him—"

"What's going on here? Who—" He peered past her, and she felt him stiffen. He stepped in front of her.

Wayne had stopped at sight of his father. But only for a split second. He lunged forward; Cleo could see the wild gleam in his eye as he struck at Jim's automatically outthrust hand. It caught and held him by the shoulder.

"Wait a minute, Wayne. What the hell *is* this?"

"None of your business. Get out of my way and stay out ... Why did you have to come back here, anyway? Who needs you?" He tore himself loose, staggered with a crash against the trash basket, and came up again with a broken beer bottle in his hand.

Cleo screamed.

But even before the door opened and everybody swarmed out—first Louie himself and behind him all his goggle-eyed customers—even before that, Wayne had come to his senses. Cleo saw the fury drain out of his face; he looked down, incredulously, at the bottle in his hand, then up again at his father.

They faced each other, dumb with sorrow.

So she needn't have screamed. And nobody needed to grab Wayne and disarm him. But she did, and they did, and by morning it was all over town how Wayne Carson had gone for his father with a broken beer bottle out at Louie's.

NINE

Mack heard the story from his secretary. Which annoyed him, to begin with. It did seem, didn't it, as if a man might expect his family to toss him a crumb or two of information once in a while, just once in a while give him some idea of what was going on. But not his family. Oh no. Not when it was information about Sally's precious Wayne. Strict censorship. Conspiracy of silence. There had been not one peep out of anybody at the breakfast table—though he was willing to bet that Marge knew all about it, Sally didn't Keep Things from her mother the way she did from him ...

At least he was glad to see that his secretary was capable of changing her expression. Carol was a smart little apple, fresh out of Athena Business College, but she seldom permitted any sign of intelligence—let alone emotion—to appear in her face. The fashionably vacant look. She must practice it in front of her mirror for hours at a stretch.

But she had been at Louie's last night, she had seen with her own eyes, and in the excitement of talking about it (she assumed, of course, that he had already heard) she allowed herself to look, for a few minutes, like a real live girl. He was grateful for this minor miracle.

As for the story itself—Well, hadn't he always felt it in his bones, that Wayne Carson was too good to be true? Too handsome. Too quiet. Too well behaved. Like those horror stories in the newspapers: the model boy who suddenly goes berserk and slaughters everybody in sight, and the neighbors are always stunned because he was one of the nicest, friendliest kids in town, why, only yesterday he'd helped them mow the lawn ... He thought of Sally and shuddered.

Let's not get hysterical, he told himself sternly. A homicidal maniac was one thing. An "emotionally disturbed" boy was quite another. Look at it one way, and some kind of a blow-up between Wayne and his father was inevitable. Wasn't it? He had been taught to hate Jim; for six years Velma had drummed hate into him. (Where love had been before. Don't forget that. It made the dynamite double-strength.) So you couldn't expect him to take Jim's return without turning a hair.

Besides, Carol's version of the blow-up was not only incomplete, it was in all probability wildly inaccurate. Mack picked up his phone and called the hotel. But Jim was not there. He left a message for Jim to call him back, and spent the next couple of hours trying to think about something else.

And then, a little after noon, here came Carol with the news that Velma Carson was in the outer office and would like to see him if he could spare a few minutes. Oh God, he thought, it must be Wayne, she must have heard too, only what she expects *me* to do about it ...

"A business matter, she said," Carol specified. She added kindly, "I don't think she's heard about Wayne. She doesn't look upset enough."

"Send her on in," said Mack. Might as well get it over with, even if smart little apple Carol turned out to be wrong for once. "You're going to lunch now? Fine. See you later."

Carol tapped away on her ice-pick heels; and in a minute or two tapped back, briefly, to usher Velma in. He didn't think she looked upset enough, either, though you couldn't ever be sure, with Velma.

Their handshake was a gingerly affair. She sat down in the chair facing him; she had a good deal of elegance, in spite of the shabbiness of her clothes. A kind of ostentatious shabbiness, or so it seemed to Mack; as if she were going out of her way to prove that she was Poor but Proud. Today she wore a navy blue suit, very neat, very shiny, and a hat that looked vaguely familiar to him. A hand-me-down from Marge? Probably. It was a hat whose spirit had been broken. The little knot of once-perky flowers in front was wilted now, and the bit of velvet ribbon drooped forlornly. But beneath it Velma's fine-featured face was still innately elegant. A maximum of distinction, a minimum of warmth. And she had kept her figure. Beautiful long legs. No doubt about it, she was still a damn good-looking woman.

"You wanted to see me on business?" he prompted at last.

"Strange as it may seem." A pause. Then she went on, almost angrily. "Believe me, it isn't easy for me to come to you for advice. You of all people. But sometimes we have to swallow our pride, we can't always afford to be proud." She had been looking down at the worn purse in her lap, clasping and unclasping it. Now she lifted her eyes to his and finished in a remarkably collected voice. "I'm out of my mind with worry."

"I'm sorry to hear that." He waited helplessly. It must be Wayne, after all.

But what she said next didn't seem to fit. "I've felt it coming on for a long time now. And fought it. Closed my eyes to it. But I can't do it any more—not if I want to live with myself. No, I've got to face the truth, no matter what it costs me."

"Yes?" He relaxed enough to assume his characteristic pose—tipped back in his swivel chair, hands clasped behind his balding head. Sooner or later this sanctimonious testimonial pitch of hers would run its course and she would get down to business.

"Yes. It's not pleasant to admit you're in the wrong. But I've got to do it, Mack. I've got to admit that six years ago I made a tragic mistake."

The swivel chair let out a startled, unmannerly squawk. "You certainly did," said Mack. "I couldn't agree with you more. I don't know of any bigger mistake a wife could make than to decide her husband's a cold-blooded murderer when he—"

"Oh, I don't mean that. That wasn't any of my deciding. I had no choice in the matter. Of course Jim's a cold-blooded murderer, it's always been perfectly obvious."

"Has it? The jury didn't seem to think so, and they ought to know. They sat through all the evidence the prosecution could dig up."

Velma gave a bitter laugh. "All the evidence! Are you serious? Why, everybody in town knew what was going on with Jim and that Fleming woman! Everybody knew that last quarrel wasn't just about money, and that the killing was no more accidental than—"

"Everybody knew nothing of the sort." Mack thumped the swivel chair straight and slammed his hands down on the desk in front of him. "The quarrel started about money, and that's *all* it was about. Furthermore, it was Herb, not Jim, that struck the first blow. It can't very well be called premeditated murder when you hit back at a man that's already hit you first."

She looked him up and down, pityingly. "That's what you say. And my, you certainly say it with conviction. What makes you so sure?"

"Because I—" In the nick of time he stopped, suddenly cold with the realization that he was within a hair's breadth of giving himself away. Or maybe not even a hair's breadth, maybe she already knew. Was there something sly and triumphant in her expression? Could this be the purpose of her visit? For a crazy moment it seemed possible. But only for a moment. Crazy. Impossible. He went on firmly: "Cleo. That's what makes me so sure. The kid was there. She overheard the quarrel, and her story was substantially the same as Jim's. You can't tell me she'd lie to cover up for the man who had purposely killed her own father."

"Maybe not," said Velma. "But hasn't it ever occurred to you that she'd lie to cover up for her own mother? She's a very devoted daughter. To her mother. And her mother, oh mercy me, what a devoted wife she was to Herb. Couldn't be called for questioning at the trial. Too grief-stricken. In a state of collapse. All very convenient. Otherwise somebody might have been rude enough—and bright enough—to suggest that she and Jim planned it together, she might even have helped him ..."

Mack stood up. "Excuse me, Velma. I'm not going to listen to this. If there's something you want to consult me about, I'm perfectly willing to do what I can. But if you've just come here to unload a lot of spiteful nonsense, then I'll have to ask you to leave."

She shot him a glance of straight venom—Lord, how that woman could hate!—but then she said meekly, "I'm sorry. Of course you're a busy man, and I shouldn't take up any more of your time than I have to. Forgive me. I didn't mean to get off on that track. I don't feel I made any mistake there. You do. And you have a perfect right to your opinion. There's no point in arguing about it. The mistake I'm talking about is … Well. The money. Jim's money."

So now we're getting down to it, thought Mack. To be sure. Jim's money. He lowered himself back into his chair. Without a word, though. Let her do the talking. She needn't expect any help from him.

"I've never touched a penny of it. I swore I never would. At the time it seemed to me a matter of principle. Because I didn't want any trace of Jim left in my life. Not the faintest trace. I never even wanted to hear his name again …"

Uh huh, commented Mack—but not out loud; he still clung to his vow of silence. Uh huh, you never wanted to hear his name again, and so you stayed here in Athena, where you knew damn well nobody was going to forget who Jim was or what a poor, wronged, noble, brave woman you were. Do go on. Tell me more.

"But I see now that I was wrong. It wasn't so much a matter of principle as of pride. Selfish pride. All this time I've been indulging myself. Just for the sake of feeding my own ego, I've deprived my boy of what he's entitled to. It's all very well for *me* to scrape along and do without rather than humble myself by accepting any of Jim's money. But I had no right to demand such a sacrifice of Wayne. I've been wrong, and I admit it. You do understand, don't you, Mack? You see what I mean?"

"Sure. I've always liked money, myself." He inspected her thoughtfully. There were little white pinches of strain on either side of her mouth. The fake heroics could be discounted. But Velma's pride was not fake. This was costing her plenty. "What made you—uh—see the light?"

"I don't know exactly. Yes, I do know. Jim coming back here, I never thought he would, I never dreamed … And then Wayne himself. I can't bear to see him so unhappy. So changed. I suppose you already know about Saturday night?"

"*Saturday* night?" She was nodding, he had not misunderstood, she had not said Saturday when she meant Sunday. He thought back to Saturday night: of course! Wayne had broken his date with Sally; there she had sat, poor baby, so pretty in her finery, with her eyes getting bigger and bigger as time passed and no Wayne, no telephone call, until Bill and Cleo finally dragged her off with them. And Mack had stewed and muttered about conceited young puppies that ought to have their ears pinned back and had secretly, hopefully thought, Well, now she knows, this will cure her ... Next morning, when Wayne called and the stars were back in her eyes—hadn't he sensed at the time that there was something pretty fishy about the explanations they gave him? All a misunderstanding, nobody's fault, now don't fuss, Daddy, please, stop *fussing*. The old soothing syrup business again. The strict censorship. The conspiracy of silence.

"Not that I blame Wayne," Velma was going on. "It was Jim's fault, forcing liquor on a boy who'd never had a drink before in his life. Typical of him." (Drunk, thought Mack. He could be a chronic alcoholic for all anybody tells me. *Don't fuss, Daddy*. Drunk.) "Of course Wayne should have had the strength to resist. He shouldn't have let Jim talk him into going up to that hotel room in the first place. But he's only a boy, an unhappy, bewildered boy—and some of it's my fault. Yes. I'm partly to blame. That's why I've come to you for help, because I thought maybe you could—" She swallowed convulsively.

"You mean you've changed your mind? You've decided to accept Jim's money, after all?"

"For Wayne," she put in quickly. "Not for myself."

"All right. For Wayne. It's finally dawned on you that there's no good reason why Wayne shouldn't have a college education and a few other advantages. Congratulations. But you can't quite bring yourself to approach Jim yourself. So you want me to be the go-between. Is that it?" She nodded, without raising her eyes from the purse in her lap. She was gripping it with both hands, no longer fidgeting with the clasp, just hanging on for dear life. He said, in a kindlier tone, "Well, I can't think of any assignment I'd rather have, Velma. Or one that would be any simpler. I know from what Jim's already said to me that he's as anxious as he ever was to provide for Wayne. For you, too, as far as that goes. So all we have to do is—" There was a knock at the door. Carol back from lunch already? Only it must be a real emergency, or she wouldn't interrupt. "Yes?" he called. "Come in."

In the instant before the door opened he had a flash of clairvoyance. He knew it was going to be Jim. And it was. Since Velma's back was to him, he did not recognize her—maybe he didn't even see her; the chair had a high back—until he was well into the room. One good look at her, and he started back-tracking, mumbling an apology. Mack started to say, "Be with you in a minute." But Velma's voice cut in with cool authority: "He might as well stay, as long as he's here. Why not get it settled, right here and now?"

Well, why not? "It's all right with me," said Mack. "Have you got a few minutes, Jim? This isn't going to take long. A very simple matter. Velma and I were just discussing the possibility of making some sort of financial arrangement with you in Wayne's behalf. She's come around to the conclusion that it may have been a mistake to reject the offer you made six years ago."

"She has?" said Jim. He sat down, warily. He kept his eyes trained on Mack. So did Velma. Apparently they were not only shying away from any direct communication; they didn't even want to look at each other. Which made it a little more complicated than he had anticipated.

"She has. I assume you haven't changed your mind? Your offer still holds?"

There was a noticeable, and, to Mack, an amazing pause. Then Jim said, rather absent-mindedly, "Sure. The money belongs to Wayne. I always meant for him to have it." He stayed on the edge of his chair, unrelaxed and hostile. "What's the deal?" he asked.

"What's the deal?" repeated Mack blankly.

"Yeah. The deal. She'll let Wayne have the money if what?"

"Why, as far as I know ..." But Mack let the sentence dwindle away to nothing. They were still not looking at each other, but at him, and he felt like an innocent bystander, caught in the cross fire of two deadly enemies. Innocent was the word, all right. He had swallowed that sanctimonious line of Velma's whole. Or pretty nearly whole. Now he looked into her hard eyes (no harder, though, than Jim's) and said, "How about it, Velma? Any strings attached?"

"One or two," she said coolly. "He's got to agree to get out of town. Right away. And stay out. And he's got to agree not to see Wayne. Now or ever. I think that's all."

For a moment Mack was too overcome by the absurdity of what he had been about to do—which was to repeat Velma's terms, as if Jim were somehow shut off and had not heard with his own ears—to take in the full, rich flavor of "the deal" itself.

"Bitch," said Jim. "Tell her from me she's a bitch."

Velma did not even glance his way. "I can't see but what it's a fair enough proposition," she said. "If he really has Wayne's welfare at heart—as he's always claiming, at the top of his lungs—here's his chance to prove it. All I want is Wayne's happiness. I see now that the money will help to make him happy, and so I want him to have it. It was wrong of me to refuse it before, and I admit my mistake freely. At the same time it's my duty to protect my boy from corrupt, criminal influences."

That did it; they dispensed with Mack as a detour and glared at each other. A dark, ugly flush rose in Jim's face. He got to his feet with a kind of murderous deliberation. "Your boy. He's my boy too, don't forget. Whether you like it or not."

"Jim," said Mack sharply. "Wait a minute. Both of you. Simmer down.

The point about Wayne is—Well, I always understood he was as opposed to accepting any help from Jim as you, Velma. Has he changed his mind, too? There's no deal unless Wayne's willing to go along with it."

"Leave that part of it to me," said Velma. "If it's presented to him in the right way, he'll understand. I'll simply admit—as I did to you, Mack—that I've been mistaken all this time. There won't be any problem with Wayne. I can convince him."

"Awfully damn sure of yourself, aren't you?" said Jim. He turned away from them and stood at the window, with his hands in his pockets and his shoulders hunched. Finally he said, "I'm supposed to agree to get out of town right away. How soon do you mean by right away?"

"Today," said Velma, without hesitation. "Tomorrow morning at the latest."

"Tomorrow morning." His voice sounded muffled and abstracted. "Give me till tonight to decide. I'll know by tonight. I need some time to—to think it over."

Velma's mouth tightened with suspicion. "If you have any ideas about getting hold of Wayne in the meantime and trying—"

"I haven't." He faced her wearily. "You want it in writing?"

"That won't be necessary, thank you. I'll expect to hear from you by nine tonight." She stood up, and added, with satisfaction, "I'm not sure you realize how much Wayne hates you. I'm afraid of what he may do if you don't leave us alone. He might even be capable of violence."

"He might," said Jim. He gave a short, harsh laugh. "I appreciate the warning."

"It's Wayne I'm thinking of. Not you. I'd die myself before I'd let you turn him into a murderer too." She smiled. "Nine o'clock tonight. I'll be waiting to hear from you." Another moment, and the door had closed quietly behind her.

There was a short silence. Then Mack said, "I take it she hasn't heard about the dust-up you and Wayne had last night. She wouldn't be warning you if she had. What was it about, anyway?"

"How do I know?" said Jim irritably. "Cleo was there. Maybe she knows. I don't."

"Well, but—"

"You heard Velma. He hates me."

"If he hates you that much, how does she figure she can talk him into taking your money? The woman's crazy."

"Like a fox," said Jim. "She talked him into hating me in the first place. It ought to be a cinch, talking him into the money."

"I wouldn't be so sure." But there was no real conviction in Mack's voice. Today had shown him how perishing little he knew about Wayne. And he himself had been half taken in by Velma's self-sacrificing pitch.

By the time she was through the kid would probably be giving her—not Jim—the credit for buying him his college education. Not only that, but Jim would have forfeited any chance to square himself with Wayne or even see him. And if, on the other hand, Jim turned down the deal, he would be doing Wayne out of the money and giving Velma the right to say I told you so. This is the kind of loving, generous father you have. When I offered to accept the money for your sake, he backed down, refused to do anything for you. He never meant to in the first place.

Neat, thought Mack, very neat indeed. Aloud he said, "You could turn her down on the deal. Take a chance on by-passing her and offering the money to Wayne directly. It might work."

"Yeah. But if it didn't work, then what? I'd have thrown away the chance to do anything for him. If I don't turn her down on the deal, at least there's a chance he'll have the money. Maybe I ought to just settle for that."

"Well ..." Mack hesitated. The money could make all the difference to Wayne. It was his only means of getting away—from his mother, from Athena and the whole sorry past. It would also get him away from Sally. Though that was strictly a side issue; Mack refused to let it affect his judgment. His judgment! What was his judgment worth to a man who told him nothing about anything, past, present or future?

He said it out loud: "How can I advise you, Jim? I don't even know why you came back here."

"You and Wayne both. 'Who needs you?' he said to me last night. 'Why did you have to come back, anyway?'" He turned his hard, lonely face on Mack and suddenly shouted, "I've got a right, haven't I? Do you think I don't know you'd all like to be rid of me—Velma and Wayne, other people too? Well, you're not going to, not till I've—Not quite yet."

"Jim. I don't want to be rid of you. My God, I'm trying to help you."

"Help me! How can anybody help me? I'm the only one. That's why I had to come back."

"Listen to me," said Mack with all the authority he could muster. "It's none of my business what you came back for. All right. I'll accept that. But I'm telling you something. If you've come back out of spite, because you're holding a grudge and want to get even with somebody—if that's it, then you're a damn fool and you're heading for trouble."

"Spite? A grudge?" A curious, startled expression crossed Jim's face. He laughed, in the old warm way. "Forget it, Mack. And forget I hollered at you, will you? You're about the only friend I've got around here. Don't you get sore at me." He put out his hand awkwardly; for a moment Mack thought he was going to open up. Thought. And hoped. Because then Mack too could open up, he could make his confession and shuck off the burden of guilt that weighed on his conscience.

But the moment passed. They could not find the right words. They could only clasp each other's hands briefly, across the gulf.

"Come over to the house tonight," said Mack. "Let me know what you decide about Wayne. Meantime, if I can get hold of him, I'll try to sound him out." On more than one subject, he added to himself. As Jim turned to the door, something impelled him to add, "Take care, Jim. I mean— Well. Take care."

TEN

"Well, how's this for a beautiful spring day?" Elroy, home from the hardware store for lunch, beamed and rubbed his hands. He didn't tip-toe any more, but he was relentlessly bent on brightening the corner where he was. And on top of that, his proprietary air; as if he had personally produced the fine weather. "Brings out the gipsy in me," he declared. "Makes me want to just get in the car and *go!*"

"So go," muttered Cleo, but under her breath, so that neither Elroy nor Mother could hear. This, of course, was the build-up (oh, clever, and oh, devious!) for Elroy's pet project—the trip, the change of scene that was going to restore everybody's perspective and put Mother out of Jim Singley's reach.

She wasn't going out of her way to play the build-up game, Cleo noticed. Mother's expression was one of polite inattention. Her eyes strayed to the dining room window, where the April sunlight danced in, and beyond, to the tender blue sky, with the budding elm branches tremulous against it. The kind of day, the time of year Mother loved best. Even the present circumstances (it was Monday, Cleo's first day in her role as vigilante) could not extinguish altogether Mother's pleasure in sunshine and balmy air and delicate green. The sorrow or terror or whatever it was that was preying on her mind had not gone away, but today it seemed overlaid with a fitful kind of gaiety.

Elroy persisted: "You'd like it too, wouldn't you, Audrey? Just pick up and light out for parts unknown."

"Why, yes," said Mother absently. "It sounds very nice."

"We could, you know. Why not? After all, I'm not indispensable. Ed's perfectly capable of running the store without me. For a while, anyway. And naturally I'd keep in touch, in case of emergency. Why don't we, dar-ling? Do us both a world of good. Nothing like a change of scene to give a person a new lease on life."

Mother gave him an odd look. "A new lease on life? I can't imagine your needing anything like that, Elroy. I always think of you as being so— so much more in control of things than other people are."

"Thank you, dear," said Elroy, though it hadn't exactly had the ring of a compliment to Cleo. "I try, of course. But like everybody else I have my times of doubt. It isn't always easy. No. It isn't always so easy ..." His neat features seemed for a moment to go somehow awry; Cleo experienced one of her pangs of embarrassed and reluctant pity for the man. "Seriously, Audrey. About the trip, I mean. All you have to do is say the word. Where would you like to go? The mountains, maybe? You've never seen the Grand Canyon, but I have, and I assure you, there's no more inspiring spectacle on God's earth. Or we could drive north to the lakes. Or south. The desert. Even as far as Mexico. You just name it, and we'll start planning our itinerary."

Mother's eyes glinted mischievously. "I thought we were going to just pick up and light out for parts unknown. There, Elroy, I'm only joking. You haven't given me time to think where I'd like to go, or even if I'd like to go or—"

"Of course we'll wait till you feel strong enough," Elroy assured her. He finished his coffee and patted his mouth with his napkin. Pussy-cat fastidious. And pussy-cat pleased with himself and the way he had pulled off his little project. "I didn't mean to rush you. But you look so much better today. Doesn't she, Cleo? Didn't I say there was nothing like rest and good nourishing food to put the roses back in her cheeks?"

"You sure did," said Cleo, and Mother shot her a warning glance. She stacked a couple of dishes and started for the kitchen, knowing that Elroy would make some excuse to follow for a word in private with her. Because she was his ally. Whether she liked it or not.

Sure enough, here he came. "Everything okay?" he whispered. "I think she seems in pretty good spirits. Don't you? She didn't *say* anything, did she?"

"Not about Jim, if that's what you mean. No word from him either, so far. It's all quiet on the home front."

"From all I hear, it wasn't so quiet out at Louie's last night. They say Wayne really lit into him, would have killed him if they hadn't grabbed him in time." He paused, but Cleo shut her mouth tight. Allies they might be, but only up to a point. He wasn't getting anything out of her on this subject. He went on, with vindictive relish. "He knows how he rates with his son, all right. If he's got any sense he'll get out of town before Wayne takes another whack at him. He might not be so lucky next time. Not that I'm condoning violence, you understand. But in a way you can't blame the boy. And then it's in the blood. A chip off the old block. Like father, like son."

"Oh, for heaven's sake!" Cleo burst out.

"All the same. That's what they're saying down town. One thing sure, Wayne's not taking any of his nonsense. Well, neither are we. He'll find out. Just let him try anything with Audrey and see how far he gets. Chances are he won't, but if he does, remember, Cleo, all you have to do is phone me."

"You can count on me, Chief," said Cleo solemnly. "They shall not pass."

Ridiculous. The whole thing ... No, not the whole thing. Just Elroy. Not the rest of it. Mother's panic, her terrible sobbing, her collapse. Cleo's own impression of Jim Singley as a man with a purpose. "Be seeing you," he had said the other night, and he meant it, they had not seen the last of him. If Cleo were not convinced of it, she would be out at the school house as usual instead of standing guard duty here in town. No matter how irritating or ludicrous she might find the idea of being in cahoots with Elroy, she was committed to it—and of her own free will; nobody was twisting her arm.

Another thing she might just as well face was that she had the jitters. Elroy made it sound very simple, and maybe for him it was. Not for Cleo; she envied him his self-confidence. In her own secret heart she was not absolutely sure that, if the time came—when the time came—she would be able to deal with Jim Singley. Any more than she was absolutely sure of what his purpose might be, or of what Mother might be feeling. And she had Wayne to thank for that. Wayne and his insinuations, the infectious germs of doubt he had exposed her to. It really was like a disease; all morning she had observed in herself the symptoms. A sense of strain. Inability to relax. Above all, a compulsion to examine and re-examine whatever Mother said or did for possible hidden meanings. On the watch every minute, and every minute hating herself for it.

A lousy, insidious disease. She went back into the dinette determined to throw it off. By this time Elroy had left for the hardware store (one hour for lunch, twelve thirty to one thirty, no more and no less, you could set your watch by him) but Mother was still at the table, dawdling over her coffee. "Have another cup with me," she said. "Live it up, Teacher. You're on vacation. Is Bill coming over this afternoon?"

"Not till about five. You're stuck with me for the afternoon. Feel like going for a ride, after you've had your nap?"

"Please. No more naps. There's a limit to everything, even Elroy's rest and good nourishing food."

"Roses in your cheeks," said Cleo. "Just get in the car and go. Brings out the gipsy in him. Olé!"

"Now, Cleo," said Mother mildly.

"You started it. Yes, and you snipe at him when he's around, too, just as much as I do. I don't understand—" Hastily, she took a swig of coffee, and with it swallowed the rest of her sentence.

But Mother said it for her. "Why I married him?" She tilted her head at Cleo and went on, in a light, teasing tone. "Elementary. I married him for his money. Everybody in town knows it. It's time you learned the truth about your mother, too. You see? When you get right down to it, there's very little to be said for me. Very little to admire."

"There is, too!" Cleo burst out. She felt her face getting red with a shame that was double-edged. She could not get rid of her doubts about Mother; they kept pushing up everywhere, tough, shameful weeds. And yet here she was, maneuvered into defending Mother against those very suspicions. Maneuvered by Mother herself, which made her seem even more devious, more open to mistrust ... "I mean, if it was the money, you did it for my sake, not your own. You had me on your hands, and no way of making a living, and—"

Mother laughed out loud. "And so I'm not to blame, after all. You're going to make me out a noble character in spite of myself, aren't you, darling? Only even you have to admit it's not very nice of me to marry Elroy for his money and then make fun of him."

"Well, of course he does get pretty ridiculous at times," said Cleo uncomfortably.

"Ridiculous?" All the lightness went out of Mother's manner; her voice, even her face, sharpened into an intensity that took Cleo by surprise. "No he isn't. No, Cleo. Don't ever make the mistake of thinking Elroy's ridiculous. No, when I laugh at him it's only because I—" She paused, in grave consideration. "Because I—Well, I have to show off, somehow or other. I suppose that's it. It's my way of showing off." She seemed satisfied with the explanation, pleased with it, as if she had made some interesting discovery about herself.

But to Cleo it was no explanation at all, it was only another bewildering turn in the maze. Unless—yes, that must be it—Mother, having married Elroy not for love but for money, must cling to this last shred of her self-respect, this faculty for making fun of him. Sort of a gesture of independence, to prove that she had not sold out quite everything of herself. Only, if that was it, why deny that he was ridiculous? Surely she didn't have to "show off" to Cleo, who was going to go on loving her no matter what. It was true: the doubts, by heightening Mother's vulnerability, heightened to the same degree Cleo's protective impulse. Even if "everybody in town" was right, and Mother had indeed been faithless with Daddy; mercenary with Elroy; weak, or wanton, with Jim Singley—even so, Cleo would still be there with her shield of anxious, steadfast love.

Surely Mother must know that. It had never been clearer to Cleo than at this moment, sitting here at Elroy's table, watching Mother as if she hoped to see past the charming, changeable face to the secrets within. Sunlight glinted on her brown hair, edging it with dark gold. She had on a hyacinth-blue blouse; just now her eyes seemed almost the same color. She sat with one elbow on the table, cheek propped against her hand, in the touching attitude of a tired child.

"I know Elroy gets on your nerves," she said haltingly. "Natural enough, I suppose, for you to resent him. Or any stepfather. But you just—you don't understand him, Cleo."

"I don't understand anything!" cried Cleo. "Don't you see, Mother? I'm all mixed up! How can I look out for you when I don't even know what it is you're scared of?"

"Scared?" Instantly the tired-child face changed, flickered into wariness. "Why ... What makes you think I'm scared of anything? Just because I got upset the other night. It was a shock, that's all. I'm over it now, perfectly all right again. Scared! Why, what in the world do I have to be afraid of?"

"Not what. Who," said Cleo, with the bluntness of desperation. "Jim Singley. After all, he did kill Daddy, and—"

"By accident. In a fight that your father started. After all, Cleo, you heard it yourself, you were right there in the kitchen. This gossip about its not being an accident—oh, I can imagine, even though I don't get around much, I know how people talk—well, nobody knows better than you how little truth there is in it."

"I—" But Cleo could not do it. She could not say I don't know because I wasn't there, I lied, I was up on the roof bawling about Mr. Rohman. Any more than she could fling in Mother's face (flushed now with excitement, or maybe anger, and her eyes were flashing) the other, even uglier half of the gossip. Though it was positively burgeoning in Cleo's mind: Didn't Mother's insistence on the accident theory constitute a defense of Jim Singley, and didn't that in turn suggest an involvement on her part? "I know," she said weakly. "All the same—"

But Mother swept on, with a grand air of assurance. Every inch the wise, kindly adult setting her child straight. (It was a role she seldom got a chance to play; she made the most of her few opportunities.) "What an idea! Of course I'm not afraid of Jim Singley. As for this notion you seem to have that it's up to you to 'look out for' me—Well, really, Cleo. I managed to struggle along on my own for eighteen years before you put in an appearance, and I'm still perfectly capable of looking out for myself. Perfectly capable, thank you, of standing on my own feet—" To prove her point, she sprang up, whirled, somehow collided with the tea wagon, and wound up on her hands and knees, looking incredulous and outraged.

After a moment Cleo asked tremulously, "Are you all right?" and Mother said, "Please. Do not interrupt the lecture. The illustrated lecture," and then they both collapsed on the floor and laughed till they cried.

Finally they pulled themselves together and went for a drive along the river road, where the willows trailed, feathery with the first faint green, and phoebes piped in voices thin and clear as the April air. It was too early for bluebells, but they got out of the car and looked for the patch Cleo thought she remembered from her childhood May basket days. In one sheltered spot Mother found a few chilly-looking, purplish anemones, and they saw a whole flock of red-winged blackbirds rocking jubilantly in a stand of cattails.

When they talked, it was of inconsequentials, and when they laughed it was over nothing in particular; they might have been two birds themselves, chirping out of sheer pleasure. There was something so direct and ingenuous about the way Mother enjoyed things … An aptitude for happiness, Cleo thought; it seemed just the right phrase for Mother. She might not be the brainiest woman in the world, or the strongest character, but she knew how to be happy, how to give life a special, lyrical quality; and that was enough for Cleo. For the moment, at least, she asked nothing more than to share in the radiance of Mother's joy. And love. She knew how to love, too, and how to be loved. Which was maybe the same as knowing how to be happy.

The afternoon was waning when they drove back to town. Away from the river there were hardly any trees, just the rich, brown, moist fields stretching on either side of the road, and overhead the dazzling blue sky with a few cottony wisps of clouds. Athena itself had a leisurely, spring-struck air, in spite of the sounds of activity—a carpet being beaten somewhere off Main Street; hammering and sawing from the business college, which was being remodeled.

Cleo let Mother out in front of the house, before she drove the car around to the garage. "You hop in and change your shoes," she said. "Elroy would have a fit if he knew I let you get your feet wet." Not that he would ever know, of course; life with Elroy was studded with such trifling secrets. He disapproved of practically everything except rest and good nourishing food, where Mother was concerned. If he had his way, Cleo thought, he would shut her off entirely from the outside world. Which most of the time seemed to suit Mother well enough; she had never been madly social, and after Daddy's death she shrank away even more from the ladies'-club, bridge and civic-improvements circuits that kept other Athena matrons bustling. Her closest friends were the neighbor kids who sometimes paused on their way past, if she happened to be outdoors working in the garden or sitting on the porch. Except for them and Cleo—and, naturally, Elroy—she led an oddly solitary life.

Cleo did not see him until she got out of the car. Jim Singley. He came around from the other side, where he must have been waiting amid the clutter of garden tools. Lying in wait, really, hiding—though there was nothing sinister in his manner, once he stepped into view. "Hello there, young lady," he said. "I saw the car was gone and figured I'd hang around a while, till you got back. Didn't mean to scare you."

It was true that she had gasped. And her heart was still knocking against her ribs like a fist beating on a closed door. So she must be scared. Not surprised, though. It was like the first time she had seen Jim, out in the school house, when she had felt that astonishing lack of astonishment.

She blurted it out: "You can't go inside. I won't let you see Mother."

"How are you planning to stop me?" he asked pleasantly. Not bothering to threaten or challenge her; just asking, out of curiosity and amusement. It was a very good question. There he stood in the garage doorway, about twice as broad and solid as she was. And certainly twice as sure of himself. She could not even get by him, unless he chose to let her past. She might, she supposed, grab up a rake and rush at him. Only it seemed such a melodramatic thing to do. Embarrassingly so—when he was not making the slightest gesture that could be called menacing. Maybe it wasn't Mother, but Cleo, he had come to see, anyway. After all, she couldn't go on dodging her long overdue explanation forever. It had obviously been on his mind the other day, at the school house. Let him have it here and now. Let him thank her, if he insisted. That too she could stand, for Mother's sake.

"I don't know what made me say that," she said, and started walking toward him, natural as you please. She hoped. "I guess you did scare me, or I wouldn't have forgotten what you said Friday out at the school house. About wanting to see me. About the time you've spent, trying to figure me out. And no wonder. You must have thought—well, I don't know what you must have thought of me. It was so crazy. One of those crazy things you get into without meaning to, and then afterwards you're ashamed because it sounds so crazy—"

"Well, yes," said Jim. "Sure I wanted to see you. Still do, in fact." She was right in front of him now. Sunlight struck one side of his face, showing up the squint lines around his eye and the strong line of his jaw (so familiar to her, so reassuring); the other side, in shadow, had a cavernous, somber look. His voice was still mild, without a trace of menace. But his next words shattered her thin hope of stalling him. "It'll have to keep, though. Right now ... Elroy's not home, is he?"

"What if he isn't? You can't see her. She went all to pieces the other night, and you're not going to—"

"I can't help it. I've got to talk to her."

"*Why?* Why have you got to talk to her?" Cleo cried frantically, because he was turning, he was setting off up the flagstone path with that purposeful stride of his. She caught hold of his sleeve. "I won't let you! I'll call Elroy, that's how I'll stop you!"

He paused. "You do and I'll—"Then the flare of anger in his eyes died out, and he said, quite gently, "Look, Cleo. You're a good kid. Only you're out of line, you're messing in something that's none of your business. I'll make a deal with you. You can't stop me from going inside, and you know it. I'm going in. But if Audrey tells me to get out, I'll get the hell out and that will be that. I give you my word."

"But Elroy—"

"Yeah. Elroy. If she wants you to call him, go ahead and do it. That's fair enough, isn't it?" Incredibly, he grinned at her. Then he headed for the house again. She had to trot to keep up with him. But Elroy—But Mother—But Jim—

There was no time left. He was already at the back door—taking no more notice of Cleo, who was still hanging on to his sleeve, than if she had been a sandbur—and Mother was in the kitchen, standing at the sink with the tea kettle in her hand, and without her shoes on. She had stepped out of them beside the door; they lay there like two small muddy canoes beached on the inlaid linoleum. At the sound of the door opening, she looked around over her shoulder, and Cleo croaked, "Mother, I tried, but I couldn't ..."

That was as far as she got. Mother neither heard nor saw her. Her enormous, deep-blue eyes were fixed on Jim; light leaped in them, an intensity of light that dazed Cleo, braced as she was for a repetition of Friday night's panic. She would have had some notion of how to deal with panic; it was at least within her experience. But this was not. This was ...

It came to her with the finality of a door shutting in her face. Jim had been right: this was none of her business. None of her business whatever.

Mother always moved quickly, sometimes with an accidental kind of grace. But now, as she turned to face Jim, she had for a moment the poise of a great lady. The tea kettle in her hand might have been a feather fan; she might have been wearing golden slippers instead of none at all; her little neck, in spite of its fragility, rose up proud and straight. She too had been right: she was perfectly capable of standing on her own feet, without Cleo or anyone else to look out for her.

"Audrey," Jim began, "I have to get it straight—"

"I know," said Mother quietly. "Yes. Of course, Jim. Yes." They did not think of Cleo as an intruder. They did not think of her at all. They had simply forgotten her. She let her hand drop away from Jim's sleeve. Its removal, like its presence, went unnoticed, and when she crossed the room and the swinging door shut behind her they did not notice that either. None of my business, she thought. She doesn't need me.

It was such a brand-new notion. Hard to grasp, after all these years of thinking of Mother as her darling little incompetent, her child-mother who didn't know how to take care of herself. But, standing there in the middle of the living room, Cleo did grasp it; with an almost parental, rueful pride she relinquished her role of self-appointed caretaker and accepted the fact of Mother's independence. She even felt a pang of amusement at the mental image of herself and Elroy as a composite, officious mother hen, clucking over a chick who neither wanted nor needed their supervision.

Only Elroy wasn't going to think it was funny. Funny! (She could hear his voice, screechy with outrage; she could feel the pale, piercing stare he would fix upon her.) Funny! None of your business! You mean to tell me you let that murdering bastard in my house, you walked out and left Audrey alone with him when all you had to do was pick up the phone and call me ...

She saw quite clearly how it would look to Elroy. The enormity of it. The betrayal of his trust in her. Unforgivable. Absolutely beyond the pale.

There was a chance, of course, that he might never find it out. Not much of a chance, though, with the collective eye of Athena trained on Jim and his doings. And this was not one of the trifling secrets Cleo and Mother were forever sharing. This encounter, this low murmur of voices from the kitchen, this whatever it was. No. Elroy was bound to find it out, he would be livid, and she could not blame him.

All the same, she was not going to call him. And when, through the picture window, she saw him coming down the street at not quite a dead run, she committed the final act of treachery. She went to the kitchen door and called through to Mother and Jim that he was coming.

There was a quick, whispered argument. Then Mother said out loud, with cool urgency, "No. I won't have it. You must let me handle this my own way." And after that footsteps and the slap of the back door shutting behind him.

Which coincided almost exactly with the opening of the front door. Elroy shot in. Jet propelled. Halfway across the room before he got the brakes on. He looked as he had looked the other time, Friday night. Face white and quivering. Wild-eyed. Topped off with that supernaturally tidy, straw-colored hair. Cleo realized that her knees were shaking.

"Where is he? What's he done to her?" He seemed literally to spin. Then Mother came in, and he stopped with his head thrown back stiffly and his hands jerking at his sides. "The kitchen! Is he out there? I'll—"

"No. He's gone, Elroy. He's already gone," said Mother. Her voice was low, rather absent-minded. In the failing light Cleo could not make out her expression, but she still had her newly acquired poise. The slightness of her figure served only to heighten the curious effect of dignity. It struck Cleo all over again—here was a woman who knew what she was doing and why; who had found her true course and would follow it unswervingly, regardless of outside help or hindrance.

It did not strike Elroy. He rushed to her, all solicitude and reassurance. "It's all right, darling. I'm here. I got here as quick as I could, as soon as I heard he was up here ... You mustn't be afraid, darling. It's all right now, I'll take care of you, I won't let him— Here, let me get your sweater. You're cold, your hands are like ice. Cleo, where's her sweater?"

"Here," said Cleo, automatically falling back into the old caretaker pattern. But as she crossed the room with the sweater, she added, "You're all right, aren't you, Mother? No need to make a fuss."

Which was a mistake—as she realized, the minute the words were out of her mouth. Elroy turned on her. "What do you mean, all right? Can't you see she's in a state of shock? Hardly knows what she's doing, and you claim she's all right! Why didn't you call me? How could you let a thing like this happen?" Mother's protest made him pause momentarily; he took a new, less hostile tack. "But maybe that's what you were doing here in the living room, trying to call me. I'm sorry, Cleo. Of course that must have been it. He got past you somehow, and then when you tried to get me I'd already left. That's it. Of course that must be it ..."

Here was her chance. It would be so easy, so much simpler, to grab the line he was throwing out to her and scramble back into his good graces. But a perverse honesty took possession of Cleo. Honor among thieves, or something. She had betrayed Elroy, but she drew the line at lying about it. Besides, scrambling back into his good graces meant scrambling back into the uneasy alliance with him. Which was out of the question, now that she had grasped the fact of Mother's independence. No. She must try to get that fact across to Elroy, must somehow or other make him understand ...

"No," she said, and Mother gave a little sigh. "I wasn't going to call you. It's true that Jim got past me, I tried to stop him and couldn't, but after that I—After that it was different. I didn't try to stop him anymore, and I left him alone with Mother, and I wasn't going to call you at all. Because—" Her throat dried up.

In the moment of deadly silence before Elroy loosed his fury, she knew that she had been out of her mind to try to explain. His eyes. The concentration of cold violence in his eyes was beyond anything she had foreseen or imagined; all that kept her from turning tail and fleeing was the state of her legs. They seemed to be dissolving under her. His words— and in another second he was flinging words at her like stones—came as a relief. Talking was at least human.

He said everything she had known he would say, screeching himself into an ecstasy of outrage. "No, no!" cried Mother, but not even she could stop him, he actually brushed her hand off his sleeve. He was *never* going to stop, thought Cleo; never going to run out of breath or bitterness. He was going to go on forever, battering her to a pulp with every last punishing word he could lay tongue to. She had asked for it—that senseless refusal to lie, that crazy notion that she could make him see—and she was getting it. All she could do now was take it. Stand her ground and take it. Only he kept closing in on her, and she could not help it, each step he took forward forced her into an ignominious backward shuffle. She was not really afraid of him physically; it was just an automatic, knee-jerk kind of reflex. A snail-pace retreat that brought her, finally, flat against the wall between living room and foyer, with Elroy's face (those eyes of his) inches from her own.

Into this nightmare scene walked Bill, come to pick her up for their supper date. Like a mirage of normality shimmering into view beyond Elroy's shoulder—Bill's open, blunt-featured face, his crew haircut and solid bulk. He stopped in his tracks, momentarily struck dumb, with his cheerful expression melting by visible degrees.

His presence (which struck Cleo as both comic and comforting) made no difference to Elroy. In a climax of invective he was snarling, "I should have known, of course. Because you've always hated me, haven't you? Simply because Audrey married me. Only I didn't realize how much you hated me, I didn't realize you'd stop at nothing. Absolutely nothing, so long as you could get back at me. No matter what it did to your own mother. This could have killed her. You know that, don't you? Don't you? Answer me. But that didn't stop you, you didn't care what happened to her—"

"No!" It came out in a wrench of relief—here at last was one point where her conscience was clear. She slid out from between the wall and Elroy and flung out her arms to Mother, who stood in stricken silence in the middle of the room. "Mud! I did it because I love you!"

"You love her. You don't know anything about love. I'm the only one that loves her." And suddenly Elroy's hand darted out and lashed against Cleo's cheek.

"Hey now, wait a minute ..." It was Bill, bumbling forward to the rescue. Mother too was across the room in a rush. "Cleo darling! Don't ..."

But it was all wasted on Cleo. With a wonderful feeling of elation and release she doubled up her fist and hit Elroy as hard as she could. In the midriff. He gave a grunt of surprise, and his face sagged incredulously. "You're damn right I hate you. I'll never speak to you again as long as I live. I'm walking out of this house right now, and I'll—"

"You sure are," said Bill. "You're coming home with me. I don't know what's going on around here, but nobody's going to slap you and get away with it. That's for sure." He turned his uncomplicated face on Elroy and added candidly, "What's the matter with you, Mr. Hild? You nuts or something?"

Elroy ignored him. "Don't let me keep you. Get out. Do you think I'd have you on the premises after what you've done today?" (He had his arms folded, prissily, across his middle, but he was not even very short of breath. So she couldn't have socked him too hard. Unfortunately.) "Not on your life. I'm not going to have Audrey subjected to any more of these performances. For her sake I'll have to ask you to leave."

"For her sake!' Cleo echoed. "Why don't you let her run her own life for a change? That's what I meant when I said—" It wasn't safe to go on. She might disgrace herself by bursting into tears in front of everybody. She marched down the hall to her room, yanked out her overnight case, and began stuffing things into it. Fierce sobs surged out of her. She could not contain them, even when she heard someone come in the door after her.

"I know," said Mother, as if there had been no lapse in time or conversation. "Of course that's what you meant. Don't cry, lamb. I know." She reached out and took Cleo's face tenderly between her hands. Which naturally made the sobs worse, only by now Cleo was past caring.

"Oh, Mud, I can't leave you alone with him! How can I?"

"How can you do anything else?" said Mother calmly. "You can't possibly stay now, and I can't leave with you because I have to explain to Elroy ... I owe it to him, you see, no matter how it may seem to you, I owe it to him. You must let me handle this my own way." She paused, as if she too were remembering that she had used the same words, earlier, to Jim. "You said it yourself—let me run my own life for a change. Is it so hard for you to believe I can?"

The slightly tilted head, the luminous eyes, the quicksilver smile, the gaiety—it was one of Mother's moments of fleeting beauty. Fleeting; and for that reason all the more poignant.

"I guess so," Cleo faltered. "Because I've always—had you figured out wrong, I guess."

"Think nothing of it. It's been going on all my life, people figuring me out wrong, and most of the time it doesn't matter. But it does with you, Cleo. You must believe what I tell you. Which is—" She took out her handkerchief and began mopping up Cleo's tear-stained face. "Namely. It's going to be all right. Really, really. I promise. There isn't time now, but I'll see you tomorrow, I'll call you in the morning, and you'll see, by then it will be all straightened out, and so you mustn't worry. Believe me. You do believe me, don't you?"

"Yes," said Cleo, from the bottom of her heart. Because the radiance was still there in Mother's face, and the strange new assurance. Even Elroy could not be blind to it much longer. Cleo hadn't been able to make him see. But Mother could. Even Elroy—like Cleo—must resign as Mother's caretaker. She didn't need one anymore.

ELEVEN

Nine o'clock was the deadline Velma had set, and nine o'clock it was, on the nose, when Mack called her to tell her that her deal was on, as far as Jim was concerned. They were in his den at home, he and Jim, when he made the call; half an hour earlier Jim had turned up and said matter of factly, "I've decided to take her up on it. Might as well. What chance have I got with Wayne, anyway? It's all I can hope for."

"I wish I'd been able to reach him this afternoon," Mack said. "If I could have gotten to him when Velma wasn't around, long enough to—"

"Probably wouldn't have made any difference. No. I might as well call it quits with Wayne. Give him whatever money I can and leave him alone." For a moment he looked past Mack, bleakly. "Go ahead and call her."

She took the news with less malicious triumph than Mack would have expected. She sounded rather tense, he thought. Could she have overestimated her powers of persuasion? "I assume you've settled it with Wayne," he said.

A barely perceptible pause. "Certainly. We're settling it now. Thank you for calling." She hung up, and Mack decided not to mention it to Jim, better not raise any false hopes.

Besides, at that moment the front door banged open and shut, and Bill's voice bellowed: "Mom! Hey, Mom!"

"She's not here!" Mack bellowed back. When Bill stuck his head in the den door, he added, "Some Woman's Club shindig. And Sally's at play practice. What are you doing here? Thought you had a date with Cleo?"

"I have. She's here with me." Sure enough, there was Cleo in the background. Both of them looked slightly flustered. Probably on account of Jim. "Hi, Mr. Singley ... Look, Dad. We wanted to ask Mom. It's okay if Cleo stays here all night, isn't it?"

Beyond his shoulder Cleo's face flushed up red as a rose. She gave a self-conscious laugh. "I guess you probably wonder—Well. I got mad at Elroy. That's how come."

"I see," said Mack. "Why, sure. Fine. There's plenty of room. Of course you can stay, Cleo. Glad to have you. Uh. Your mother's recovered, I guess, or you wouldn't—"

"Oh, she's all right again. She's perfectly all right, Judge McVey." But the message, Mack realized, was for Jim. Who sat stiff and still, his eyes fastened on Cleo, as hers were fastened on him. She spoke with great earnestness. "Mother's just fine. Otherwise, of course, I wouldn't have left, no matter how mad I got at Elroy." She remembered Mack and her manners. "Thanks very much, Judge McVey."

"Make yourself at home, honey. You're welcome to stay as long as you like."

After that the kids left to go to the movies, and after that there was a longish silence. Trust Jim not to break it. Mack got up and mixed them each another bourbon. "You were over there this afternoon," he said. "Weren't you?"

"Yes," said Jim. Period.

"Did you see Elroy?"

"No," said Jim. Period.

Just so had he behaved in the witness stand six years ago, giving straight answers to the questions they put to him, volunteering nothing, refusing to make a display of his feelings. It had struck Mack at the time that he was a risky kind of witness; his reserve—while it commanded respect—might very well have backfired. Too cool a customer, the jury might have decided. Cold-blooded.

Well, they thank God hadn't.

And quite a bit emerged from Jim's monosyllables, after all. The picture of this afternoon's happenings was clear: Cleo left on guard, and failing in her assignment—for of course that was what she and Elroy had quarreled about. She had let Jim get past her, and Elroy had found it out. In a way, it was ludicrous, the picture of Elroy Hild as a knight in shining armor, galloping full tilt to the defense of his invaded castle, his lady menaced by this intruder from the dark past. But in another way ...

Audrey wasn't beautiful, at least not in the ordinary sense of the word. Mack had never been able to figure out whether she had any brains or not. Or any integrity. Amazing, how little he knew about her. Of course, she hardly ever got any farther from Elroy's house than the front yard. You never saw her downtown. Yet he discovered that he had a far more distinct mental image of her than of lots of women he saw all the time. That fragile little neck. Heartbreaking. And then the eyes. It wasn't so ludicrous, the idea of Audrey as one of those haunting legendary ladies for whom men fought and died.

Herb Fleming and Jim had fought, all right. And Herb Fleming had died. For her? There was nothing solid to substantiate such a legend. Audrey's name, though it might have been in everybody's mind and on everybody's lips privately, had not been mentioned in the courtroom. Besides, she had wasted no time in marrying a different husband.

Which was all well and good. Jim had still come back to Athena to see her. No getting around it. It was why he had stalled Velma off on her deal—not for time to think it over, but for time to see Audrey. And now, having seen her …

Over the edge of his glass Mack took a curious look at Jim's face. A guarded, proud face. Had it changed since this morning? Was some of the tension gone, some of the harshness? He caught Mack's eyes on him, and suddenly smiled, with such rare and open warmth that Mack's guilty heart lurched. He's leaving town tomorrow, he thought; I may never get another chance, I've got to get it off my chest, I can't stand not to.

"Jim," he said, "there's something I have to tell you, something I've been—"

The phone at his elbow cut in shrilly. He took a deep breath and answered it.

"Judge McVey?" The voice at the other end of the wire came at him in a rush, trembling, barely under control. It was a moment before he recognized it as Wayne's. "I know you talked to my mother a little while ago, and I just wanted to tell you—I just want to get this straight with you, that's all. I've got something to say on the subject too, don't forget. And another thing, they can just stop shoving me around like I was a football or something. You can tell him that from me."

"Wait a minute, Wayne. I thought it was all settled. Your mother said—"

"I know what my mother said, and I don't care. She doesn't need to think I'm going to take any of his damn money. Because I'm not."

"I see," said Mack. "I want to talk to you, Wayne. Where are you?" Not at home, certainly; a juke box blared in the background.

"What is there to talk about? I don't want his money, that's all. You can tell him so from me. I'd have told him myself, only he's not at the hotel."

"Your father's here with me. Wayne. Listen to me. We both want to talk to you. Not just about the money, we'll skip the money if you feel that way about it. Calm down, and come on over here. Or, if you'd rather, tell me where you are, and we'll meet you. Anywhere you say."

"I don't want to see him! I don't want money or anything else from him! Why doesn't he leave me alone? He's probably not there, anyway. He's probably—"

"He's sitting right here beside me. Do you want me to put him on the phone to prove it?"

"No!" yelled Wayne. "What do I care where he is? Tell him from me he can go to hell."

"Wayne …" But the line crackled and went dead.

There was nothing for Mack to do but hang up too. He turned help-lessly to Jim. "Well. He's not buying Velma's deal, if that's any consola-tion. He's too worked up to make much sense. Claims he doesn't want to see you, and yet he went to the hotel looking for you—"

"Is he still there? Where is he?"

"God knows. Maybe The Snackery. There was a juke box going."

"Drunk?"

"No," said Mack, after a moment of consideration. "Just disorderly. I don't think he knows himself what he wants, or what he's going to do."

"What do you mean, what he's going to do?" Jim's tone was edgy, al-most hostile; Mack felt an answering flare of nervous irritability.

"How do I know? I told you he wasn't making sense. If I could get hold of him maybe I could—"

"Well, let's get hold of him then! My God, Athena's not such a me-tropolis as all that. There's not more than half a dozen places for him to be. Let's go find him."

"I'm not so sure we should," said Mack slowly. "For one thing, look how he blew up when he saw you last night. Another scene like that isn't go-ing to do anybody any good. Besides, I've got a feeling he may turn up here, after all. What if we miss him, and he finds nobody here? He'll go looping off again, more worked up than ever. Let's give him ten or fif-teen minutes before we start beating the bushes."

It was a long, uneasy ten minutes. Jim paced the floor. Mack managed to stay in his chair; he could not keep from fidgeting. The silence op-pressed him, but so did his one or two forlorn attempts at conversation. He wished to God Jim would stop pacing. (As Jim no doubt wished to God he would stop fidgeting.)

"We could split up," Jim said abruptly. "We don't both have to sit here and wait. Why don't I go take a look around town, and if I find him ..."

"I think there's more chance he'll talk to me than to you. So if you do spot him, don't try to talk to him. Call me, and I'll get there as soon as I can. That's the best way."

"Sure." Jim was already in the hall, heading for the front door, with Mack close behind him. The relief of doing something cheered them both. They went out onto the porch together; Mack had turned on the porch light, and it made a pool of almost theatrical brightness in the night, blanching the bridal wreath bushes that banked the porch and twisting the branches and trunks of the maples into weird shadows. The house was set far back from the street, with a big, old-fashioned, hedge-bordered yard.

As Jim started down the porch steps, Mack had another thought. "You want to take the car?" It was right there in the driveway; the kids had gone to the movies on foot. "You can have it if you want it."

Jim paused on the bottom step. "But then you won't have it, if I do happen to find him and call you. No. I'll do just as well without it. Thanks, anyway. Thanks for everything, Mack."

The light fell sharply on his uplifted face, with its lines of sorrow and strain. "Don't worry," Mack said. "We'll get him straightened out. Could be we're just making a mountain out of a mole hill, anyway, and he's already—"

The shot cracked out of the darkness, an incredible whip lash of sound. Jim flinched from head to foot and then stood frozen, his face still lifted toward Mack, only now it was blank, no expression whatever. For an instant Mack was too dazed to do anything but stare back at him. It was as if lightning had struck them both.

Then Mack recovered his senses. "Jim! Are you hit? For God's sake get out of the light ..." He was down the steps, yanking at Jim, half-dragging him across the porch and into the safety of the house, still uncertain whether or not the shot had found its mark. It seemed terribly important to get the porch light turned off.

"What in the hell?" said Jim mildly. He leaned against the wall and closed his eyes.

"Somebody took a shot at you." Impatiently Mack looked him over. "What's the matter with you? If you're shot why don't you say so?"

"I'm not," said Jim. "Lay off, will you? They missed me. Whoever it was, they're not going to win any prizes for marksmanship."

"That light. You were a sitting duck. Whoever it was ..."

Their eyes met, shifted, met again. Jim said, quite loudly, "Wayne was a dandy shot, even as a kid. I used to take him out hunting. He was a dandy good shot even then." His face went white, and still Mack found it impossible to look away from him.

"We've got to report this, Jim. No choice in the matter. We have to call the sheriff."

"Why do we have to? Why can't we wait till after we've found Wayne—"

"Look, Jim. Somebody tried to kill you. I don't care who it was, you're not going to give them another chance at you. I won't permit it. Not just because I happen to be a judge and presumably on the side of the law, but because I'm a friend of yours—and of Wayne's too, when it comes to that. Whether he's in it or not, you'll only be making it worse for him by trying to stall."

It worked. There was a moment when he thought it might not, but in the end Jim gave up and nodded.

When he came back from phoning, Mack said, "He'll be right over. Sheriff Wohler. Don't know if you know him or not. He asked did we see anybody? Or hear anything, after the shot?" He peered out at the peaceful darkness. Idiot. As if Jim's enemy were still there, obligingly waiting to be discovered. Long gone by now, of course. And he had been too intent on getting Jim inside to see or hear anything else. "I'm not even sure which direction it came from. Are you?"

"That way," said Jim, and pointed to the driveway side of the yard. "They could have fired from the other side of the car. Or from behind the hedge."

"The car—" Mack began, but Jim broke in on him. "Chances are he doesn't even own a gun. Does he?"

"Not that I know of. I don't think he hunts anymore. But it wasn't necessarily his gun. It could have been—" Mack swallowed. "It could have been mine."

"What do you mean it could have been yours? How could he—"

"The car, Jim. I keep it in the car, in the glove compartment. Ever since I was held up on that trip I made a year or so ago. Marge made such a fuss, and I decided myself it wouldn't hurt to have a little protection. So I bought a .38. The glove compartment's usually locked, but it wouldn't be hard to break the lock."

"He'd have to know about the gun," said Jim.

"It's no particular secret, and Bill and he use the car often enough."

"No particular secret." Jim pounced on the phrase. "So plenty of other people could know about it too."

"Sure. Sure they could. Practically everybody in town. Look. We're getting way ahead of ourselves. Whoever it was, we don't know they used my gun. It's just a notion. I wouldn't even have thought of it, except that the car's there in the driveway and— But for all we know, my gun's right where it belongs, locked in the glove compartment."

It wasn't, though. As Sheriff Wohler very quickly discovered. The compartment door hung open, its lock broken ("No trick at all," the sheriff pointed out. "You could do it with a nail file.") and the revolver conspicuously missing. They recovered the bullet; the sheriff dug it out of the porch pillar where it had embedded itself. But there was no sign of the gun in the driveway or along the hedge. Of course they might easily have missed it in the dark, Mack told himself hopefully.

"Looks like he took it with him," said Sheriff Wohler, who liked to spell things out. "You better stay out of sight, Mr. Singley. Watch out he don't take another shot at you." He was a barrel-shaped man with a hard, jovial face, blunt in thought and speech. He did not get many ideas; those he got he hung on to. "That boy of yours. Wayne Carson. I heard you and him had some kind of a scrap last night, out at Louie's. That so?"

"If you want to call it that," said Jim.

It was obvious that the sheriff did want to, and Jim's account of last night's episode did nothing to change his mind. "So you don't know what was eating on him," he said. "Looks to me like we better find out. Seen anything of him tonight?" And after Mack told him about the phone call from Wayne, he nodded and hitched up his pants with an air of resolution. "Yep. That's the first thing to do. Get a hold of Wayne."

There was no denying it. Mack did the best he could. "I'd like to talk to him when you find him," he said. "If it's all right with you. I know Wayne, and—"

"So do I. But sure, Judge. I got no objection. I'll call you as soon as I get a hold of him. Yep. I know Wayne too. He runs around some with my boy." His voice took on an edge of bitterness. "These kids nowadays. Can't tell what they're liable to do next."

TWELVE

As soon as the door closed behind Sheriff Wohler Jim said, "Come on. Or do you want to wait here while I go?"

"To look for Wayne, you mean? Listen, Wohler may not be a mental giant, but he's competent. As a matter of fact, he's a pretty good guy. He'll find Wayne."

"I know it."

"Then why not let him do it?"

"Because he's made up his mind Wayne did it."

"Let's face it, Jim. There's a damn good chance Wayne did. And if he did, there's no sense trying to cover up for him. It doesn't make any difference whether you call him 'sick' or 'bad.' Either way, you can't leave him running around loose."

"All right. I know it." Jim turned impatiently, his hand on the door knob. "I've got no intention of trying to cover up for him if he did it. But if he didn't do it, he ought to have a chance, there ought to be somebody to believe him ... And this sheriff of yours, he's made up his competent mind. He's not going to change it no matter what Wayne says or does. You can sit here and wait for him to call you if you want to. I'm not going to."

"But Jim—" Mack began. The protests that sprang to his lips died there. Like the sheriff, Jim had made up his mind; it would do no good to point out to him the rashness of haring off like this in search of a crazy boy who might be carrying a gun. In which case, Mack's presence would probably do no good either. "Okay. I'm with you," he said, never mind why, and he followed Jim out to the car. "Let's try Velma's house. He might just possibly have gone home. Wohler will cover the places down town first, anyway. No point in just following him around."

If Wayne had gone home, and if Velma knew that he was in trouble, they would of course get nowhere with her. She would lie herself to hell and back to protect him. "I'll do the talking if you don't mind," Mack said as they stopped in front of the Carson place. "There's a chance she doesn't know yet what's up. If so, let's keep it that way."

There was a light on in the living room. Velma must have been watching from the bay window; Mack barely had time to press the bell before she was at the door. "Wayne," she said at once. "Is he with you? Where is he?" She peered past Mack at Jim, and her mouth hardened. "I know he went to find you. What have you done to him?"

Luck, then, was with them. If she had known what was up, she would never have said that.

"Nothing," Mack told her. "We haven't seen him. We're looking for him ourselves. Isn't he here?"

She shook her head, and he felt a pang of reluctant pity at the uncertain, groping way her hand lifted toward her mouth. "I talked to him on the phone," he said. "He sounded pretty upset when he called me. I tried to get him to come over to the house, but he—"

"Jim's not to see him," Velma said sharply. "That's part of the agreement, that Jim's not to see him. I should have known better than to trust you, either of you."

"Cut it out, Velma. The agreement's off, and you know it as well as I do. It's off because Wayne's not buying it. You found out you couldn't talk him around, after all. You might as well admit it."

"I'll admit nothing of the kind. I didn't expect him to see things in their proper light right away. I didn't myself. So why should Wayne? But he will, in time, after his first reaction wears off and he has a chance to think it over. He'll see."

"I wouldn't count on it if I were you. Not even if Jim gets out of town and leaves you with a clear field. The way you planned it. I think you're still going to have trouble with Wayne." Which was putting it very mildly indeed. Again he felt the pang of pity. All too soon now Velma would understand just how much trouble everybody was going to have with Wayne. Well. That was Wohler's department, not his. "Why are you so scared to have Jim and me see him, anyway? We want him to agree to your deal too. That's why I tried to get him to come over, so I could talk to him, try to—"

"I know exactly what Jim would try to do, thank you." Even in the half-darkness he caught the vindictive light in her eye. "He's ruined everything else for me. But he's not going to ruin Wayne. I don't care what I have to do to stop him."

She slammed the door.

Neither of them spoke till they were back in the car. Then Mack said, "We can try the hotel. Not that I think he'll be there. But if Ernie Brewer saw him when he was there earlier, he'll tell us all he knows and then some."

He was right on both counts. Ernie was talking breathlessly into the phone when they walked in: "I'm telling you, Wohler was just here, that's how I know, and—Listen, I got to go now. I'll talk to you later." He hung up and turned to them, bright-eyed, his withered little monkey face alive with excitement. And he went right on talking. Hardly missed a beat. "You fellows looking for Wayne too? Well, he ain't here now, but he was before, and like I told the sheriff, I said to myself at the time there's a boy with something on his mind and whatever it is it spells trouble, that boy is spoiling for trouble I said to myself, it even crossed my mind maybe I'd ought to call you, Judge McVey, only the thing of it was, it wasn't any of my business—"

"You shouldn't have let that stop you," said Mack. "What do you mean, he had something on his mind? What did he say?"

"It wasn't anything he *said* exactly. It was the way he *acted*. The way he *looked*. Wild," said Ernie with relish. "He had this wild look about him. Oh, I could feel it in my bones, I said to myself I wouldn't put anything past that boy, he's just not responsible."

"He was asking for me?" Jim asked, with commendable patience.

Ernie nodded and took a long breath. "That's right. Asking for you, and when I said you'd gone out and far as I knew you hadn't come back, he gave me this wild look and said did I mind if he went up to your room and checked, so I told him go ahead—I couldn't hardly say no, and anyway I figured it was all right, being's I knew good and well you weren't there. So then when he came down he says did I know where you were and then, real quick, before I had a chance to answer he says he must be at Judge McVey's, that's the only friend he's got in town—" The glance Ernie darted at Jim was at once apologetic and inquisitive. When he got no response he went on. "So when I says something like I don't know about that, he could have gone out to Louie's for a glass of beer ..."

(You would, Mack commented to himself, you nosey little bastard, you couldn't resist trying to pump him about what happened out at Louie's last night, could you?)

"And?" prompted Jim. "Then what?"

"Well, he didn't say anything much to that. Just gave me kind of a funny look. And then he headed for the door."

"Is that all?" said Mack. "Doesn't sound so wild to me."

It wounded Ernie's pride. "Maybe not. But you didn't see him. I told you, it wasn't what he said so much as the way he acted. Besides, there was one other thing that I don't know whether it's even worth mentioning. Happened while he was still standing there at the door. Didn't amount to much." He let them wait a moment; then he added virtuously and craftily, "Matter of fact, I didn't mention it to the sheriff. Oh, I thought of it all right. But the thing of it was, why drag Hazel into it if I didn't have to? Lord knows she felt bad enough as it was, she didn't mean any harm, hadn't any idea Wayne was there or she never would have—"

Mack exploded. "Jesus, Ernie, have a heart! What about Hazel? Tell it straight, will you?"

"Why sure, Judge McVey. I didn't know if you'd be interested, was all. Hazel don't ordinarily work so late, but the Woman's Club, they had their dinner here tonight, of course the ladies had all left by then, but Hazel was still here, clearing up in the dining room. And her sister. We'd got her in to help out, so there was the two of them, talking back and forth, you know how people will, especially womenfolks ..."

"I know," said Mack through clenched teeth. "What did they say?"

"Well. It was about Jim and—" Ernie swallowed; he kept his eyes fixed, almost desperately, on Mack. "There's word going round that Jim was over to see Mrs. Hild this afternoon. That's what they were talking about. Hazel said she had it on good authority, and she'd just like to been a little mouse, she'd give a lot to know what went on there. One thing about it, she said, we could stop wondering what Jim Singley came back here for, he came back to see Mrs. Hild, and this proved it. Not that it surprised her any, she always had said where there was that much smoke there had to be some fire ..."

It was clear, from Jim's set face, that he was not going to contribute to the conversation. That left Mack. "I see," he said. "Well, I don't know that it matters so much. After all, Wayne's certainly heard this kind of talk before. From his mother, if nowhere else. This has been her pitch all along."

"Yeah. But the thing of it is, he hadn't heard about this afternoon before. Because he come on back to the desk and says to me, real low but keyed up, 'Is that true? Did he go over there today?' And of course I says, 'Lord, Wayne, you can't prove it by me. I heard it, sure, but it don't necessarily mean anything.' 'Oh yes it does,' he says. 'Means plenty to me. I know what it means, all right. You don't have to tell me.' He had this wild look in his eye. And then he beat it. Through the door like a bat out of hell. The last I saw of him he was headed toward Main Street."

Which—though Ernie delicately refrained from pointing it out—was the way he would have to head if his destination was the McVey house.

"He didn't make any phone calls from here, did he?"

"Phone calls? Nope. Just talked to me, like I told you, and it wasn't so much what he said, it was the way he looked—"

"I know. Wild. Okay, Ernie. Thanks." Jim had already turned toward the door, and Mack followed him.

"Hey, wait a minute, Judge McVey," Ernie sputtered. "Is it true he's got a gun? From what the sheriff said I kind of got the idea he stole your gun and—"

"I expect you kind of did," said Mack, and kept on walking. Before they were through the door, Ernie was reaching again for the phone.

Back in the car, they sat in silence for a moment. "You see what I mean," Jim said abruptly. "They've got it all doped out ahead of time. Wayne did it, and that's that. Before they've even found him. Before he's had a chance to say a word."

"Yes. All right." But—Could you blame them? Mack stared straight ahead of him, struggling for the cold, clear view. He too had found Ernie supremely irritating. All the pop-eyed dramatizing, all the lurid feelings-in-his-bones could be divided by at least two with no damage to the facts. And the sheriff's hidebound preconception of Wayne as a juvenile delinquent—that too could be partially discounted. But not entirely. There still remained enough hard facts to make Wayne the logical suspect, and Mack's experience had taught him how rarely crimes turned out to be complicated or surprising. Most of them were just exactly as elementary as they seemed at first glance. There was always the chance, though, always the chance. A damn slim one, in Mack's opinion. But then he wasn't Wayne's father, and he furthermore had never been accused of murder or served a prison term or ...

He sighed. "All right," he repeated. "Now where? Wohler must have covered all the likely spots in town by now. Of course, for all we know he may have picked him up, too. Let's drive past the court house and see if anything's cooking."

Nothing was. No light in the sheriff's office or anywhere else in the court house. No sign of Wohler's car. So what was left? Where would I disappear to, Mack asked himself, if I were a distraught boy, possibly with a gun I wanted to get rid of, possibly with nothing of the kind, only a load of misery?

"It beats me." He looked sideways at Jim. "Unless he's taken to the woods."

"He might," said Jim thoughtfully. "He always used to like it down by the river. It's an idea. He just might."

There were no flies on Sheriff Wohler; the same idea had struck him. A couple of minutes after they turned off on the river road, their headlights picked up his car, lumbering along in the ruts. "It's a small world," Mack murmured, but to himself he added that it was not small enough, if Wayne really was intent on hiding out they were going to have the devil of a time finding him. It might take days, even with the posse Wohler would organize, even if he called out the ...

Ahead of them Wohler's car slowed and bumped to a stop. They heard him shout something, saw his car door open and his burly figure emerge and edge forward in a cautious but resolute advance. By this time Mack too had cut down to a crawl; suddenly Jim whispered, "There he is," and before Mack had the brakes on he was out of the car and streaking down the rough road.

It was Wayne, all right. He made no move to run or hide; he simply stood there in the glare from the sheriff's headlights, which by some trick made him look smaller than he was, and younger. A gawky, vulnerable kid. It was doubtful whether he could see Jim, who had stopped back of the sheriff, out of the light. Mack stopped there too.

"Stay back, you guys," said Wohler without turning his head. "He may still have the gun."

"Gun?" said Wayne. "What gun?" He turned a dazed face, very pale, on the approaching sheriff, and he offered no resistance to the search that followed. It was a quick, thorough search, and futile.

"What did you do with it? Throw it away? You had plenty of chance to." The sheriff put away his own gun and took hold of Wayne's arm. "Well. We'll go into all that when we get you into town. Come on. We've got plenty to talk about, you and me."

"Wayne," Jim began, but Wohler cut him short.

"Hold it, Mr. Singley, just hold everything. You and the Judge both. Time enough to see what's what when we get to my office."

"I'll ride with you and Wayne," said Mack firmly. "Jim, you can drive my car back. We'll see you in the sheriff's office."

Wohler gave a short laugh. "What's the matter, Judge? Scared I'll rough him up on the way in?" And as he herded Wayne—still dazed, stumbling a little, but docile—into the car, he added, "Not that he don't deserve it. But you don't need to worry. I got no objection, Judge. Come ahead."

THIRTEEN

"No," said Wayne for the umpteenth time. "No, I didn't steal Judge McVey's gun. I didn't try to kill anybody."

Though it was an idea, now that they mentioned it. It certainly was an idea. Once more his eyes made a tour of the sheriff's office—dreary institution-green walls, fly-specked calendar, Mississippi river crack in the ceiling, all uglified even more by the harsh overhead light—and settled on his father's stony face. It's his fault, Wayne thought, why did he have to come back here, anyway? Well, of course, to see Cleo's mother. The little woman with the eyes. *You didn't think it was to see you, did you? He never really cared anything about you. You know that, don't you? Sure, you've always known it.*

"No," he repeated, and tried to swallow another of those inopportune yawns that kept overtaking him. "I didn't do it."

Did they believe him? Not the sheriff. He had seen right off that there was no chance of convincing Sheriff Wohler. That Spring City deal, still galling him. Even though his own son had been in on it. Correction. *Because* Jug Wohler had been in on it. Up to his neck: it was Jug who had swiped the car; the rest of them were just drunk and disorderly. And the sheriff knew it. He had let them get by with it on account of Jug. He couldn't forgive anybody for that. Must have been biding his time ever since, waiting for just such a chance as this. And here it was. Oh brother, not the sheriff.

Judge McVey was trying to believe him. For Sally's sake, maybe. (Who knew why? Who cared?) Anyway, give the Judge credit, he was trying. The folding chair creaked under him every time he shifted his weight—and that was pretty often; his usual relaxed air showed signs of wearing thin. His big, egg-shaped face was almost comically grave. He kept patting the top of his bald head, as if to comfort himself. Not a bad guy, the Judge. There he sat, trying to believe. It wasn't his fault he couldn't quite make it.

"But you knew about the Judge's gun. You knew where it was. Didn't you?" Very tough, the sheriff. He ought to be on television.

"Sure. Who didn't? Everybody heard about how he was held up and bought a gun for protection. I knew he kept it in the car. Bill told me."

"Did you ever see it before tonight?"

Oh, that sheriff, he was full of tricks. "You mean when did I stop beating my wife?" It sounded smarty. Wayne knew it and couldn't help it, any more than he could help the goddam yawns, which didn't make a good impression, either.

"Okay, wise guy. Answer the question."

"I never saw the gun at all! Tonight or any other time. How many times do I have to tell you, I didn't do it, I didn't—"

The door opened. Wayne's voice dwindled to nothing. He closed his mouth, and then his eyes. Mother. Somehow or other he hadn't realized that of course Mother must hear about this, this wasn't trivial or easy to hide like getting drunk or even the Spring City thing. There was no possible way of keeping the knowledge of his disgrace from Mother. Shame flooded him. Double shame; because he could not suppress a tiny, selfish pulse of hope. Maybe she'll believe me, maybe she'll ...

"What's the meaning of this? Why wasn't I informed?" Mother demanded, with such frozen fury that even the sheriff turned red and blinked. "What right have you to use such methods, Mr. Wohler? Oh, I know now that it was you on the phone, trying to pry information out of me without telling me why you wanted it. Without even identifying yourself. Trying to trap me into incriminating my boy, my own son ... And you!" Her glance raked across Wayne's father and the Judge. "I should have known when you two came pussyfooting around looking for Wayne that something was wrong. Why didn't you tell me? How *dare* you not tell me!"

"Now, now, Velma," said the Judge, and ponderously, impressively he got to his feet. "You didn't give us a chance to tell you much of anything. Even if we had intended to. Which I'll admit we did not. We figured you'd hear about it soon enough—"

"Soon enough! My boy is arrested for murder, and you don't bother to tell me, you figure I'll hear it soon enough!"

"Not arrested." The sheriff stood up, too. Already he was recovering from the jolt of Mother's entrance. Making like the official again. "Not arrested, and not murder, Mrs. Sing—Mrs. Carson. Nobody's been murdered. We're questioning Wayne, is all. We know he had it in for his father, on account of the way he went for him last night, and so—"

"What?" she whispered. She sat down on the edge of the folding chair the Judge set for her. She said, with great composure, "Start with last night. I want to hear everything."

So she heard everything. From the sheriff mostly, who naturally had to make a few detours here and there, to "question" Wayne. "What did your father do that made you so mad last night, out at Louie's?"

"Nothing. I was having a—conversation with Cleo. He came along and interrupted. That's all."

"A conversation? What about?"

"A private conversation."

Pause. "We can ask Cleo, you know."

"You do that. Go ahead, if you think she'll tell you. I don't. It was private. Between her and me." Let them think he'd been trying to lay Cleo. Fine. Great. Let them tell Sally, too. He wouldn't have a prayer with Sally after this, anyway. He yawned violently.

The sheriff dropped the subject of last night and got back to his recapitulation of tonight. Now and then Wayne sneaked a look at Mother; the idea of meeting her eyes terrified him, and yet when it finally happened she seemed to stare right through him, she was listening with such intensity that she did not see him at all.

A final detour: "What were you doing down there by the river? Why did you go there? You were scared by what you'd done, you were running away. Weren't you?"

"Sure. You bet. How many miles was it you had to chase me before you caught me? I was so out of breath I lost track."

"You asked for that one, Wohler," said the Judge. But he didn't look happy about the way Wayne had answered. "He wasn't doing any running."

"All right, he wasn't doing any running. He didn't have to. By that time he'd ditched the gun." He switched back to Wayne. "That's how it was, wasn't it? You headed for the river, to get rid of the gun."

"I never *had* the gun! I headed for the river because I wanted to get away from people yammering at me and yanking at me and pushing me around like I was a— I just wanted to be some place where there weren't any *people!*" He paused, embarrassed by the passion in his own voice. But he had to go on, and now he turned quite openly to Mother because she was the only one who would maybe believe him. Again he had the curious feeling that she did not see him at all, that she was staring through him as if he were a pane of window glass. "I didn't do it! I can't help it if nobody believes me. I did not do it!"

Into the silence his father spoke. Four astounding words: "I believe you, Wayne."

They rang in Wayne's ears like a clangor of bells. Caught off guard, he found himself looking straight into his father's eyes. Instantly he looked away. But he could do nothing about the flush that rose in an aching flood to his face and neck. Or about the inner flood, either; it welled up in all its treacherous, spontaneous power. *I believe you, Wayne. I believe you.* He stared at the floor. He realized, with horror, what would happen if he tried to speak.

"It's a little late to be saying that, isn't it?" said Mother. "It might be more convincing if you hadn't already screamed murder to the sheriff."

"Velma," the Judge began.

But she clipped him off before he got any further. "Of course Wayne didn't do it. I know perfectly well he didn't, and fortunately I can prove it."

It jolted him out of his preoccupation with the floor. He looked up; there was Mother, composed but tense, not leaning back in her chair, her shoulders straight, her chin high. The Judge's hand remained on top of his head, arrested in the middle of a pat. Wayne's father watched her warily.

At last the sheriff stopped goggling and said, "Prove it? You can prove it?"

"Certainly. He couldn't have done it. He didn't even go past the McVey house tonight. I know because I followed him. If you had taken the trouble to inform me of what was going on when you should have, you could have spared yourself and everybody else all this nonsense. Instead, you had to—"

"Now wait a minute. You say you followed him? Why?"

"Because I was worried about him. He was all upset when he left the house. As a matter of fact, we were both upset. On account of our discussion about Jim's money." (Discussion, thought Wayne. How understated could you get?) "I had a feeling he was going to see Jim, and I didn't want that to happen. I didn't want it under any circumstances, and certainly not with Wayne in the state he was in. I knew it would only get him even more wrought up. So I followed him. To keep him away from Jim if I possibly could. I stayed out of sight, of course. In the first place, I didn't know for sure that's what he had in mind. And then he would have resented it, he would have felt I was spying on him."

The sheriff nodded. "Okay. Where did he go first?"

"To the hotel," said Mother promptly. "Just as I had suspected. I waited across the street and watched. I knew Jim was at McVey's—or at least he had been a little while before, when Mack phoned me. So I thought that's where Wayne would go next." The sheriff was giving her a very fishy stare. She ignored it. "But he didn't. Instead, he went into The Snackery and made that phone call to Mack. Not that I knew then it was to Mack. But of course I suspected as much."

"Yeah. Then what?"

"He turned off Main Street. North. So I was positive he was going to the McVey house."

"Well. Didn't he? He admits himself he went past there."

"But don't you see? That's because he was so wrought up, and it was in his mind to go there, and so he thinks he really did!" Her hands opened outward in triumph at this explanation. No one spoke or moved. Like the others, Wayne listened with rapt attention. "When the truth is that he didn't get within four blocks of the McVey house! He kept going, quite fast, for a block off Main Street. Then all at once he stopped short. As if he were thinking. And then he doubled back and cut through the vacant lot and went right on going till he hit the river road where it comes in there by the cemetery. That's as close as he ever was to McVey's house tonight. So how could he have stolen Mack's gun and tried to shoot Jim? He couldn't have. It's impossible."

"Yeah. Unless you—Uh. All this time you were following him, the way you tell it, there was probably somebody that saw you, wasn't there? In case we wanted to—uh—check on it. I mean, there you were right on Main Street part of the time, so somebody'd be pretty apt to see you. Wouldn't they?"

"I rather doubt it," said Mother coolly. "I don't remember seeing anyone in particular. Of course I was concentrating on Wayne. But it was late enough so there weren't many people out. I really rather doubt it, Mr. Wohler."

"So there's just your word for it."

"That's right. Just my word for it." She faced him arrogantly. Not turning a hair. Daring him to call her a liar.

Which she is, thought Wayne. She's lying in her teeth. For my sake. To get me off the hook. Because she thinks ...

It must have been clear, even to a meathead like the sheriff, that he was no match for her, he was never going to break her down. But he was a stubborn man. Doggedly he took her through her story again, step by step. Just where, Mrs. Sing—Mrs. Carson, and just when? She did not falter once. At ten minutes of ten, when the shot was fired, Wayne had been at the other end of town, he must have been passing the cemetery just about then. No, she had not followed him any great distance on the river road. It was a place he headed for quite often, when he was upset or wanted to be alone. Once she saw that he had given up the idea of seeing Jim, she had turned around and gone home.

"But you didn't mention any of this to the Judge and Mr. Singley when they came looking for Wayne, later on. You didn't tell them—"

"Certainly not. Why should I? That was my whole point, to keep Wayne away from them."

"You didn't mention it to me, either, when I phoned you."

"Well now, really, Mr. Wohler! Did you expect me to? You didn't even identify yourself. As soon as I realized what was going on—because I got worried again and called Mr. Brewer, and he at least had the decency to tell me—then of course I came up here right away."

Oh, she had all the answers. Neat. No loose ends. She had taken care of everything—including Wayne himself, with the bit about his being too wrought up to know whether he had gone past the McVey house or not. He wasn't going to argue with her, of course; he wanted off the hook too much. She hadn't overlooked that point either ...

Because she thinks I did it. She doesn't believe me. That's why she's lying. Because she thinks I'm lying. And it doesn't bother her. Just so I get by with it, that's all that matters to her.

Shocked and fascinated, he stared at her. She seemed to him an utter stranger, only of course no stranger would lie like this, coldly and brilliantly lie for his sake. It was more than he had ever expected from her, far more—No. It was somehow less. He had expected her to believe him. Not lie for him. Just believe him.

"I don't see how you can hold Wayne any longer," his father was saying. He stood up, as if to signify that, for his money, the show was over. Or maybe he felt that it gave him an advantage to be looking down at the sheriff. "What kind of a case have you got against him, anyway? Mack and I were both there when you found him. He didn't have the gun, he made no move to run or hide, it was plain enough right then that he didn't know what you were talking about. And, aside from what his mother has been saying, he's told a straightforward story himself. It satisfies me. I believe him."

"Yeah, Mr. Singley, but you're his father—"

"I'm also the guy that got shot at. Remember? And I refuse to press charges against Wayne. I'll tell you something else, Sheriff Wohler, if you insist on holding him I'll—"

"Now just a minute, Jim," the Judge put in smoothly. "Let's not get worked up over this. I'm sure the sheriff's willing to listen to reason." (It didn't look that way to Wayne. The sheriff had gotten to his feet, slowly and belligerently; nobody was going to tell him how to run his business. Only Judge McVey was too quick for him. A real smoothie.) "I agree with you, Mr. Wohler, this whole thing is getting on too much of a personal basis. Too many emotional involvements." (Mr. Wohler looked first startled, then flattered.) "I think it would be a good idea if you and I could talk this over privately, without interruptions from either of Wayne's parents. Suppose we adjourn to my offices down the hall. We can put Wayne in the inner office for safekeeping while we have our discussion in the outer one. How does it strike you? Meanwhile, Jim and Velma here can—"

"Don't worry, Velma. I'll wait outside," said Wayne's father. He and Mother glared at each other briefly. Then he followed Judge McVey into the hall; Wayne, while he was being shepherded out by the sheriff, could hear their low, earnest voices.

Mother said as he went past her, "It's going to be all right, dear. It's just as I said, you couldn't possibly have done it. The whole thing's ridiculous." But she was still looking through him in that strange, glassy way. She still didn't believe him.

He sat where they put him, in Judge McVey's inner office, and waited. He did not worry or hope. He did not even think much. There was a silver-framed picture of Sally on the Judge's desk; he looked at it and waited. A low mumble of voices—mostly the Judge's—reached him from the outer office. No words, though. The sound had a timeless, hypnotic quality, like the singing of locusts. The Judge was supposed to Have Influence, Wayne recalled idly. Maybe he was Bringing Pressure to Bear on the sheriff.

When they opened the door Wayne rose politely. The movement jolted him back into reality, and into a moment of panic anxiety. Then he saw that it was all right, the sheriff had surrendered.

"Well, Wayne, we've talked it over, the Judge and me, and we've decided ..." Yeah. We killed the bear. But anyway, Wayne was off the hook. Released. Free. (Again he felt a spasm of belated panic at the way it might have been. The way it had been, six years ago, for *him*. Jail. Prison. Bars. The terrible grinding away of yourself, day after day after ... The dead weight of knowing that no one believed you.) "No hard feelings, I hope," the sheriff was saying. He even shook hands with

Wayne, though you could tell it hurt him to do it.

The Judge opened the outer door and called, "It's okay, Jim! Wohler's not going to hold him!" And thank God, thank God, Wayne managed to get out into the hall in time, because it was dark there and they couldn't see each other's faces. That wouldn't have been safe, not safe at all. Somehow or other the one word he said—"Thanks"—came out sullen-sounding, as if he begrudged it, but he didn't dare go on because if he did ...

Then Mother was there, making a big deal of it, her boy, her model son, virtue triumphant, all that jazz. And they were back in the sheriff's office, where the sheriff—surrender or no surrender—couldn't resist one parting shot. "I'd just like to know—" and the way he bore down on each word, you'd think he was pounding in nails—"I just wish somebody would tell me one thing. If Wayne didn't do it, who did?"

The silence must have gratified him. It was quite a sizable chunk of silence. "Yes," the Judge said at last. "Well, now look, Sheriff, it's just a question of finding the gun. I know it's not going to be easy, but you'd be surprised how often—"

"Skip the pep talk, Mack," said Wayne's father shortly. "He's not very apt to find the gun, and you know it. Frankly, I don't give much of a damn who did it. For one thing, I don't think whoever it was meant to hit me. They just wanted to scare me. Well, I'm leaving town tomorrow anyway, so they can quit worrying. But I'm no red hot favorite around here, Mr. Wohler, in case you hadn't noticed. You've got a good many more to pick from than just Wayne, when you put your mind to it ..." His eyes flicked across the room to Mother. Flicked away again. Wayne might even have imagined it.

"I'm sure you're right," said Mother. She smiled at him and then, just as sweetly, at the sheriff. "I'm afraid I can't be of any help to you, Mr. Wohler. I simply have no idea who it might have been. But then that's your responsibility—isn't it?—to find out ... Come along, Wayne dear. It's late, and I know how tired you must be."

Automatically he took her arm and started out with her. They had reached the doorway when the Judge said, "I'd still like to talk to you, Wayne. I know it's late, but if you feel like it I wish you'd come over, after you've seen your mother home." Very smooth, very courteous. But there was a hardness, almost a challenge, in the Judge's eyes.

He could feel Mother stiffen beside him. His own neck was suddenly rigid; his nod was so slight that he was not sure the Judge caught it. But she did. And he knew that she would never forgive him for this, either. Not for this. Not for anything, ever.

FOURTEEN

"You think he'll show up?" Jim asked.

"Wayne? I doubt it," said Mack. And hoped not, he might have added. He had regretted his suggestion that Wayne come over, even while he was making it. Because what he had in mind was confession, and for confession two people only were needed. The cast was complete right now: himself and Jim. And the scene was right, too: they were settled in his den with their drinks. Alone at last. That in itself was a major achievement, for of course everybody was on deck, waiting to hear the news, when they got home from the court house. Sally and Marge. Bill and Cleo. Mack had been downright curt with all of them—even Sally, who (naturally, naturally) burst into tears when she heard that Wayne was in the clear. She was so happy, she sobbed. She was so relieved. Okay, okay, Mack had said shortly, run along to bed now. Good night. Everybody. Jim and I are beat; all we want is a night cap and a little peace and quiet. Please; no more yakking tonight.

Well, it was the truth. He *was* beat. It had been uphill work with Wohler; he was not only mule-headed by nature, but tonight he had had the courage of his convictions to sustain him. Which was more than Mack had. Oh, he was inclined to believe that Wayne was telling the truth, all right. But he wasn't dedicated to the proposition. Not the way Jim was. *I believe you, Wayne.* It was Jim that had stopped Wohler. While he knew of course that Velma was lying, he also knew what a tough time he would have, breaking her down. Still he would have tried—he was just mule-headed enough—if he could have counted on Jim to press charges. Without that, even Wohler had to admit he was licked.

Jim took a sip of his drink and said, "I thought Wohler acted like he had some kind of a grudge against Wayne. Has he?"

"A grudge? Not that I know of." Mack added, with sudden irritation, "He didn't have to have a grudge. Good Lord, Jim, the kid went out of his way to make him sore! All that smart alecky stuff. I'd have been sore too."

"Yes. But he wasn't lying. I still know that much about him, I can still tell when he's lying and when he isn't. It's something he does with his shoulder, he kind of hunches it, when he isn't telling the truth. I know. I do it myself."

Okay. So he didn't hunch his shoulder. He didn't look you in the eye, either, when you said you believed him. And no wonder. Even if he wasn't lying tonight, it must have shamed him to hear you say that. He never did as much for you. Yes, and afterwards, when he trotted off after Velma, without bothering to say so much as thanks to either you or me ... Oh, don't worry, he won't come over here. I knew he wouldn't when I asked him, that's why I did it, to show him up. Velma's going to grab the credit for getting him off. She's got him where she wants him now. Right under her thumb. He'll take your money, maybe, but that's all you'll ever get a chance to give him. You've seen the last of Wayne, and good riddance, if you ask me ...

In the middle of this mental tirade, Mack remembered that he himself sometimes found it hard to look Jim in the eye. He too had cause for shame. Wayne at least had the excuse of youth and divided loyalties; with His Honor it was a simple matter of moral cowardice. And now that his hour of confession—so long dreaded, so long yearned for—was at hand, here he sat, sweating and dumb, like a novice actor tongue-tied by stage fright.

He closed his eyes and plunged. "Jim. I have a confession to make— I mean, there's something I have to say, because if you're leaving town tomorrow I'll never have another chance and I can't—"

And the door bell rang. He was saved, he was lost. He sprang up wildly.

"Wayne?" said Jim. "It's Wayne. He's turned up, after all." They both headed out of the den at once; for a ludicrous moment they were jammed side by side in the narrow hall, helpless as sardines, and when that crisis was past, Jim couldn't seem to work the lock on the front door, so in the end it was Mack who let Wayne in.

He looked mortally tired. As he had a right to be, Mack thought; on top of everything else, Velma must have been raising hell with him. And yet here he was. You had to hand it to the kid. Here he was. Once they were back in the den, Wayne sat down tensely, on the edge of his chair. He was still avoiding Jim's eyes. "You asked me to come over, Judge McVey," he began quietly enough. "You said you wanted to talk to me."

"Well, yes. Well." Mack rummaged in his mind. Velma's deal: that was safest. "For one thing, we still have to get this business about the money straightened out. I suppose by now your mother's convinced you she's right and you've decided to accept it?"

It was as if he had touched a match to gasoline. "What do you mean 'by now?' What makes you think she's convinced me? She didn't before!"

"That's true. But there's been a good deal going on since then. I thought—"

"You thought I'd do anything she said from now on. Just because she got me off the hook up there at the sheriff's office. You didn't even expect me to come over here. Did you?"

"Frankly, no," said Mack. "Congratulations. I'd just like to set you straight on one point. It wasn't your mother that got you off the hook. It was—"

"I don't care who it was! She was lying, anyway. She didn't believe me.

She thought I did it. That's why she lied."

"Obviously. But your father wasn't lying. He believed you. For no good reason. He believed you, and he said so, and you can just damn well give him credit for it! You can just damn well—" Mack could not understand his own anger; Wayne and he seemed in perfect accord on the subject of Velma, so what were they arguing about? He finished in a voice of thunder: "You can just damn well quit pretending he isn't here!"

Wayne flushed. "I know he's here, all right." Then he shot one queer, defiant glance in Jim's direction and added, sullenly, "I know you believed me. I— Thanks."

What was Jim supposed to say to that? You're welcome? Wayne didn't give him a chance. "But I still don't want the money if you—I don't care what she says! All at once there's nothing wrong with your money. You're a murderer and all the rest of it, but I'm supposed to take everything I can get out of you. I can't do it! How can I, if I don't know for sure—Don't you see that I have to find out?"

A cry for help. There was nothing beseeching in Wayne's voice or manner; he sat on the edge of his chair and glared about him with fierce scorn. Nevertheless, a cry for help. And it meant ... By God, thought Mack, it meant that there was some hope for Wayne! He wanted to "know for sure." He wanted to "find out." So Velma's word was no longer gospel truth to him; she had not succeeded, after all, in sealing up his mind against all doubt of his father's guilt. He did doubt. He must. Otherwise what would there be for him to "find out?"

"You want proof that I'm not a murderer." Jim's voice was very low. "I can't give you proof. All I can give you is my word."

And still Wayne would not look at him. But suddenly his face quivered, and Mack knew what he was remembering. "I believe you, Wayne." His word had been enough for Jim. But Jim's was not enough for him. No matter how much he might want it to be, it was not enough.

Mack cleared his throat. "You're overlooking something, both of you. It's not just Jim's word. It never was just that. It's Cleo's word too. She told the same story. And it was her father that was killed."

"Yes. But it was her mother that—" Wayne gulped. "You didn't come back on account of me or Mother, you didn't make any move to see either of us. But you went to see Cleo's mother this afternoon."

After a slight pause Jim said, "Yes."

"So that's why Cleo lied. To cover up for her mother. To keep her out of it. That's what we were talking about out at Louie's. Cleo did lie, I'm sure of it—"

"Only not on account of Mother." The voice came from behind Mack; he swivelled, and saw Cleo standing at the open door. No telling how long she might have been out there in the hall. They had been too intent, the three of them, to notice. Pale and serious, almost stately in her pink flowered robe, she moved forward. She added, fantastically, "On account of the beef stew."

"Beef stew," Mack echoed, and she nodded, his ears had not deceived him.

"I didn't really mean to lie. I just kind of got started, and then I couldn't stop."

"Do you realize what you're saying, Cleo?" As he got ponderously to his feet, Mack saw that Jim had closed his eyes. No help for it now. Nothing to do but go on. "You weren't telling the truth when you backed up Jim's story? You committed perjury?"

"But not on account of Mother," she repeated. "I have to tell Wayne, because he thinks I did it to protect her. Don't you see that I can't let him go on believing that? It's just something his mother made up, and he swallowed it along with all the rest, only now he wants to find out the truth, and— Well, he's got a right. I have to tell him."

"Tell me." Wayne's voice was rough. "How much of it was a lie?"

"All of it," she said, and Mack's heart sank. He listened, appalled and at the same time fascinated, while she plunged ahead, through the crazy-quilt pattern of cause and effect. Glee club practice. Mr. Rohman. Up on the roof, bawling her eyes out. The beef stew for Daddy's supper ... "When I went into the living room Jim was there, bending over Daddy. He said, 'I didn't know you were here,' and I said, 'Oh yes, I was in the kitchen fixing supper.' It just slipped out. Because, you see, that was where I was *supposed* to be. And then he said, 'So you must have heard us fighting,' and I said yes, and after that—well, you see, by the time I realized, it was too late. I couldn't take it all back, so I just kept on saying I'd heard the fight."

It had to be true; it was too bizarre to be a fabrication. Mack felt a wild impulse to laugh. Justice, he thought, complete with blindfold. It took a muddle-headed kid's lie to convince the jury of the truth. If only—for Jim's sake, and for Wayne's—she could have gone on lying forever!

Was there nothing to be salvaged from the ruin, nothing at all? "Still, you must have believed Jim's story," he said slowly. "You must have, Cleo. Even though you didn't actually hear the fight. You were just a kid, and you were scared, you had your guilty little conscience and all that. But if you really thought Jim killed your Dad on purpose you'd have broken out and said so to somebody, somewhere along the line."

"Well, of course," said Cleo impatiently. "Of course I believed him." She turned to Jim and added, "You knew, I guess? I always had a feeling you knew ..."

For the first time, Jim was startled out of his stony-faced silence. He sounded tired. "I suspected it. One or two little things. But I wasn't ever sure. And I couldn't figure out why. Then when I saw you the other day out at the school house you were so—"

"I was afraid you were going to thank me." She blushed. "I couldn't stand it, to have you thank me. I wasn't ever going to tell anybody, only I had to prove it to Wayne, that it wasn't on account of Mother."

"You think you've proved it to me?" Wayne leaned toward her, handsome, hateful, triumphant; every inch Velma's son. He even sounded like her. "Well, you haven't! Because I know he was over at your house this afternoon, and don't try to tell me it was to see you. It was to see your mother. Wasn't it? Wasn't it?"

Cleo's temper snapped, visibly and audibly. "Yes it was to see my mother! And no I don't know what they talked about! Mull that over in your busy dirty little mind. Make anything you want to out of it. Run home with it to Mama, she knows all the answers."

"Shut up!"

"I will not shut up! You started this, you had to find out the truth, you dragged it out of me. I don't care whether you like it or not. I don't care what you think about my mother, either. She had nothing to do with it, Jim told me so, and—"

"He told you so, did he? When?"

"Cleo honey," Mack began, but she was past stopping.

"Right after he called the doctor for Daddy. While we were waiting for the doctor. He said we must look out for Mother, she had nothing to do with it and we must keep her name out of it. There! Now you've got it all out of me. Every solitary thing I know and don't know. Now are you satisfied? Now will you leave me alone?" Her voice wobbled off into a sob. She looked scared now, instead of angry; like a child frightened by the irreparable damage she herself had done.

Only the damage was not irreparable. It came to Mack (at last, at last, how obtuse could you get?) that with his bit of truth he could repair—at least in part—what Cleo had destroyed with hers. His bit of truth. His confession. His mouth went dry with excitement. "Wayne," he croaked. "Listen. I—"

"No!" It was a long, tearing gasp. The next instant Wayne was out of his chair, out of the room. Jim, almost as quick, was after him like a shot. The front door slammed. Once. Twice.

Silence. "Judge McVey," quavered Cleo. The tears were running down her face. "I didn't mean to—"

"I know," said Mack. He patted her absently. "There, honey. There."

It seemed to him that he was the one who needed comfort. Cleo had made her confession. But not Mack; his still oppressed him, as wearisome a burden as ever. Once again he had missed his chance to get rid of it.

He sat down heavily. He envied Cleo.

FIFTEEN

Eight o'clock in the morning, and all was quiet—not to say comatose—at the Athena Hotel. The dining room lay hushed and empty; though breakfast was available there, the Athena's few guests often preferred to gulp their coffee and doughnuts at the counter of The Snackery. Out in the kitchen Hazel dawdled over a cigarette, marshalling the strength for her chambermaid duties. Ernie Brewer presided at the front desk, with his little dog beside him on her stool and yesterday's paper spread out in front of him. Not that he was reading it; he was too busy reliving last night's stirring moments. A shooting, right here in Athena! And Ernie himself had played quite a considerable part in the excitement, without having to set foot outside the hotel. Yes sir, they had all turned up here—Wayne and Jim and the Judge and Wohler, and Ernie had told them ...

The telephone beside him broke in on this soul-satisfying reverie of "I said" and "he said." A keyed-up voice answered his announcement: "Athena Hotel, good morning."

"Is that you, Ernie? Listen, is Jim Singley there?"

"He hasn't come down yet this morning. I can call him if you—"

"No. I don't want to talk to him. I just want to know if he's there. Are you sure?"

"Sure I'm sure," said Ernie rather edgily. "I saw him come in last night, way late, must have been two A.M. or past, and he hasn't gone out since. Unless he's jumped out the window, and I guess I'd hear about it if he had. Who is this, anyway?"

"Elroy Hild," said the voice, and Ernie froze to attention like a bird dog. "Listen, Ernie, will you do me a favor? I wouldn't ask you, only I—"

"Yes?" prodded Ernie, when the silence lengthened out.

"Only I don't know where else to turn," said Elroy, and he sounded even more keyed-up. As if he were talking through clenched teeth. "I don't dare leave her alone unless I can count on you. He might come back here, and I can't afford to let that happen. I'd stay home myself, only Ed's out of town, I've got nobody to tend the store for me. You see the fix I'm in, Ernie? You understand what I'm talking about?"

"Sure, Elroy, sure. Only ain't Cleo there? The way I heard it, she was staying home this week to look after her mother." When there was no immediate response, he added, with dignity, "Not that it's any of my business, of course."

Elroy said, "Cleo's still in town. But she isn't staying here anymore. This is just between you and me, Ernie ..." Ernie's chest swelled at the phrase; it was one of his favorites. "… but Cleo and I had a disagreement yesterday. A very serious disagreement. She's not here now, and she won't be in the future. I'd rather not go into it just at present. 'How sharper than a serpent's tooth.' That's all I have to say. 'How sharper than a serpent's tooth.'"

Ernie would figure that out later. "What was it you wanted me to do?" he asked.

"If you'd just let me know when Jim Singley leaves the hotel. Just give me a ring at the hardware store, so I can get home and keep him away from her. It's important. Vitally important. Can I count on you, Ernie?"

"You bet you can," said Ernie, from the bottom of his heart. "No trouble at all. I'll be right here at this desk all morning, and he won't get by me. Don't worry about a thing, Elroy. The minute he heads for the door I'll call you."

It struck him as kind of pitiful, how grateful Elroy was. He wasn't a fellow you warmed up to, somehow; didn't seem to know how to make friends. But Ernie couldn't have resisted an assignment like this, no matter who asked him. It would have taken wild horses to drag him from his post. Here was drama, and here was he actually on the inside, playing a role of vital importance. His brain buzzed with conjecture, busy as a bee in clover. He sat bolt upright, his hand, his throat already tingling in anticipation of the moment when he would reach for the telephone and deliver his clipped message: "Your party just left. Heading north …" Beady-eyed with vigilance, he watched the stairway and waited for Jim Singley.

Cleo also waited. For the call from Mother. It was a relaxed, sub-surface kind of waiting at first. She slept until almost nine, and came downstairs to find all the McVeys gone about their various business. (To her secret relief; she had no impulse to rehash last night's happenings.) Judge McVey had already left for his office, Sally for school; according to a note from Bill's mother, she and Bill had gone down town, back soon, Cleo was to make self at home. She poured a cup of coffee and settled down in the quiet, sunny kitchen.

Mother would probably call about nine thirty. By then she would have everything straightened out, and when Cleo saw her she would explain it all. It was going to be all right. Really, really.

Sure enough, at nine thirty the phone did ring. Only it wasn't Mother. A complicated message for Mrs. McVey about the rummage sale.

Well, then, any time between now and ten. But the waiting was no longer quite so relaxed. And it was not sub-surface at all; she was aware of it now. She grew increasingly aware of it as the hands of the cat-face clock journeyed jerkily between nine thirty and ten and the phone remained mute. She poured another cup of coffee. Lit another cigarette. The purr of the refrigerator, which she had not noticed before, began to get on her nerves. So did Bill's absence. He might at least be here, she thought irritably, he might at least show a little interest.

She didn't like the idea of calling Mother herself, on account of Elroy. For all she knew, he might be home this morning instead of at the store, and if so it would be just her luck to have him, not Mother, answer the phone. Which would be embarrassing, to put it mildly. Matter of fact, that must be why Mother hadn't called—Elroy must still be home, and Mother was waiting to get in touch with Cleo till the coast was clear. Of course. That had to be it ...

Embarrassing, to get embroiled with Elroy, even just by phone. She was so delicate she couldn't stand a little embarrassment? It would be a sight easier to stand than waiting around like this, wondering what on earth was going on. She picked up the phone and made the call.

She let it ring time after time—much longer than made any sense— but there was no answer. No Elroy. No Mother. No answer. Her hand felt cramped from gripping the phone so tightly. Her heart thudded.

"Hi, Keed!" Bill breezed in, beaming. Then he took a good look at her and said, "What's wrong? What's the matter?"

"I can't understand it," she faltered. "Mother said she'd call me this morning, only she hasn't, so I tried to call her just now, and nobody answers. I just can't understand it. She promised, Bill. She knew how upset I was about Elroy, and she said I mustn't worry, she'd call me, she'd see me this morning. It's so funny, for nobody to answer. I mean—"

"Yeah." Bill stood close beside her, thinking. "Would Elroy leave her alone? He made such a big deal out of having you stay with her. Looks like he'd get somebody else, now that you're off the list. Or else stay with her himself."

"He might not. Because Mother was different yesterday, after Jim was there. She was—I don't know—changed. Do you think I would have left her, otherwise? She said she had to handle it herself, she owed it to Elroy to explain to him—whatever she had to explain—and she was going to explain to me too, this morning." She stopped, aware of how snarled up it sounded. Was Bill getting any of it, any of it at all?

Well, anyway, he was trying. He frowned. Chewed on his lip. Breathed heavily. "Okay. So maybe Elroy's down at the store. We can check on that easy enough." He reached for the phone, and in practically no time was speaking into it. "Hello, is Ed there? ... Oh, that's right, I forgot, he's out of town ... No, never mind, Mr. Hild, I'll see him when he gets back. Thanks."

He hung up and turned again to Cleo. "He's there, all right. Must have been sitting right on the phone. Anyway, he didn't waste any time answering."

"But then where's Mother? Why doesn't she call me? Why doesn't she answer? There's something wrong, Bill!"

"Now let's not catch fire, honey. Let's— Maybe she was out in the yard or something, and didn't hear the phone. Give her one more try before you call out the Marines."

He was so big and calm and easy-going. He almost convinced her that she was blowing up a storm about nothing and that this time Mother's voice would be there: "Of course, lamb, I was just going to call you …"

It was not there. Only the senseless, mechanical bell, shrilling into a vacuum. She hung up and said, "I'm going over there." Her legs felt queer and unsteady.

"Okay," said Bill. "I'm going with you."

Elroy's house showed no outward sign of "something wrong," Cleo thought as they went up the flagstone walk. It looked as trim and stylish as ever, with its picture window sparkling in the morning sun and a robin cheerfully splashing in the bird bath. Again she misdoubted her own fears; there was no disaster except in her mind.

But no one answered the door bell, and when they tried the door they found it locked. "You got a key?" asked Bill. Cleo shook her head. She had never needed a key. Mother was either there to let her in (she so seldom left the house) or she didn't bother to lock the door.

"I'll go around to the back," Bill said. "You wait here."

She waited obediently. Surely for quite a long time? Bill must be finding the back door locked too. She had no impulse to follow him and see for herself. The task of getting in was his. Hers was waiting, as she had been told to do. Her mind felt extraordinarily blank, incapable of registering anything beyond superficialities—the robin giving his wings a last flirt and swooping off; the neighbor's dog barking.

Then, through the picture window, she saw Bill inside the house, moving with what struck her as strange, incongruous haste, down the hall toward the bedrooms. Still she waited, suspended in blank-minded space. He was coming back now, down the hall, across the living room, toward the front door. As he opened it, he said something; Cleo had no idea what. All she heard was the harsh, snoring sound that came from Mother's bedroom. Not so much snoring as tearing, as if a piece of cloth were being ripped into strips. A sound of disaster.

She started toward it. "No," said Bill sharply. "Don't go in there. Cleo. Stay here. I've already called the doctor." His face alarmed her. So stern, and not a bit of color in it. Again she did as she was told.

"The doctor?" she said stupidly. Her clumsy brain fumbled at making the connection between the doctor, and Mother, and the harsh snoring sound. Now and then there was a break in its rhythm; it would stop entirely, and with it Cleo's own breathing, her very heart seemed to skip its beating. Bill had hold of her arm. She could feel him holding his breath too, and letting it out in a rush of relief each time the sound started up again.

"He'll be here right away," he said. "Five minutes. Not even that long. Right away."

She made no response. Listening absorbed her. It obsessed her. Her glance, straying aimlessly around the living room, fell on the litter of papers at one end of the sofa. Bright-colored travel folders. Elroy's beloved maps, on which he had started plotting the trip that was going to restore Mother's perspective. It took Cleo a moment or two to identify them. In her distracted state ... But that wasn't the only reason. Every single folder and map had been savagely crumpled up.

"Here's Doc," said Bill, and drew her with him toward the door. "Thank God. Here he is."

For an hour after Elroy's call, Ernie kept his vigil, every nerve at the ready. It was past nine when Jim finally came down the stairs. Ernie's hand, itching for action, moved toward the telephone—and then stopped, because Jim did not seem of a mind to leave the hotel, after all. Usually he went right on past the desk. Not this time.

"Morning, Ernie." He looked the way he had when he came in, six, seven hours before. As if he'd been put through the wringer. Backwards *and* forwards. Well, naturally, when a fellow's own boy took a shot at him ... "Did Wayne—Did anybody call me?"

Wayne? He expected Wayne to call him? As for Elroy's call, that didn't count; he had said in so many words that he didn't want to talk to Jim. "Nobody so far," Ernie chirped. He decided not to mention anything about last night. Not yet. Work into it gradually. "Looks like another nice day."

"Why, yes. Yes, it does." And then he went on to say that he'd be checking out today, along about one o'clock, if that was okay.

It didn't exactly surprise Ernie. Still ... "You're paid up for a week," he pointed out. "I thought you was going to be around for a while. You mean you're leaving town?"

"That's right," said Jim, with finality. He wasn't what you'd call an easy man to pump. He didn't even give Ernie a chance to ask where he was planning on locating. "How about some breakfast?"

"Sure thing," said Ernie, and hollered for Hazel. He bustled around as long as he could, getting Jim settled in the dining room, and he dredged up every last opening he could think of. But it didn't do him a lick of good. Jim wasn't talking, and that was that. Forlornly, Ernie admitted defeat and retired to his post at the desk.

He toyed with the notion of making an interim report to Elroy. It would be easy enough; Jim needn't hear a word if he talked low, and picked a moment when Hazel was clattering dishes. Still, Elroy's instructions had been explicit. "If you'd just let me know when Jim Singley leaves the hotel." Most likely it was nothing to him where Jim ate breakfast, or if he ate it at all.

He was certainly taking his time. Dawdled over his scrambled eggs, over his newspaper, over his coffee and cigarettes. Ernie got the feeling that he was stretching it all out on purpose, waiting for something. Maybe for Wayne to call him? The Lord only knew.

And when he got through dawdling in the dining room what did he do but wander into the lobby and dawdle some more—beyond the Christmas cactus and the ferns and the snake plants, far enough away so that a person couldn't strike up a conversation with him. Not and make it look casual, anyway.

Finally, when Ernie had just about given up, he came over to the desk and said, "If anybody calls, I'll be back in half an hour." Again he didn't wait for Ernie to get out two words. Just turned and made tracks for the door.

Like a steel spring released, Ernie's hand shot out and connected with the telephone. He cleared his throat and wet his lips.

And no one answered. After all the waiting and watching and debating and holding back—what a fizzle! Incredulous and indignant, Ernie stared at the phone as if it were responsible for cheating him out of his dramatic climax. But it was Elroy who was responsible. To set all this machinery of intrigue in motion and then walk off and leave it …

No. It wasn't like Elroy. A fussbudget. A regular old woman. He wouldn't pull such a trick on Ernie or anybody else. Except in a case of extreme emergency. The idea fired Ernie with fresh excitement. And with resolve. Having undertaken to keep Elroy posted, was he going to give up just because their original plan hit a snag? Not on your life. A glance through the window told him that Jim had almost reached the corner; it was anybody's guess which way he was going to turn when he got there. He might be heading for the court house to see Judge McVey. But he might just as well turn left, toward Elroy's house. It was up to Ernie to get the message through.

Besides, if there was a case of extreme emergency he wasn't going to miss it. He slammed the telephone down and took off like a hare for the hardware store.

Extreme emergency was right. He saw that the minute he hit Main Street. There was at least a score of people milling around the entrance to Elroy's store. Other storekeepers, several women with shopping bags, the beauty shop girl, the idlers from the pool hall. Even old man

Schultz, who was too cranky to care what went on, had his head poked out of his shoe repair shop. But for all the crowd, there was an abnormal hush. A shuffling of feet; a respectful, doomful murmur of voices. Ernie pushed his way up alongside of the beauty shop girl. He was just in time to see Elroy. The McVey kid was helping him into his car. He looked all shrunk up, and he kept stumbling; Bill was halfway carrying him.

"What happened?" whispered Ernie urgently, but it wasn't until Bill got the car started and drove off that he got any kind of an answer. Then the hush lifted and grew into a confused, subdued buzz.

"She committed suicide. Mrs. Hild. Took enough pills to kill a horse ..."

"I didn't hear him say she was dead. He just said ..."

"As good as. They took her to the hospital, but ..."

"It was Cleo and the McVey kid found her. Busted down the door and ..."

"Tough on Elroy. Did you see his face when he ..."

Ernie drank it in in gulps. He could have put in his two cents worth, too. What Elroy had said to him: "It's important. Vitally important." But for the moment he was too drunk with drama to do anything but listen. Later on. There would be no lack of opportunity.

It seemed to him that the other name was all around him, like wind rustling through a corn field. "Jim Singley," somebody whispered behind him, and to the right, and to the left, "Jim Singley. Jim Singley."

SIXTEEN

Now and then a child whimpered. The little Keller boy (according to Mrs. Jenks, who worked in the hospital kitchen); he had a broken leg, and he was in the room right above the waiting room, and now and then he whimpered. Poor kiddie, said Mrs. Jenks.

Mrs. Jenks brought them coffee. Personally she favored a nice cup of tea herself, but everybody to their own taste. Maybe Cleo would like something *with* her coffee? A nice piece of toast, maybe? If so, all she had to do was say the word.

"Not now, thank you," said Cleo, and Mrs. Jenks plodded back to the kitchen. There were four of them in the waiting room—Cleo sat on the couch, with Bill on one side of her and his mother on the other; Elroy stayed at the opposite end of the room. As far away from Cleo as he could get. Most of the time he paced. Often he muttered. Now and then he slumped down in the wing chair, which was covered in flowered cretonne, to match the couch.

Cleo knew that he blamed her. They had not exchanged a word; none was necessary. Or even possible. Not after the look he gave her when he first came in, with Bill practically holding him up. One withering glare, which apparently disposed of her as far as he was concerned. He took no further notice of her. His muttering seemed to alarm Mrs. McVey; whenever it began she would pat Cleo and start up a jumpy little conversation about how attractive the new slip-covers made the waiting room, and the new drapes too, so much more attractive than the old ones.

He blames me, Cleo thought. If Mother dies it will be my fault for letting Jim in the house yesterday. She took all those capsules on account of Jim. If she dies I killed her, Jim killed her, she killed herself ...

No. Always, at this point she hit the same road block of solid, unreasoning negation. No to everything. Most of all, no to Mother's dying. She wasn't going to die. No no no. The doctor said she had a chance (maybe they always said that?), now be a good girl, Cleo, don't make a fuss, I'm going to do my best. The nurse said it was too soon to tell, there was always a chance, Doctor was doing his best. Mrs. Jenks said something *with* her coffee and (the little Keller boy, not Cleo) poor kiddie.

She was being a good girl. No fuss. It was as if the little Keller boy was doing her crying for her. Besides, he was going to be all right. That made him, for Cleo, a kind of talisman; crying for her, bringing her luck. She drew a superstitious comfort from his fretting.

People came and went. The only two that made much impression on Cleo were the Presbyterian minister and Judge McVey. The minister came to offer Elroy the solace of the church in this dark hour of tribulation. (Those were his actual words; he and Elroy had much in common.) He also fixed Cleo with his piercing eyes and said, "God's will be done."

She mulled it over in her mind while the minister went back to pace and pray with Elroy. God's will be done. Another road block. Another big immovable No. It was Mother's will that must be done. She did not want to die. She could not want to die. She had been *happy* when Cleo left her yesterday afternoon. The memory of her radiant face was as vivid as fire. No connection with the woman they had carried out of Mother's bedroom this morning when the doctor came. Thick-faced; insensate; making that sound of disaster with every breath. Cleo knew the true from the false. "It's going to be all right. Really, really ... You do believe me, don't you?" Passionately Cleo believed—now, as she had believed then. Mother's will be done. And Mother's will was to live.

"She seemed quite calm last night," Elroy was explaining brokenly to the minister. "She had been upset. Earlier. But I got her quieted down, she seemed so much improved, so calm —It was an unnatural calm, of course. I should have realized it at the time."

"We cannot foresee these things. We must not reproach ourselves," the minister proclaimed.

"All the same," Elroy said, and wrung his hands. "And then this morning when I looked in on her. It never entered my head. I was relieved to see her so sound asleep. Relieved! I could have saved her then, I could have—"

"We must not abandon hope," said the minister.

"Hope. Hope." Elroy stared vacantly at the rug for a moment. Then he resumed his lament. "It never entered my head. I was careful not to disturb her, it was early when I left for the store—"

"You left her alone, with Jim Singley still in town?" said Cleo. It shocked everyone, including herself; certainly she had planned nothing of the sort.

Elroy did not look at her. But he answered her. With dignity. "I took precautionary measures. Naturally. I made arrangements with Mr. Brewer to notify me when—the party in question left the hotel." He turned his haggard face toward the minister and cried beseechingly, "I thought that was where the only danger lay. I never thought that Audrey, Audrey herself—How could I have been so blind? I loved her so. How could I have failed to see?"

"We must put our trust in God," said the minister. "He will not fail us in our hour of need."

On the other hand, Judge McVey offered brandy. He padded in—he was surprisingly springy on his feet for a man of his weight—whisked the bottle out of his pocket, and told Cleo firmly, "Here. Warm up your gizzard." And he was right, she felt a glowing spot in her interior. Elroy declined, though Cleo had a momentary impression that he was tempted. But his distrust of the judge as a friend of Jim Singley's won out. "No, thank you," he said primly, and turned his back on the proceedings.

Well, it was his loss. Not so much the brandy, Cleo thought, as Judge McVey himself, who had a quality of built-in comfort. Part of it was simple physical size (his big warm hands clasping hers; his broad solid shoulder to lean against.) But not all of it. Judge McVey projected his own inner security. He held out no hollow promises: things were bad, and they might get worse. He knew it, and he still refused to panic. He seemed to move, calm and sensible, among the nightmare terrors that haunted Cleo—not in the least blind to them, not underestimating them, but not giving way to them either. And making it possible, just barely possible, for Cleo to do the same.

He produced, besides the brandy, other crumbs of practical comfort. He had managed to snatch a few words with the doctor. "Remember, Cleo, she's got a chance," he said matter-of-factly. "Doc told me so himself. He'd have no reason to say it—not to somebody like me—if it wasn't true. The next hour ought to tell the story. She's got a chance. It's lucky you kids turned up when you did."

"Yes, but I left her yesterday. It's my fault, because yesterday I—"

"Hush," said Judge McVey, with authority. He cast a glance toward Elroy's back, still turned to them, and lowered his voice. "Jim told me a little about yesterday. A very little, I'll admit. He's outside now." At Mrs. McVey's gasp of alarm, he added quickly, "Don't worry, he'll stay outside, he's not coming in. He told me you'd figure it was your fault, Cleo. He said to tell you not to. So I'm telling you. From him. From me, too."

It was extraordinary, the effect of this flat statement. It evoked, for Cleo, a sudden clear picture of Jim: he would be sitting on the bench in the hospital yard, waiting it out in stony self-containment. Even so— and even after the way Cleo had blown her top to Wayne last night— he had a thought for her, and a few words. Kindly words, in their laconic way. She saw the very tilt to his head, one side of his face in sunlight, the other shadowed and somber, the way it had been yesterday in the garage. That queer juxtaposition of the known and the unknown, the reassuring and the sinister. What he had said to Judge McVey (and she heard him saying it: "Cleo will figure it's her fault. You tell her not to.") had the same quality of doubleness. Kindly as it was, it carried with it other, darker implications. How could he be so sure that it was not Cleo's fault? How, indeed, unless he knew that it was his own?

There he sat on the bench outside the hospital, with whatever he knew about Mother locked inside him. And he must know a great deal more about Mother than Cleo did. From six years ago—because he had come back to Athena. From yesterday—because he was here, waiting. The murderer returning to the scene of his crime? It was one explanation. He was responsible for Daddy's death. And if Mother died ...

No. She was not going to die. Of course not. Even though the little Keller boy was not crying.

Mrs. McVey was. Sniffling quietly into her handkerchief, as she had done at intervals ever since they got here. However long ago that was. She was a nice little woman, Mrs. McVey; nice and normal, with her little fits of sniffling and chatting. For Cleo's sake, in both cases. She hardly knew Mother, so the tears couldn't be for her; and the chatting was to distract Cleo from Elroy's muttering.

He had started again. Mrs. McVey mopped her eyes and took up her burden, with dogged brightness: "It's such a pretty day. Nothing like spring, I always say. Look, Cleo dear, how green the grass is getting ..."

A sprightly accompaniment to Elroy's broken lament. "I should have realized, because I knew of course how upset she was, in the afternoon. But then afterwards, I got her quieted down, I thought she was going to be all right. I'll never forgive myself. It never entered my head, this morning when I—"

Judge McVey was listening quite attentively, Cleo noticed. He even got up and paced a bit with Elroy, so as not to miss anything. But of course he hadn't heard it before. All at once Elroy turned on him, snarling. "You're no friend of mine. What are you doing here, pretending to sympathize? Go and sympathize with him, the way you did when he murdered Herb Fleming. Go and tell him he's murdered her too. It's what he came back for, the only reason he came back, to hound her to death. You're his friend, not mine. Get away from me!"

"All right," said Judge McVey affably. But he didn't leave the room. He settled down in the big chair close to the sofa, and after a while Elroy unclenched his hands and seemed to forget he was there.

Mrs. Jenks trudged in with more coffee. Time crawled by.

When the doctor came in, Elroy had subsided in the wing chair, with his eyes closed against those twin eyesores, Cleo and Judge McVey. He jerked upright, shuddering, at the doctor's touch on his shoulder. "Mr. Hild. Mr. Hild, she's—"

"No no no!" Cleo was on her feet; she felt that she was shrieking. Only there was no sound at all. Silence, deathly silence. The little Keller boy was not crying. She could not get the screams past her aching throat, and she put her hands up to her ears to keep from hearing what the doctor was going to say. Because the little Keller boy was not crying. "No no no!"

Everything floated. Elroy's stupefied face and behind it the wing chair; the doctor's outstretched hands as he floated across the room toward her; even the floor under her feet could not be trusted, it set up a leisurely tilting that made escape impossible. The doctor was in his shirt sleeves. No gold watch chain looped across his stomach, this time, to gleam in the lamp light. "God Almighty, Jim, he's not hurt," he had said. "He's dead ..."

Those words of six years ago were louder in her ears, and realer, than what he was saying now. "It's all right, honey. She's going to pull through."

Bill grabbed her and hugged her. Mrs. McVey was laughing and crying at the same time. Judge McVey hugged everybody except Elroy. But it took the little Keller boy to convince Cleo. When she heard his thin whimper again she knew that it was true, Mud was not going to die, Mud's will be done.

"You're sure?" Elroy croaked from the wing chair.

"I'm sure," said the doctor. "She'll make it, Mr. Hild. We got to her in time. She's in no shape for any of you to see her yet, and won't be for hours. But you can set your mind at rest, she's going to pull through."

In a burst of glory, Cleo started toward Elroy. He did not see her. He stared, glassy-eyed, at the doctor; at last he lurched to his feet, all shrunken and disheveled. "But she doesn't want to live," he said, and stumbled out of the room.

"Wait," cried Cleo. "Elroy!" She followed him to the front door, but when he paid no attention she stopped on the steps and watched him till he turned the corner. He moved erratically, like a ramshackle mechanical toy; his arms flapped as if on worn-out springs.

"I'll pick him up in the car," said Bill. (Because he was there, watching too; steadying her. The same quality of built-in comfort, like his father.) "Don't worry, I'll look after him. You stay with Mom and Dad." She was aware of them coming up behind her as Bill took off for the car. They stopped short and waited. So did Cleo.

Jim was crossing the sunny yard. His shadow strode beside him, elongated and lonely. From the foot of the steps he said, "I saw Elroy leaving. Is she—Tell me. For God's sake tell me."

Judge McVey told him, and his face turned white as plaster. Cleo saw the sweat gleaming on his forehead. His hand groped out and caught hold of the broad stone stair railing. He sat down on it, abruptly.

"Hey now, Jim." The judge hurried down to him. "Take it easy. I said she's going to be all right."

Jim lifted his head from his hands and asked—as Elroy had asked—"You're sure?"

Cleo heard her own voice rising, shrill and uncontrollable, above the judge's. "It's not true, what he said, that she doesn't want to live! No, no, no! I don't believe it. Jim!" She ran down the steps and knelt beside him so that she could look into his face. "You know it too! It's not true, what he said!"

"Who said? Elroy?" Jim's eyes glinted.

"Hush, Cleo dear," Mrs. McVey was chattering nervously. "Elroy was upset, or he wouldn't have said it. You've been so brave all along, you mustn't cry now ... Of course she wants to live. The way it could have been, she must have taken those capsules by mistake. Not on purpose at all, just by accident ..."

Absently, Jim brushed the back of his hand along Cleo's cheek—a curious, tentative gesture that heartened her. But only for a moment. When he spoke it was Elroy's words again. "My fault. I should have known."

SEVENTEEN

It was the tranquil hour of sunset. The last, golden rays of light slanted across the grass like a benediction. Bird songs sounded pure, and golden as the air. Mothers called their children home to supper.

Judge W. F. McVey stepped along at his usual springy though unhurried gait, bent upon an errand of mercy. He was carrying a bowl of potato salad to Elroy Hild. Poor fellow, Marge had said, she couldn't bear to think of him in that house all alone, nobody to fix him a bite to eat. She couldn't invite him for supper, of course, on account of Cleo. (Who had fallen asleep from brandy and exhaustion after they got home from the hospital. But there was no telling when she might wake up.)

"But Mack, do you think you should?" Marge protested when he offered to make the delivery. "I mean, the way he turned on you at the hospital. He may not even let you in the door."

Which was perfectly true. Mack's impulse to check up on Elroy (he admitted it to no one but himself) was part of this hunch he had, this peculiar feeling ... Not about Elroy so much as about Jim. He had this peculiar feeling that Jim was up to something. He didn't know what, or even why.

He had left Jim sitting there on the hospital steps. No thanks, he didn't want to come home with Mack. Not right now. Later, maybe. Sure he was all right, he was fine. He just didn't feel very sociable right now. Then he had asked, "You didn't hear anything from Wayne today, did you?"

Mack hadn't. Not through lack of trying. But Velma had answered the phone when he called, and had curtly given him to understand that Wayne was asleep and that she had no intention of disturbing him.

It seemed that Jim hadn't heard from him either. "I thought maybe he'd call me. Last night, you know, when I caught up with him—he wouldn't talk to me then, or listen to me. But I asked him to call me this morning, and somehow I thought maybe he would. He never will, I guess, after what's happened today. I can just hear Velma ..."

Mack couldn't argue with him. Velma would make the most of this opportunity: Audrey's suicide attempt, coinciding as it did with Jim's return, was all she needed to prove that she had been right from the beginning. How could Wayne doubt her now?

"Look here, Jim," Mack had said, "you're not planning anything foolish, are you? I mean, it won't do you any good to go messing around with Velma. You'd just be asking for more trouble than you've already got."

After a moment of blank staring, Jim had laughed. "You mean she might take another shot at me? You don't need to worry. I know better than to go messing around with Velma. I sure ought to, by this time. I'm not planning anything."

All the same, Mack had this hunch. And of course he still had his confession to make. Somehow he must wangle another chance, in place of the one he had missed last night. Somehow he must make it up to Jim. As he turned up the flagstone path to Elroy's house, Mack heaved a great sigh.

The drapes were pulled shut across the picture window, but there was a light on in the living room. Mack rang and waited for what seemed like a long time. He began to imagine, uneasily, that he was being watched. Then the door opened and Elroy said, "What's happened? They promised to let me know when she regained consciousness ..."

At first glance he looked considerably more composed than when he left the hospital. His clothes were restored to their usual state of phenomenal tidiness: jacket neatly buttoned, tie and collar straight. And of course not a hair out of place; to the best of Mack's recollection that straw-colored coiffure had remained undisturbed through the worst of Elroy's distraught moments.

"No, no, nothing like that, as far as I know," Mack said. "I'm sure they'll call you the minute she comes to. I just brought over some salad Marge fixed for your supper."

"Oh," said Elroy. He peered at the bowl in Mack's hands. After quite a long pause he added, without warmth, "Thank you. It's very kind of you, I'm sure."

Mack took a step forward, half expecting Elroy to bar the way. But he drew aside docilely, and Mack moved on in. "Let me put this in the kitchen for you."

How quiet the house seemed, almost hushed. And as tidy as Elroy—except for a litter of crumpled papers on the sofa in the living room. The kitchen looked unused, as if it belonged in a model house where no one had ever lived.

"I realize I owe you an apology," Elroy said suddenly and rapidly. "It was inexcusable, the way I spoke to you at the hospital this afternoon. Inexcusable. Even in my distracted state."

"Forget it. I know what a strain you were under. It was perfectly natural for you to blow up."

"No excuse," Elroy insisted. "I should have controlled myself, no matter how great the strain ... Yes. Terrible. The strain. Nobody knows how terrible. Very kind of you, I'm sure." He fixed his eyes on the salad bowl. His face quivered; Mack thought, with dismay, that he might be going to burst into tears. "Everyone's been very kind, Judge McVey. More than I deserve. A person never realizes, except in time of trouble, how many friends, how kind ...”

What friends? It occurred to Mack, not for the first time, that Elroy was a singularly friendless man. There was something old-maidish and stilted about him that put people off. Always had. Men and women both. He went through all the motions: church, lodge, business clubs. Contributed to worthy causes. Served willingly and conscientiously—as treasurer, usually, or in some similar thankless capacity. But the reality, the heart-warming comradeship was lacking. He had been eminently eligible as a bachelor, and yet girls—belles or wallflowers, it didn’t seem to matter—had never showed much interest in him. Two or three dates, and they dropped him. Until all at once Audrey Fleming married him. Strange.

Well, there it was. He felt he had friends. He didn’t know the difference. Didn’t realize that right now he was not only embarrassing Mack but exasperating him, producing in him an aversion that he was ashamed of but could not suppress. Another angry outburst would have been easier to take than this flow of apology and gratitude.

To shut it off, he said, “Don’t mention it. You ought to try to get some rest, Elroy. From what Doc said, he doesn’t expect her to come out of this for several hours. Maybe not till morning. You ought to eat something and then lie down for a while. Try to get some sleep.”

Elroy uttered a short, startling sound, like a laugh. “Yes, of course. Sleep. Rest in peace. How can I sleep? I keep thinking about her, when she comes out of it—” Where was it now, that first false impression of composure? There was a glaze of terror in Elroy’s eyes. He shuddered. It was as if all that held him together inside his neat clothes was a mechanism of jangled wires and rickety springs that might break down at any moment and send him flying in all directions at once.

He ought to have a sedative, Mack thought, I’ll call Doc as soon as I get home. Aloud he said, “It may not be that bad, Elroy. She might not have meant to take an overdose. It could have been by accident. A mistake.”

“A mistake? How could it be by accident, when she took the whole bottleful? Or nearly the whole bottleful. All that were left from when she was sick last week. That’s all that saved her, you know. Did you know that? Too much of an overdose. She threw some of it up, and that’s why she didn’t die the way she wanted to.” Again the startling, laugh-like sound. “That was the only mistake. Too much of an overdose.”

“But it still doesn’t mean she’s going to feel the same way when she comes out of it,” Mack argued doggedly. “Look at all the would-be suicides that change their minds at the last minute and call for help. With lots of them it’s just a passing impulse, and they’re glad to wake up and find themselves alive instead of dead.”

He stopped, aware that Elroy had not heard a word. The glazed eyes were still fixed on Mack; the tidy head was inclined politely in his direction. But Elroy was impervious to incoming messages. At the same time he seemed to be struggling to communicate a message of his own. His hands jerked out toward Mack; his mouth worked convulsively and brought forth at last—what else, from Elroy?—a platitude.

"I loved her. Not wisely but too well."

The odd thing was that it did not sound ridiculous. For the first time Mack felt a surge of genuine compassion. Before he could speak (not that he had much idea of what he was going to say, anyway) the front door bell chimed. At once Elroy's false front of composure was restored.

"I expect that's Velma Carson. She called and said she was coming over. A wonderful woman. So kind. Everyone's been so kind ..."

"In that case," said Mack, "I'll just nip out the back door. Take care of yourself now, Elroy. Anything Marge or I can do for you, let us know."

It set off another spate of gratitude. And before Elroy hurried off to usher in his next caller, he added one of his especially sincere—and especially clammy—handshakes. It had its usual effect on Mack. Compassion oozed away; aversion oozed back. He wiped his hand on his trousers and headed for the door, pausing only long enough to make sure that it was indeed Velma who had rung the door bell.

Her voice reached him clearly: "I do hope I'm not intruding, Elroy. I just felt I had to let you know in person how deeply I sympathize. No one can understand better than I what you must be suffering—"

Oh you bet, thought Mack. They had so much in common, Velma and Elroy. It was going to be a regular We-Hate-Jim orgy. On a high-minded plane, naturally; no vulgar truth-telling.

But then who was he to throw stones at other hypocrites? He let himself out quietly and stood a moment on the back door step, looking up at the translucent sky. The sun was all but gone; there was a little new moon, tissue paper, and one last gilt-edged cloud. What was he but the essence of unadulterated hypocrisy, passing himself off as Jim's best friend, never once admitting to the underhanded role he had played on that night six years ago? No matter how he tried to rationalize it ...

Underhanded it would certainly have seemed to Jim—though in all probability he would have seen, once he cooled down, that it was to his own advantage. At first glance, though, he would have seen just one thing: Mack had known that Herb Fleming was cheating him before he knew it and instead of telling him about it had been fixing to help cover up the cheating. He would have taken an understandably dim view of Mack's presence on the stairs, and of the check in his pocket. A check made payable to Jim's dishonest partner and signed by his best friend. W. J. McVey, Esquire. That sterling citizen, that able member of the bar, whose name happened to be up for District Judge.

Mack made his way down Elroy's flagstone path without seeing it; he forgot that supper was waiting for him at home; the balmy spring air changed, for him, to the iron-cold, black winter evening of six years ago.

It had been late enough for Main Street to be deserted, all the stores closed. So there was no one to see him enter the street door beside the garage and start up the dark, closed stairway that led to the Fleming apartment. With the check in his pocket. Because earlier that day, in the morning, Herb Fleming had come to Mack's office and spilled the whole sorry story. Dumped it in Mack's lap, in effect, by asking for the loan so he could straighten out the firm's accounts before Jim got wise to what he'd been up to. One thing about Herb Fleming, he had the born salesman's instinct for the right pitch. It had gone like this: "You're a friend of Jim's, you'll be doing him a favor by keeping him from breaking up our partnership. Because that's what he's apt to do if he finds out the money's missing. It will ruin me, I'll admit, but it won't do Jim much good either. He's not good at selling and I am, he needs somebody like me as much as I need somebody like him. We've got a nice little business going. It would be a shame to break it up over a few lousy bucks that I didn't really steal in the first place, I just meant to borrow it temporarily, only I got in deeper than I expected. You know me, Mack, I'm not a crook ..."

Granted that Herb was a slick talker, there was still considerable truth in what he said. Without him on the selling end, Jim wouldn't have had anywhere near as profitable a business. And Herb *wasn't* an out-and-out, confirmed crook. He had his weaknesses—lack of judgment, an indiscriminate friendliness that had drawn him into too much drinking, too much gambling. But calculated dishonesty, never. Surely, Mack had decided after an afternoon of due deliberation, Herb Fleming was worth taking a chance on. Give him a break, and his first offense might well turn out to be his last. He was such a good guy basically, warmhearted, well-meaning, sociable, everybody liked him ...

And of course that had been Mack's other reason. With his name up for District Judge, it wouldn't hurt a bit to have a fellow like Herb—popular, a big wheel in Rotary and Lions Club—solidly on his side. Not that Herb suggested anything like that, or even thought of it. But Mack did. It had already sneaked into his mind, even while he was putting on his cautious lawyer's act with Herb, refusing to commit himself without his afternoon of precious due deliberation. Which in a way had condemned them all—Herb to death, Jim to prison, Mack himself to six years of guilty conscience.

The stairway smelled of gasoline and oil from the garage on the street floor. Halfway up, Mack had heard the voices raised in violent anger and had realized that he was too late, Jim had already found out about the missing money. What to do? Barge in, cheerily waving his check, while Jim was in the middle of calling Herb a drunken, thieving bastard? And while Herb, who as a matter of fact didn't sound any too sober, was taking a poke at Jim? Mack heard the thud, Jim's grunt of surprise, and his voice: "So that's how you want it. Think you're tough, do you? Okay." And then the crash, and Jim again: "Come on, get up on your feet, I'll teach you to steal from me ... Can't you take it, tough guy? Had enough already?"

Footsteps up above; and Mack, suddenly horrified at the prospect of being discovered, lurking there on the stairs, eavesdropping, had turned tail and fled. Down the stairs. Home. He still had the check in his pocket. He still had his good intentions. (At the moment Jim was in no mood to listen to the reasons why he shouldn't break up his partnership with Herb. But later on, when he cooled down—as he was sure to do—later on, Mack would go to work on him.) And he still felt like an honorable man.

He had torn up the check that night, when he found out Herb was dead. He had switched his good intentions to another track: Of course he would speak up in Jim's behalf if his word was needed. No matter how embarrassing it might be, or how damaging to his personal ambitions. And it would have been damaging for him to get involved in a murder trial, with the district judgeship in the offing. Especially when public feeling was running high, and when the defendant happened to be a good friend of his. Besides, there was that smack of underhandedness, shadiness, in his own role. Conniving with a man who had admittedly misappropriated funds. Sneaking up a dark stairway, listening to the quarrel without making a move to stop it, haring off to avoid being discovered. No. It wouldn't have cinched the judgeship for him. But of course he would have spoken up ...

Only right from the start there had been Cleo speaking up in his place, relieving him of the responsibility, convincing with a lie where he might have failed to convince with the truth. Cleo had made it possible for him to keep his pretty little skirts clean. And impossible for him to feel like an honorable man.

He found, rather to his surprise, that he was back again in front of Elroy's house, approaching it from the opposite direction. So he must have been walking round and round the block. He crossed the street and sat down on the church steps. Somehow he didn't want to go home just yet.

Velma must still be in there, commiserating, convincing Elroy, and herself as well, that what she was feeling was sympathy instead of hate, compassion instead of triumphant spite. You had to hand it to her. Velma was a woman who could rationalize anything she did. Even taking that shot at Jim last night—assuming that Jim was right and she actually had done it. She was capable of it, all right, whether that shot had been a genuine attempt on Jim's life or a fake one, meant simply to scare him into leaving town. Either way, Velma would have no scruples. Anything to keep him away from Wayne ...

Wayne. Mack suddenly came to attention. Here was his chance—wasn't it?—to by-pass Velma and talk to Wayne alone. If he couldn't repair the damage Cleo had done last night, he might at least persuade the kid to take Jim's money. Take it and get the hell out of here, before Velma turned him into a spineless Mama's boy or a no-account drunk. There was some good stuff in Wayne to be salvaged, Mack admitted to himself; given any kind of a break, he'd be all right. It wasn't too late for Wayne. Certainly it was worth a try. In the middle of hoisting himself up off the church step, Mack saw Jim turn the corner at the end of the block. He was walking smoothly and quickly, obviously a man with a fixed destination. Which was—oh, Mack's prophetic hunch—Elroy's house.

Elroy won't let him in, thought Mack. He'll slam the door in his face, he'll raise all kinds of hell.

But when the door opened there was no eruption, only the murmur of their two voices, neither of them loud enough for Mack to catch what was being said. After a moment Jim stepped inside and the door closed behind him. The whole transaction had made hardly a ripple in the evening stillness.

EIGHTEEN

Velma took a long breath and closed her eyes. But when she opened them again Jim was still there, standing there at Elroy Hild's front door, looking Elroy in the eye. He was even smiling a little, that insolent smile of his.

"You," Elroy said, and then, rather shrilly, "what do you want?"

"There's something I want to talk to you about." Jim's glance skipped past him to the chair where Velma sat, rigid with outrage. "It's a private matter."

"I'm busy at the moment," said Elroy.

"Then I'll wait," said Jim, and stepped neatly past Elroy and into the living room. He made himself comfortable on the sofa. "I don't mind."

Elroy remained on his feet, hands clenched at his sides. All at once he burst out: "I'm sorry, but I do mind, I'll have to ask you to leave. I— There's nothing I care to discuss with you."

"I'm sorry too, but I'm not going to leave. Of course you can always call the police."

Velma jumped up. "I think you should, Elroy. After all, this is your house, you have a right to protection. You don't have to put up with—"

"No," said Elroy sharply. "Please. It's not a matter for the police. Not yet."

"No. Not yet," Jim agreed.

It jolted Velma, the way they were looking at each other. For an instant she had a strange illusion of another, deeper exchange between them—more than threat and counterthreat—an understanding that escaped her. An illusion, of course, and quickly gone. The next moment Jim's glance switched from Elroy to her, and she was engulfed in a wave of acute and unreasonable embarrassment. It was the sardonic gleam in his eye that did it; she felt as if she had been caught out in some bit of silliness. Damn him, oh, damn him, what right had he to make her feel like this? There was nothing silly about her calling on Elroy in his hour of trouble; on the contrary, it was an act of courage and high-minded charity for her to admit that she had been wrong in her judgment of Audrey. Elroy had recognized it as such; they had both felt uplifted—until Jim came and spoiled it all, turned it into a travesty of itself. So that now all she wanted to do was get away from here, escape before Jim could completely destroy her cherished inner vision of herself ...

There he sat, perfectly well aware of what his silence was doing to her and Elroy. Counting on it, in fact; using it as a weapon. Sure enough, Elroy gave way under the pressure. "Why can't you leave me alone? Haven't you done enough harm around here? You've accomplished what you came back for. You've ruined Audrey's life all over again, hounded her to death—"

"She's not going to die, Elroy. Didn't they tell you?"

"Certainly they told me." Elroy's voice cracked. "I was the first person they told, naturally. And I'll be the first, when she starts coming out of it, they'll call me the first thing. They promised. She hasn't regained consciousness, I know she hasn't, they promised to call me—"

"I didn't say she had. Calm down. Naturally they'll call you. Naturally you're planning to be there, when she starts talking. That's the way I figured it."

Velma could hold back no longer. "This is outrageous! It's inhuman. You have no business coming here, badgering Elroy, at a time like this!"

"I have more business here than you." His level gaze shifted to Elroy. "You want Velma in on this? It's nothing to me, either way."

By some miracle of will power Elroy had pulled himself together. He said, with an approximation of his usual precise manner, "I don't know what you're referring to by 'this.' If you're under the impression that I had anything to do with the attack that was made on you last night—"

"I'm not." He smiled wolfishly at Velma. "That's all settled, as far as I'm concerned. No, Elroy, it's not that at all."

"I see. Well, then, whatever it is, and I intend to find out—No, I don't want Velma subjected to any unpleasantness on my account. She's suffered enough at your hands as it is ... No, Velma, I insist. You're very kind, but this is something I must handle myself."

Her protests were mechanical. But then so were Elroy's expressions of gratitude. Mechanical and hurried, as if he too were anxious to have her go. All the time she could feel Jim's eyes, watching, mocking.

When she was outside, on the path, she found a handkerchief in her purse and wiped her hand; Elroy's, clasping hers in farewell, had been slippery with nervous sweat. But he had not wanted her to stay. And he had definitely not wanted the police. His attitude had seemed to her an odd mixture of dread and eagerness, as if he knew what kind of an ordeal lay ahead of him and wanted to get it over with.

It was about Audrey, of course. (She's not going to die, Velma thought. Yes, but she doesn't want to live. It's a worse punishment this way. Poor woman. Ah, poor woman.) They were both in love with Audrey, each in his own way.

If you could call Jim's way love. Primitive animal attraction, the lowest common denominator. Oh, Velma knew; she had seen it flashing between them. More than once; but the first time was the most vivid. A February-thaw day, full of false spring warmth that sucked up the dirty, lacy-edged snow drifts and turned the side roads into wastes of shining mud. Velma, stopping in at the garage on her way home, saw them before they saw her: Jim was kneeling, unfastening Audrey's overshoes for her, she had on that tacky old coat she used to wear and her arms were full of groceries. Velma remembered the bunch of celery sticking up out of the biggest sack, and the nervous sound of icicles dripping from the eaves outside, and then their two faces. She knew the look on Jim's face; it used to be there for her, before she and Jim were married. Afterwards too, for a little while. Only Velma had never looked back at him as Audrey was doing. The woman apparently had no shame; she didn't care what showed in her eyes, she even seemed to be proud of it. An embrace could not have been more revealing.

That was Jim's way of loving Audrey Fleming, Audrey Hild, whatever you wanted to call her. Illicit then, and illicit now, a jealous, violent lust that had brought him back after six years with his mind set on destruction.

How terrified Audrey must have been by his return! Even if she wasn't in on it when he killed Herb Fleming—But she was, she must have been. Velma felt a thrill of exultation. Of course! That was the purpose of Jim's visit to Elroy; to betray her as his comrade in murder, because he could not forgive her for having married Elroy. It explained everything—his air of insolence, Elroy's nervous dread (he must suspect, perhaps he even knew), his refusal to call the police. "Not a matter for the police. Not yet." Of course!

She walked faster, more buoyantly. (Poor Audrey. More to be pitied than censured. At last, at last, she was suffering for her sins. Poor suffering Audrey.) Once more the wonderful sense of being uplifted possessed Velma. Let Jim smirk at her, let him try to make something silly and false out of what had been a noble impulse on her part. The truth would prevail; he could not destroy her inner vision of herself.

He could not win Wayne away from her, either. From the security of today she could look back calmly at the frantic anxiety of last night, when she had been unable to keep Wayne from making that return visit to the McVey house. She had fought it tooth and nail, because she knew that Jim would be there too, but it was no use ... Some of the things Wayne said to her would rankle as long as she lived. "He believed me. You don't. You think I shot him, that's why you lied. He knows I didn't do it." The two of them against her. Always, always, the same intolerable pattern. Come on, Wayne, let's you and me go fishing. Or hunting. Or down to the garage. You and me. Leaving her the extra, leftover one, forever shut out of their private circle. And forever unable to understand why, or even exactly what she was shut out of.

Ah, but this time it had not worked. Wayne had come back to her, after all. Wayne was hers. Her boy, now and forever, amen.

On a wave of triumph, she turned up the walk to her own house.

She heard him coming down the stairs as she entered. There was only the one dim light in the hall. And it was chilly; nothing short of midsummer's fierce heat could penetrate the big, gloomy house. His face, peering down at her from the stairs, was sullen with misery. And with something else that she could not name, and chose to ignore.

"There you are!" she said cheerily. "You must be starved. Come on down, dear, I'll have supper ready right away."

Wayne had spent the day holed up in his room, and of course Velma understood, she herself had found it impossible to face her job at the bank today. She had not intruded, except when she took up a tray of lunch for him. (And, incidentally, the news of Audrey's attempt at suicide. For it was better—wasn't it?—that he should hear it from her than from an outsider. In view of its significance. Much better.)

"Where have you been?" he asked.

She was unprepared for the hostility in his voice; his attitude earlier in the day had been one of weariness and apathy. "Wayne dear, why are you looking at me like that? I went out for a while. I just—"

"Where? To see Judge McVey? Are you still trying to work that deal of yours?"

"Wayne," she said patiently. "You know I'm not. I told you last night. You don't want to take any money from your father, and that's the end of it. When have I ever tried to force you into doing anything you didn't want to do?"

"Oh, brother," he said. He came on down the stairs. "Then why won't you tell me where you've been? Don't try to kid me. I can tell. Something's happened. You're hiding something from me."

"Nothing's happened. I'm hiding nothing from you. I told you, I went out for a while." Her eyes shifted away from his, she could not have said why. "I'm sorry to be so late with supper—"

"Oh God," he said violently. "Stop being *sweet*, will you? Is Cleo's mother dead? Is that what you're looking so pleased about?"

Cold with fury, but determined not to show it, she took off her coat and hung it in the hall closet. Her hands were shaking. "She's not dead. She's going to recover. I'm not pleased about it, and I don't suppose she is either. If you can't speak to me civilly, please don't speak to me at all."

"How do you know? Who told you?"

He was standing right behind her; she had to turn and face him. "Elroy," she said shortly.

"So that's where you were. I don't understand how you—" There was a strange, marvelling expression on his face. "You went to see Elroy Hild. Why?"

"Why?" she repeated, and then, sharply, "Why not? Why shouldn't I pay a neighborly call on Elroy? I've known him for years, we go to the same church, it's the natural thing to do, to offer my sympathy."

"You hate her," said Wayne.

"No. Not anymore." With gentle dignity she explained that she no longer saw Audrey as an enemy, but as a fellow-victim, and as she talked she felt assurance returning to her, a healing tide of conviction. It had really happened like this: her visit to Elroy had sprung from the noblest of impulses, her heart was cleansed now of all bitterness. She finished on a note of near exaltation. "It's not for me to hate Audrey. Whatever wrong she did, she's already been punished many times over. No, Wayne. I pity her. From the bottom of my heart I pity her."

There was no immediate response from Wayne. He still watched her with that expression of mingled curiosity and wonderment. Finally he said, "Okay, Mother. If you say so. How'd it go over with Elroy?"

"What?"

"It went over, I guess. He's just dope enough to—"

"I'm not going to listen to any more of this, Wayne. I've tried to make allowances because I know how hard it's all been on you. But you owe me a little consideration too."

"Sure. All that I am or hope to be. Et cetera."

It was too much. She lashed out coldly: "You seem to think it's so peculiar that I should go to see Elroy. Well, it may interest you to know that your precious father went to see him too. He's there right now, and whatever his reason is, you can be sure of one thing, it's not to offer sympathy."

"He's at Elroy's? But I thought—I thought he was leaving town today."

She saw, with exquisite pain, how the thought of Jim made his face come alive as it never did for her. And he took a tentative step away from her, toward the front door. "That's right. Run to him. Run straight to him. It's what you've always done, and this is once when I want you to. I want you to hear what he's saying to Elroy. I want you to find out for yourself just exactly what he is, yes, and what she is too—"

"What do you mean? What are you talking about?"

"Go on." She pushed him toward the door. She was beside herself. "Find out for yourself. You don't believe me, you never have, he's always been God to you. Well, maybe this will teach you, if you hear it from his own mouth ..."

When he was gone she leaned against the wall, trying to control the gasps that shook her from head to foot. They sounded like sobs, but they were not; Velma never wept, even in the cruelest moments of disaster. And this was a moment of elation. Not sobs. Gasps of triumph, the triumph that would so soon be hers.

Of course. Of course. Only she had never known before, she would not have believed it: how much like disaster triumph could feel.

NINETEEN

Now, thought Elroy as he closed the door behind Velma. Now. An unearthly peace spread through him. The terrible journey was almost over. Its end no longer appalled him; he had foreseen it, he was prepared for it, he even welcomed it.

"Now," he said, and he turned toward Jim Singley. "Now will you be good enough to explain the meaning of this intrusion?" As if he did not already know. But the ritual demanded that he ask. He had to follow the ritual.

"All right," said Jim. "Let's start with what I said before—that I figured you were planning to be at the hospital when Audrey starts talking."

"What of it? If I feel that my place is at my wife's side when she regains consciousness, that's my business. I fail to see why it should concern anyone else. Least of all you."

"I'll tell you why. Because I'm figuring on being there too."

"You what? If you think for one minute I'll let you go near her—"

"You've got it the wrong way round, Elroy. I'm not going to let you go near her. Not by yourself. You can go back to the hospital when they call you if you want to. Only I'm going with you."

The ritual called for a high-pitched laugh. Elroy uttered it. "You're crazy."

"Look, Elroy. Let's stop stalling. You know as well as I do what this is all about. We both know what she told you last night, that she was going to—"

"She told me nothing! Nothing. She was too upset to talk." He still had moments when with one part of his mind he believed this. Deep, deep he had buried it, Audrey's voice saying what he could not bear to hear.

"She wasn't upset when I left her yesterday afternoon," said Jim steadily. "One thing sure, she didn't have anything like suicide on her mind. Cleo knows it too. She's the one that started me thinking."

"Cleo," said Elroy. He remembered that he hated her. "Oh, of course, Cleo. You think you can get her to lie for you again, the way she did before. Well, let me tell you, it won't work this time."

"It doesn't have to. It's nothing like the way it was before. Nobody's going to die this time on account of me—or on account of you, either."

So sure of himself. Nobody's going to die. She's going to pull through, the doctor had said, long ago and far away, this afternoon. She'll make it, Mr. Hild. And he had foreseen then the shape of the present moment. The ritual had been imposed upon him then.

"On account of me!" he echoed sharply. "Are you saying it's *my* fault that Audrey tried to kill herself?"

"Not exactly," said Jim. "I don't think she tried to kill herself."

He said it so quietly, without emphasis. And of course Elroy was prepared for it. Still—he thought in a detached way—it was strange, the almost complete absence of impact. Jim was not even looking at him; lazily his eyes followed the wisp of smoke from his cigarette. Sitting there so relaxed, so sure of himself, so impervious to danger. *Because he thinks it was Velma last night.* Elroy almost chuckled.

He said with great composure, "Let me see. Where does that leave us? Maybe you're suggesting that it was an accident?"

"Doesn't seem likely," said Jim. "She didn't just take one or two extra. She took the whole works."

How easy, how simple it had been. Because he had given no sign. Except for that first, animal cry of anguish that burst out of him. "No, Audrey! No! You can't!" It was his one concession to the pain that rent him, and when he saw how it distressed her he left the house—the shock, he told her, please, a few minutes by himself, and he would be all right, he would get over the shock. And what happened then had a sleepwalking quality, all gliding and unreal and flawless. Until the shot itself, which was not flawless. He knew, even while he was making his swift, stealthy escape back to Audrey, what he must do and how he must do it. Very simple. Very easy.

From then on what he presented to her was an image of love sublimely understanding and unselfish. (A false image? No, no; everything he had done sprang straight from the extremity of his love.) He would not stand in the way of her happiness. Sorrowful resignation; the unfailing care and devotion he had always shown her ... We won't talk about it anymore, darling, take your sleeping capsule, go to sleep. She took the first one herself, trusting him, even weeping a little for the cruelty she could not help inflicting. For once, for once, she had wept on his account. And then, half an hour later—when the drowsiness was taking hold of her—Here, darling, I've fixed you a rum toddy. Lots of lemon, the way you like it. It will put you to sleep in no time, drink it down, there's my good girl. A sleepy protest: Oh, bitter ... But trusting him, obeying him, maybe in the end even loving him a little; he could still see the dreaming smile that flitted across her face when he bent to kiss her, and the last quiver of her eyelids.

"Then you're accusing me of trying to kill her," he said to Jim. "That's more your style than mine, isn't it? Murder. May I ask what motive I might have had? Audrey is my wife. I love her very much. Why would I want to kill her?"

"Because she's going to leave you," Jim answered. "She's going out to the coast with me. We'd be on our way right now, if this hadn't happened. We'll still go, as soon as she's able. She's coming away with me. She told you so last night. I don't know what else she told you, because I don't know why she married you. There wasn't time yesterday, before you came home. I should have stayed with her then. But she didn't want it that way, she said she must—"

"Of course she didn't want you to stay." In spite of all he could do, he was trembling, almost screeching. Here it was again, what he could not bear to hear—from Audrey first, and now from Jim. "She never wanted any part of you. All she wanted was to get rid of you, any way she could. Why do you think she went all to pieces Friday, when you turned up the first time? Because she can't stand the sight of you!"

"That was my fault too. I should have let her know ahead of time. Only I couldn't understand, I couldn't believe—" Jim's voice thickened. "I had to find out."

"You had to find out. You had to get even with her, you mean. You had to spoil everything for her. You couldn't let her be happy. It wasn't enough, what you did to her six years ago. You had to come back and ruin all I've done for her, the life I've made for her—"

"She told me you've been good to her," said Jim awkwardly.

"Good to her!" It was too much; Elroy felt his control snap. "Why, you— What did she ever get from you but trouble and disgrace and sorrow? I've given her everything it's humanly possible to give. I've devoted my whole life to her, my whole soul—Good to her! Do you realize what I could have done to the two of you if I'd wanted to? They wouldn't have let you off with manslaughter, I can tell you. And her name wouldn't have been kept out of it, either, she might very well have been tried along with you, if I'd told what I could have!"

Jim sprang to his feet. "What are you talking about? She had nothing to do with it. She wasn't even there!"

"That's right, she wasn't even there. You were the actual murderer—"

"No! It's not true. I never meant to kill him."

"You never meant to kill him," mimicked Elroy. "You were fighting about money, just money, so help you, not another thing but money. Do you think I don't know the truth? The money was just an excuse. You were fighting about Audrey."

Jim said between his teeth, "We never mentioned her name, either of us. I don't care whether you believe me or not—"

"And I don't care whether her name was mentioned or not, you were still fighting about her." Jubilantly Elroy saw his advantage and pressed it. "Admit it. Why don't you admit it?"

"Admit it? No, I—Listen. Do you think I haven't been over it a million times? How I killed him without meaning to, even though I—All right, there were times when I wanted Herb the hell gone, maybe I even wanted him dead. But I never—"

"Maybe not. But let me tell you this, Jim Singley, it wouldn't have looked so good for either you or Audrey if the jury had known about those evenings when Herb didn't happen to be home and you sneaked off to meet each other. No, it wouldn't have looked so good. It wouldn't have been so easy to make them believe you fought about money or that you never meant to kill him."

Jim took a step forward, hands clenched, face darkly flushed, and Elroy's heart leaped with triumph. "Well?" he demanded. "Do you deny it? You needn't. Because I know. I followed her on those drives she used to take, I know how you used to just happen to be driving along the same country road ..."

That too he had done out of love. Love from the moment he first laid eyes on her, the fragile creature who had seemed to him like a wild, sweet bird. Forever out of his reach, he had thought at first; he had no hope of capturing her, it was enough that he should now and then catch a glimpse of her quick-changing face, the marvelous eyes, the figure delicate as a child's. At first. Even in the next phase of his enchantment, when he no longer depended on chance, but arranged little encounters that would look like chance—even then, he never hoped, or dreamed of hoping. There was her husband. There was (he slipped into the next phase imperceptibly: watching, following) Jim Singley. Then, during the course of Jim's trial, it came to him—that with the crumbs of information he had hungrily stored up he might capture his bird, his fabulous, unattainable bird; and hope burst in him like a rocket.

"So that's it," said Jim. He took another step. "You followed her, so you knew about her and me. You could have talked—and you would have, if she hadn't married you. That's it, isn't it? You blackmailed her into marrying you. It's the only way you could get her, and you did it, you son of a bitch, you did it. I ought to have guessed. But I got all screwed up, sometimes I even believed maybe I hadn't meant anything more to her than that ... The way you figured I would. You thought you were safe, you thought I'd never come back. Why, I ought to—"

"Kill me? Yes. Why don't you?" said Elroy softly, and in his eagerness he moved forward, within easy reach. How perfect, if this was to be the pattern, how perfect beyond all imagining! "You got away with it before. Go ahead. You can always say it was an accident, you didn't really mean to."

Jim stared at him curiously. "You'd like that, wouldn't you? You wouldn't even mind dying, if it meant getting even with me. And God knows you deserve to die. But no, Elroy, no, I'm not going to kill you. Why should I? You're already finished, anyway. Or will be, the minute Audrey starts talking."

Then it would have to be the other less perfect way, thought Elroy. A pity. Still, it would serve, it would snatch from Jim the victory he was so sure of. How stupid he was, really, not to see what a dangerous man he was dealing with. The most dangerous man in the world—one with nothing left to lose. Stupid of him. Fortunate for Elroy.

"You're awfully sure of yourself, aren't you?"

"Why not?" said Jim. "I know what she's going to say. So do you. I just want to make good and sure you don't get another chance at her. That's why I'm going to the hospital with you."

"Another chance at her! Are you suggesting that I'd harm a hair of her head?" Elroy cried in outrage. He could not understand why Jim was looking at him so queerly, with something approaching awe.

"My God, Elroy, you tried to *kill* her. Of course I'm suggesting. How do I know you won't try it again, to keep her quiet? Or maybe you've got some notion of twisting what she says around, making out she's lost her mind—"

"Nonsense," said Elroy briskly. He had no intention of going to the hospital at all. The call from the doctor was to be a signal, nothing more; when it came he would know that it was time. The climax of the ritual. The end of the journey—for Elroy, but for Jim as well, since he had insisted on barging in. As for his having tried to *kill* Audrey ... Jim made it sound violent. It had not been. No violence. No pain. Sleep. He had put her to sleep, his darling, because the shot had missed and there was no other way to save her from Jim. He had sat beside her, watching her sleep, and after a while he had tiptoed out of her room. One last moment of savage grief in the living room, when he saw the travel folders and crumpled them up ...

"We were going on a trip," he said in a faraway voice. "I was going to take her out west, when she felt strong enough. The Grand Canyon. There's no more inspiring spectacle ... Or wherever she wanted to go. Whatever she wanted to do. Anything. All she ever had to do was say the word." When he closed his eyes, it seemed almost possible again. They could still go, he and Audrey, he could still take care of her, watch over her, wait on her hand and foot ...

But when he opened his eyes, there was Jim Singley. Standing guard over him. Waiting, as he was waiting, for the phone to ring. Only they didn't have to wait. Excitement flashed through him. Now. It could be now, just as well as not.

He smiled and drew the gun out of his pocket.

TWENTY

As soon as he saw Velma leave, Mack began to get uneasy. Though why he should regard her as a deterrent to trouble was a point that escaped him. From his post on the church steps, he watched her progress down the street; she moved, as usual, with decision and considerable grace. Which signified exactly nothing. She would move that way if she had left Jim and Elroy locked in mortal combat.

The melodrama of the phrase made him feel a bit sheepish. Did he seriously believe that any such situation existed behind the drawn curtains of Elroy's house? It looked so bland and well-groomed, straight out of one of those gracious-living advertisements. All right. But Audrey had come within an ace of dying there last night, presumably by her own hand ... Presumably? Into his mind sprang the memory of Cleo rushing down the hospital steps, and her impassioned face lifted to Jim's: "It's not true, what he said, that she doesn't want to live! I don't believe it. Jim! You know it too!"

And right now Jim and Elroy were in there together. They might not be locked in mortal combat. But they weren't exactly a gracious-living team either. Mack knocked out his pipe and stood up. After a minute or two he crossed the street; the atmosphere of serenity remained unimpaired. No angrily raised voices. If they were having a quarrel Jim would be hollering, wouldn't he? Yes, and another thing, he wouldn't appreciate Mack's meddling in what was none of his business. After all, Elroy had admitted Jim of his own free will, so why should Mack take it upon himself to play the busybody?

No. He would stroll around the block once more. Walk off his uneasiness.

It didn't work. He got jumpier and jumpier; back again in front of Elroy's house he even found himself mistrusting the quiet. Too much quiet. Not reassuring at all. Ominous.

So he was a busybody. He wasn't going to stand by this time and let Jim get into a mess of trouble. He turned in at the flagstone walk. Ring the bell. Make some excuse: I seem to have mislaid my pipe, I was wondering if I left it here ...

But at the last moment such a feeling of foreboding gripped him that he ditched his little social tricks. This was no time to be ringing door bells and making excuses; he knew it, never mind how. By the pricking of his thumbs, maybe. By the thudding of his primeval heart. He tried the door; it was not locked, and he entered quietly.

He saw at once that he was in the presence of a maniac. Elroy was standing at the far end of the living room, with the gun in his hand. (Mack recognized it. His missing .38; he had bought it through Elroy in the first place. So it was not Wayne or Velma last night, but Elroy.) There was a chilling smile on his face. His eyes were over-bright, almost shimmering, and they were fixed on Jim, who stood not far from the foyer, with his back to Mack, as yet unaware of his presence.

"You're right," Elroy said. "I'm already finished, anyway. Nothing to lose. And we both know what she's going to say. So why should either of us be there? Answer: no reason. Neither of us to hear her, neither of us to have her."

A maniac. A maniac's meaningless gabbling. But the gun wasn't meaningless. Mack made his voice loud and authoritative. "Elroy." (Instantly Jim's head jerked around. "Mack! Get out of here. Go back!") Instead, Mack moved forward into the room. "Elroy," he repeated. "Cut it out. Put that down and listen to me. You hear me, Elroy?"

The shimmering stare did not shift from Jim. "I hear you. You keep out of this or you'll get it too."

He probably means it, thought Mack. He kept on moving forward as if he thought nothing of the kind. And he kept on talking; he had read somewhere that this was advisable, under such circumstances. "You don't want to shoot me, Elroy. What good would it do you? Come on now, use your head. Let's talk sense ..."

The gun waggled at him. (He can't be a good shot; he missed Jim last night.) Another step, and Mack was right beside Jim, who turned on him. "Will you get out of here? Mack, you damn fool, you want to get yourself killed?" He reached out a hand, and Mack knocked him sprawling and stepped between him and Elroy. (Why didn't he fire the instant Jim moved? He should have. Would have, if he knew what he was doing.)

"Stay where you are," Elroy said in a high, tight voice. "I'm warning you. I mean it. Why shouldn't I kill you too?"

He was aware that behind him Jim was picking himself up, so it was now or never, the one chance was to rush Elroy and hope to God it worked.

"Why? Because you are a man of honor," he said majestically, and plunged across the room.

There was just time, before he heard the shot and felt himself spinning, for him to think, Now what in the *hell* possessed me to say a thing like that? What in the hell ...

He did not black out. He had a rather pleasant little floating spell when he thought he was going to. But as he crashed backwards, taking Jim down with him, he saw Elroy turn the gun on himself, and he heard the second shot.

Then Jim was crawling out from under him, cradling him in his arms like a baby. "You damn fool," he said. "I told you to stay out of it."

"No. Elroy's the fool. And a lousy shot. Missed you again." Mack laughed, rather giddily. "This time, Jim, I didn't let you down—"

"Shut up," said Jim. He went over to the phone and made two calls. One to the sheriff's office. One to the doctor.

In spite of the pain spangles in his shoulder, Mack managed to get up off the floor and into a chair. There was Elroy, stretched out on the gray carpet with his head tipped to one side. The small dark trickle under his temple. The gun beside him; he seemed to be pointing at it with distaste. My Lord, Mack suddenly thought, I must have been out of my mind, I walked right *at* that madman with the gun in his hand ... Cautiously he touched his shoulder. It felt a little sticky. He kept his hand pressed against it. Hans at the dike.

He was floating, balmily, when all the racket started. First the sheriff charging in, giving them a knowing, so-it's-you-again look, grabbing Jim; and before Mack could get out a word a boy's voice hollered from the foyer, "No! He didn't do it! I was right here, the door was open, and I saw—"

Wayne. Mack felt no particular surprise at seeing him there. And he saw with great clarity the kindling warmth that lit up the boy's face as he plunged across the room to Jim.

"Dad," he cried. "You didn't do it. Dad!"

"Of course not," said Mack in his most imposing Judge's voice. Which was pretty damn imposing, in case anybody asked. "I saw it too. I mean I heard it. I can clear this whole thing up. Greatest of ease. Just so happens I was in the key position. There I was on the stairs—"

"Shut up, Mack," said Jim. "You're not making sense."

"I beg your pardon," Mack began. But here came the doctor, and everything kept wobbling and blurring before his eyes, and the point he had in mind swam away from him like a fish.

It was all right, though. Wayne saw it too, he thought. He was right there in the foyer, the door was open, so there's his word for it, not to mention mine. Wayne knows Jim didn't do it ...

"I can explain everything," he told the doctor owlishly. "Man of honor."

The doctor didn't think he was making sense, either. He nodded indulgently. "Sure, sure," he said. "Now let's see what we have here."

THE END

The Little Lie

By Jean Potts

ONE

Mr. Fly stood in the downstairs hall, listening to them quarrel. Going at it hammer and tongs—both of them, for once. Usually these occasions were too one-sided to suit Mr. Fly: Chad just let her blaze away at him without firing back more than a shot or two. This time, though, he was giving as good as he got. Their voices snarled together like static. It made the argument hard to follow (and besides, Mr. Fly had missed the beginning), but it livened things up considerably.

"In my own house. After all I've done for you." Dee always managed to drag that in. Couldn't forget the room rent she hadn't charged Chad when he ran out of money, and wasn't about to let him forget it, either. Like Mr. Fly, he occupied a room on the second floor, which she rented out to paying guests; unlike Mr. Fly, Chad also occupied a place in her affections—an enviably secure place, in spite of these occasional little crises.

"And I've done nothing for you?" he was saying now. "The work I've put in at the shop, the money I've saved you, yes, and made for you too—that doesn't count? Is that what you're saying?"

"Of course it counts. I didn't mean—"

"Well, then, shut up about all you've done for me. You've worn that needle out. Let's stick to the point. This crazy notion of yours that Erna and I—"

"My own sister-in-law. In my own house. Erna, poor thing, it's about what I'd expect of her. But I trusted you, Chad. It never crossed my mind you could do a thing like this to me—"

"I couldn't. I haven't. You're sick in the head. You're making it up. Because for some reason, God knows why, you've got to pick a fight with me every once in a while—"

Static again. Mr. Fly leaned yearningly toward the closed living room door, straining to sort out the tangle of angry words. But he stayed where he was, one foot planted on the first step of the staircase, hand on the banister. If any of the other roomers chose this moment to come in, or if one of the two combatants charged out of the living room, he would present the clear and blameless picture of a man on his way up to his own room, minding his own business.

A rumpled, stocky, not-very-young man—he glanced at himself in the hall mirror—burdened with a brief case full of ninth-grade themes which he would spend the rest of the afternoon correcting. Automatically he swiped at his bushy gray hair; it sprang back, forever intransigent. Absently he noted a rip in the shoulder of his suit jacket, and the wad of stuffing exposed by it. Erna would fix it for him, if he remembered to ask her. Or Dee herself, when it came to that. Never anything but obliging, for all her brusque manner. He liked her, admired her, wished her well. And the same went for Chad. Otherwise he would not have bothered eavesdropping on them. He was no vulgar, undiscriminating snoop. He was a student of human nature.

Chad's voice emerged, momentarily free of interference. "This is too much. This time you've gone too far, even for me. The things you can make yourself believe! I've had it. I mean it, Dee. Maybe it's what you've been trying for, all along, to push me to the point of no return. If so, congratulations."

She blurted out something. Could she be crying? Something about "love." There was a muffled reply from him, and Mr. Fly decided they had probably reached the making-up stage. But no. Here was Chad again, very clipped: "I'm getting out of here. I'm leaving. I know when I'm licked. And I am, God help us both, I see now it's no use, it's never going to work with me or anybody else. There's only one person you've ever really loved. Only one thing you've ever really wanted ..."

It was typical of Mr. Fly's luck that at this crucial juncture the kid next door should rev up his motorcycle, producing a racket that obliterated all other sounds. When the shuddering, stuttering crescendo of his departure had faded and died, there was nothing left to listen to; the living room was a vacuum of silence.

Then there was a small, smart sound—like a slap, exactly like a slap—and Dee said, in a tone that made Mr. Fly shiver, "That's a lie. How dare you, oh, how dare you! It's a lie, it's not true, you're lying."

"I wish I were," said Chad, so close to the door that Mr. Fly thought it best to start climbing. Just as he reached his own room on the second floor, he heard the living room door slam open and shut, and the fast, hard thud of Chad's footsteps. His room was directly across from Mr. Fly's; that door too slammed open and shut, and there followed twenty minutes or so of intermittent, muffled commotion. Could he have been serious when he said he was leaving? Mr. Fly hadn't thought so, but it certainly sounded like drawers being yanked open, hangers jangling, a suitcase being dragged out.

All right, so he was packing. But that still didn't mean he would really leave. On second thought he would decide to apologize for whatever it was he had said to Dee, and she would forgive him, and they would make it up the way they always had before. Just another lovers' quarrel. Nothing to worry about. It would all work out to the happy ending that Mr. Fly firmly believed in, personal experience to the contrary.

He sat down at the small table that served him as a desk, opened his brief case, and tackled the first theme. "How I Spent My Spring Vaction."

Funny, he thought as he inserted the missing "a" in his large, untidy handwriting, funny how in all the schools where he had taught—so many, so many—they made the same mistakes, over and over again. Just as they made the same jokes about his name. He hadn't heard a new one for at least a decade. Yet the kids themselves never failed to be convulsed by their own witticisms. As if nobody else had ever thought of them, or ever would again. Like the group he had heard sniggering in the hall this morning.

He sighed and pressed on, pencil poised for mistakes. Mr. Fly accepted his name, along with the other things that had happened—or had not happened—to him, with resignation.

At six o'clock he emerged from his room, headed for his lonely dinner at one of the town's two eating establishments that were within his financial means. The diner or Ye Olde Corner Tea Shoppe. Again he carried his brief case, now packed with clippings, notes, and the photographs he had taken on his tour of the English cathedrals nine years ago. He always went prepared to the meetings of the Self-Culture Club, of which he was an enthusiastic member. Maybe tonight he would be able to work the discussion around to a showing of his treasures.

The door to Chad's room stood open, revealing the dresser stripped of all personal belongings, the table uncluttered by the usual stack of books and magazines. A vacancy. A room to let.

Well, Mr. Fly had guessed as much. But he still refused to believe the worst. Just because Chad had cleared out his room, packed up bag and baggage in a momentary huff, it didn't necessarily follow that he had actually gotten in his car and driven off. He could be downstairs right now, making it up with Dee. Probably was.

But he wasn't. The front door bell rang while Mr. Fly was plodding down the stairs, and here came Dee to answer it, chic in a garnet-red dress, her color high, a festive sparkle in her eye. Yes, come to think of it, Mr. Fly recalled hearing something about a dinner party she was giving tonight.

It was the Bascombs at the door. Mr. Fly sidled down the stairs in an unobtrusive way, smiling tentatively in case anybody noticed him. Not that anybody was likely to, what with all the effusive greetings and the kisses. They were great ones for kissing, the Bascombs.

"Where's Chad?" cried Peggy Bascomb. "Chad, come on out here! I want to—"

"He's not here," Dee broke in. "Isn't it a shame. Except it isn't, really. It could be marvelous. He got this call from New York about a job, they want him there for an interview first thing tomorrow morning, so of course he was off like a shot ..."

"Something good, I trust?" boomed Howard Bascomb.

"Oh, very good. Better than anything either of us even hoped for. Keep your fingers crossed, everybody."

She was looking her best, which was very good indeed. Her hair was long and dark, and she wore it pulled back severely, in a style that suited her, in spite of the imperfections of her features. Her jaw, for instance, was too square, and her nose a shade too long; when she was in a bad humor it gave her face a heavy, drooping look. But tonight she was all charm and animation: red lips parted in a dazzling smile, dark-blue eyes glinting with excitement.

Give her credit, thought Mr. Fly, she was carrying it off with flying colors. Who was to see or understand the touch of strain in the angle of her head, the slight tightening in the cords of her neck? No one but Mr. Fly, watching her from the stairs where, earlier, he had stood, listening. Now as then, she was unaware of him, too busy ushering the Bascombs into the living room to notice when—still smiling tentatively, just in case— he edged his way down to the hall and out the front door.

More guests were coming up the steps to the wide porch. He scuttled past them down the walk, but he could still hear her proud, bright voice greeting them, explaining Chad's absence and the job interview in New York.

It hurt him to hear her. He hurried on.

TWO

How easy it had turned out to be, after all, the ordeal of a dinner party that, for a cowardly few minutes, Dee had thought she would have to call off. Why, she had come close to enjoying it, toward the end! Not at the beginning, admittedly; but once she was past the first hurdle—and the worst; Peggy Bascomb had the sharpest eyes and ears on the eastern seaboard—she knew she could make it home free.

She kicked off her pumps and padded around the living room, gathering up highball glasses and emptying ashtrays into the fireplace, where the remains of a fire still winked. A successful evening. How successful only she knew.

And not so much as a twinge from her New England conscience. But then it had been such a little lie, a fib, a half-truth. For Chad had almost certainly gone to New York. And he would undoubtedly find a job there, if not tomorrow morning, then next week or next month. More than a half-truth. Two-thirds of a truth. The other third ...

It went through her, cruel as a knife. He's gone, he's left me, I've lost him. Chad, oh Chad.

The point of no return: her fault, as he said, for pushing him to it; or his, for going on to such unforgivable lengths? Either way, they had reached it. For the moment nothing mattered but the stab-thrust of loss.

Six months ago she had opened the door and seen him standing there in the autumn dusk. A thin, dark man. "… Chadwell Johnson, I'm looking for a room for the weekend." And that might have been the end of it, except for the accident that had smashed up Chad's car and his leg, written finis to his job in New York—which was only a stopgap, anyway—and stretched his stay on through the winter. A winter like no other; an affair like none of the others.

Except that it too had fallen to pieces. She leaned against the wing chair, waiting for the pain to ease.

All right, she could bear it. But only if she kept it to herself. This was not like the other times, when she had welcomed the solicitude of her friends, poured out her griefs in many a therapeutic heart-to-heart and steeped herself in comforting reassurances: It's not your fault it didn't work out, Dee, you're lucky to be out of it, he's simply not in your class.

True enough, the others had all been obviously, basically unsuitable. They were married to somebody else. Or they were drunks, or boors, or weaklings, or neurotics. Call it bad luck or bad judgment; maybe it was the brief disaster of her teen-age marriage—long ago though it was, and all but forgotten—that had set the pattern for her, and kept her in it ever since.

Until Chad. No one would say he was not in her class. No one would call him unsuitable. Even his financial difficulties, which might so easily have led to ruin, had instead only provided further proof of his rightness. Dee (and no doubt all her friends) had expected the worst when she offered him credit; it was so often the kiss of death, that sort of arrangement between a man and a woman. The toughest test of all, and Chad had passed it. He owed her nothing in the way of money. Quite the contrary: during his convalescence he had worked harder than Dee herself at her antique and gift shop, sanding and rubbing down furniture hour after painstaking hour. And for years to come she would be profiting from the attic full of goodies he had discovered on one of his foraging trips.

She stared at the tray of glasses in her hands, but what she saw was Chad. He lay in the hospital bed, pale and remote, until his eyes flicked open, suddenly, alarmingly alight. He waited for her at the foot of the staircase, blinking up at her through dancing shafts of sunlight, balancing on his "walking cast," his hair coarse and vigorous and black, like a horse's mane. The fear; she had felt it even while she was running down to meet him, the fear that underlay all her other feelings about Chad. Yes, she had sensed that he was dangerous, right from the start.

Almost like a premonition of this afternoon, almost as though she had foreseen that some day he would say the unspeakable, tell her what she could not bear to hear.

She must put it out of her mind. Blot it out. Blot it out. Forget what was lost and think of what she had left. Her house, her beloved house; though the second-floor rooms were rented out and the top floor had been converted into an apartment for Erna and Oliver, the downstairs remained hers, unchanged from her own and Oliver's childhood. Her shop. Her share of good looks and charm, even now when she was in her late thirties. And she still had—

The knock at the door was Oliver's, two light taps, one heavier. She set down her tray and hurried to let him in.

"Hi, Dorothea." He never used her nickname, nor she his. "I was hoping you'd still be up. Party's over, I take it?"

"All over. Everybody's gone. Come on in and have a nightcap."

He had spent the evening, as he often did, in his repair shop, tinkering with some mysteriously stricken radio or television set, patiently coaxing it back to health. He wore his work pants, and that disreputable old zippered jacket made of shiny nylon that would probably never wear out. It gave him the look of a nobleman in disguise. Oliver should have lived in the days of plumed hats and doublets. His face was narrow, much darker than Dee's, almost swarthy, and it had a romantically mournful cast quite at variance with his cheerful, easy-going temperament.

He sprawled in the big striped chair that was his favorite, feet cocked on the hassock, and watched while she poured them each a brandy. "Cheers," he said, rather absently. "Where's Chad? Folded up already?"

"He's—" The little lie was for other people, not for Oliver. She could not tell even him the whole truth about her quarrel with Chad, of course. No need to; Oliver would never press her for more details than she cared to volunteer. But no need, either, to keep up the brave, false front she had hung on to throughout the party. With Oliver she could give way to honest misery and accept his simple, ungalling sympathy.

But he was going on without giving her a chance. "Listen, Dorothea, I'm glad I caught you alone. There's something I'd like to ask you about. If you've got a minute, that is."

"Of course." She sat down across from him and waited. Another of his financial problems? Poor Oliver, they were more or less chronic with him, and he usually brought them to her. He was the older by a year, but Dee was the one who had inherited, along with the house and the family furniture store, their father's head for business. Oliver's share of the estate had long ago dribbled away into ill-advised commercial ventures and the childish extravagances that both he and Erna found irresistible.

"Well," he said, "I got this letter from Gus. Erna's brother, you know."

She knew, all right. Not that she had ever met him, God forbid. But Erna was forever talking not only about Gus but the rest of the tribe, all of them still out there in the wide open spaces where Oliver had found her and where he should have left her, in Dee's opinion. "Yes?" she prompted, in a carefully noncommittal tone.

"He sent it to the shop. Didn't want to get Erna stirred up, I guess, till he'd sounded me out. Anyway, there's a repair shop up for sale out there. The guy that's run it for twenty-odd years wants to sell out and move to Florida. Gus says it's a good little business, the only one in town. He thought of me when he heard it's going to be on the market. Thought I might be interested."

"You mean—" Her throat tightened uncontrollably. "You mean, leave Rushford? Move out there permanently? But this is where you belong, this is your home! I don't see how you can—" She could not go on. The choking sense of betrayal. The panic.

And she had startled him with her intensity, put him on the defensive. "No need to get into such a sweat. Sure, Rushford's my home, but in a way it's my home town out there too. Don't forget, we lived there for almost a year when we were first married. Erna's always talked about going back some day. She'd jump at the chance."

"I'm sure she would. But I didn't know you felt the way she does. I thought you liked living here. Of course it's not like when we were kids, with the whole house to ourselves, but it hasn't been too bad for you, having the apartment and all ..."

"I never said it was bad. It's been fine. Great." Oliver flushed slightly. He was inclined to be touchy about how little rent he paid for the top-floor apartment—and that little at his insistence; Dee accepted it only to save his pride. "Who's talking about the apartment, anyway? The point is, the business, whether or not it would be a good business move. That's where I need your advice. Maybe I shouldn't even consider it. What do you think?"

"How do I know what I think?" she said irritably. "Did he give you any figures? What's the asking price? What's the volume of business? How much could you get for your shop here?"

"Yeah, I see what you mean." Facts. Figures. They invariably made Oliver nervous. He took a sip of brandy and assumed what he no doubt thought was an astute expression. "Nothing to go on without the figures. As I say, Gus was just sounding me out. Kind of a trial balloon, in case I might be interested. He can get all the dope for me if I want him to. It wouldn't hurt to ask, I guess." He eyed her doubtfully.

"Suit yourself. It probably wouldn't hurt to ask. On the other hand, if you're not really interested, why waste his time and yours?"

"I see what you mean," he said again. Very subdued now, crestfallen.

"I didn't mean to snap at you like that, Oliver. I'm sorry." Not very sorry, though, and not for more than a second. Again the sense of betrayal swept through her, and the panic. He could actually consider leaving, could sit there and calmly, casually, ask her what she thought of the idea … And he was the one she had felt she need not lie to! "I suppose I am in sort of a sweat tonight. I mean, to have you come up with this notion, on top of Chad leaving—"

"Chad leaving!" He sprang out of his chair and stood beside her, his eyes darker than ever, stricken with alarm and remorse. "For God's sake, Dorothea, why didn't you tell me? Here I've been yakking away at you— What is it with Chad? What happened?"

"It's all right. Really. Not what you think." Her head came up proudly. Once more the little lie rolled out, smooth and plausible and familiar. As easy as turning on a tap.

"How about that!" Oliver was properly impressed. "Good for Chad. I didn't know he had a solid line on anything."

"He didn't either, until this afternoon. Of course he's been answering every ad that looked remotely possible." This was where she inserted a little laugh. "You should have heard him floundering, trying to place the one they were calling about! Too funny. It does sound right up his alley, Oliver, I don't know all the details yet, but …" This was the place for a tremulous, hopeful sigh. She supplied it.

"Great. Terrific." He was back in his chair now, no longer worried. "You know, though, I kind of figured Chad might decide to stay here in Rushford. It wouldn't be the first time a guy chucked the rat race and settled down in a place like this. And he seemed to get such a charge out of everything, the small town bit, and working with you in the shop. Fit right in everywhere. But maybe it wouldn't have worked in the long run." He gave her his sudden, flashing grin. "If he does land this job in New York—Who knows, Dorothea, you could be the one to leave the old homestead, not me!"

An unexpected twist. An exciting idea. "Could be," she agreed, past the ache in her throat. "Why not, if that's the way the ball bounces? You can't tell, I may wind up farther away than New York. Chad's got no special ties there." Or anywhere else, as far as she could discover. When he came east from California a year ago, Chad must have made a complete, clean break of it. He sometimes mentioned California friends—no family; he was an only child, orphaned in his teens—but he had evidently kept in touch with none of them. And he had not been in New York long enough to put down new roots.

"That's so," said Oliver. "It could be anywhere. California. Isn't that where he came from originally?"

She nodded. And she speculated, not for the first time, as to what, if anything specific, lay behind that unqualified change of course in an otherwise smooth life. Woman or job trouble? A fiasco-marriage like the one she had suffered? "I just went stale on everything and decided to pull out and start over again." That was as much of an explanation as he ever gave her, and she had resisted the temptation to probe, strong though it was. Two could play at that game: she had no wish to uncover the bad spots in her own past.

It didn't matter anymore. After this afternoon nothing about Chad mattered anymore. The point of no return.

"I was just thinking," Oliver was saying. "If you should leave—of course it's all still up in the air, anybody's guess—but if you should happen to leave—Well, what about the house, for instance?"

"The house?" She was silent a moment; where was he heading? "I could sell it," she said, feeling like a traitor. "It would probably bring a pretty good price."

"Probably. Or, here's an idea. If you'd rather not sell, maybe Erna and I could run it for you. Taking care of the rooms, renting them out, so on. It would be good for Erna. Give her something to do."

Ah. So that was it. Ah.

"And you'd still have the house," Oliver went on eagerly. "I don't see why we couldn't work something out, if you wanted to."

Over my dead body, thought Dee. Certainly Erna needed something to do—something more than drink beer and cry on the shoulder of whoever happened to be around. Chad's shoulder today; at least that was his version of the incident that triggered this afternoon's quarrel, and now that she had her perspective back Dee admitted to herself that it was probably true. Pity, only pity for Erna and her muzzy tears, had prompted him to put his arm around her. In a way Dee had known it, even while she was lighting into him ...

Be that as it may, Erna wasn't going to get her corn-fed hands on the running of the house. She was Oliver's wife; let him figure out some other way to keep her out of mischief.

Gus's letter, though; she remembered it and said thoughtfully, "I think you've got something, Oliver. It's our house, after all, and I'm not sure I could bring myself to sell it, turn it over to strangers after all these years. Yes. I really think you've got something. I don't see why it wouldn't work out fine for everybody. The only thing is, if you go ahead and look into this proposition Gus wrote you about, and then if you decide you like the sound of it—"

"I'm not all that keen about it. I'd just as soon hold off on it till we see what's going to be with you and Chad."

"Well. If you're sure you don't mind." Absolutely, he assured her. The whole thing was pretty damn iffy, anyway. "Why don't we leave it like that, then? Just let it ride for the time being. Wait and see what happens."

"Right. Meantime, let's not mention any of this to Erna. The business about the house, or Gus's letter, either. If it works out, fine. If it doesn't she won't be disappointed."

"Yes. Much better not to get her hopes up." The conspiratorial smile they exchanged warmed her; she stretched luxuriously. "By the way, I do hope you and Erna weren't hurt because I didn't ask you to tonight's party."

"Good Lord, no! What makes you think we would be? We don't go around with your crowd. Never have."

"I know. But Erna seemed a little upset this afternoon, and I just wondered. She didn't say anything to you at dinner?"

"I didn't come home to eat. When I saw I was going to be stuck I just grabbed a bite downtown. She sounded all right when I called her." He paused, added cautiously, "How do you mean, upset?"

"It was probably my imagination. Forget it. I shouldn't have mentioned it." And might not have, except that she had to make sure Erna knew nothing about the quarrel. The chances were all against her knowing: Dee had held her fire until she got Chad to herself, downstairs. But better safe than sorry, especially with somebody like Erna, who was apt to spill out everything she knew or didn't know to Oliver. She wouldn't have waited. One whiff of trouble, one overheard word, and she would have been on the phone, sharing the wealth with Oliver.

His face showed clearly that nothing of the sort had happened. He looked—her conscience smote her briefly—nervous and puzzled and embarrassed, as he often did when she brought up the subject of Erna. "You mean one beer too many?" He got heavily to his feet. "What time was this? Because she sounded okay when I called her around five."

"Oh, it was long before that. I'm sure she's all right by now. You know how she gets sometimes, and I just wondered if it was something I'd done. I never mean to hurt her feelings, Oliver. You know that."

"She'll be better once Marilyn's home for the summer. She always is. She's kind of at loose ends, with Marilyn away at college, and only the apartment to take care of. It's not enough to keep her busy. I suppose what she needs is half a dozen other kids to look after, and a twenty-room house to keep clean ..."

And forty acres to plow before breakfast every morning, and a herd of cows to milk, and threshers to cook for, and a few hundred chickens to feed. You could take the girl out of the country, but you could never take the country out of a girl like Erna. Oliver should have known better than to try.

"It's not your fault," he assured her anxiously. "Nothing you did." The light caught flecks of white in his dark hair and sharpened the touch of melancholy in his face. It had been there even when he was a boy; time had not dulled its poignancy for her.

"You're such a comfort to me, Oliver," she said, and held out her hands impulsively. "What would I do without you?"

"Or me without you?" he said as he kissed her goodnight. "Sleep tight, now. Wake up bright in the morning light."

He always said that. Part of the goodnight ritual that dated back to their childhood. But before the door closed behind him he added, "Let me know, won't you, how Chad makes out. His appointment's in the morning, you said? Then you'll probably hear from him before evening."

"Yes. Of course. I'll let you know."

She felt cold and hollow. If only she had not had to lie to Oliver too! She could not back out now. She could not stand still, either. She had no choice but to go on.

THREE

Saturday was Erna's day to go to the supermarket. Any other day would have done as well, and with only Ollie to cook for, grocery-shopping was no big deal, anyway. But she couldn't seem to get out of the habit. Back home they had always gone to town on Saturday to do their trading, as the old-timers called it; and usually the kids stayed in for the evening, to go to the movies or the public dances that were held in the old Bohemian Hall, and ...

A far cry from Rushford with its picture-postcard primness, its sedate elms, its tight New England faces, its suffocating *littleness*. But then Erna herself was a far cry from the red-cheeked, tow-headed girl who used to dance the night away and work the day away without ever getting tired. Nowadays she was tired most of the time. She hadn't expected to keep the peony cheeks and cornsilk hair—they were Marilyn's now, and rightly so—but what had happened to that leaping, sparkling spring of vitality? How could it have dried up on her already?

She pushed her shopping cart over to the fresh fruits and vegetables and peered despondently at the cartons of blistered, mean little tomatoes, the topless carrots and radishes in cellophane, the bundles of limp rhubarb. Didn't look as if they had ever been near dirt or sun, ever been attached to living green leaves. But the strawberries smelled real. So real, so good that tears sprang to her eyes. That was the other thing, she never used to cry like this, for no reason. The tiredness and the tears.

"Hi, Erna. How are you?"

She turned and saw Peggy Bascomb, smart and flat-bottomed in her stretch pants; eyes unfathomable behind big round sunglasses; evidently in one of her chatty moods. She didn't always put herself out for Erna. Which was all right, of course; they were more acquaintances than friends. Erna was never quite at ease with Dee's set. They had such a clipped, bright way of talking. They were so glossy and sure of themselves.

"What a pretty dress," Peggy was rattling away. "Did you make it yourself? I envy you, having the time to sew. Well, and the know-how. I'm hopeless at that sort of thing. All thumbs." Before Erna could do more than flush with pleasure, she was off on a different angle. "Tell me, how's Dee? I haven't seen her all week, not since we were there for dinner, and I'm dying to know about Chad and the job. Last time I called her she said it was still hanging fire, but that was two or three days ago. Has she heard any more?"

"Nothing for sure. I mean, he calls her, of course. Practically every day. They're interested in him, no doubt about that. But it's not the kind of job where they hire somebody right off the bat. I don't know how many different ones have interviewed him, and they're not through yet. He's got an appointment Monday to see somebody else, another one of the higher-ups."

"But that's a good sign!" cried Peggy. "It sounds to me as if he's practically in. Otherwise the big shots wouldn't waste their time on him. He'll make it, I'm betting on Chad. He's a great guy."

"He sure is. Luckiest thing that ever happened to Dee, him coming along the way he did. I mean—" She probably shouldn't have said that. Talking out of turn again.

But Peggy didn't seem to think so. "I know what you mean, dear. It's about time Dee got a break. When I think of some of the pills she's been mixed up with, the utter pills! And she's so sensible about everything else. I can't understand it. Especially after that mess of a marriage. I never knew the kid, whoever he was, it was before my time, but I gather it was pretty much of a shambles."

"Terrible," Erna assured her. "Not that I knew him, either. It was all over by the time Ollie and I got here—that's why we came, you know, we were just getting started back home, Marilyn wasn't but a month old—anyway, he'd already pulled out. Dee went all to pieces. Kind of a nervous breakdown. It was the doctor that called us, said she needed somebody, and of course there wasn't anybody but Ollie. So we picked right up and came. It was a good thing we did, too, the shape she was in. Oh, you wouldn't believe it! She was nothing but skin and bones. Wouldn't talk, wouldn't eat, just sat there in that little sewing chair, rocking from morning to night, back and forth, back and forth ...”

Even now, it gave Erna the shivers to remember her first sight of Ollie's sister, Ollie's home. Such a raw March evening, the trees in the yard bare, the grass frostbitten, and not a light on inside the big, drafty house, empty except for the skinny, huddled, rocking figure. She hadn't answered when Ollie called her name, hadn't taken any notice of Erna or the baby, just went on hugging herself and rocking. Something cold and foreboding had crept into Erna's bones then and there, and to this day it had never quite thawed.

“I knew it must have been bad,” said Peggy. “Just the fact that she never talks about it.”

“Never. I don't even know where she met this boy, he wasn't from around here. Somebody said he was from the south, a migrant worker of some kind, but I don't know. Somebody else said he was with a carnival. It didn't last more than a couple of weeks, and she finally got one of those Mexican divorces. By then she'd snapped out of it, pulled herself together and got interested in the antique business. And that summer she started renting out rooms, and Ollie got a job, and we fixed up the top-floor apartment, and we never went back the way we planned to.” She sighed. Eighteen years, she thought. “Funny how things work out, isn't it? Now it looks like Dee will be the one to leave. As soon as Chad gets settled—”

“Well, good for her,” said Peggy crisply. “I don't mean I won't miss her. We all will. But she's got a good thing going with Chad. Too good to pass up, if you ask me.”

“Oh, me too, me too. I'm all for it.” She hadn't let herself think about it much, and neither Ollie nor Dee had said a word. Maybe she hadn't believed it. Now, with Peggy accepting it so matter-of-factly, her mind took off like a bird set free. She saw herself running the house—unless Dee decided to sell it—busy every day with the cleaning and laundry; and then the yard work, she would get rid of that lazy boy and take care of the lawn and the flower beds herself, put in a garden patch out back so they could have their own tomatoes and fresh stuff ... And if Dee did sell and they had to move, well, there again it would be her own place, hers and Ollie's. They didn't have to stay in town. Might find a small truck farm, why not, or a place where she could raise chickens. A tingle of excitement ran along her arms, right down to her fingertips.

It lasted after she and Peggy parted (“Tell Dee I'll be calling her, awfully nice talking to you, dear, when will Marilyn be back?”) and through the trip home with her load of groceries. It had done her good, visiting like that with Peggy, so nice and friendly, not a bit high-hat. Her thoughts kept darting ahead to how it would be if Dee left—no, not if, when Dee left—and then back to how it had been when she and Ollie were first married, the first time she saw him: he had been the stranger at that Saturday night dance, the Yankee boy passing through, headed for the west coast in his old jalopy, landing there instead of in some other town only because a thunderstorm had stopped him from going on. Oh, she could see him, just as plain, standing by the door, trying to act as if it didn't bother him, not knowing anybody.

Well, that hadn't lasted long; all the town girls went into a buzz over him, so dark, and with a sad look about him somehow, romantic. But in the end it was Erna he singled out. "Excuse me, may I have this dance?" And at intermission, "Would you care for a coke?" They sat in a booth at Joe's Joint, with the jukebox blaring in the background and the dance crowd whooping it up, such a racket she couldn't hear half what he said. It was partly the way he talked. Different. She didn't even have his name straight at first. Oliver Morris. He did something funny to the "o" in Morris. She had never known a boy named Oliver before; he had never known a girl named Erna. It was part of the miracle.

He never made it to the west coast. He drove her home in the jalopy (she had gone to the dance with her brothers, who naturally didn't expect to be stuck with her once they got her there) and they sat in the porch swing, whispering and kissing, until the thick stars began to blink out in the lightening sky and her father came to the door in his night-shirt and asked Ollie how he wanted his breakfast eggs.

They held off making love until the third night. He did, rather; from the start she had been all his for the asking. Did he know that, even now? It was the truth. Yes, right from the start: never mind the rules she had lived by before she met him, or her mother and father, or the fact—as she thought, that first night—that he would drive off in his jalopy next day and never look back.

Well, he hadn't. He had stayed on, as love-struck as she, and there had been the third night, and all the other nights of that long-ago golden spring. They were married the end of June (Marilyn was already started, but just barely); Ollie got a job in the filling station; they set up housekeeping in a bungalow that belonged to her father, and would in time have belonged to them. It was on the edge of town, Pop put in a new furnace for their wedding present, painted the whole place inside and out. He thought a lot of Ollie, all her folks did, everybody. The way things turned out, she, not Ollie, was the misfit. But she didn't know it then. Rushford was just a name to her. She had floated through the happiest days of her life without even knowing that was what they were. Like a bee in clover. Too bemused with here and now to believe there could ever be anything else.

But of course if she had known about being a misfit and the Rushford chill in her bones, she wouldn't have been so happy. And no amount of foresight would have kept her from marrying Ollie. She didn't regret it, and never would. It was her fault, not his, and she only wished, she only wished ...

Again she brightened, remembering her chat with Peggy. As she turned in at Dee's house and trudged up the walk, she noticed, with a thrust of sharp pleasure, how green the lawn was getting, how fast the elms were leafing out. No two ways about it, it was a pretty place, especially this time of year: the wide-porched white house with its banks of bridal wreath bushes looked comfortable and inviting. The long, lonesome winter was behind her; who knew what might happen before the summer was over?

In the hall she met Mr. Fly, off for one of his bird walks, binoculars and camera strung around his neck, his pocket bulging with the brown paper sack that contained his crackers-and-cheese lunch. So seedy-looking, with his hair every which way and his desperately cheerful air. She remembered hearing somewhere that the school board hadn't re-elected him—to the surprise of no one, probably including Mr. Fly himself. Another misfit, she thought; two of a kind.

She made a joke of scolding him about the rip in his jacket. "I told you I'd mend it for you. What do I have to do to get it off of you, hogtie you?"

"I keep forgetting."

"Don't poke at it. You're making it worse. If you can't spare the time now, bring it up when you get back. It won't take me but a minute ... Pretty day, isn't it?"

Mr. Fly agreed, at considerable length. Poor fellow, give him an opening and you were apt to be stuck for the next half hour. Not that it mattered to Erna; she had the time, more than she knew what to do with. The difference between her and Mr. Fly was that she wasn't willing to settle for bird walks.

When she got to the third floor, Dee was just coming out of the apartment. "Oh, there you are. Grace finished the ironing this morning, and I brought yours up. I didn't like to leave it in the hall, so I took it inside. I hope you don't mind."

"Of course not. Why should I?" No reason: it was Dee's house. And Grace worked for her; no reason—as Dee had long ago pointed out—why she shouldn't do all the laundry while she was at it. Less bother for her than having Erna putter around in the basement doing hers separately. There wasn't enough to make that much difference. "Thanks for bringing it up. Are you in a rush to get back to the shop? Come on in, and I'll fix you a sandwich."

"I've had lunch, thanks. A cigarette would be nice, if you've got one." She perched on the kitchen step-stool and watched while Erna put the groceries away. "No, I'm in no rush. Nothing much doing at the shop. I might as well have closed up and gone to New York for the weekend the way Chad wanted me to."

"He did? For Pete's sake, why didn't you say so?"

"Of course he did," said Dee sharply. "I should think that would go without saying."

"Well, sure. I didn't mean—" Somehow or other she was always putting her foot in it with Dee. "You could still do it, Dee! Why not? Just hop in the car and go. If anybody comes looking for rooms Ollie and I can take care of them. It's not so far, you could make it by dinner time, easy."

"I wouldn't say easy. And I'd want to get back before too late tomorrow ... No, it's not worth while. I'd rather wait and make a real weekend of it." Subject dismissed. She turned her attention back to Erna. "What on earth were you thinking of, girl, buying all those strawberries? Unless you're having company for dinner—"

"No." Erna flushed. Like a fool. Like a criminal. "They smelled so good," she said apologetically.

"All right, but four boxes! Oh well, it's your business."

"I thought you might like some."

"They give me a rash. Otherwise I'd love a box. They do look delicious."

"Yes," said Erna heavily. But not as delicious as they had in the store. They didn't even seem to smell the same. She had paid too much for them, too. At least Dee needn't know about that. "I ran into Peggy Bascomb. We had quite a little visit."

"What did she do, pump you about Chad?"

"Well, naturally she wanted to know if you'd heard any more about the job and all." Pumping. Erna added, with a flash of spirit, "After all, she's a friend of yours. Be kind of funny if she didn't ask. I didn't know it was a state secret."

"Don't be silly, of course it isn't. I just know how Peggy is, that's all." Smiling, Dee stubbed out her cigarette and stood up. Not a wrinkle in her crisp pleated skirt, and her waist was as trim as a teen-ager's. "I'm not blaming you for anything, Erna! I'm sure you didn't tell Peggy a thing I wouldn't have told her myself."

But when she was gone Erna wondered. She stood still, staring at the four boxes of strawberries, feeling thick and dull and vaguely ill at ease. Maybe she had talked out of turn to Peggy. Not about Chad. But all that stuff about Dee's marriage and the nervous breakdown; what had possessed her to rake that up? Just because Peggy was so nice, so friendly and flattering ...

It wasn't a compliment about my dress, she thought suddenly. She meant it looks homemade. It does, too.

She put the rest of the groceries away, folded the sack neatly and stacked it with the others in the space beside the refrigerator. The kitchen was spotless. So was the rest of the apartment; she had cleaned every inch of it yesterday. Dinner was hours away, and Ollie had taken his lunch today, and—oh God, oh God—there was nothing to do, nothing whatever to do.

She might as well have a beer.

FOUR

Monday was drizzly and glum, discouraging after the fine weather of the weekend. Business at Dee's shop was dull, in fact dead, until late in the afternoon, when—just as she was about to close up and go home—here came a trio of pre-season tourists, large, leisurely ladies in plastic raincoats with time on their hands and nothing on their minds but getting in out of the wet. They browsed for a good half hour, oh-ing and ah-ing and asking questions; Dee felt she deserved a medal for hanging onto her patience and her smile. The bell had hardly stopped jangling behind them before she was clicking off the lights and reaching for her coat.

She dashed across the street to her car, and—still another delay—Peggy Bascomb popped out of the drugstore. "Hi, Dee! Haven't seen you in ages. How are you?"

"Fine. Except I'm late, and Chad's supposed to call me at home. Browsers at the last minute, wouldn't you know, I thought they'd never leave. They wound up buying a big two boxes of note paper."

"I won't keep you," said Peggy, and then proceeded to do exactly that. Some long involved story about how Howard might have to postpone his vacation because his boss's wife was sick; they didn't know whether to cancel their cruise reservations or try to change them, and if they didn't get away before August they'd be stuck unless Howard's brother could switch his plans and come earlier ... Dee edged closer to her car. Kept her hand on the door handle. Rattled her keys. At last Peggy broke it off. "What's the matter with me, running on like this? I know you're dying to get home. Give Chad my best, and call me after dinner, won't you, let me know what gives. Any time. We'll be home all evening."

Dee was already behind the wheel, all set to zoom off. She fumed when she had to wait for the light at the intersection; remembered she was out of bread and decided against stopping for it. She was late enough as it was. She must hurry. She did hurry, and it was only as she was running up the steps of the back porch that she realized the absurdity of her own behavior.

There was no rush. Chad was not going to call, tonight or any other night. It wasn't true. She had made it all up. What kind of a dope was she, acting as if she herself believed her fabrications? They were for her friends' consumption, not for hers.

Yet the urgency of the past three quarters of an hour had not been feigned. Not at all. The itch of impatience had been as genuine as if it were based on absolute reality. Was it a tribute to her powers of persuasion that she had been taken in by her own lies—she who was supposed to be so strong-minded? Or was it a sign, a proof of weakness that she had turned out to be so suggestible? One theory was as unnerving as the other.

A nice situation Chad had gotten her into. Too bad he couldn't have seen her scurrying home, all a-twitch for fear of missing his mythical phone call. It wouldn't have surprised him in the least. "The things you can make yourself believe," he had said to her, and here she was, confirming his disgraceful theory for him, behaving as if it were true. It wasn't, of course. Nervous strain, that was all that was wrong with her, the nervous strain of having to invent explanations for Peggy Bascomb and the others.

But she felt so shaken that she lit a little fire in the fireplace and even poured herself a glass of sherry to sip while her casserole dinner heated in the oven. She hardly ever drank alone, disapproved of it on principle—look at Erna—but tonight seemed to call for emergency measures. While she sipped, and later, while she ate, she eyed the telephone, which squatted there on the end table, sneering at her. Sooner or later she would have to pick it up and dial Peggy's number. Otherwise Peggy would call her, wanting to hear the latest on Chad. If not Peggy, then someone else. There was no escaping the tyranny of her friends—and her relatives; Oliver and Erna couldn't leave it alone, either. Couldn't forget Chad themselves, or let her forget him.

But she had to! It was fatal to remember him and their last quarrel; her only chance of surviving the blow he had dealt her lay in total, permanent obliteration. Blot it out. Blot it out. And after a while she did manage to get her treacherous mind under control; she leaned back and finished her coffee, once more capable of calm, coherent, constructive thought.

It was not perfect, the explanation that rolled out when she called Peggy an hour or so later. But it would serve. It would give her the respite she had to have. And Peggy swallowed it whole. "California!" she shrieked. "They're sending him out to California! Oh Dee, I had no idea there was any chance of anything like that! I mean, of course it's wonderful he's got the job, but California's so far away … It's permanent? It's not just for a while? But Dee darling, if you go all the way out there, when will we ever see you, either of you?"

This was the part that wasn't perfect. But she was prepared for it; she had decided on a note of tremulous levity. "You mean when will I ever see Chad. That's what worries me. I don't see how I can get away till the end of the summer, and by then he may be all tied up with some other babe ..."

"That'll be the day. Anyway, what do you mean you can't get away till the end of the summer? You could fly out for a few days. At least for a weekend."

"I know. He's hoping to get some time off, and of course if he does he can fly back here. What makes me sick is that I could have gone to New York this past weekend just as easily as not. If only we'd known they were going to spring this on him—Well, it's too late now. He's leaving on an eleven o'clock flight tonight, they want him out there bright and early in the morning."

"Cheer up, dear. It'll all work out, wait and see if it doesn't. How about dropping in for a drink tomorrow? No point in holing up and brooding."

"I'm not, really I'm not. It's a marvelous opportunity for Chad. I just haven't had time to get used to the idea, that's all. I haven't even told Oliver yet. You're the first person I've called."

And the only one she would need to call, she thought as she hung up. Leave it to Peggy to spread the word. Except for Oliver, of course, and Erna. But now that the trial run with Peggy had succeeded, she had no qualms about the others. It was like anything else, she thought as she headed for the third floor: practice made perfect. And though Chad-in-California might not be the final solution, it certainly eased the pressure of Chad-in-New York.

Next morning friends kept calling her or dropping in at the shop to verify the news—Peggy had done her work well—and to commiserate and congratulate. It was like the end of that first dinner party; again she found herself rather enjoying the general fuss and her own skill at embellishment.

By ten thirty things had begun to quiet down. She ordered coffee from the drugstore, as she often did, and settled down at her desk, behind the screen near the back, to go through the mail while she drank it. The bell jangled again just as she was opening the coffee carton; she peered around the screen, and there was Oliver, of all people, he hardly ever showed up at the shop.

"Hi," she called. "What's on your mind?" He made a throat-clearing sound, not really an answer, and took a couple of steps toward her, laboriously, as if he were slogging through mud. Her voice sharpened. "Is something wrong? What's the matter?"

"Nothing. That is, I—" She could see his face more clearly now; it had such a strange, frozen look that her heart gave a lurch of alarm. Erna, she thought, she's done something crazy like burn down the house.

Again Oliver made the throat-clearing sound. He was holding something in his hand, a thick, rolled-up newspaper, thrusting it at her like a club. "I just wondered if you—Have you seen—?"

"What's the matter with you? I don't know what you're talking about." She jumped up and went to meet him. It was the New York newspaper; copies reached Rushford about this time. The headline read: 66 Killed in Jet Crash. The story was familiar: Two hours after taking off from La Guardia for Los Angeles ... Crash occurred in a rural section of Ohio ... Farmers reported hearing an explosion ... Fog blamed ... No survivors ... List of victims ...

The name leaped out at her. Johnson. No initials or first name, no indication even of sex. Passenger lists were so often sketchy. Johnson. Johnson.

"It wasn't Chad's flight?" Oliver was saying pleadingly. "You didn't mention the flight number or even what line. It wasn't Chad's? Dorothea?" She lifted her head, and he stopped talking. For a dazed moment they stared at each other. The last thing she remembered was Oliver's stricken El Greco face against a background of dazzling, spinning blackness.

His face was also the first thing she saw when she came to. She seemed to be more or less stretched out on the Victorian love seat she had never been able to sell, and he was bending over her fanning her with the newspaper. She could see the shine of sweat on his forehead, and below his jawbone a little dark patch of stubble that he had missed when he shaved this morning.

"I'm all right," she whispered. She felt queerly peaceful.

The phone rang and he picked it up. She stayed where she was, listening to his subdued voice: "Yes, Peggy, yes, I'm here with her. I came over as soon as I saw the paper ... I'm afraid so ... No, apparently nobody heard the news report, or if they did they didn't make the connection ... All right, maybe a little later ..."

Then he came back. "I'll take you home," he said. "As soon as you feel like it. You're better off at home." After a little while, when she sat up groggily, he put his arm around her. It was this gesture of warmth and tenderness that shattered her. Bent forward, hands locked between her knees as if the pain that overwhelmed her were physical, she gave way to violent, convulsive weeping. "No, oh no—Chad, oh Chad—"

She had lost him. In that first outburst of grief—and it was genuine, she was strangling with it—she let go of the fact that she had invented Chad's flight to California. Nothing mattered but the loss itself. For the moment it stood alone, divorced from how or when or why; the only reality. Then, as the sharp edge of sorrow gradually dulled and her sobs slacked off, she felt again the queer peace, the release. She was done with inventing, finally freed from the kindly tyranny of her friends' curiosity.

She was through with Chad.

FIVE

"Well!" Erna said in that hearty voice of hers, when she opened the door to his tap. "I was wondering if you were going to go off without even telling me goodbye."

Mr. Fly beamed back shyly and lifted his hand in quite a dashing flourish. "Not goodbye. Au revoir. After all, it's only for two weeks. Then I'll be back for summer school." And after that it really would be goodbye; Rushford would merge with all the other towns where he had taught for a year and not been re-elected. Erna, the members of the Self-Culture Club, the waitress at Ye Olde Corner Tea Shoppe who sometimes chatted with him when she wasn't too busy—they would all shake his hand and urge him to keep in touch, but a year from now he would be little more than a comic name to them. There was no use pretending otherwise. Yet Mr. Fly did pretend; as he accepted Erna's invitation to come in for a cup of coffee he felt the familiar flutter of optimism once more lifting its bedraggled wings. He had made friends, real friends like Erna, here in Rushford. In plenty of other places too; it was just that, moving around as he had done—a rolling stone, a regular gypsy—he hadn't had time to make them as permanent as he would have liked. Next year might well be a different story entirely. Why not, if he found the right spot? And he might: a nice little niche where he would settle down in quiet security, after all his roaming; a snug harbor for the declining years ...

"I might even decide to get out of the teaching profession," he heard himself saying expansively, as he stirred cream into his coffee and watched Erna cutting a generous wedge of cake for him. Chocolate. His favorite. "Try my hand at something else for a change. That's why I'm so delighted at the prospect of spending this couple of weeks in New York. The city of opportunity. I've always found it a stimulating place to visit. Who knows, maybe I'll wind up living there permanently."

"Not me," said Erna. "I wouldn't take it as a gift. Dee said you're going to stay with friends there?"

"A second cousin of mine. That is, I'll be staying in her apartment. She's going into the hospital for an operation, and I'm to look after her pets. She's a great animal lover. Three cats, I believe, and two dogs. I'm delighted at the prospect," he repeated firmly. "It will give me an opportunity to explore the possibilities. And I'll still have my room here. It's very kind of Dee to hold it for me and not charge me for the two weeks I'll be away. She suggested it herself. Very kind of her, I must say, especially now, in her time of trouble."

Erna nodded dolefully. "Yes. It was terrible about Chad. Terrible. I can't get over it. You've got to hand it to Dee, she's bearing up pretty well, considering."

"She's never had any—well, any official notice?" He risked a glance at Erna's face; as far as he could tell she saw nothing out of the way about the question. He answered it himself. "No, of course not. It's not as though she were the next of kin. I don't know that you could even call her his fiancée."

"Well, I don't know what else you'd call it. They were planning on getting married. She was planning on going out there, as soon as he got settled in California." Tears welled up in Erna's eyes, which—now that Mr. Fly thought about it—looked puffy, as if she might have been crying quite a bit lately. "Now she'll never go—out there or anywhere else."

Mr. Fly knew from past experience that it didn't do to show too much sympathy at moments like this one. A comforting pat, even a kind word, might send her off into a real spell of the weeps. He took a bite of cake (delicious) and waited for the tears to dry up from lack of encouragement, as they usually did in a matter of seconds. Easy come, easy go. His own feelings about Dee's "time of trouble" were ambiguous. How did he know what had happened after Chad packed up and drove off in such a hurry? He might very well have called Dee and patched up the quarrel. Which only Mr. Fly knew about; he had not breathed a word to a living soul. If so, then all the rest was true—the job negotiations, the shift to California—and Chad had indeed crashed to his death in the fog along with all those other people. There had been a Johnson among them. But it was not an uncommon name, and the first incomplete list was the only one the paper had published ...

And Dee had lied about the job at the beginning. There was no getting around that; no dodging the possibility that, having invented her first pride-saving story, she had added one installment after another. By popular demand, so to speak; pressured into it by the interested friends who were rallying around her now, commiserating with her over the final, tragic chapter. It wasn't that simple for Mr. Fly, who was also a friend of hers, but who knew about the quarrel and who therefore could not help wondering how much was fact and how much fabrication.

A muted sob from Erna jolted him out of his preoccupation with his secret problem. The tears, far from drying up, were brimming over; she bent her head and covered her face with her broad, stubby hands.

"Now, now," he said nervously. "Mustn't give way. We're all going to miss Chad—"

"It's not just that. Everything else, Marilyn and everything, the whole summer without her—"

"Without her!" echoed Mr. Fly. "But she'll be home next week." It dawned on him that this time Erna was not just crying into her beer. No beer to cry into, for one thing; he could always smell it. His conscience smote him. She had been unfailingly kind to him, never too busy for a sociable chat or a little favor. The closest friend he had in Rushford, maybe in the world. How could he have been so obtuse? He pushed back his chair, sloshing coffee and scattering crumbs, and scuttled around the table to stand beside her. Distress made him more uncoordinated than usual: he reached out to pat her shoulder, discovered he was still clutching his fork, and wound up dropping it on the floor under the table instead of on it. "Oops," he said, and then, deciding against any attempt to retrieve it: "What is it, Erna? You told me yourself Marilyn was coming home. What's happened?"

She gave a great sniff and lifted her head. "She's going to Europe." He realized she was trying to smile. "Isn't that—Isn't that wonderful?"

"Europe! Of course it is. Wonderful." He crouched over her anxiously while the rest of the story came quavering out. This college teacher of Marilyn's was all set for a summer abroad with his wife and three children, except that at the last minute the girl they had lined up to take along as a baby-sitter had backed out—she was a friend of Marilyn's, they lived in the same dorm—so they had offered Marilyn the job, a small salary in addition to all expenses including transportation. No, they weren't flying, they were sailing next week from New York, with Marilyn occupying the space originally reserved for the other girl; she already had her passport and would be home for the weekend, just long enough to pack ...

"The chance of a lifetime. We couldn't ever afford anything like that for her. These people she's going with, she's baby-sat for them before, and she's crazy about them." Erna swallowed hard. "Oh, and her boy friend's going to be over there too, for part of the summer. She'll have a ball. You can imagine how thrilled she is. Way up there on cloud nine." She managed a real smile this time; for a moment she looked like a smudged version of Marilyn, of the very pretty girl she must once have been herself. Not that she was unattractive now. But the first bloom was gone. Time had darkened her hair and thickened her figure and coarsened her skin. And then the lonesome, homesick look in her eyes—it was what Mr. Fly had noticed first about her, what he had instantly recognized.

"You'll miss her," he said huskily. "I know how you've been counting on this summer."

"She's eighteen. The same age I was when I met Ollie and we got married and had Marilyn. I remember how Mom bawled when we left to come to Rushford." She looked past Mr. Fly, off into space. "Like she knew we'd never be back. We didn't know it ourselves, we weren't planning on staying ... But Mom had the others. The boys were still home. Marilyn's the only one I've got."

"Now, now. It's not forever. Just this summer."

But she shook her head. "Next summer it'll be something else. Another job, or she'll decide to marry Don. They might not wait that long. He's transferring to another college, in Chicago, next fall and she's pulling all the strings she can think of to get into some school out there too, so as to be near him. If that doesn't work she might just quit school and marry him. It wouldn't surprise me. He's a real nice boy. No, Mr. Fly, I'm not kidding myself about how much time Marilyn's going to spend at home from now on. I knew good and well this summer would be the last. That's why I—" She sat slumped and hopeless, not crying any more, just staring into the emptiness ahead. "I'll have to get used to it, I guess. Somehow or other I'll have to get used to it."

Mr. Fly stood silent, mentally riffling through his well-worn stock of platitudes. Time heals all wounds? What can't be cured must be endured? The sun will shine again? Always darkest before the dawn? None of them seemed to hit quite the right note.

The best he could offer was a switch in the subject. "Before I forget, Erna, I wondered if I could ask a favor of you."

"Sure. Of course." She actually brightened up a bit. "Something needs mending?"

"No, no, I'm all packed, ready to go. I just thought if there should be any mail for me, anything that looks like it might be important, maybe you'd forward it to me in New York. There probably won't be, but I'd like to leave you my address, just in case. Don't bother with magazines or anything like that. Maybe you'd hold them for me."

"Sure. Be glad to. Just write it down so I'll have the address."

He had already done so; after a moment's fumbling he found the card in his pocket, and she planted it under the recipe box on her kitchen cabinet. "Many thanks," he said. "The telephone number's there too. If by any chance you should get to New York while I'm there—"

"Who, me? What would I be doing in New York?"

"You never know. Anything can happen." It was Mr. Fly's basic tenet; at times it was all that sustained him. "If by any chance it should, be sure to call me. I'd be delighted to hear from you. I must be getting along now, or I'll miss the bus," he added with a look at his watch. "Tempus fidgets ..."

A hurried handshake, a regretful glance at his unfinished piece of cake, and he was scurrying down the stairs to his room to pick up his zip bag and brief case. At the last minute he remembered Chad's book, the collection of true-crime classics Chad had lent him a couple of months ago. A great reader, Chad; this was a book he had brought with him when he came to Rushford for the famous weekend that had stretched to six months. On its flyleaf was scribbled the name Quentin, and below it a New York telephone number.

Provocative, thought Mr. Fly. Lately he had found himself speculating more and more about Quentin. A friend of Chad's? Somebody he had run into unexpectedly and whose name and number he had jotted down in the first place that came to hand? Quentin could be either Christian or surname. Or, for that matter, the name of a store. It might not even be Chad's writing, might have nothing whatever to do with him.

But Mr. Fly saw no harm in doing a little research, as long as he was going to be in New York anyway. He tucked the book into his brief case and zipped it shut.

After all, you never knew. Anything could happen.

SIX

The following Friday evening, when Dee got home from the shop, she found Erna waiting for her on the porch. Now what, she thought, and resigned herself to another session of fantods: Erna, poor thing, had been in a twitch all week, ever since the business about Marilyn came up. If it wasn't "What will I do without her?" it was "Should she take a warmer coat?" or "Supposing she gets sick way off there in Paris or somewhere?"

There she stood, stocky and un-chic in her loving-hands housedress, red-faced, flustered, and—why should Dee so often have this effect on her?—momentarily tongue-tied, unable to come out with whatever it was she had on her mind. Eventually she made it: "Could you come up and have supper with Ollie and I? There's something I—That is, if you're not busy—"

Dee was busy. As usual these days; her friends were solidly united in their drive to keep her from brooding, with the result that she would almost have welcomed an evening to herself. There was no letup in the invitations—many of them purportedly impromptu—to dinner, cocktails, bridge parties. Tonight it was a cook-out at the Bascombs'; Howard's birthday. "I'm awfully sorry," she told Erna. "Otherwise I'd love to. Is it something important? I don't have to leave for half an hour."

"I was afraid you'd be busy. No, it'll keep, I guess." An awkward pause. "Maybe you could run up for a little while after you get home from the Bascombs'. Ollie'll be here then."

Dee gave her a sharp look at that. A family conference? Was Oliver in one of his financial fixes? But Erna had never been included in such discussions before; they had all been strictly between Oliver and Dee. "Look, Erna, if there's something wrong—"

"No. Honest. Nothing to worry about. We'll tell you all about it later."

Dee had no choice but to leave it at that. But all evening she was a little abstracted. She kept remembering Erna's face, with its high cheekbones and deep-set eyes; the expression on Erna's face. She hadn't seemed upset exactly, at least not in the usual way. More excited than upset, and not altogether unhappily so. As if she were bubbling inside. That letter from Gus; could Oliver have weakened and told her about it, after all? Dee's heart sank at the thought.

She left the cook-out as early as she decently could, pleading a headache which would no doubt spur everybody on to more strenuous efforts to cheer her up. They were so kind. They meant so well. But in a way the sociability underlined the fact of Chad's absence: he haunted every party because he had been as much a part of the crowd as Dee herself, they had become an entity, Dee-and-Chad, as much as the Bascombs or any of the other married couples. She kept thinking of that poem: "If to be left alone were to be left alone ..."

No. Her friends were right. It must never be permitted to happen. To be left alone meant to be left at the mercy of what she could not afford to remember about Chad. Blot it out. Blot it out. Remember only how she had loved him, not how she had lost him.

She turned into the driveway. There was her house, tranquil, drenched in moonlight. The third-floor windows were lit from within: Erna and Oliver waiting up for her.

Oliver opened the door to her and switched off the television. Erna offered refreshments. Coffee? Beer? A drink? Finally she gave up on that angle and sat down on the sofa beside Oliver. She still had her bubbling expression. Oliver looked a bit effervescent himself, in a tentative way. It couldn't be financial difficulties, then. He was always shamefaced about them.

"All right, what's up?" asked Dee, since neither of them seemed capable of calling the meeting to order.

They both started to answer at once. Then they both shut up. Finally Erna blurted out something about having had a letter from her brother. Dee's eyes flew to Oliver at that; he was staring fixedly at his feet. "It's about Pop," Erna floundered on. "My father. His heart. According to what Gus says, he's in pretty bad shape."

"I'm sorry to hear that," said Dee carefully. Her only acquaintance with Erna's father was through the snapshots Erna showed her now and then: Pop posed, a chunky old boy in overalls, against a stand of corn as tall as he was; or, stiff in his Sunday suit, he stood planted in front of the silo, his hands clamped on the shoulders of a couple of towheaded kids. Gus and his family had moved in with him after his wife's death; his other sons were scattered around the county on farms of their own.

"The doctor says any time, it could happen any time. They're not letting on to Pop, of course, and he's not letting on, either. All the same, Gus can tell he knows. The way he's acting lately. The things he says. As if he's—" The tears that were always on tap with Erna welled up; her voice quavered. "As if he's getting ready, sort of settling everything in advance."

"I see," said Dee. On the one hand, tears. On the other, the bubbly effect. Oh yes, she saw, all right. Again her eyes shifted to Oliver, who sat hunched forward, still engrossed in his own feet. In the end, though, he found the courage to speak up.

"He wants us to come out there," he said bluntly. "He's never sold the bungalow, the house he fixed up for us when we first got married. He's made up his mind to sign it over to us now."

"You mean provided you move out there and live in it?"

"No, though of course he'd like to have Erna closer home, where he could see her more often. And of course it would suit her right down to the ground." He gave Erna a husbandly smile and reached for her hand.

Off she went, into a long, breathless, jumbled spiel about a half-section of land, chickens, dairy cattle, truck gardening ...

"How about you, Oliver?" Dee broke in at last. "Your business isn't farming. It's repairing radios."

"But that's the other thing!" cried Erna, and here it all came, in an exuberant rush, the big news about the repair shop. Dee did not stop her. At least it was not Oliver who had told her; he was looking at Dee now, and in earnest, sending her urgent, pleading little messages.

Silence at last. Dee said dispassionately, "Well, of course it's an idea. But you're not doing too badly here in Rushford, are you, Oliver?"

"I'm not doing all that well. The competition's going to get worse when the new appliance store opens in the fall. They're going to have a repair service. No kidding, Dorothea, this past couple of years I've scraped along, and that's just about all." He and Erna exchanged another dreamy smile. "And I wouldn't be going to a place where nobody knows me. I made out okay when we were out there before. We've always talked about going back some day. Well, maybe this is the time to do it."

"Oh, I'm not saying it isn't. Not at all. I've never interfered in your business, you both know that, and I don't intend to start now. I just think you ought to take a long hard look before you leap. A long hard look from every angle. This isn't something to decide off the top of your head. There's too much at stake. You'll be pulling up all your roots, starting out fresh—and you're not kids anymore, let's face it, we're none of us getting any younger." She flashed them a smile of her own, and drew one in return from each of them. Erna's was none too hearty. "Think about it, that's all I ask. Think about what you'll be cutting loose from and what you'll be getting into."

"Well, sure." Oliver's eyes slid away from hers; he rubbed his jaw nervously. "Naturally we're not going to make a snap decision. But I can't see that we've got much to lose ..."

"Maybe not. I know you've had some setbacks with the shop, Oliver. Everybody gets a tough break now and then. Or makes an error in judgment." She paused, almost imperceptibly; but Oliver got the point. "All the more reason why you should think twice before you jump feet first into something new. In spite of the setbacks, you've got a going business, one that's made a living for you for eighteen years. That's a pretty good record, isn't it? And you've got a reasonably comfortable apartment for very little money—"

"If we leave," Erna put in, flushing at her own boldness, "you could rent it to somebody else for at least twice what we pay."

"Possibly. And I realize that out there you won't be paying any rent at all. Taxes, of course, and maintenance ... By the way, do you know what sort of condition the bungalow's in? Has it been sitting there empty all these years?"

"Oh no, Pop's been renting it right along. He hasn't let it run down."

"Good. No problem there, then. As a matter of fact, it's something you might consider yourselves, once it becomes your property. Renting it out, I mean. You might find it's more profitable to do that than live in it yourselves. The extra money could make all the difference as far as Oliver's shop is concerned."

"But we'd have our own place!" cried Erna. "We'd have the extra money I could make raising chickens, and the garden, and—It would be our own place!"

"Yes." After a brief silence Dee stood up. "I've always thought of this as your own place. The whole third floor was done over with you in mind. I know that technically the house belongs to me, but believe me, I've never thought of it as anything but Oliver's home. If I had realized you felt like this about it—"

"Erna didn't mean it that way." Oliver was on his feet, his forehead creased with the familiar anxious frown. "Dorothea, please, you know we both appreciate all you've done for us. Erna, you didn't mean it that way, did you, honey?"

"I'm sorry. I just meant—I just—" Here came the tears again. Erna kept her head down, fumbling in her pocket for her balled-up handkerchief.

"Never mind. It's all right, dear," said Dee. "I guess I'm a little on edge nowadays. Let's not talk about it anymore tonight. I've already said more than I had any right to. After all, it's your business, not mine, whatever you decide. I'm not trying to influence you one way or the other, truly I'm not, though there's no denying I'll miss you more than I can say, especially just at this time ..." She blinked bravely and headed for the door.

All right, she thought when she was downstairs, getting ready for bed, she had put on an act. Hammed it up. Pulled out all the stops. But it was for their own good. Somebody had to point out a few home truths to Oliver, or he'd wind up without a penny to his name. Left to himself, he would have gone broke long ago—not because he was lazy or stupid, far from it, but simply because he was impractical about business matters. When she thought of the harebrained schemes he had gotten sucked into, the good hard-earned cash he had thrown away ...

But this beat everything that had gone before. Why, he must be out of his mind to imagine he could make a go of it out there at the end of nowhere! And Erna, poor creature, with her chicken-raising dreams of glory. "Our own place," if you please. Couldn't they see that the old man was bribing them—none too subtly, either—dangling that famous honeymoon bungalow in front of them in one last attempt to get the whole tribe gathered around him before he died? And there was only Gus's word for the repair shop that was on the market and that was supposed to be such a red-hot bargain. It would take more than one man's say-so to convince Dee. But not Oliver. Always ready to buy a pig in a poke.

Even if it did turn out to be the sound business proposition Gus said it was, Oliver would be taking more of a chance than he seemed to realize. He might think he had a second home town out there, might have fond recollections of living there for almost a year and "making out okay." But he hadn't been running his own business then. He had been a lovesick kid from New England, as much of a novelty to the Midwesterners as they were to him. Now, approaching forty, he would be a not-very-successful outsider moving back—thanks to the helping hands of his in-laws—and expecting to pick up where he had left off.

Oh, it was natural enough that he should see it like this, through a haze of nostalgia. What else could you expect, with Erna incessantly harping about "back home," never making the slightest effort to adjust to Rushford? A misfit from the start; and now she wanted to drag Oliver to a spot where he would be as much of a misfit as she was here. As a matter of fact, Erna herself might find the reality something less than the paradise she remembered. Eighteen years was eighteen years for everybody.

A good point, thought Dee, unpinning her hair and picking up her brush. A point she must remember to make when Oliver discussed the matter with her in private, as he undoubtedly would; experience had taught him the value of her advice and the dangers of making decisions on his own. Her reference tonight to errors in judgment—that had hit home, it had made him wince. As well it might. Poor Oliver, she wouldn't mention it again unless she had to.

For his own good, she repeated to herself as she snapped off the light. Oliver was her brother, her only close relative; she couldn't stand by without lifting a hand to stop him from making the worst mistake of his life.

In the middle of the night she woke, sobbing, sweating, trembling. The recurrent nightmare of years ago, back again, as terrifying as ever, at once vivid and obscure. Yet how could it be the same? For Chad had been in this one, Chad and Oliver and Erna ... As always, the pattern eluded her. Somehow that made the terror more real. It was several minutes before she could summon enough courage to turn on the light. There was the comforting familiarity of her room: the soft green rug, the white ruffled curtains, the gooseberry wallpaper and gleam of polished wood. And there was her bottle of sleeping capsules in the bathroom medicine cabinet. The doctor had prescribed them to help her through the shock of Chad's death. Such nice dependable little capsules. A couple of them would put her back to sleep in a jiffy. As soon as the trembling eased off—and it would, in a minute—she would go into the bathroom and take them. It was all right, it was all right, nothing to be afraid of.

She left the light on and waited—motionless, sleepless, wary—for the terror to recede.

SEVEN

Slowly, regally, the ship began to slide away from the pier, where Erna stood waving her blue scarf, her eyes glued to Marilyn. She too was waving—wildly, both hands—leaning over the rail, laughing and waving. In the sparkling noon sunshine paper streamers floated out in lazy twirls; voices called back and forth; there was a burst of brave music from the ship's band; a deep-throated, thrilling hoot. It was a perfect sailing day: balmy and breezy, with tufts of festive white clouds dotting the brilliant blue sky. It had been very festive in the Wests' stateroom too. Champagne and flowers and last-minute bon voyage telegrams; the West children hopping with excitement; a welter of relatives and friends milling and chattering.

Erna hadn't had such a good time in years. And to think that she had been of two minds about coming! Yes, she had kept on with her objections and excuses from the time the subject first came up till the bus pulled out for New York with her on it. She didn't like New York. She had never been there by herself. (And it had to be by herself; Ollie was tied up, handling the tape recording and amplifying system for the Masonic banquet.) She didn't have anything to wear. She would only be in the way. Between them Ollie and Dee had talked her into it, and thank the Lord they had.

By now the crowd on the pier was beginning to thin out and Marilyn was recognizable only by her pink dress. She probably couldn't see Erna's scarf anymore; all the same, Erna kept on waving it, while the pink dress dwindled to a brush stroke, to a dot, to nothing.

"Mom! I was afraid you wouldn't come!" she had cried when Erna walked into the stateroom. Her face lit up like a Christmas tree. "I want you to meet my mother." So proudly, as if Erna were a queen. And at the end, when the all-ashore call came: "Mom, oh Mom!" and the last half-tearful hug, the childhood trick of nibbling Erna's ear ...

Remembering it, Erna felt her heart melt all over again. The ship was moving faster; soon even it would be out of sight. She edged away toward the taxi place, aware of an ache in her arm, a buzz in her head from the champagne, and an empty letdown feeling.

This was what she had been afraid of. This was why she had come prepared: the slip of paper with Mr. Fly's telephone number and address on it was tucked in her purse, his mail—so far there had been nothing worth forwarding, only ads and a couple of magazines—in her tote bag. Her bus back to Rushford was not due to leave until midafternoon; there was plenty of time for a little visit, in case Mr. Fly was in. She headed for the nearest phone booth.

Mr. Fly was there on the front stoop, waiting to welcome her when she got out of the cab. He had one of the second cousin's dogs in tow, a stout, elderly creature with moth-eaten spots in its long black coat. Mr. Fly himself was exuberant. His bushy gray hair stood even more on end than usual; his clothes looked as if he had been sleeping in them; his tie was wildly askew.

"Didn't I say anything could happen?" he cried triumphantly, as he ushered her inside. "You were so sure you'd never turn up in New York, and yet less than a week later here you are! Come in, come in, sit down and tell me all about it." He cleared a chair for her and added anxiously, "I'm afraid it isn't as tidy as it might be."

Erna didn't argue the point: a whacking understatement. In the first place, Mr. Fly's second cousin owned far more furniture than she had space for. The dark little living room was as crammed as a secondhand store. And as dusty. Second Cousin had obviously and understandably given up long ago. It wasn't just the furniture, it was the knickknacks on top of the furniture. There was an ancient smell of cats, and all the upholstered surfaces had a layer of dog and cat hairs.

"Very cozy," said Erna valiantly, and at once Mr. Fly brightened again. Yes, cozy; he couldn't ask for a more comfortable spot, and the pets were wonderful company—each one a distinct personality—and New York was as stimulating as ever, no telling what might materialize in the way of a job. But enough of his affairs; what about Erna?

She had always found him a sympathetic listener. Now, as she sipped the rather muddy coffee he pressed upon her, and munched the crackers and cheese, she poured out the details of her morning's adventure, happily reliving it in the telling. Mr. Fly seemed to enjoy it as much as she. He sat on the edge of his chair, too absorbed to notice that one of the cats was gnawing his shoestrings or that the other dog—a soiled-white poodle type—was begging for bites.

"I wouldn't have missed it for the world," she finished. "Of course it's not the same as having Marilyn home for the summer, but it helps. And anyway, I won't mind the summer so much if—" She hesitated. Nothing was really settled yet, about moving "back home," and wouldn't be settled until they found out more about the shop that was up for sale. Though as far as Erna was concerned, she was ready to pick up and move tomorrow, shop or no shop. Ollie would be too, if it weren't for Dee. She kept saying it was their business, not hers, but she knew good and well how much Ollie depended on her judgment when it came to money matters. Oh, he might still be talked around into going—at least Erna hoped so—but it would take longer, without Dee's approval.

"You were saying?" prodded Mr. Fly. "Down, Snowdrop, you know it's not polite to beg."

"This is just between you and me and the lamp post," Erna said, and went on from there. It was a great relief to get it all off her chest; there hadn't been time for more than a few hurried words to Marilyn, and no one in Rushford would understand how she felt. Not even Ollie. In a way, Ollie least of all. Dee was his sister, the only family he had, she had been more than kind to both of them. Sometimes Erna felt smothered by her kindness. But how could she say such a thing as that, especially right now when Dee was reeling from the blow of Chad's death? How could she explain her own deep, irrational conviction that if they did not get away they were doomed? It sounded crazy to Erna herself. "I'm just dying to go," was the way she put it to Mr. Fly. "If it doesn't work out I just don't know what I'll do. I don't see how I can stand it."

"No reason why it shouldn't work out," said Mr. Fly thoughtfully. "If worst comes to worst, you can threaten to go by yourself."

Her jaw dropped. "You mean—You mean leave Ollie? Oh, but I couldn't!"

"No, but you could threaten to," said Mr. Fly. There was something about his expression that made Erna think of an elf. "That would bring him around. I'd be willing to bet on it."

"Well, but supposing—" She gave a sudden, nervous giggle. "I'd never have the nerve." Her eyes darted away from his in confusion, and lit on her tote bag. "Oh, while I think of it, here's your mail. There wasn't anything that looked important, but I thought as long as I was coming I'd bring it along."

"Thanks for taking the trouble." Mr. Fly took the little bundle and began flipping through it. "I appreciate—Hello! Here's one that isn't for me." He fumbled a letter out of the packet. There was a moment's silence while he stared at it. Finally he cleared his throat and said, "It's a letter for Chad."

"Chad? But how could I have—It must have gotten mixed in by mistake, slipped in between a couple of yours. I didn't pay much attention, I just—That's what must have happened." He handed her the letter; it was a little spooky, somehow, to see Chad's name and below it the familiar Rushford address. The postmark date was too blurred to make out, but the return address was fairly clear. "Looks like H. A. Quentin," she said. "Somebody here in New York. Some friend of Chad's that doesn't know he's dead. It's handwritten. A personal letter. I wonder—I guess the best thing is to send it back with a note?"

Mr. Fly was too busy rummaging through a stack of books on one of the overloaded little tables to answer. When he found the one he was looking for he brought it over to her, open to show her what was written on the flyleaf. Quentin. And a telephone number. She blinked at it, uncomprehending.

"It's a book I borrowed from Chad," he explained. "The same name. Quentin. They must have run into each other before Chad went up to Rushford, and he jotted down the number ..."

"We could call him up, then," said Erna. "That might be better than—" She stopped, at an involuntary sound of protest from Mr. Fly, and was astonished to see the slow, thorough flush that was rising to the roots of his hair. "What's the matter? Why not?"

"Because." He turned even redder. "Because I already tried it. Mr. Quentin is no longer with them. It's an office number. I already called it."

"You did? Why in the world? Oh. Well, naturally. You figured it must be a friend, and he might not have heard about Chad." Yes, it was typical of Mr. Fly—lonesome as he was—to snatch at any opportunity for human contact, no matter how many times removed.

He was nodding gratefully. "Yes. Exactly. There aren't many Quentins in the phone book. Of course I didn't have the initials, and I only checked Manhattan. He could live in New Jersey, Long Island, any-where."

"It's a Manhattan address on the letter," said Erna. "And we've got the initials now. H. A. Maybe he's just moved and it's a new number. Could-n't we ask Information?"

"It's an idea. Of course if he has an unlisted number—"

"No harm in trying, is there?" She cast a glance around, and spotted the telephone on a sort of desk, embedded in a clutter of knitting and miniature pictures. "It seems more friendly, calling him instead of just returning his letter. Don't you think so?"

"Yes. Exactly," said Mr. Fly rather absently. "Unless it's something Dee would rather handle herself. She might, if she knows Quentin, or even if she's only heard about him through Chad."

Erna thought it over. Then she shook her head. "No. I think it would just upset her. It gave me kind of a turn, seeing this letter. Brought it all back. And she's told me more than once, she didn't know any of Chad's friends or his folks, or anything about them. Of course he had-n't been in New York very long, chances are he didn't know many peo-ple here. But he never mentioned anybody out in California either. That's where he came from. Chad was a funny guy in some ways, you know. Kind of closemouthed."

"Yes," said Mr. Fly, in the same absent tone. "Let's see, what's that ad-dress again? I'll try Information."

Erna's guess turned out to be right: the Quentin number was a new one, too recent to be listed in the directory. Mr. Fly noted it down on the envelope, said, "Thank you very much," and stayed where he was, his hand still resting on the telephone. After a moment he picked it up again and dialed.

It wouldn't have surprised Erna if there had been no answer. After all, on a weekday afternoon Quentin was more likely to be in an office than at home. But the phone couldn't have rung twice before Mr. Fly was say-ing, "Mr. Quentin?" and launching into his explanation. He didn't get far—just the part about the letter, the book, and how he was a friend of Chad's from Rushford—when the voice at the other end broke in. From where she sat Erna could catch only a mechanical, meaningless gabble; it was by the look on Mr. Fly's face that she knew something very strange must be going on. His face, and the sharp, squeaky way he spoke. "What? What's that? You did?"

More of the gabble—Quentin seemed to be quite a talker—and then Mr. Fly was writing something else down on the envelope and speak-ing again, not so much of a squeak now; more like a croak. "I see ... Yes ... Thank you very much." He hung up and turned toward Erna; he looked numb, and though his chin kept waggling up and down, not a word came out. Not one solitary syllable.

Erna stood it as long as she could. "Well? What is it?" she burst out. "What's the matter with you? You didn't even tell him about Chad being dead!"

"He told me," Mr. Fly began. He waved his hand helplessly. "He said he saw Chad yesterday."

"He what? But that's—"

"That's what he said." Once started, Mr. Fly gained momentum; above the ringing in her ears—a regular clangor of shock and amazement—Erna heard him going on in pretty much his normal, schoolteacherish voice. "Chad called him and they had a drink together. He said Chad's fine, just fine, all set up over a new job he landed a couple of weeks ago and an apartment he's just moved into." Mr. Fly paused briefly. "Here in New York. He gave me the address. He said not to bother about the letter, no point in forwarding it now that he's back in touch with Chad. It was just a note asking what went on and when Chad was coming back to town. I gathered they're not very close friends. He said something about knowing Chad's wife better than he did Chad—"

"His wife!" gasped Erna.

"It sounded to me as if she might be dead, as if she died out there in California. I don't recall exactly how he put it. 'Now that she's gone,' I think he said, he and Chad had rather lost touch. But Chad did drop him a note from Rushford, telling him about the accident, only Quentin never got around to answering it till now. He's free-lancing these days. Writing magazine articles."

"But I don't understand ... Not dead at all. It wasn't him, then, on that plane that crashed. It was all a mistake. Oh, Mr. Fly, thank God, thank God!" She sprang up, in a surge of belated belief and joy. "I can't wait to tell Dee ..."

"No! Wait. I mean—" Mr. Fly was flushing again. In his agitation he took hold of her arm. "Listen to me, Erna. Before you tell Dee—before you tell anybody—we must consider the circumstances. Don't you see how peculiar they are? Doesn't it occur to you that somebody is—well, not telling the truth?"

His earnestness had a sobering effect on her fuddled wits; now that she stopped to think, she saw that he was right. "Lying," she specified. "Somebody's lying." Quentin? But why on earth should he say Chad was alive if he wasn't? Another moment of mental groping, and she said painfully, "It's not the first time Dee's picked a lemon. After all she did for Chad. And he acted like he was so crazy about her. To think of him stringing her along like this, making up all this tale about a job in California. Not a word of truth in it. A pack of lies."

Mr. Fly's eyes skipped away from hers. He shifted uneasily from one foot to the other. "You don't think it's possible that Dee made it up herself?"

"Dee? But why should she ..."

"Well. The fact of the matter is," said Mr. Fly. He took a deep breath and squared his shoulders. "The fact of the matter is, Erna, I have a confession to make. As fate would have it, I happened to overhear—No. I eavesdropped. I stood on the stairs and listened for all I was worth. It was the day Chad left, that afternoon, and when I came home I heard them in the living room. They were having a quarrel. Chad said he was through, it was never going to work out, and he was getting out of there, leaving and never coming back. That's what he did, too. Inside of half an hour he was packed up and gone."

"He walked out on her," whispered Erna.

"Yes. Exactly. She was having a dinner party that evening, if you remember, and naturally everybody wanted to know where Chad was. I heard part of that, too. The first guests were arriving just as I went out for supper. When they asked about Chad, Dee told them he'd been called to New York for a job interview."

Erna was silent for a moment, staring at him. "And after that everybody kept on asking, and she kept on—fibbing." How could she do anything else, once she had committed herself with the first little lie? The calls from Chad, the progress reports, the trip to California had all sprouted from the one stem; and chance had completed the cycle with the plane crash and the passenger named Johnson. "She may even believe it herself by this time, that it was Chad on that plane."

"It's quite possible," said Mr. Fly. "In any case, I think you would be extremely ill-advised to tell her Chad is alive. Or anybody else, for that matter. I repeat, anybody at all. For one thing, you would be exposing her as a liar and, even more humiliating, as a woman scorned. For another—"

"Oh, don't worry, I won't tell. Not even Ollie. Why, she'd kill me, and I can't say I'd blame her, if she ever found it out. Not to mention what she'd do to you if she knew you spied on her and Chad. Eavesdropped, I mean. Don't you worry, Mr. Fly, nobody's going to hear it from me."

"Thank you," said Mr. Fly. "I certainly had every intention of keeping it to myself. It was only through circumstances beyond my control that I was forced into telling you."

"I know." She added, with a little laugh, "I wonder what Chad would say if he knew he's supposed to be dead."

"So do I," said Mr. Fly. "Can I offer you another cup of coffee?"

But it was time for her to leave, she discovered when she looked at her watch. Mr. Fly bustled around helping her collect her belongings and hailing a cab for her. The last she saw of him he was standing on the stoop, disheveled and shabby, both arms flailing in a windmill wave.

It had been a day, all right. But throughout the long bus ride back to Rushford she didn't even doze, much less sleep as she had expected to do. There was too much to think about. Literally too much; her mind seemed to jump like a grasshopper from Marilyn to Chad to Dee to Mr. Fly. It was funny how some of the things he had said kept coming back to her. Consider the circumstances. And before that: No, but you could threaten to.

Poor Dee, she thought—and realized, to her shame, that there was something exciting, even a little pleasurable about feeling sorry for someone like Dee. The shoe had so often been on the other foot. Erna, poor thing. Even when Dee hadn't said it out loud, Erna had known she was thinking it. Poor, stupid, helpless Erna.

The difference between being pitied and pitying ... Erna had never seen it until today: how great the difference was, how much more blessed it was to give pity than to receive it.

EIGHT

It had been quite a day for Mr. Fly, too. An unexpected guest—or, for that matter, an expected one—would have been excitement enough. But Erna's call was only the prelude to the shock of what transpired during the course of her visit. He should have been prepared for it; after all, throughout the past month he had speculated frequently and lengthily on the possibility of Chad's being alive. But speculation was one thing; confirmation quite another. The thump of reality had hit him as hard as Erna.

He felt shaken and restless; it was an effort, after she left, to settle down to his routine chores. He got through them, conscientiously if automatically: the daily visit to his second cousin in the hospital, the feeding of his four-footed charges, the two separate walks with Snowdrop and Sooty, whose jealousy of each other made a combined outing not only nerve-wracking but futile. His one break with regulation was to eat dinner at a nearby cafeteria. He could not face his own cooking tonight.

Back from this unwonted fling, he sat on the stoop and searched his soul. Part of what he found there was guilt. First of all, on account of the eavesdropping. But at least until this afternoon Dee's secret had been safe with him. Now Erna knew it too. Could she be relied on to keep it to herself? She had promised. She meant to. But then so had Mr. Fly. That was how much good intentions were worth.

Now that it was too late, he saw how easily he could have parried the "circumstances beyond his control." He could have only pretended to dial

Information. Erna wouldn't have known the difference, she would have believed him if he had reported no telephone listing for Quentin. And that would have been the end of it as far as she was concerned. He could have volunteered to return Quentin's letter—a perfectly natural suggestion, sure to be accepted by Erna—and he would have been left to do what he chose about it, and furthermore with his conscience and Dee's secret intact.

He took the letter out of his pocket and peered at the address he had jotted down on it. Chad's address, gladly and freely offered by Quentin. "I don't think he has a phone yet, he's only just moved in, and I don't have his office number. But here's the address, if you want to get in touch with him ..."

And that was the other product of Mr. Fly's soul searching. The curiosity. If anything, it was stronger than the guilt. In one sense they overlapped, for it seemed to Mr. Fly that the most likely means of exorcising his guilt feeling was to satisfy his curiosity. Rationalization? Maybe. All the same, Chad's reaction—if he were informed of his own purported death and of Dee's grief, which gave every appearance of being genuine—Chad's reaction might well be to hasten back to Rushford to patch up the quarrel. The lovers would be reunited. The happy ending so dear to Mr. Fly's heart would be accomplished, thanks in large part to Mr. Fly himself.

What could be better, from everybody's point of view?

The possibility of a different reaction from Chad was hardly worth considering, in Mr. Fly's opinion. He had seen the way they used to look at each other, Chad and Dee. He knew love when he saw it. No, probably Chad had held out this long only because he wanted to be able to say, when he called Dee, that he was satisfactorily established. Now that he had found a job and an apartment it was just a question of time, anyway. A word to the wise, a little nudge from Mr. Fly, was all it would take to trigger him into action.

He had Chad's book as an excuse; never in his life had he failed to return a borrowed book. And the business about Erna's bringing him the letter from Quentin by mistake, the phone call to Quentin, would explain how he had come by Chad's address. All valid and straightforward. With any luck, he wouldn't have to mention the eavesdropping episode; and even if he did have to, what was a moment or two of embarrassment compared with the opportunity to do Chad and Dee a favor they would never forget? They were friends of his, both of them. Look at the way Dee was holding his room for him. Look at the other books Chad had lent him, and the little chats they used to have when they met in the hall or on the stairs.

Strange, this reluctance he felt about approaching Chad. Yet even while he was puzzling over the strangeness of it, another department of his mind was busily composing an appropriate note. It should be casual in tone; no particular urgency except that he would be returning to Rushford in ten days or so, if Chad cared to give him a ring at the following number, et cetera. The next move would be up to Chad. No response from him would end the matter; Mr. Fly had no intention of pushing in where he was not invited.

Darkness had fallen while he sat there on the stoop, too absorbed in thought for his usual exchange of pleasantries with the stoop-sitters at the rooming house next door. He rose stiffly—his back seemed to be kicking up quite often lately—went inside and wrote the note to Chad. He mailed it that night before he went to bed. Before he had a chance to change his mind.

The call from Chad came on the second morning, early, while he was still sipping coffee and working his way through the Help Wanted columns. (Nothing promising so far, but then things always slacked off a bit in the summer. You never knew. Anything could happen.)

"Hello there, Mr. Fly," Chad said cordially. "I just got your note. Never expected you to turn up in the big city! How are you?"

"Very well, thank you. I hope you didn't mind my taking the liberty of writing you—"

"Not at all, not at all. Glad to hear from you. How about coming around for a drink? I'll be home about six, if you could make it tonight."

It was that simple. Nothing to it. Mr. Fly couldn't imagine now why he had felt the slightest hesitation. Chad couldn't have sounded friendlier. Less on account of Mr. Fly, of course, than because he was hoping for news of Dee. But even so ...

The apartment house was over on the east side, one of the imposing, glassy buildings that were springing up like machine-age mushrooms all over town. Mr. Fly was there on the stroke of six. In honor of the occasion he had washed his nylon shirt and brushed the worst of the cat and dog hairs off his suit. His own hair continued to defy discipline, and the anonymous stain on his lapel had not responded to sponging as well as he might have wished. However.

He pressed the bell above the neat new Chadwell Johnson label, the door opened, and there stood Chad with his hand outstretched in welcome. Again Mr. Fly felt the thump of reality. More of a whack than a thump this time, and utterly illogical: how—having talked to Chad on the phone —could he possibly have entertained the slightest remnant of doubt that the man was alive? He hadn't, really. It was just that seeing was different from hearing. More conclusive, somehow.

"Come on in," Chad was saying. "It's still pretty messy, I'm afraid. I haven't had time to get settled yet."

"Very nice," said Mr. Fly hollowly. Afterwards, he found it impossible to remember anything about the room, except that it seemed large, perhaps only by comparison with his second cousin's quarters. It must have been at least partially furnished, because he found a chair and sank into it. When he recovered enough of his breath, he added, "You're looking very well, Chad. A little thinner, maybe. But very well."

Quite a little thinner, actually, he thought when Chad brought the Scotch-and-sodas and settled down opposite him. One might almost say a lean and hungry look. Probably it made him even more attractive to the fair sex. Not that he could be classified as the traditional tall, dark and handsome. Dark, yes; but he was of barely average height, and his features were far from perfect. Rather lopsided nose, sallow skin, a tight, guarded cast to his face. Mr. Fly sighed. No use trying to analyze that kind of charm. People either had it or they hadn't.

There was a good deal of preliminary small talk. Chad was sorry to hear that Mr. Fly would not be a member of the Rushford High School faculty next year; if he heard of any likely openings he would certainly get in touch. He himself had been lucky enough to land in a spot with what seemed to be excellent prospects. Yes, New York was quite a change after Rushford. It took a while to get used to the pace, but on the whole he was glad to be back. Yes, very stimulating.

A pause that threatened to turn into a permanent halt. Then Chad to the rescue: "You said Erna was here? How the hell did that happen?"

He had opened up a two-pronged vein—Marilyn's trip abroad, the possibility of a move westward for Ollie and Erna—and Mr. Fly explored both leads thoroughly, aware that Chad was listening with more than perfunctory interest. Naturally enough: it was only one step from Dee's family to Dee herself. They were getting warm.

"I can't believe they'll ever really go," said Chad. "Poor Erna, it's probably just a lot of wishful thinking."

"I wouldn't be too sure about that. I've only heard her version, and of course she sees it through rose-colored spectacles. But she can't be making up the part about the house. And the fact remains that Ollie's business isn't getting any better, no, and isn't likely to. Granted that he might not do any better out there. But at least they'd have the house, plus several acres of land that could be used in any number of ways. That's more than they'll ever have in Rushford."

"I know, but—" Whatever the "but" was, Chad decided against divulging it. Instead, he refreshed their drinks, and when he delivered Mr. Fly's he did not go back to his chair at once but stood in the middle of the room, his eyes fixed on the floor, his profile unsmiling and tense. After a couple of false starts he broke the deadlock. "You haven't mentioned Dee." He was looking at Mr. Fly now, accusing him.

"No. I didn't know if you—"

"All right. I'm asking. How is she?"

"She—" It was his fierceness that rattled Mr. Fly. He had envisioned the scene in a variety of ways, but this was none of them. All the same, he managed to dredge up one of his lines. "She's bearing up fairly well, considering."

"Considering? Oh. You mean because I walked out on her? Yes, I suppose it was a blow to her pride. I'm sorry about that." He took a gulp of his drink. "I'm very sorry."

"That is not what I meant," said Mr. Fly. "The fact of the matter is, Chad, you're supposed to be dead. Everybody in Rushford thinks you were killed in a plane crash."

There. It was out. In resounding silence they stared at each other; Chad with his mouth ajar and the glass in his hand tilted within a hair's breadth of spilling. "What?" he said at last. "But I don't understand ..."

Mr. Fly explained it to him, briefly and—except for the eavesdropping episode—fully. When he was through Chad heaved a deep sigh, crossed to his chair and sat down. The way he moved made Mr. Fly think of a sleepwalker, and when he spoke his voice had a muffled, faraway sound.

"I see. Yes. It's like Dee. The sort of thing she would do. She's very proud, you know. And always before she was the one who did the walking out. I recognized the pattern. I saw what she was up to when she picked that last quarrel with me. I beat her to it. I wish now I hadn't. It wouldn't have hurt me to play it her way."

Remorse, thought Mr. Fly; a step in the right direction. "These things happen," he offered hopefully. "The course of true love never runs smooth." There was no response from Chad. He pressed on. "She does love you, Chad. If you could see how she's been grieving—"

"Over my death? But she made it up! She knows perfectly well it's a lie!"

"There was somebody named Johnson on the plane ..."

"Well, it wasn't me. Whatever Dee says. Whatever she believes or doesn't believe. I suppose it's possible she's convinced herself, along with everybody else in Rushford. But I have never called her or written to her since the day I left." He paused, and added, suddenly fierce again, "I've thought about it often enough, God knows. But I didn't do it."

"Better late than never," said Mr. Fly boldly. "You could still do it, you know."

"And make a liar out of her? She'd never forgive me for that." He added morosely, "She'll never forgive me, anyway."

"She might, if you gave her a chance." Perhaps he had gone too far? The look Chad turned on him was hard, sharp, piercing as a fish hook.

"Of course it's none of my business. I don't mean to be presumptuous. And I'm not setting myself up as an expert on matters involving the fair sex. Far from it. I've never been married—"

"I have been. I expect Quentin told you? Yes. He was a friend of my wife's. She wasn't what Dee and I quarreled about, if that's what you're thinking. Though Dee used to try to make something out of my past. I wasn't being secretive, I just didn't care to—She died. That's when I decided to pull out of California and come east. No mystery about it. If Dee hadn't picked at it, I probably would have told her. After a while she gave up on that angle and found something else."

"I'm very fond of Dee," Mr. Fly faltered. "Nothing could please me more than—"

"Yes, Mr. Fly, I get the message." Chad laughed, not unkindly. "If I thought it would work, believe me, I'd call Dee this minute. But it's not that simple. Do me a favor. Take my word for it."

"Certainly," said Mr. Fly with dignity. "I have no intention of meddling. Or of spreading tales. Let me assure you, Dee will never hear about this from me. Neither will anyone else."

"I hope not." Chad was giving him the fish hook look again. "There's Erna, though. She might talk."

"I don't think she will. Frankly, I think she'd be afraid to. She's rather in awe of Dee, you know."

"Yes. That's so. All the same, I wish she didn't know." He peered down at his glass, rolling it between his palms. "Well. No help for it. I'm depending on you, Mr. Fly. In the first place, to keep this to yourself. In the second place, to let me know if Dee—if Erna should do anything foolish."

Mr. Fly rose and held out his hand. "I give you my word on it. I'll be in Rushford for another month at least. If anything happens I'll call you."

"Good. In the meantime, let's hope for the best."

The best, thought Mr. Fly wistfully on his way home; to him the best would still be reconciliation, reunion, the happy ending he had pictured in such glowing colors. It was not to be. At least not yet.

But was it ruled out entirely? Chad was still being stiff-necked about the quarrel, whatever its basis. But he had thought of calling Dee "often enough, God knows." He would call her "this minute, if I thought it would work." That proved how he felt about her. And he was obviously anxious not to lose touch; he had given Mr. Fly his home and office telephone numbers, had charged him with the responsibility of keeping the line of communication open.

No, the situation was by no means hopeless; Mr. Fly's spirits lifted, as buoyant as ever. It was going to take more time than he had anticipated, that was all. Eventually love would triumph. Yes indeed. Always and forever, love would find a way.

NINE

The minute the mail came that morning Erna hightailed it down to the shop with Gus's letter. It was addressed to Ollie, and it was full of figures about the repair shop that was up for sale. Too many figures for Erna. While he read it aloud, she stood hugging her arms close to her body as if for warmth, her eyes fixed on his face. Down payment, amortization, gross receipts—no, she couldn't follow the technicalities. All she had to go by was Ollie's expression. He was frowning. But that might only be a sign of concentration; Ollie was no great shakes when it came to figures, either. It wasn't till he came to the end that she knew for sure. "Sounds like a pretty good deal to me," Gus had written. "Think it over and let me know."

Ollie looked up then, and his face broke into a grin. "A pretty good deal. How about that? Old Gus practically going overboard."

She hugged her arms tighter, trembling with relief. It was all right, it was all right: Gus was the last man on earth to take a chance. His "pretty good" was anybody else's "great."

"Oh, Ollie," she whispered, and burst into tears.

"For Pete's sake." Ollie cast his eyes heavenward. But then he dug up some Kleenex for her and stood close to her, still grinning, while she pulled herself together. "Okay? Look, honey, let's not spread the news till I've had a chance to tell Dorothea about this. I mean, she ought to be the first one to hear it."

"Sure. Of course." It was a good thing he had mentioned it, though; otherwise she might have been tempted to tell Mr. Fly, who was back from New York for his summer school session, and who was coming down the front walk when she got back to the house.

He greeted her with his usual wistful, puckered-up smile and one of those would-be gallant flourishes of his arm. "You're looking bright and cheerful this morning. What's the good word?"

"It's such a pretty day," she said. As indeed it was: sunshine dappled the lawn, shimmered in the elms overhead, flashed against the white porch pillars. In the lilac bush a wren teetered its tail and poured out its miniature heart in joy.

Having quoted the line about what is so rare and so on, Mr. Fly asked if there was any further news from Marilyn.

"Not since the card from Paris." He knew something was up, all right. And after all, the secret they shared about Chad far outweighed Gus's letter ... No, if she could keep the big secret—and she had, not a word, even to Ollie—then surely she could keep the little one, especially since it was for only a day. Not even a day. By this evening she would be free, like the wren, to break out with her own glad tidings to Mr. Fly and the rest of Rushford. Meanwhile, to fend off temptation, she asked, "How about you? Any new job nibbles?"

"I think I mentioned my interview next week. A consolidated school. But then I'm very fond of the country, you know, and in some respects a school of that type offers more scope than a place like Rushford. More variety. More of a challenge." It was a pep talk she had heard before, but she listened sympathetically while once more Mr. Fly exhausted the subject.

This chat, like all their others nowadays, wound up on a surreptitious, whispering note. "You haven't heard anything more from Chad?" "Not a word. You haven't either, I suppose?" Head shakes, a thoughtful silence, a sigh in unison. "And if Dee has, she's not letting on. But then if they didn't make up of course she wouldn't ... Well, mum's the word. Absolutely. Me too."

Mr. Fly still clung to his hope of a reconciliation, though even he admitted that the longer it was postponed the slimmer its chances became. Erna, who had never been as optimistic as he, was by now convinced that Dee and everybody else in Rushford had seen the last of Chad. Okay; he had been crazy about Dee; still was, according to Mr. Fly. But the fact remained that he had walked out on her. Chad wasn't the type to do that over some trifling little disagreement. And another thing, he wasn't the type to be left floating around loose in New York long. Not that he was so handsome—Ollie had it all over him when it came to looks—but just the same plenty of women would be more than happy to latch on to him. Dee certainly hadn't hung back.

That didn't mean, though, that she would take him back now. Erna didn't pretend to understand her, but anybody with half an eye could see how proud Dee was. After all, she had begun her whole structure of lies simply because she was too proud to admit that Chad had pulled out on her. No, forgiving and forgetting wouldn't come easy to Dee. Chad was probably better off not calling her.

Poor Dee, she thought as she went up the stairs, and again she felt the shameful little throb of complacency. It was one more thing she could forget about, once they were out of Rushford and back home. Oh, and the forgetting would come so easy to her, so blissfully easy! She let herself into the kitchen, which no matter what Dee said had never seemed like hers, and which at this moment was replaced, in her mind, by another kitchen in another country. The one in their bungalow. Yes, it was all plain as day to her, down to the last square in the linoleum, the last nick in the woodwork; and through the window she saw, not the tidy New England scene, but the alfalfa field in bloom, rolling on over the rise, purple as mountains at dusk.

In the afternoon she went for a walk around the loop, as it was called, a pleasant lane that meandered off into the woods beside the brook, angled past a stretch of pasture land, and finally curved back into town at the other end. Erna used to bring the Girl Scout troop assigned to her out here for wienie roasts and hikes. That was back in the days when Marilyn was in grade school instead of college, before the tiredness got so bad and Erna was still trying to fit in somewhere or other.

She had really tried. She had done her best with whatever "activities" were open to her in Rushford. There weren't so many. Nothing in her background or temperament suited her for the civic-minded, culture-conscious Womans Club; even less for the country club set with their afternoons of bridge and golf, their expensive lunches and cocktails. That left things like PTA and church. When she thought of the cake sales, the rummage sales, strawberry socials, Thanksgiving bazaars, sewing circles ...

She had loved her little band of Girl Scouts, though. And her Sunday School class; she used to take them on picnics too, skating parties in the winter. The more kids swarming around the better, as far as she was concerned. But it hadn't worked very well, having them at the apartment. There wasn't much space, and Dee's paying guests might complain about the racket, and you couldn't blame Dee for not wanting the yard littered up with cook-outs or ball games. Somehow, with Marilyn growing up and all, it hadn't seemed worth the effort anymore. A couple of years ago, when she had that spell of flu, she had let the Sunday School class go along with everything else.

Nobody seemed to care much, one way or the other. The kids probably missed her for a while. Then they forgot. The minister did come to call once, as it happened on an afternoon when Erna had had an extra beer or two. He never came back. Now, when she met the sewing circle ladies on the street or in the store, they pinched out a chilly little nod, sometimes even a smile, and scuttled on their way.

Eighteen years, she thought, and not a single real friend to show for it.

There had been old Mrs. Larsen, who used to visit with Erna—maybe only because she didn't belong with the others, either—when she came in from the country for church doings. How long ago was it she died? Marilyn's third grade teacher, but she got married and moved away. One or two others who had moved away.

Ollie didn't realize. At first he had said comfortably, "Give 'em time. It takes a while to get acquainted." Now it was: "What do you mean, no friends?" He had his hunting and fishing cronies, fellows he had grown up with; once in a while he and Erna went bowling with another couple, or had dinner together. But ... He didn't realize, he just didn't know how it was.

Well, it was over now, or as nearly over as made no never-mind. No friends meant no regrets. On either side: Rushford would be as indifferent to her absence as it had been to her presence, and for Erna herself the day she left town would be one of the happiest of her life.

She scrambled down the bank, thick with bushes and ferns; here was her favorite spot, a big flat rock to sit on, the brook gurgling by, its depths tobacco-brown, its surface glinting with sunlight. Farther on it grew more boisterous, whipping itself into a froth as it brawled uproariously over stones and fallen logs. But at this spot it paused to catch its breath. Minnows switched their tails in the shelter of the rock, dragon flies skimmed past, the willows bent down to dabble their fingers in the water. As Erna dabbled hers: icy, in spite of the sun. The tree trunk back of her was plushy with Pullman-green moss. She settled against it and smoked a cigarette.

The pasture was the other place on the loop where she always paused. The road curved suddenly out of the woods and into a clearing that reminded her—not much, but a little—of home. It was a stony pasture, bright with daisies and Indian paint brush. Beyond it, at the foot of the wooded misty hills, nestled a weather-beaten old farmhouse. Today sheep were grazing there; one of them lifted its foolish face to survey Erna briefly, then got back to work. The sun beat down, bees hummed in the clover, overhead a crow flapped. She stood still for a minute or two, looking, and at the next bend she turned back for a last glimpse.

There. She had said all the goodbyes there were for her to say in Rushford. The brook and the pasture were the best she had to remember.

We're leaving, she whispered to herself, *we're going back home*. Somehow this farewell pilgrimage of hers made it really true. Jubilation seized her. She was the wren in the lilac bush, she was the roistering brook. She broke into a plunging, joyful run.

But one look at Ollie's face when he walked in at supper time, one look, and she knew. She was in the living room, watching the news on television, all cleaned up, fresh housedress, lipstick, hair brushed, waiting till he got there to have a festive beer. She didn't hear him on the stairs. Didn't even hear him come in through the kitchen. All at once there he was in the doorway, and right away she knew.

He had a wilted, hangdog look, and there was a tired slump to his shoulders. His eyes skidded away from hers. "Hi," he said warily.

She stayed where she was, not answering, just waiting to see whether or not he was going to get up enough nerve to look her in the eye. It seemed not. He took off his jacket and hung it over the chair back. Lit a cigarette. Ran his fingers through his hair. Turned back toward the kitchen and asked over his shoulder, "Want a beer?"

"No thanks," she said. "I want to know what Dee said."

He did look at her then—the scared, pleading, sorrowful look that she remembered from other quarrels. Ollie hated to fight. So did she. Usually.

"Oh. Well. We went over the figures." He swallowed nervously.

"Did you tell her we're going?"

"I told her—That is, I showed her Gus's letter. We went over the figures, and ..." She waited stonily. He needn't expect any help from her. "All the figures. Not just from that end, this end too. Because it's like Dorothea says, the only way to get the whole picture is to make a comparison. Draw up a balance sheet. Get it all down in black and white—what we've got here as against what we can expect out there." Dee's phrases, of course; his confidence grew as he quoted them, his voice took on an echo of her crisp, no-nonsense tone. "And when you do that, take a long hard look at both sides—Erna honey, it may not be quite as good as it seemed at first glance."

"Gus said a pretty good deal. That's good enough for me."

"I know, but that's only half the story. After all, Gus doesn't know, except in a general way, what the situation is here. He'd be the first to admit it. It's a question of comparison. We'd have to borrow for the down payment, don't forget. You've got to figure in the interest. Not only that, but the intangibles. There's bound to be changes, you know. We can't expect to go back and find everything just the way it was. It's been eighteen years."

"I know how long it's been," she said bitterly.

That stung. He was silent a moment, biting his lip. But he went on quoting Dee: her words, her quiet, reasonable tone. "In the first place, we're different. We're not kids any more. And I wouldn't be working for somebody else the way I was then, I'd be on my own, running my own business. It might not be so easy, starting over again at this stage of the game. At least Rushford's my home town, everybody knows me here—"

"And Dee's here to tell you when to blow your nose." She got heavily to her feet and moved toward him. "She's talked you out of it. Hasn't she? You've changed your mind about going."

"I didn't say that. I just—"

"You don't have to say it. Do you think I don't know? I'm not that dumb. Whatever she may think."

"She doesn't think anything of the kind!" He was getting sore. She could tell by the way his nose pinched in. Good. "She's never said one word against you. No, and she didn't talk me out of it, either. All she did was point out a few plain, common-sense facts that I should have seen for myself."

"Sure. The figures. And the intangibles. We mustn't forget the intangibles. Like what a lousy businessman you are, what a flop you'd be without her to keep you straight. Oh, I might have known how it would be, when you said you had to tell her first. You didn't tell her at all! She told you! And you let her do it. You know why? Because you've got no more backbone than a jellyfish. That's what you are. That's what I'm married to. A worm. A jelly—"

"Shut up!"

They were face to face now, heads thrust forward, glaring at each other. She saw the mean glint in his eye, and exulted.

"Jellyfish!" she yelled.

He slapped her, a healthy smack that sent her stumbling against the couch. It shocked him as much as it did her; more, to judge by his dazed expression.

"I'm not taking it back," she warned him. "You can beat the daylights out of me and I still won't take it back. Not till you stand up to her for once in your life and—"

"Oh for Christ's sake! It's not a question of standing up to Dorothea. She's not against the deal. She just doesn't want us to do anything we'll be sorry for later. Can't you understand that? Erna. Erna honey." He was beginning to look like himself again, warm and gentle, with the touch of sadness that had so often melted her. She hardened her heart against him, cringed from his pleading outstretched hand as if in fear of another blow. He flushed painfully.

"I understand enough," she said. "You were all for going this morning, before you talked to her. Now you're not. Of course she's against it."

"What do you mean, of course?"

"I mean ..." She cast about in her mind. No question about the conviction. Solid as a rock. But where had it come from? "I mean whatever I want she's against. It's always been that way. She always—"

"What? You must be out of your mind. How can you say such a thing, after all she's done for us?"

"I don't care!" she cried passionately. But she did. She was ashamed of herself, remembering what pains Dee had taken, when she was having the apartment done over for them, to get everything just the way Erna wanted it; the furniture she had offered so freely, Ollie's favorite chair, the rugs and the grandfather's clock he was so fond of, she had given them their pick of anything in the house. She had helped nurse Marilyn through her mastoid; when Erna broke her collarbone, had pitched right in and done the housework; had more than once—though nobody ever said so flat out—helped Ollie out when he needed cash. There was no forgetting the kindnesses; they weighed like a yoke on Erna's shoulders.

So did the loneliness, the friendless, discontented years of feeling like an exile. But was any of that Dee's fault? Of course not; if anybody was to blame, it must be Erna herself. Something blind and stubborn had risen up in her, a resistance against Rushford and everybody in it. Something cold, the bone-deep, bone-hard chill that had crept over her when she walked in and saw Dee for the first time, huddled in that little sewing chair, rocking back and forth.

From then on nothing was quite the same. Nothing. The chill spread everywhere, sometimes even into bed with her and Ollie. He might not know it, but she did. Yes, God help her, she sometimes pretended, play-acting from memory where once reality had consumed her. She couldn't let on to Ollie. He never let on to her, either, whatever he may have guessed.

And the doctors could spout all the fancy explanations they wanted to, Erna knew why there had been no babies after Marilyn. The chill had got in and shriveled the life out of her, that was why. If they had stayed back home where they belonged, if they could go there now ...

"... thinking about going away herself," Ollie was saying nervously, keeping an anxious eye on her as if she were some kind of wild animal who might jump him at any moment, "for a while at least. It's hard for her here just now, too much to remind her of Chad. Of course she couldn't leave the house with nobody to run things, but if we were here— Maybe you'd feel different about Rushford if you had more to do, you're always saying there isn't enough to keep you busy ..."

"It's too late for that now. Ten years ago it might have made a difference, even five years ago. She needn't think she can bribe me now. She'd never really go, anyway. It's just talk, to keep us from going." Chad, she thought, and felt her mouth curving into a cruel smile. Chad. That particular angle had slipped her mind. Should she use it, her secret weapon? Would Ollie believe her if she were to come out with it? Would it somehow boomerang and destroy more than she aimed at?

"Don't look like that," he said sharply.

She would be breaking her promise to Mr. Fly. He would be one of the casualties; no way of leaving him out of it. He was, after all, one of the few friends she could name in Rushford. The brook, the pasture, and Mr. Fly. And at the thought of him something else stirred in her memory.

"Like what? What do I look like?"

"Not like yourself. Erna. Erna honey, you know I want you to be happy." So troubled he looked, so sad and loving, so defenseless against her and her secret weapons. Because she had more than one. Oh yes, she could pick and choose; she had never realized how powerful she was until now.

She stood straight, unmelting, her arms folded across her breast as if to contain the excited thud of her heart.

"You can suit yourself, Ollie," she said. "Go or stay, just as you please. But either way, my mind's made up. I'm getting out of here. Whether you come with me or not, I'm going back home."

TEN

"You're not taking her seriously, I hope," said Dee. "You know better than that, Oliver. You know perfectly well Erna would never leave you."

"The hell she wouldn't. She's started packing. Had the bedroom closet all turned out when I got home from work tonight."

She couldn't help smiling a little. How gullible he was, what an unsuspecting alarmist! Like Chicken Little, hurrying to her with his tidings of doom. "Well, but surely you can see she's only bluffing."

"Bluffing?" He lifted his eyes from his scuffed loafers and peered at her in forlorn hope.

Tonight they were sitting—as befitted the gravity of the situation—in the study, a small, square room which opened off the living room and which was furnished much the same as in the days when Papa used to work here of an evening, going over the accounts from the furniture store. Roll-top desk, sectional bookcase, brown leather chairs and sofa, somber-patterned rug. As a child Dee had assumed that this room was what was meant by the expression "a brown study." The one touch of bright color was the crocheted afghan folded across the foot of the sofa.

On the wall behind Oliver hung the oval portrait of Grandfather Morris. A square, Yankee face, blue-eyed like Dee's and like Papa's before her. Indeed, except for the handlebar moustache, the portrait might almost have been of Papa. Oliver got his look of dark, exotic melancholy from their mother's side of the family. He claimed he could remember her—a dress with fringe that she had worn, the jazzy tunes she had played on the piano—but for Dee there was nothing left of her at all. She had been much younger than Papa; had died much younger, too. Only twenty-seven, thought Dee, and once again wondered what sort of person she herself would have been, with a mother instead of without one. They might be entirely different, she and Oliver both.

"I'm not so sure she's bluffing," he decided gloomily. "It didn't look like it to me."

"Wouldn't be much of a bluff if it did," Dee pointed out. "I'm not blaming her, mind you. If I were in her place, I'd probably do just about what she's doing. She wants her own way. Naturally. But when it comes to a showdown, she's not going to give you up, not for anything."

"I wouldn't bet on it. I'm not such a bargain." He was staring at his shoes again, sitting hunched forward, hands knotted together between his knees. After a moment he added, very low and shamefaced, "There's something I didn't tell you. I—Well, I slapped her."

"What? Oliver, you didn't!" Instantly there sprang into her mind a memory of that last afternoon with Chad, her hand lashing out, stinging against his face.

Oliver nodded dolefully. "She got me so mad. I never did such a thing before in my life. She's not going to forget that in a hurry. Well. Neither will I."

"No, I suppose not." Though Erna, like Chad, had undoubtedly deserved it. She may even have wanted it. The peasant mentality. "Don't be too hard on yourself. She's not going to hold it against you forever, just because you lost your temper once in however many years it's been—"

"Nineteen. Nineteen years ago since I took off in that good old jalopy. California, here I come. Only I never made it. We were married the end of June."

And not a moment too soon, according to Dee's arithmetic. Poor Oliver, he never had a chance. Trapped into marriage so young, stuck with a wife and baby before he knew what hit him. What was one little slap compared with that?

By the time his letter to Dee arrived it was all over, a fait accompli. She had read it in this very room, sitting in this very chair. "Letter from your brother," Mrs. Covey told her at noon when she came home from the store. They were still running it, she more than Oliver, though he went through the motions till the jalopy and the travel itch got too much for him—making a go of it too, young as they were—and Mrs. Covey was still there, keeping house for them as she had done since before Papa died. An ungainly old woman, shambling of gait, top-heavy of figure; deaf as a post, and very nearly as impassive.

She had been putting up strawberry preserves that sultry June day. The smell, thick and sweet, sickening, spread from the kitchen through the whole first floor. From the elms outside came the muted sobbing of mourning doves. The smell, the sobs, the letter in her hand. "The wedding's all set for tomorrow." A tomorrow which by then was two days past. He had held off writing Dee until old Woodrow, their guardian, came through with his consent. "I hope he hasn't already told you. He promised to leave it to me. Wish you could be here, but we decided not to wait ..." The casualness of it. The finality. And at the end the cruelest cut of all: "I guess you knew when I left I might not be back. It's different for you, you've got the store and the house, and with your head for business you'll make out okay."

Oh, how could he, how could he? She had known nothing of the kind—about his trip, the store, the house, any of it. He was going away for the summer, that was all. Doing what lots of boys did when they got out of high school, jaunting off to see a bit of the country before they settled down at a job or college. While it was true that the house and the store were hers, or would be when she came of age, she had never once thought of them as anything but theirs, hers and Oliver's. Never once had she suspected that he might think otherwise, might not share her feeling of family solidarity, might live his life anywhere but in Rushford.

Even now, it shook her to remember that June of nineteen years ago. "Let's have a brandy," she said. "Would you get it? It's in the sideboard—"

"Sure. I know." He sprang up and returned in a moment with bottle and glasses. "She's never liked it too well in Rushford," he said. "I don't know exactly why. She never got used to it, somehow."

Never tried, thought Dee. Made up her mind at the start not to like it simply because it wasn't a Midwestern farm. The peasant mentality again: dead set against any and all change. "Poor Erna," she said. "Maybe if she just went back for a visit she'd get it out of her system. Have you suggested that?"

"She's not buying it. She says when she goes it'll be for keeps. Says she's wasted enough time as it is. Wasted," he repeated and blinked as if in pain. "I don't think it's a bluff, Dorothea. I think she means business. And of course if she does—"

After waiting a moment Dee asked gently, "If she does?"

"Well, of course if she goes I'll go too. What else can I do? Hell, if it means that much to her, I've got no choice."

"I suppose not." She took a sip of brandy. But brandy too reminded her of the day the letter came. She had not gone back to the store. While Mrs. Covey—impervious to all but strawberry preserves—measured and stirred and sealed in the kitchen, she had fetched a bottle of Papa's brandy from the sideboard and had sat here in the study, getting drunk for the first time in her life. It had been a memorable experience. In some ways, a sobering one ...

"What's funny?" asked Oliver.

"Nothing. I was just thinking about the night you came home drunk from choir practice. That's where you claimed you'd been. Choir practice. The minister and his wife were here, I remember—"

"So do I." He grinned. "Believe me, so do I."

"We heard this thumping noise out in the hall, and when I opened the door there you were, crawling up the stairs on your hands and knees. With your shoes tied around your neck, for some reason."

"Sure. So as not to make any noise. It was the first time I ever got drunk. Port wine. I've never cared much for it since. What put that into your head?"

"I don't know. Let's see, Papa was dead then, it must have been the winter before you went out west. Our last year of high school, when we were still running the store. Crazy, we were such a crazy pair of kids."

Oliver had been the leader in those days, more daring than she, more openly rebellious both before and after Papa's death. On one or two thrilling occasions he had even defied Papa. That basketball trip that Papa objected to; Oliver had gone anyway, he was the star of the team, oh, how proud she had been of him, her handsome, dashing, heroic big brother ...

"Maybe," he said now. "But we'd never had much of a chance to cut loose. Papa was pretty damn strict with us, if you remember."

There was an understatement for you. Strict. Church was the only social activity Papa had really approved of for his children. Sunday school, plus two interminable sermons, plus Bible study and choir practice during the week. Straight home from school every afternoon, supper at six o'clock sharp, bed at nine thirty. No company without his presence as supervisor. No outside parties without his arrival on the stroke of eleven to escort them home. And yet it wasn't the rules that Dee had minded so much; agonizing though they were, they indicated a form of concern. Besides, they could—on rare, delicious occasions, and at Oliver's instigation—be dodged. No, it was the aloofness, the impersonality, the feeling that she was less a daughter than a duty. Well, it worked both ways. In the end she had stopped hoping for warmth or praise from him; had wound up thinking of him less as a father than an oppression, an all-encompassing power of veto.

His will, leaving her both house and store, had been a belated act of faith in her; at least and at last he had recognized her head for business. But by that time ...

"I don't know that we were so crazy," Oliver was going on. "After all, we kept the store going. You did, rather. I wasn't much help. I never expected you to sell it, you know. You were so set on keeping it at first."

"Maybe I just wanted to show everybody I could do it." Not such an implausibility, at that. Her act of rebellion, in answer to Papa's act of faith: to prove she could run his precious store and, having done so, get rid of it. But the main reason was Oliver. The day after his letter came, she marched down to the bank and told old Mr. Woodrow, their guardian, that she had decided to put the store up for sale. This, coming on the heels of his own recent correspondence with Oliver, all but unnerved him. Had she given the matter sufficient consideration? Was she quite sure? Quite. And had she—ahem—heard from Oliver? Certainly. Of course she knew about his marriage. Had known for some time. Even before that, she had been thinking seriously about selling out. After all, she was only eighteen, too young to be tied down with so much responsibility. If she got a good price for the store—and she saw no reason why she shouldn't, in view of past offers—she would be free to travel, go to college, whatever she chose.

"Anyway," she said, "I've never regretted selling it. I'll say this much for old Woodrow, once he saw my mind was made up, he pulled himself together and got down to business. I didn't lose any money on the deal. And I've had a lot more fun with my little shop than I ever would have gotten out of the store."

"I always hated the place myself," Oliver confided. "Even now I'd rather not go in there. It still smells the same, you know? Varnish or something. Takes me back to all the hours I put in when I was a kid, Saturdays and after school. He claimed it was good for me. Kept me out of mischief. Maybe. But I sometimes think it's a wonder we didn't go even more haywire than we did. I mean—" He shot her a glance of apprehension. To this day they shied away from discussing the circumstances of Dee's "going haywire." The usual phrase for it was her nervous breakdown. As for what brought it on, that was not mentioned at all. It happened. It was over. The less said the better.

For she had chosen—not college or travel—but disaster. Chosen? It might have been deliberate. She simply did not know. She simply could not remember enough of what she had done in those feverish months— let alone what she had thought or felt. There were the nightmares. Now and then there were splinters that worked their way to the surface of her mind, sharp but insignificant, easily flicked aside. The rest she kept buried, decently out of her own sight and everybody else's.

Except Chad's. She had not succeeded in hiding it from him. He had seen—No. He hadn't. It never happened. Blot it out. Blot it out. And anyway, Chad was dead.

"You know," she said suddenly, "sometimes I even forget his name, that boy I—" Married? Ran away with? Whatever it was, the annulment canceled it, and the boy with it. He was part of the nightmares, though. Faceless. Nameless. Disaster. "I didn't just go haywire. I must have been crazy as a loon. Maybe I still am."

"Yeah. And maybe I'm Queen Elizabeth. Look, Dorothea, everything's changed since then. You've changed. Grown up. You're a different person now. Dorothea! Hey, now," he cried, in consternation. "Don't cry. Please don't cry."

"I'm not." But she was; she covered her face with her hands and felt the tears rolling down. "I'm sorry. I'll be all right in a minute. I just—"

He bent over her, smoothing her hair. "It's my fault. Bringing up all that old stuff. I should have known better."

"No. It's not that. You don't know, Oliver, you don't know what it's like!" She gave a gulp of terror and pulled away from the comfort of his hand. "Why did it have to happen? Why couldn't I have kept Chad ..."

"There," he said helplessly, "there," and when she composed herself enough to look up at him, his face was drawn with compassion and distress.

"Poor Oliver," she said. "You've got your own troubles. I don't often do that anymore. I'm all right now. Really. I'm through crying."

Yes, she was through crying. He said goodnight presently, and left her sitting there in the brown study, smoking a last cigarette. Dry-eyed and quiet. Beyond crying.

Indeed, she could almost have laughed, remembering what he had said with so much naive conviction: "Everything's changed since then. You've changed ... You're a different person now."

ELEVEN

This time it was not a case of eavesdropping. Mr. Fly was right there in plain sight—overlooked, perhaps, as the scene progressed—but still there, practically a captive audience. For there was only one way out of the basement: the narrow stairway leading up to Dee's kitchen, and getting to it would have meant not only crossing the stage, as it were, but actually interposing himself between the two protagonists. An unpardonable intrusion; and if as seemed likely they had forgotten his presence, an acutely embarrassing reminder.

He was there first (for what that was worth), and on legitimate business. In return for the several favors Dee had done him lately, such as holding his room for him without charge during his stay in New York, he had offered to get her garden furniture out of storage and ready for another summer's use. So there he was in the basement, scrubbing plastic cushions, when Erna hove into view, feet and thickish ankles first, then her blue checked dress, finally her broad face with its topping of streaked blondish hair.

"Hi!" she sang out. "Got yourself a job, have you? I'm looking for our trunk. Did you see it, back in the store room? Lord knows what kind of shape it's in by now, but I thought I'd take a look at it just in case it's usable."

"I'll help you haul it out," said Mr. Fly, straightening up and wiping his hands on his dungarees. He did not ask any of the questions that trembled on the tip of his tongue. No need to. Erna had already reported to him the details of her threatened departure; if Ollie had given in and agreed to go with her, she would have said so by now.

It made Mr. Fly a little nervous to think that in her eyes he was not merely a friend but a collaborator, an instigator. Because that was where she had gotten the idea in the first place—from him, the afternoon she came to see him in New York. Yes, it was his chance remark that started her off, and the worrisome part was that, having started, she might not stop …

Nonsense. Of course she would never actually leave Ollie. It was only a threat, a wifely little stratagem to bring him around to her way of thinking. As it was bound to do, sooner or later; the wonder was that he had held out this long. The trunk would crack his resistance. Packing a trunk was, after all, a pretty spectacular operation.

Between them they dragged it out of the small dark store room and into the laundry area where there was room and light enough for proper inspection. It didn't look too promising: the outside battered and covered with dust, the inside stained and smelling of mildew, empty except for a few newspaper scraps and mouse mementoes.

"I don't know if it's worth the trouble," said Erna, wrinkling her nose. "It seems sound enough, but it's going to be some job, cleaning it. I just don't know."

Neither did Mr. Fly. They were still debating the pros and cons when Dee, home from the shop for lunch, clattered down the stairway.

"There you are," she said to Mr. Fly. "How's it going?" But it was the trunk that caught her eye. "Don't tell me, Erna! You're not counting on using that old relic!"

Erna flushed and turned defensive. "Why not? It doesn't look so bad to me."

"Well, but—No, really. Look, the lock's sprung, it won't even close. Why, you'd never get it up the stairs in one piece, let alone halfway across the continent."

Now that she mentioned it, the lock didn't seem to work right. But Erna said stubbornly, "That could be fixed, the lock. Otherwise all it needs is a good cleaning."

"It's up to you, of course. I just don't—If you're bound and determined to take a trunk, I'll buy you a new one. Honestly, Erna. I'd be glad to."

"Thank you very much," said Erna, "but that won't be necessary."

Right then and there Mr. Fly knew there was going to be trouble. He even had a split-second premonition as to what kind of trouble. It was something in Erna's tone that warned him, a dry, level note of assurance he had never heard her use before, certainly not to Dee. Then there was her stance: hands on hips, head tilted at what might almost be called a belligerent angle. None of this was lost on Dee; her eyes sharpened, her face tightened up a bit. They stood, one at either end of the dratted trunk, taking each other's measure; and between them stood Mr. Fly, facing the stairway but cut off from it by them and the trunk. He began an unobtrusive, diplomatic retreat toward the laundry tubs behind him.

"Whatever you say," said Dee, and turned toward the stairway. "May

I ask how soon you're planning to leave?"

"As soon as I get my things packed." Erna spoke casually, over her shoulder; she had moved around to the front of the trunk and was tinkering with the lock.

As for Mr. Fly, he stopped in his tracks. I? My? His heart sank at the implication. Impossible. Unthinkable. She would never leave without Ollie. She was only bluffing.

"I take it you're going on ahead of Oliver then," Dee was saying. "It will take him a little while, I should think, to wind up his affairs. The only reason I ask—"

"I know why you ask, all right." No doubt about the belligerence now; the flicker in Erna's deep-set eyes was openly hostile. "You don't need to rub it in. If Ollie decides not to go, it'll be your doing. Nobody else's. You've done your best to talk him out of it."

"I've done nothing of the kind. He asked for my advice and I gave it to him. I don't understand your attitude, Erna. What kind of a sister would I be if I failed to point out the risks as I see them? It's his business if he wants to go ahead and take them, but at least he'll be doing it with his eyes open. As for rubbing anything in, the only reason I asked about your plans is that I'd like some idea of when the apartment will be available so I can see about finding another tenant. Or trying to, anyway. I have a right to know, haven't I?"

"Then don't ask me, ask Ollie! I don't know what he's going to do!" Erna flung it out, a cry of misery. "There. Does that make you happy, that we've hardly spoken to each other the last two days?"

It shouldn't have given Mr. Fly such a jolt. After all, she had poured it all out to him: the argument, the slap, her ultimatum. He should have guessed, just from the sight of Ollie's face—longer, more soulfully sad than ever—the time or two they had met on the stairs. Ridiculous to assume that so serious a quarrel had been patched up in so short a time. Yet Mr. Fly had assumed it. Now, backed up against the laundry tubs, he was aware of a further sinking of the heart, another pang of foreboding.

"Certainly it doesn't make me happy. Why should it?" Dee looked very pale and, as always in contrast with Erna, very fine-drawn. The trimness of her waist, for instance; her slim neck, the intricate elegance of wrist and ankle. "On the contrary, I'm sorry if you and Oliver have had a falling out over this. You say you don't know what he's going to do. Surely that depends on you?"

"You mean ... He can make up his mind for himself! Me, I'm getting out of here. If it has to be without him, then that's the way it has to be. God help us."

For Mr. Fly the last spark of hope winked and died. It was not just the tremor of truth in Erna's voice that convinced him, it was the desolation in her face. It had to be genuine; Erna was no actress. And this was no bluff. Maybe at the start, but not now. However muzzy her original intentions, they had crystallized in the last two days. Ollie's mind might not be made up. Hers was.

There was a rather long silence. Then Dee said gently, "I see. I only wish I had realized before this how unhappy you've been here in Rushford. I thought it was just—you know, a spell of homesickness now and then. A little trouble adjusting. I could have done so much more, if only I had seen in time—"

"I'm not blaming you." Erna flushed uncomfortably.

"Oh, but I think you are. Maybe not consciously. But it was because of me that you came to Rushford in the first place. I think you've always resented that, always held it against me for getting sick."

"No! I never!"

"I said not consciously. Then when things worked out the way they did and Oliver decided to stay, that somehow or other got to be my fault too. Just as you're blaming me now because he's having second thoughts about leaving. It's my doing. I've done my best to talk him out of it. Those were your very words. A minute ago."

It was clearly too complicated for Erna, this permutation from self-blame to counterattack. After a moment of bewildered blinking she grabbed for the only certainty in sight. "Well, it is your doing! He was all set to leave till you started in on him. Going over the figures, all that. I don't want to hear about them. I don't care how much money Ollie makes or loses on the deal. I just want to go!"

"Yes. So I gather. It's perfectly all right with you if Oliver winds up without a cent of his own, living off of handouts from your father. You don't care what happens to him, just so long as you get what you want." Dee kept her voice down. Her hostility, unlike Erna's heated outbursts, was cold as death, all the more virulent for her self-restraint. Mr. Fly shrank back, shocked at the sudden ugliness of her face. She went on, still low-pitched and controlled. "You're willing to go to any lengths, aren't you, to get your own way. Including blackmail. That's what it amounts to. You're blackmailing Oliver into leaving against his better judgment."

"Blackmail?" faltered Erna. "I don't—I—"

"All right. I'll put it another way. You're pulling the oldest female trick in the book, you're trading on sex to keep him in line. As I might have known you would. What else have you ever had to trade on? It's how you trapped him into marrying you in the first place, and now you're—"

"You shut up!" yelled Erna. "Don't you talk to me like that! Who do you think you are, telling me I trapped him? What right have you got? Ollie and me ... You don't know anything about it!"

Mr. Fly was both impressed and surprised. Who would have thought it of Erna? Ordinarily she was so unsure of herself, so inadequate and what was more so helplessly aware of it. Not now. Honest outrage lent her the authority she usually lacked, and the dignity. She took a step or two toward Dee. She looked strong, and she looked threatening.

But though he himself found her imposing, Mr. Fly did not expect Dee to react as she did. For a moment she actually seemed on the verge of buckling at the knees and collapsing. With one hand she reached for the wooden stair rail to steady herself; with the other she brushed the hair back from her temple—a confused, weary gesture that was as as un-characteristic as the shakiness of her voice. "I'm sorry. Please, Erna, I shouldn't have said that. I don't know why I ... I didn't mean to ..." She lifted her head a little; there was a touch of slyness about her now, as if she were watching Erna, calculating the effect on her. "Of course I haven't any right. I can't think what made me say such a thing, I know it's not true, I just ... Please, Erna. Forgive me."

She should have left it at that. Though Erna did not respond in words, her fists unclenched, and the angry flush in her cheeks began to fade. After all, she had a soft heart, and apologies didn't often come her way, certainly not from Dee.

But Dee made the mistake of pushing on. "It's no excuse, but I'm not really myself these days. I'll get over Chad eventually, I suppose, but I get the strangest feeling sometimes. Like the other day in the shop— Never mind."

At the mention of Chad, Mr. Fly closed his eyes. Through a buzz of ap-prehension he heard Erna asking, a little too politely perhaps, "The other day in the shop? What happened?"

"I shouldn't have mentioned it. I found myself sitting there, rocking, rocking. It gave me the shivers, somehow."

"Yes. Did you tell Ollie about this?"

"No, of course not. Forget I mentioned it to you. I'm sure I'll be all right. Really. Just delayed reaction, I suppose." Mr. Fly opened his eyes: she was trying, bravely, to smile. "I can't help it, I dread the thought of be-ing all alone. Chad's death, and now—"

"Chad's death," repeated Erna. Her face turned cruel. "If you feel an-other nervous breakdown coming on, Dee, don't you think you ought to see a doctor?"

"Who said anything about a nervous breakdown? I simply—"

"Because I can tell you right now, this time it's not going to work. With Ollie, maybe. Not with me. You can rock yourself to death as far as I'm concerned. It won't keep me from leaving."

"And you claimed a minute ago that you never blamed me. My God," whispered Dee, "how you must hate me. All these years, and I didn't realize how much. Believe me, Erna—No, of course you won't believe me, but I'll say it anyway. I haven't the slightest intention of trying to keep you here, either you or Oliver, against your will. I should have known better than to expect you to understand. You couldn't care less, I see that now. My problems are my own. I'm the one that has to learn to live with them, and if I can't, then ... I'm sure I'll manage somehow. It would have been a little easier, not to be left alone until I'd gotten over Chad's death, but—"

"Chad's death." Erna thrust her stony, cruel face forward. She laughed; and at the sound Mr. Fly's prophetic soul, secretly smoldering until now, erupted into open flame. He croaked out a warning, but it was too late; nothing less than an act of God could have stopped her. "Who do you think you're kidding with your tale of woe? Chad's not dead. He's alive, and you know it. You've been lying about him all along, making up the whole thing so nobody would know he walked out on you ..."

"Erna!" screeched Mr. Fly. "You promised." He scuttled forth from the shelter of the laundry tubs, flailing his arms. They had forgotten him, all right; their expressions made that clear. Dee was gray with shock; Erna wheeled toward him awkwardly, a guilty flush drenching her face and neck.

Dee gave him no more than the one abstracted glance. "Chad? Alive?" The words rattled out. He saw how her chin was trembling, in spite of her rigidly clenched jaw. Saw the stunned look in her eyes—was it possible that she had really believed in Chad's death?—and felt again the obscure pain that had gripped him weeks ago, when he had heard her clear, proud voice greeting her dinner guests, explaining about Chad and the job in New York.

"Well, he is," said Erna, shamefaced yet defiant. "No more dead than I am. Right there in New York where he's been all the time. The California business was just something you made up, like the phone calls from him. Whatever Johnson it was in that plane crash it wasn't Chad."

"How do you know this? Did you see him?"

"No, but—" Erna caught her breath and, just in time, kept her eyes from switching to Mr. Fly. "I know. Never mind how. That part of it doesn't matter. None of the rest of it matters, either, except that I'm sick and tired of hearing you carry on about Chad being dead when you know and I know it's a lie. You had a fight and he walked out on you, that's all."

"I see." Dee was still mortally pale, but she had herself under control. "And what did we fight about? I suppose you overheard that too, along with everything else."

"What do you mean, overheard? I didn't—"

"You know perfectly well what I mean. You obviously took it upon yourself to eavesdrop on a private conversation that was none of your business. You must have been in the hall that day, listening at the door, eating up every word."

Mr. Fly spoke up bravely. "You're making a mistake, Dee. It wasn't Erna. It wasn't like that at all. I happened to—"

But she rushed on, paying him no more heed than she would have paid the buzzing of a gnat. "And ever since then you've been having the time of your life, telling everybody in town. In strictest confidence, of course. Oh, I can hear you! 'This is just between you and me and the lamp post, but ...' You hate me that much, don't you? You've been waiting for just such a chance as this, ever since you came to Rushford. Why don't you admit it?"

For a moment Erna could not get out a single word. She stared, open-mouthed but speechless, into Dee's glittering eyes; she swallowed a couple of times and finally found her tongue. "No, no, I never! Not to a living soul, not even to Ollie. Honest and true, Dee, I never meant to, only you made me so mad—"

Dee laughed contemptuously. "Mr. Fly seems to know all about it. If you didn't tell him, who did?"

"Let me explain," he began, once more prepared to do his duty. "This is all my fault. I'm the one who heard you quarreling with Chad, quite unintentionally, I assure you, and then, through a chain of circumstances beyond my control I found myself with no choice but to acquaint Erna with the situation ... I take the full responsibility, and I furthermore give you my word of honor that it has reached no one else's ears, either through Erna or me, and never will."

"Spoken like the gentleman you are, Mr. Fly. Congratulations on your loyalty. Erna's very lucky to have you for a friend. I only wish I trusted her as implicitly as you do." She gave him a withering smile and started up the stairway.

"Wait!" he cried. "Don't go yet! You've got to believe me! I haven't told you—"

"You've told me enough, both of you. We all know where we stand. I see no point in further discussion." Her heels clicked briskly on; in another moment the door at the top of the stairs opened and closed with finality.

"Later," quavered Mr. Fly. "I'll explain it all to her another time, when she's not so upset. She'll listen. I'm sure she'll believe me, once she hears me out."

"You're not to blame," said Erna. "You did your best." Suddenly she shivered.

TWELVE

Had she eaten lunch or not? The question occurred to Dee after she got back to the shop. She could not for the life of her remember. She might have come straight here from the basement. On the other hand, she might have stopped in the kitchen and automatically eaten the sandwich she had been making when she thought of Mr. Fly at work on the garden furniture and went down to see how he was making out. And to offer him lunch, in case he hadn't already had his.

A tuna fish sandwich on rye. She didn't feel at all hungry, so maybe she had eaten it. Not that it mattered, one way or the other, except as a symptom. What else might she have done, or not done, all unbeknownst to herself?

There was the study, too. If that was where she had gone when she left the basement—again she wasn't sure—she couldn't have stayed there for more than a few minutes. It was only one thirty now; she had closed the shop and gone home for lunch at noon. There was no telling, of course, how long the scene in the basement had lasted. One moment it seemed to her brief and violent as a thunderclap; the next it stretched out to impossible lengths. So this recurrent flicker of memory about the study might be rooted in reality. Certainly it was vivid enough: the small brown room, the cracked leather of the chair arms, the pain that racked her as she sat there listening to the mourning doves, breathing in the smell of brandy and something else, unbearably sweet and heavy, strawberry preserves ...

No, no! That had been another time, another June. Nothing to do with today. She had never even heard of Chad back then, and he was at the heart of today's disaster. Chad. Chad. She must get hold of herself and stop mixing everything up like this. She must forget the nonessentials and focus her mind on Chad.

She was not through with him, after all. She had been so sure, that day weeks ago when Oliver came in with the newspaper and the name of Johnson leaped out at her. Yes. She had believed the myth of Chad's death just as, earlier, she had come to believe the lies from which the myth had sprung; and to her the shattering of it was as great a shock as to the townful of people she had deluded. Greater: there was no dupe like a self-made one.

"No more dead than I am," Erna had said, and Erna was unmistakably alive, a living, breathing, hating presence. The break between them was open now; surely, after today's scene in the basement, she would lose no time in spreading the word. She may already have done so. The whole town may have been laughing at Dee behind her back all this time, pretending to sympathize with her over Chad's death while they were secretly enjoying the spectacle she was making of herself.

Her stomach churned at the thought. Her hands went clammy with cold sweat.

It couldn't be, it couldn't be. One among her circle of friends would have been careless enough, or kind enough, to betray the knowledge they shared. Or Oliver. He could never in the wide world have kept such a thing from her. Wouldn't, even if he could.

But Mr. Fly knew. Erna must have told him. (His attempt to present himself as the eavesdropper was of course not to be taken seriously; Dee dismissed it as a typical Mr. Fly gesture. Poor, misguided, chivalrous fellow.) He came as close to being a friend of Erna's as anybody in Rushford: the logical one for her to tell. But he was also a friend of Dee's, so if Erna had kept her mouth shut until now it must be thanks to Mr. Fly. "You promised!" he had cried when he came charging out of the corner. Too late to stop her, though. By then nothing could have stopped her. And nothing would, from here on in. Nothing short of—

The bell jangled and Peggy Bascomb bounced in, fresh from the beauty parlor, smelling of hair spray. "Is it too light, do you think? If it's too light, Howard's going to have a fit ... Dee! What's the matter? You look like death warmed over."

Was it that bad? Over the love seat hung an oval, gilt-framed mirror; she turned to it and saw a face gray as cement, heavy-jawed and dull-eyed. That bad. Worse when she tried to smile.

"I've had sort of a jolt, Peggy. Though why I never realized it before this—Well, I didn't. It simply never occurred to me that she hated me."

"Who? What are you talking about?"

"Erna. She does, she really hates me. You knew it, I expect. Probably everybody did. Everybody except me."

"Erna hates you?" Peggy was staring at her in what certainly looked like genuine astonishment. "Listen, Dee, you'd better sit down. Here. Let's sit down a minute. Try to relax, dear. Try to pull yourself together. What makes you think Erna hates you?"

"The things she said. Oh Peggy, the terrible things. About Chad and me." They were sitting side by side, Dee with her hands over her eyes; through her fingers she stole a glance at Peggy's face. It showed nothing different: open surprise and concern. And her arm around Dee's shoulder maintained its steady, friendly clasp, neither tightening nor slackening. "I can't tell you. It's too ..."

"Sh. Never mind. Whatever it was, you mustn't let it get you down. You've been so brave about Chad, bearing up the way you have, you can't give in now just because Erna—I must say, I wouldn't have believed she could be so mean. And after all you've done for her and Ollie. Why on earth should she hate you?"

"She's never liked it here in Rushford. Never fit in, somehow."

"Well, but that's not your fault!"

"According to her it is," said Dee. She let her hands fall to her lap. Her voice was calm now, and grave. "It was because of me, because I got sick, that they came here in the first place. Apparently she's always held that against me. And now she blames me because Oliver's not completely sold on moving back west the way she and her family want him to. Can you imagine? She claims I'm trying to talk him into staying here. Everything's my fault, according to her. Everything."

"I don't understand it. You've always gotten along so well together. Not that you had a great deal in common, of course, but still ... To think that all the time she's been harboring this grudge, rankling away inside and hiding it, that's the thing, never giving the slightest indication of how she really felt. It's scarey, Dee."

"I thought maybe it was just me," said Dee. "That it was obvious to everybody but me."

"I mean really scarey. Erna of all people. She seems like such a simple soul, you know. Not too sharp, but goodhearted. Good Lord, Dee, if she's really gone around the bend she could be dangerous!"

"Oh now, Peggy, I didn't say around the bend ... I admit it shook me up, the way she lit into me, some of the things she said. But who knows, maybe it was something I said that set her off, without meaning to, of course. Everybody has frustrations. She was probably just taking hers out on me. I expect she'll be all right, once she gets away from Rushford, back with her own people."

"The sooner the better, if you ask me."

"Yes, I'll be just as glad myself. Poor Oliver, I'm not at all sure it's a wise move for him as far as business is concerned, but in view of Erna's attitude I don't see what else he can do. After what happened today, I realize there's nothing I can do for either of them. If Erna really is on the ragged edge, I'll only make matters worse. She's Oliver's wife, his problem. He's got to work it out for himself. I only hope he can."

"She's a problem, all right. The part that gets me is Chad, starting in on you about Chad." Peggy's eyes took on an added gleam: sympathy plus curiosity.

"Forget I mentioned it. That's what I'm going to try to do," said Dee decisively. "Forget it. Put it out of my mind. She was beside herself. She didn't know what she was saying." She stood up and smoothed her hair. "I'm going to put the whole thing out of my mind and get busy sorting that batch of silverware I bought the other day. I have a feeling it was a mistake. Might as well find out for sure."

"All right. I'll be on my way." At the door she paused. "I can stay, if you want me to, Dee. All you have to do is say the word. I mean, if you—"

"No, really, I'll be all right now. It's done me good to talk to you. Bless you for stopping in. Just what I needed. I'm better now. Much better." She added, out of gratitude, "Your hair's just right, dear. Not a bit too light."

Once more alone, she took another look at herself in the mirror. Yes, better. The talk with Peggy had at least reassured her as to whether or not the story of Chad's non-death was already going the rounds. One way or another it would have reached Peggy's ears, if only because she was one of Dee's closest friends. Quite apart from the fact that she drew gossip to her like a magnet. But an actress she was not; she couldn't have been pretending in the scene of a moment ago. At some point there would have been a false note, a betraying gesture or word, and Dee had been watching, she wouldn't have missed it.

Strange as it seemed, Erna must have kept her mouth shut. So far. Not for much longer, though, and when she did start talking ...

Well, Peggy herself had come up with the notion—and with very little guidance from Dee—that Erna must be halfway around the bend. Possibly dangerous. Certainly not to be believed.

It was something on the plus side. But it was not enough to balance Peggy's curiosity. Now that it was aroused, she would find a way of satisfying it, no matter what. Might even seek Erna out and ask her what she had said about Chad. And though she was predisposed not to believe it, she would make it her business to check just in case, would track Chad down—it wasn't as though he was hiding—and find out for herself.

Chad's name shouldn't have been mentioned, then? But that would have meant giving up even the slight, stopgap advantage of discrediting Erna in advance. It was all Dee had in the way of an advantage. And it was not enough. Once Erna started talking nothing would be enough. The whole town would know that Dee had lied about Chad, and why. She would be a laughingstock, a figure of ridicule, scorn, pity. She could hear them: Not dead at all, never left New York. Seems they had a fight and he walked out on her, poor thing, she made it all up, halfway believed it herself.

If in addition Erna had overheard the climax of that last quarrel with Chad ... For a precarious moment it threatened to surge up from the depths of Dee's memory like some prehistoric monster heaving to the surface, refusing to stay buried in the slime where it belonged. She fought it down, her hands clamped on the back of the love seat, her forehead cold with sweat, her ears ready to burst from the throbbing, shattering roar that was part of what she must not remember. The background part. Not Chad's voice; he had stood close to her, speaking with deathly quietness. Yet sound and fury had filled her living room, climbing up and up while Chad spoke the unspeakable, receding into the distance when he was through. After the rip of violence, the hush; and then her hand lashing out against his face.

A motorcycle, she thought. That's what it was, the kid next door and his motorcycle; and with this triumph of recollection the crisis was past, she had the monster once more under control. There was further relief in the certainty—well then, the near-certainty—that Erna could not have overheard the entire quarrel. Surely, surely, the motorcycle had drowned out Chad's voice at the end.

But again it was not enough. It would not stop Erna from telling what she knew. She must be stopped, and quickly; before she stripped Dee of everything that made life worth living. The line had been crossed today, down there in the basement. Mr. Fly—who knew too, but who did not hate Dee—could no longer help her. It was a miracle that he had managed to keep Erna quiet this long. Today's open flare of hostility marked the end of the miracle.

There was only one way to stop Erna. With a peculiar, profound feeling, almost like release, Dee sat down at her desk and bent her mind to what she must do.

THIRTEEN

In the afternoon Erna set to and cleaned house. It was either that or get drunk; she knew it and governed herself accordingly. And at least no one could accuse her of slovenliness; she would be leaving the place spick-and-span—for Ollie, if he decided to stay on by himself, for Dee and her next tenants if he didn't.

What really counted, though, was that good hard work kept her mind off things that didn't bear thinking about. Other things besides Ollie, and God knows she had worn herself to a frazzle in the last few days, worrying over which way he was going to jump, and over when, if ever, the spell of wintry silence that prevailed between them was going to break. (It was his turn. She had already spoken her piece. Couldn't back out now even if she wanted to. Which she didn't. Besides, he had hit her.)

But the quarrel with Dee was different. It made her ashamed of herself. In spite of the cracks Dee had taken at her—and the sting of them would never be forgotten or forgiven—she still had no business blurting out the stuff about Chad when she had promised not to. She had broken her word to Mr. Fly out of pure meanness, just to get even with Dee, without giving one thought to what damage she might be doing him.

None, as it turned out, but she hadn't foreseen that Dee was going to pick her as eavesdropper and tattletale. She wasn't going to change her mind, either; Mr. Fly could talk himself blue in the face for all the difference it would make to Dee. "How you must hate me," she had said ...

Damn right I do, thought Erna, wringing out her mop. Or did, for a while there. But no more than you hate me. Not as much. You didn't mention that part of it. You've got a way of turning things around to suit yourself.

That was another thing. The quarrel with Dee had left her with a sense of something basically out of kilter, something turned inside out or upside down. But what? What? She had almost grasped it, down there in the basement, only then it had slipped away from her, lost along with her temper and what little reasoning power she possessed.

Dee's wits were so much quicker and sharper; often before she had had this befuddling effect on Erna. Often before had made her feel like some big dumb animal lumbering along ten steps behind. All the same, today was different. Shame; and a deeper confusion, an uneasiness that now and then congealed into icicle stabs of fear. Real fear, even though it had no name, no focus or shape. There. She felt it again, a sudden, mindless shiver. Though why she should be afraid, or what she should be afraid of ...

It beats me, she thought, and got back to her scrubbing. Whatever it is, I'll be out of it in less than a week. Out of Rushford and the whole sorry mess. Meanwhile, thank God for an apartment to clean and dinner to cook.

Not that they either of them had much appetite these days. Ollie had never been a big eater; now all he did was pick at his food. Erna herself wasn't much better. Nothing tasted very good, somehow. Nevertheless, dinner to cook.

She was at the stove, starting the stew, when she heard his footsteps on the stairs. Early; it was only four thirty. Out of the corner of her eye she saw him open the door and come inside. "Hello," she said, without turning around.

"Hello," he said from the door.

And that would about wind up the evening's conversation. He might ask her to pass the salt at the dinner table. She might inquire if he wanted more coffee. If he didn't go back to the shop after dinner, they would sit in the living room, their silent wilderness made all the more desolate by the yackety-yak of television. Then they would go to bed and lie tense as tightrope walkers, immobilized by the dread of inadvertently touching each other.

This was what they had come to. This was the way they lived nowadays. If anybody could call it living.

She did not hear him move away from the door. But she sensed his nearness, even before she felt the stealthy fumbling at her apron strings and the warmth of his breath against the back of her neck. She stood motionless, giving no outward sign; inside, her blood was bounding. Then, as her apron dropped to the floor, she let the stew spoon clatter out of her hand and turned. There was his narrow, urgent face, his hand on her breast, the blessed, living heat of him. The silence broke without words: she drew his dark head down into its place in the hollow of her neck, and who knew whether the half-sob she heard was her own or Ollie's or theirs together?

They stumbled through the living room and fell onto the bed like survivors of a shipwreck making for the shore, the beautiful, longed-for, remembered shore. Yes, it was like that, like paradise regained, all the more precious for having been lost.

In due time Erna opened her eyes and saw, with a faint pang of surprise, the pine branches swaying stiffly outside the window. Somehow she had expected the cottonwoods of home, the sky and wind of that other place, that other summer. So long ago, yet she felt almost like a girl again, and Ollie's face in the dusk looked touchingly young, all the anxious lines smoothed away as if by magic. An old married couple like us, she thought, and gave a purring little laugh.

He stirred, smiled. And sniffed. From the kitchen there was wafted the unmistakable smell of something burning.

"Oh Lord," she murmured. "The stew."

Ollie heaved himself up off the bed. "I'll see to it," he said, and she let him, she just lay there too comfortable to move, with the breeze ruffling in across her bare thighs and the shadows shifting on the ceiling and the delicious drowsiness creeping over her.

After quite a while—she was beginning to feel a little guilty, but not enough to help—he came padding back with a loaded tray. "Burnt to a crisp," he reported cheerfully. "I brought us a picnic."

Propped against the pillows, they wolfed the sandwiches and gulped the cold foaming beer. Nothing had ever tasted better. Afterwards they lay quietly, snuggled together like cats, whispering now and then about nothing. Twilight came on, cool and limpid; beyond the pine branches the sky was watermelon pink.

The tap on the door brought Erna out of a light doze. Dee's tap, her signal, louder than usual, as if it had been repeated more than once. Ollie heard it too. "I left the light on in the kitchen," he said under his breath. "I'll have to—"

"Don't let her in." Erna, stricken by a Dee's-eye view of things, reared up in alarm. The reek of burnt stew in the kitchen (and Ollie was not a tidy sandwich-maker); the trail of discarded clothing that must be strewn through the living room; the beer bottles and rumpled bedclothes and Erna without a stitch on. Not that Dee was likely to get as far as the bedroom, but supposing she did. Squalor beyond her wildest dreams. "Make some excuse."

"Sure. Okay."

Off he went; she draped the bedspread around her and listened. Dee's voice was unintelligible; Ollie's rang out heartily. "I'm catching a cold or something. Folded up early ... No, not really asleep yet ... Erna's in the shower ... Yeah, aspirin. Don't worry. I'll be all right tomorrow. See you then ..."

Back in the bedroom, he said, "Well, it was all I could think of. What the hell, as long as it worked."

"What did she want?"

He shrugged. "I'll have a talk with her tomorrow. After we've decided just when we're leaving and so on."

"We?" she whispered. "You're not staying, then?"

"Without you? You know me better than that." He sat down on the edge of the bed and settled cozily against the peak of her drawn-up knees. Trapped? If Dee was right, it didn't seem to worry Ollie. Maybe he didn't realize. And Erna might be in the same fix; trapped along with him, and too happy to care.

Because she hadn't known, any more than she had known, nineteen years ago, that he was not going to drive away in his jalopy and leave her without a backward glance. She hadn't held back then on account of the uncertainty. Or this afternoon, either. That was why pine trees instead of cottonwoods had surprised her, because all the rest was so much the same.

"Unless, of course," he added, smiling, "you don't want me to go with you."

Not want him? Ollie, oh Ollie. She drew her hand down the long curve of his jaw. The miracle repeated: he had not gone away and left her then; he was not going to let her leave without him now. The sense of her own luck swept over her in a great, breath-taking wave. Whereas Dee, poor woman ...

If she chose to lie about Chad, that was her business. She had a right to whatever cold comfort she could get out of saving her pride. Look at it one way, she wasn't even lying.

Chad was as lost to her as though he had literally died. Why should Erna—rich, lucky Erna—strip her of what little she had left?

No reason. She would never tell anyone, not even Ollie. If he heard about the quarrel at all, it would be from Dee herself, as much or as little as she wanted him to hear. Let her twist it around to her heart's content.

Again Erna felt the flick of intuition, something basically out of kilter. And again the little shiver.

But here was Ollie, full of his plans for winding up things in Rushford, swinging a loan, whether to sell their furniture or move it …

She pulled the bedspread closer around them both. Poor Dee, she thought luxuriously, poor poor Dee.

FOURTEEN

One of Mr. Fly's problems was that he had no telephone to call his own, either in his room or at school. Yesterday afternoon he had used the one in the principal's office—recklessly; aware that somebody, including the principal, might stroll in at any moment. Nothing of the sort had happened, thank God, but Chad's office had reported him out for the rest of the day, was there any message. None, thank you. No point in it, no number where Chad could reach him. Dee's phone, which he had used on special occasions in the past, was of course out of the question this time, either for incoming or outgoing calls. During the evening he had tried Chad's home number several times, from the phone booth in the drugstore, but without success. The drugstore closed at ten o'clock.

And opened at eight thirty. Mr. Fly, jumpy after a restless night, was there at eight thirty-one, ready with his assortment of change and the number written on a slip of paper in case of a lapse of memory. Once the clickings and whirrings were over, he waited, sweating slightly and counting the rings. Seven. He was beginning to lose hope when Chad's voice came on, hurried sounding.

"Chad? I hope I didn't wake you."

"No, no. Just going out the door. Heard the phone and came back. Who is it?"

Mr. Fly identified himself and began his prepared speech. "I attempted to reach you several times yesterday—"

"What's the matter? What's happened? Is Dee all right?"

"Yes. That is, I think so. I haven't seen her this morning. Not since early yesterday afternoon, in fact. I thought it best to call you in view of the unfortunate situation which arose at that time."

"Please," said Chad.

"Yes. The fact of the matter is that she and Erna became embroiled in a disagreement in my presence, as it happened, through circumstances beyond my—"

"You mean they had a fight. And Erna told her about me."

"Yes," said Mr. Fly, jarred into brevity for once in his life.

"Oh God." After quite a long silence Chad added heavily, "It figures. Go on. Who else has she told?"

"No one as far as I know. Possibly Ollie. My own feeling is that there is little cause for concern on that score. The only reason I called you is that you asked me to keep you informed of any untoward developments. In spite of her indiscretion yesterday, I don't believe Erna has any intention of circularizing what she knows."

"Why not, if she blurted it out to Dee?"

"There was a certain amount of provocation," said Mr. Fly delicately. "We all lose control of our tempers on occasion, say and do things we later regret. That's quite a different matter from deliberate, sustained malice."

"I suppose so ... You haven't told me yet what started them off."

"To the best of my recollection, it began with the trunk, Erna's trunk. Did I mention she's definitely leaving?"

"She's not!" It was like an explosion in Mr. Fly's ear. At the same moment the operator broke in, requesting more money; the rattling of coins mingled with Chad's voice, sharp with anxiety: "Ollie? Ollie's leaving too?"

"There seemed to be some question about that. In Erna's mind, that is. Dee was apparently taking it for granted that if Erna goes he will too."

"Of course he will. She's got him by the balls," said Chad. Seemed to say. Mr. Fly preferred to think he had misunderstood. "Erna's not just bluffing, by any chance?"

"No. She's determined to go, even if it means leaving Ollie. Rightly or wrongly, she blames Dee for trying to dissuade him from going. Very bitter. One thing led to another, until finally—"

"Okay, okay. I get the picture. It's one hell of a mess."

"Personally," said Mr. Fly, "I take a less pessimistic view. I have greater faith in Erna than you seem to have. She'll hold her tongue from now on, I'm convinced of it. Quite apart from the fact that she'll be leaving Rushford soon, anyway. So I can't see that any great harm has been done. On the contrary, this quarrel may turn out to be of positive value to both her and Dee. There's something to be said for clearing the air."

Chad groaned. No other word for it. Then he said wearily, "Never mind. The question is, what to do, what to do about Dee ... You haven't seen her yet today, you said. And it's not absolutely final about Ollie. If, by some miracle—Are you going to be around tonight? Somewhere where I can call you?"

"That's the difficulty, you see. Unfortunately, I don't have access to a telephone of my own. I'll be glad to call you again if you want me to."

"I'm not sure where I'll be. No, that won't work. How about Erna's phone? She already knows about me, anyway. If you could arrange to be up in her apartment, I could call you there, say about seven thirty. How about it?"

"I don't see why not." Mr. Fly's imagination caught fire. "If someone else is there and I can't talk freely, I'll say Wrong Number. That will be your signal to tell me where you are, so I can call you back as soon as I can excuse myself and get down here to the drugstore."

"Good. Fine. About seven thirty, then. Meanwhile, of course, mum's the word with Dee. I appreciate this, Mr. Fly. Thanks a lot."

"A pleasure," said Mr. Fly truthfully. He set off springily for home. His summer school classes did not start until ten today, so there would be time to see Erna now and tell her about the telephone rendezvous scheduled for this evening. His interview with Dee would probably have to wait until later in the day; perhaps after lunch he could stop in at her shop for a little chat. A perfectly natural gesture on his part, if only because she was still laboring under the mistaken impression that Erna, not he, had overheard her final quarrel with Chad, and it was his duty to set the matter straight. Now, of course, he had the added responsibility of observing her state of mind and reporting back to Chad.

A pleasure indeed. Even more so if he might prove to be instrumental, however indirectly, in bringing about a reconciliation. And why not? Chad had not given him much opportunity this morning; wistfully he remembered some of the phrases he had hoped to work into the conversation. But surely it was a good sign, that Chad should show so much concern for Dee. That had been his first thought: "Is Dee all right?" Yes, thought Mr. Fly, it augured well. You never knew. Anything could happen.

Erna cheered him still more. Just the sight of her face, when a few minutes later she opened her door to his tap. He was prepared for depression, self-reproach, shame over yesterday's scene with Dee. Instead: "Erna, you look positively blooming," he exclaimed in honest surprise. "Radiant as a bride!"

She gave him a rather embarrassed smile and went over to the sink to set down the burnt-out pan she had been scouring. "Time for a cup of coffee before you go to school? It's all ready." She poured them each a cup, and her face broke into a different, open, beaming smile. "I ought to look good this morning. That's how I feel. Why not? We're going home, Ollie and me."

"He's decided! He's going too! There now. I knew he would. No question about it in my mind." Or in Dee's, he might have added. And very little in Chad's.

"Well, believe me, there was in mine. I haven't been worth shooting these last few days. But it's all settled now. He called Gus long distance last night, that's my brother, Gus, told him to go ahead from that end, and he was going to the bank first thing this morning to see about a loan. Oh, Mr. Fly, the relief, I can't tell you, I just can't tell you!"

"How's Dee taking it?"

"That's the other thing. Ollie went down to talk to her right after breakfast—after all, the least he could do—and she was sweet as pie about everything. Told him she'd thought it over and decided it was a pretty good idea, wished us luck and so on. She even offered to go to the bank with him if he wanted her to. He didn't, but all the same. Couldn't have been nicer, he said. And after the way I acted yesterday. Makes me feel like two cents, more so than I did before, I mean. Well, at least she knows I didn't blab all that stuff about Chad to Ollie. I didn't tell him anything about the fight, and neither did she. I know Ollie, he couldn't have kept it from me if she had."

"It's best that way," said Mr. Fly. "Least said soonest mended."

"You're telling me! What a blabbermouth! I could kick myself every time I think of it, breaking my word to you like that. Not to mention what I did to Dee. I wouldn't blame you if you never forgave me, either of you."

"If I remember correctly, Dee made some remarks she's undoubtedly regretting too. Though in a way it may be healthier to get these things out in the open. As I said to Chad this morning—"

"Chad? You talked to Chad?"

It was a thoroughly gratifying response, aside from the fact that it provided Mr. Fly with the opening he had been looking for. He launched at once into the details of his conversation with Chad, and Erna listened with flattering attention. She did not interrupt until he got to the part about using her phone. "I hope you don't mind my taking the liberty ..."

"Well, of course not. It'll work out fine, because Ollie won't be here. He wants to get everything finished up at the shop, so he's not coming home for dinner, I don't expect him before ten."

"Good," said Mr. Fly, though he felt a pang of regret that his wrong-number gambit would not be necessary. "In the meantime I'll make it a point to see Dee. As I would have done, anyway, to try to disabuse her of the idea that you eavesdropped on her and Chad."

"You don't have to on my account. I don't care if she thinks it was me." She stirred her coffee thoughtfully. "It does sound like Chad's still got her on his mind. Wonder what would happen if he ever got up the nerve to call her himself? She'd probably just hang up on him. Whatever that last scrap of theirs was about, it must have been a dilly. But that doesn't necessarily mean they'll never make it up. Like Ollie and me."

"I consider it a distinct possibility," stated Mr. Fly. "And may I add that nothing could please me more. For the present, however, I have no choice but to abide by Chad's wishes. He made it quite clear that he does not want Dee to know we have been in communication, and I have no intention of—"

"Oh, me neither," said Erna. "Don't worry, I've learned my lesson."

She had, too, he thought during his ten-minute walk to school. In addition to which, she was too absorbed in her own happiness to bother about anything else. It was misery, more than spite, that had driven her to yesterday's outburst. Now that her fondest dreams were coming true, she could be trusted to do no more damage. Besides, she and Dee were accustomed to keeping their distance; in all likelihood they would each be inclined to avoid the other's company today.

It turned out that he was wrong about the latter premise, as he learned when he dropped in at Dee's shop after lunch. She was in the middle of a telephone conversation with Erna, and though Mr. Fly hovered tactfully near the door he could not help hearing what she was saying. This was clearly all right with her; she waved him in cordially, meanwhile making no effort to lower her voice. "... owe you an apology, too, Erna, I was just as much of a stinker ... As long as Oliver will be working late tonight, why don't we have a drink together? ... No, you come downstairs, you're probably all at sixes and sevens, what with the packing ... Fine, any time between five and five thirty, I'll see you then."

She hung up, and Mr. Fly said, "I hope I'm not intruding. I was just passing by, and it occurred to me you might not be too busy for a few minutes' conversation. You're looking very chic, as usual."

What a pleasure it was to pay compliments, especially, as in this case, sincere ones! Dee's dress today was cornflower blue, a good color with her eyes; nubbly material, with a little stand-up Chinese kind of collar. No jewelry except for the silver bracelet Chad had given her for Christmas; sleek chignon; the right amount of the right shade of lipstick. Yes, very chic. But Chad would be expecting more tonight than a superficial report on her costume. It was her state of mind that concerned him. Conscientiously Mr. Fly applied himself to his role of shrewd observer-in-depth.

And decided that a different compliment—"You're looking very well," for instance—would have meant stretching sincerity a bit too far. It wasn't a matter of trembling hands or jittery gestures. It wasn't even the heavy, drooping effect that marred her face when she was angry or disturbed. What, then? Tension in the line of her neck, a drawn look around her eyes, as if she hadn't slept well—but surely that was understandable, after yesterday's stormy episode. Mr. Fly wondered if he might not be seeing signs simply because he was on the lookout for them.

"Won't you sit down?" said Dee. "No, I'm not busy, I'm just sitting here waiting for customers. It's been a slow day so far. Probably just as well, considering the shape I'm in."

"You're not feeling well?"

"Would you be, if you'd behaved as badly as I did yesterday? Disgraceful. And in front of you, too. That makes it even worse. I suppose it's no use telling you I'm sorry, but—"

"Please. These things happen. My own view is that they're not entirely without value. Something to be said for clearing the air."

She gave him a strange, searching look; he remembered the groan that had been Chad's reaction to this sentiment. "If it's any consolation to you," he went on, "Erna's not proud of herself, either."

"I know. I was just talking to her. She was quite decent about it, really."

"I'm sure she was. Very decent." Here was his opportunity: he proceeded at once with the unabridged explanation which would at least clear Erna of eavesdropping and tattling. But Dee broke in when he was barely past the preamble.

"It doesn't matter. I don't hold it against either of you, whoever did what. If you don't mind, Mr. Fly, could we just skip it? The whole thing's too, too embarrassing ..." After a moment's pause, she surprised him— and raised his flagging hopes—by asking, very low and fast, "Which of you saw Chad?"

"I did, and—" His mind swirled with the possibilities. Which was the telling phrase, the magic word that would convince her of Chad's undiminished love and open the way to reconciliation? In the end the best he could stammer out was, "And he had only the kindest of words for you, Dee. I assure you, only the kindest."

"Thank you," she said, and for an instant it seemed that her face might come to life. (He realized now that that was the sign he had not been able to put his finger on at first: the empty, dead look in her eyes.) But then the door bell jangled. In came a talkative woman looking for a candlestick to match the one that had been handed down to her from her great-grandmother. There was nothing for Mr. Fly to do but depart.

He walked back to the schoolhouse, deep in a mental rehearsal of the report he would make to Chad this evening. The look in Dee's eye must be mentioned, of course. But not exaggerated. Already its disturbing quality was beginning to lose ground, in Mr. Fly's incurably sanguine mind, to more promising observations. She had seemed, on the whole, her usual calm and collected self. Had asked after Chad; without the customer's interruption, might well have gone on to reveal more, much more. Then there was her willingness, and Erna's, to forgive and forget. That too was a good omen.

Yes indeed, thought Mr. Fly, his account to Chad would show more items on the credit side than the debit. On the whole, on sober second thought, the outlook was far from discouraging. Quite the contrary, in fact. Quite the contrary.

FIFTEEN

"I'd just as soon have a beer," said Erna, who had obviously, and predictably, fortified herself with more than one in advance. She had appeared on the dot of five fifteen, dressed in one of her pink, loving-hands jobs, with the tracks of the dusting powder puff on her neck and a film of nervous sweat on her upper lip.

"Oh, but I made Manhattans! Especially for you," said Dee. "I thought you liked them. Whatever you prefer, of course."

And on second thought a Manhattan was of course what Erna preferred. She sat with her thick ankles genteelly crossed, taking dainty sips and smiling anxiously every time her eyes met Dee's. The conversation limped at first. Nice weather they had been having. Marilyn's last letter: she was fine, fine and dandy, having a ball. The new motel that was going up west of the junction.

But, having sipped her way through half a drink, Erna struck off boldly for deeper waters. "I'm real glad you called me today, Dee. I'd hate for us to wind up on the outs. Over nothing, too. Because you don't need to worry about me blabbing what's your business. So help me, I'll never breathe a word." She raised a solemn, meaty hand.

"I know you won't," Dee assured her. "As soon as I calmed down and thought it over, I knew you wouldn't."

Give Erna credit, she hadn't told Oliver. Yet. Whatever they had been doing last night that kept them from opening the door to Dee, talking wasn't it. Rage filled her at the memory of that conversation with Oliver, through the door that remained shut between them. Felt a cold coming on, did he, and Erna was in the shower. The humiliation of it, the consuming rage. To be treated like that, as if she were a nuisance, a nosey in-law pushing in where she wasn't wanted ...

Don't think about it. Blot it out. Blot it out.

This morning when she inquired solicitously about Oliver's cold, he had looked at first startled and then shamefaced. No talent for deception. She had seen at once that he didn't know about Chad, or even about the quarrel between her and Erna.

Of course it was just a question of time before Erna forgot her good intentions and spilled the whole story not only to Oliver but to everybody in town. Look at the way she had spouted it out yesterday, never mind her promise to Mr. Fly and no doubt to herself as well. That was proof, if any were needed, that she could no more keep a secret than a sieve could hold water. Sooner or later it was sure to happen again. Under the pressure of circumstances—an extra beer, the right question asked by the right person, a moment of pique, a childish bid for attention—Erna could be counted on to give way. She operated on impulse, not calculation; an animal kind of instinct, not controlled logic.

Just a question of time; and time was not unmanageable, it could be kept on Dee's side.

"You've been awfully good to us," Erna was going on earnestly. "I'm not going to forget it, and neither is Ollie. He thinks the world of you. Always has." She was down to the last sip, and the cherry, which she disposed of juicily. "Always will. No, Dee, you just don't forget things like that in a hurry. The apartment, and when Marilyn had her mastoid. Things like that. You just don't forget."

"It's worked the other way too, you know. And I've been glad to do whatever I could. After all, you're my family, you and Oliver. All the family I've got." The corn is green, thought Dee. But that was how Erna liked it. "I'm ready for a refill," she added, and stood up. "How about you?"

"Oh, well. Might as well be drunk as the way I am," said Erna, handing over her glass. "There's nothing like a Manhattan to hit the spot."

It was the second one that was going to do that, according to Dee's reckoning. Her bottle of sleeping capsules stood ready and waiting in the kitchen. Two of them dissolved in Erna's second Manhattan ought to be a sufficiency, in view of the beer foundation provided by Erna herself, and her lack of resistance to any drug more powerful than aspirin. She didn't believe in taking pills; seemed to consider them in some obscure way immoral.

This time Dee put the cocktail shaker on the tray along with the two full glasses. (Two cherries in Erna's.) The dividend system would help things along: no clear line of demarcation between the end of one drink and the beginning of the next.

Back in the living room she said cheerily, "Here we are. Happy days."

"Happy, happy days," echoed Erna. Her eyes misted with easy, sentimental tears. "I know they will be for me and Ollie. I just hope—I just wish—Maybe I'm talking out of turn again but it seems like such a shame for you and Chad to break up. I mean, a couple like you, just made for each other. I thought sure nothing was going to go wrong this time."

Oh, the pain of it, thought Dee, alas and alack. Except that the pain of it was suddenly real, so real that for a humiliating moment she could almost have wept as muzzily as Erna. The piercing sorrow, the yearning for what she had lost. Chad, oh Chad ... "Well, it did go wrong," she said curtly. "As you pointed out yesterday, Chad walked out on me."

"Yesterday," Erna mumbled. Emboldened by more of her Manhattan, she pressed on. "Never mind he walked out on you. So what? I bet all you'd have to do is say the word and he'd be back. He as good as said so to Mr. Fly. Said if he thought he stood half a chance he'd have called you long ago."

"I know all about what he said to Mr. Fly." She didn't, though; thanks to the candlestick woman. Yes, thanks. Because what was the use of dwelling on the impossible? Why was she letting Erna maunder on like this? As if Chad's calling her would have made things right! "I'm afraid it's not quite as simple as you and Mr. Fly seem to think."

"Maybe it is and maybe it isn't." Erna leaned forward, flushed and intent. Gone was the shyness that usually clamped down on her in Dee's presence. Gone too the ladylike airs she had put on at first. Now she sat with her knees comfortably spread; as for the sips, they had turned into something very close to gulps. "If you mean I don't know what it was came between you and Chad—"

She couldn't know. That much at least Dee had been spared. Stupid though Erna was, she wouldn't be making a pitch for reconciliation if she knew. Wouldn't even be here. And if she didn't know then neither did Mr. Fly. It was share and share alike with those two. No matter who had done the actual eavesdropping, there was thank God a gap in it. Be grateful for small favors, Dee told herself, meanwhile unobtrusively replenishing Erna's drink.

"—all right, I don't know. Thanks. Don't know and don't care. But I bet whatever it was it can be patched up. It's been my experience that these things pass, you may think they won't, but they do, they pass over. Like Ollie and me, oh, we've had our scraps too, don't think we haven't. But somehow in the end it passes. It all passes over." She illustrated with a large, vague gesture. "That's been my experience," she added, and sank back in her chair like a fighter on the ropes.

Dee sat straight and tense with the effort of holding down the wild, soaring impulse to laugh. She mustn't, she mustn't, if she got started she might not be able to stop. It would be like the excruciating fits of giggles that used to overtake her and Oliver in church when, one on either side of Papa, they could not resist the exchange of glances (Oliver's cross-eyed) that perpetuated their state of crisis. To this day church and giggles were inseparably united for her; and certainly Erna's contribution to the proceedings smacked of the mid-weekly prayer meeting. She had been testifying, Sister Erna. "Me and Ollie." "It's been my experience."

Not only testifying but handing out advice to the lovelorn, giving Dee, free of charge, the benefit of her superior wisdom. She was an authority, of course: the complete, successful woman who had snagged a husband for herself, never mind how, and hung on to him, ditto. In contrast to Dee with her history of abortive marriage and wrong choices right up to the final, galling failure with Chad. Oh yes, the implication was there, clear to Dee if not to Erna, and it was a scream, absolutely hilarious, she mustn't get started or she would laugh till she cried ...

Erna roused up and delivered still another clincher. "You think about it, Dee. You just think about it."

"I will. I am." It shouldn't be long now; Erna was having a little trouble focusing and her face had a numb look, as if she had suffered a slight stroke. Meanwhile, this conversational tack was as good a way to pass the time as any. Quite a fitting finale, in fact. "But I don't see exactly what else I can do. Are you suggesting that I get in touch with Chad? I don't even know where he is."

"Sure. Why not? What have you got to lose?"

"Nothing, I guess, but—"

"False pride. Where does it get you?" Erna fixed her with a glazed eye and heaved forward to connect—by divine guidance—with her glass. "Nowhere. That's where. Somebody's got to make the first move."

"I see what you mean." No more dividends, Dee decided; it wouldn't do for Erna to pass out down here. The sooner her thoughts turned toward home the better. "Are you sure you're all right, dear?"

"Fine. Why? Say the word, that's all. Say the word and he'll be back. Wanta bet?" She drained her glass, hiccupped, and added in a voice that was suddenly unslurred, sober-sounding, "It's the other way round. I haven't got it all figured out yet, but I do know that much. It's the other way round."

"What? What do you mean, the other way round?"

But the spark of lucidity had already flickered out. "Huh? Why do you keep interrupting? I don't think it's very nice, the way you keep interrupting ... Oh Jesus, I'm cross-eyed. How did I get this way? All of a sudden I feel so—I better lay down somewhere: I'll be all right if I can just lay down for a while. Oops. Sorry. Excuse me." She had surged to her feet without warning and crashed against the cocktail table; there was a shattering of glass and a thump as the shaker hit the rug.

Dee leaped and grabbed her just in time. For a moment she sagged, boneless and unmanageable as a mattress; then Dee got her propped against the chair back. "It's all right. I'll help you, you'll be more comfortable upstairs. Come on now, Erna, hang on to me and you can make it."

Apparently the sharpness of her tone got through. Erna shook her head groggily, drew a sobbing breath, and together they began the lurching, lumbering journey to the door. The worst stretch was crossing the hall; once they reached the stairs Erna had the banister to hang on to. All the same, she stalled a couple of times, just slumped like a broken-down horse until Dee cracked the vocal whip enough to get her going again. They met no one on the way. Not that it would have mattered if

any of the paying guests—there were three of them besides Mr. Fly—
had popped out to see what was going on. But none of them did, either
because they were not there or because they preferred to stay in their
rooms and listen.

Erna wheezed and panted and apologized. Dee shoved and cajoled and
bullied. Somehow or other they made it to the third floor apartment.
Through the kitchen, which smelled pleasantly of soap and coffee, and
into the living room, where the grandfather's clock was bonging out six
thirty and the curtains swelled inward in the evening breeze.

"Why don't you stretch out right here on the couch? Just take a little
nap and you'll be right as rain."

"Sorry. Excuse me." Erna stumbled obediently to the couch and collapsed on it.

But she had another unexpected spark of lucidity when Dee, having
closed the windows, paused beside her on her way back to the kitchen.
Erna lay like a felled tree, her pink dress twisted above her knees, her
arms flung up on either side of her head as if someone had her covered
with a gun. Then Dee saw that her eyes were open, and aware. "The
other way round," she said in the same clear-cut tone as before. "Don't
hate me, Dee. Please. You've got no call to hate me."

She shivered; and so, eerily, did Dee. For a macabre instant they were
united in terror. Seemed to be. Afterwards Dee put it down to nerves, a
trick of her own overwrought imagination.

Before she could answer—what was there to say?—Erna's eyes
dropped shut and her face lapsed back into numb vacancy. She did not
stir when Dee, on some obscure impulse, straightened her dress and
slipped the loafers from her broad peasant feet.

In the kitchen she did what she had planned to do, quickly and automatically, as if it were one of those routines too familiar to require con-
scious thought. Before she left she turned the catch on the door so that
it would lock behind her.

Then she went downstairs, not hurrying, not dawdling, and let herself into her quiet living room. Her hands, as she cleared up the wreck-
age of the coffee table, were steady as rocks. She felt peaceful and pu-
rified. And safe. At last and forever, safe.

SIXTEEN

With a practiced swoop, the waitress in Ye Olde Corner Tea Shoppe
delivered Mr. Fly's coffee and removed his chicken croquette plate.
"Going to Whatsis Club tonight, I suppose?" she observed chattily.

"Self-Culture," said Mr. Fly. "I'm afraid I'll have to forego tonight's meeting. A conflicting appointment. I may be able to drop in later, if my schedule permits."

"Uh huh. That's how it goes. Sure you won't change your mind about dessert? There's rice pudding."

There always was, and on occasion Mr. Fly had been hungry enough to eat it. "No, thank you," he said. "I'm a bit pressed for time."

This was not the literal truth, but he liked the sound of it. Now and then, while he was drinking his coffee, he glanced at his watch; promptly at seven he rose from the teetery little table with its quaint candlestick-type lamp and its vase of artificial flowers. The walk home would take no more than ten minutes. Another five to stop off in the bathroom and brush his dentures, and he would arrive at Erna's with a nice little margin of time before his telephone rendezvous. If Chad's call came punctually at seven thirty, he could count on reaching the Self-Culture Club meeting well before the discussion—Egyptian Art Treasures—was over.

For some reason his thoughts took on a faintly melancholy tinge as he trudged along the familiar tree-lined street. Dusk falling, lights going on in the houses, families gathering around the supper table. It was a lonesome time of day. He couldn't help remembering with what high hopes he had come to Rushford less than a year ago, what faith that this time he had found the right niche. Yet now, as so often before, he must pull up his roots, such as they were, and move on to another town, another job, another set of flimsy hopes. And he didn't know where, he didn't know where. No word so far from the consolidated school which was—admitting it, he felt a hollow pang, like hunger—his last and only chance as a teacher.

There were other professions, of course. Any number of them. Never too late. Besides, no news was good news. Always darkest before the dawn. And though Rushford had turned out to be a disappointment as far as his personal destiny was concerned, his presence here need not be without its effect on those who had befriended him. Erna, for one, was not going to forget him and the role he had played, however small, in making her dreams come true. If in addition he could contribute toward a reconciliation between Dee and Chad then he would undeniably have left his mark. In years to come they would remember, with gratitude, the name of Mr. Fly. "If it hadn't been for him we might never have gotten together again. He was only here the one winter, a quiet sort of man, a rolling stone, but we owe him more than tongue can tell."

Why shouldn't it be that way? Why shouldn't fate have drawn him to Rushford for the purpose of weaving him into the endless complexity of her pattern? For there was a pattern, Mr. Fly assured himself; obscure though it might seem at times, there had to be a pattern, in which even the most insignificant life had its use as a thread.

His flagging spirit lifted, like a sail catching the breeze. This time he would speak out plainly to Chad; in a few well chosen words he would state it as his considered opinion that Dee regretted no less than Chad himself the breaking off of their relationship and that all he needed to do to end this unhappy situation was to make whatever overture seemed most appropriate to him. The decision was Chad's: a letter, a telephone call, even an unannounced visit. Far be it from Mr. Fly to proffer unsolicited advice. He was simply reporting his impression of Dee's state of mind, as gleaned from firsthand observation.

He squared his shoulders and quickened his step in anticipation, no longer an outsider but a man assigned by fate to his own specific, unique place in the over-all scheme of things.

There was no answer to his tap on Erna's door. He waited and rapped again, more loudly but with the same result. Strange, he thought; she must be expecting him, she couldn't have misunderstood the time. True, he was a little early. Not that early, though. A bare ten minutes before the appointed hour of seven thirty.

Then he remembered, with a slight sinking sensation, that Dee had invited her to come down for a drink—"any time between five and five thirty." Could she still be downstairs, two hours and certainly more than two drinks later, unmindful of the passage of time and her previous commitment? The answer, unfortunately, was yes. Fond as he was of Erna, Mr. Fly could not deny that she was inclined at times toward overindulgence. If this was one of the times, she had put him in something of a predicament. To go after her and remind her of their arrangement would be to risk disclosure to Dee: he supposed he could invent some other excuse for breaking up the cocktail party, but Erna might be surprised, or shamed, or simply loose-tongued enough by now to let the truth slip out. On the other hand, to take no action at all might mean missing Chad's call and with it his big opportunity.

A predicament indeed. He did not grasp its full magnitude until he tried the door—the circumstances justified what would ordinarily be an unpardonable trespass—and found that for once Erna had locked it behind her. The discovery started him sweating. He had a painfully vivid mental image of himself standing here helpless while on the other side of the door the phone pealed time after unanswered time.

Unthinkable. After a frantic, futile moment of knocking and rattling the door knob, he calmed down and faced the fact that he had no choice but to go downstairs and get Erna. All right, if he had to, he had to. But let him at least go prepared with some excuse that would both convince Dee and, if God was good, keep Erna's tongue from running away with her. He leaned against the door and closed his eyes, the better to concentrate.

And into his consciousness there crept, instead of the inspiration he sought, a faint, unmistakable odor. He straightened. Stiffened. Sniffed. No, it was not his imagination; the wonder was that he had not noticed it until now.

He broke for the stairs and plunged down them like a load of logs loosed into a chute, to hit the front hall just as Dee was emerging from her living room. A last-minute grab at the newel post was all that saved him from colliding with her. He hung there, panting and incoherent. "Dee! Erna! Where is she? The door, I can't get in, you must have a key, quick ..."

She did not say a word. Stunned, perhaps. Even in his distraught state, he was struck by the look she gave him, a look compounded of despair, irony, even—though surely he was mistaken here—a bitter kind of amusement.

It had a sobering effect on him; he realized that he had omitted the crucial point. "Gas. I smelled gas." He added urgently, "Is she up there, Dee? Where is she?"

"I'll get the key." She laid the sweater she was carrying over her arm, and her purse, down on the hall table and turned back toward her living room door. "Let's not panic, Mr. Fly. I won't be a minute." She was composed, quick-moving, competent. None of Mr. Fly's wild waste of energy for her. No superfluous questions, no flustered gestures or gasps. Thank God for her cool head! Thank God he had caught her in time!

Here she was, back with the key in her hand. Up the stairs they went: Dee in the lead, moving with that enviable economy, Mr. Fly still breathless and stumbling.

"I'm afraid Erna had a little more to drink than she could handle," she explained crisply over her shoulder. "My fault, I suppose, for not realizing what a head start she had on beer. When she started falling apart I helped her upstairs and got her settled on the couch. It never occurred to me she wouldn't be all right as soon as she slept it off. Otherwise of course I wouldn't have left her alone. I simply didn't realize ... Was she expecting you?"

"I beg your pardon? Oh. She may have been. More or less. That is, she had suggested that I drop in for a cup of coffee this evening. Nothing definite, you know. Nothing special."

"I see. She didn't mention it to me."

They were at the top of the stairs by now. When Dee unlocked the door, the smell gushed out; undaunted, she moved swiftly to the stove and turned off the two open jets. She started toward the living room. And then, for the first time, she faltered. Her hands fluttered up to her throat; her eyes trembled shut. "Please," she whispered. "Would you—"

So it was Mr. Fly who took over in the living room. Anxiety lent him, for once in his life, a glassy kind of coordination; he surged past Dee, past the couch, on to the windows, which he flung open. Lit by the floor lamp, the room looked cozy and familiar. Erna lay stretched out on the couch, peaceful in her pink dress, arms curved above her head, one foot dangling over the edge. He bent over her, dizzy from the hammering of his heart. Her mouth was a little open. Did her breast rise and fall, or only seem to because he willed it to? Was it her pulse he felt, or only his own, pounding away in the fingers he pressed against her wrist?

At last he let out a croak of triumph and relief. "She's breathing! I can feel her pulse, she's alive …" He swiped clumsily at the tears that were running down his face.

"I'll call the hospital," said Dee, who still hovered like an uneasy ghost in the doorway. She drew a long breath, stiffened as if to attention, and jerked herself forward into the living room. By the time she reached the telephone, which stood on a little table opposite the couch, she was moving with her usual sureness and grace. And her voice, talking to the hospital, was once more brisk; her report on the situation admirably clear and concise.

"They're sending the ambulance," she told Mr. Fly when she had hung up. "Right away. There's nothing for us to do in the meantime, they'll take care of everything when they get her to the hospital. I told them—well, you heard me—about the drinks, and how long it's been. Not much more than an hour since I brought her up here. I thought she was out cold, but she must have roused up enough to turn on the gas after I left—"

"By mistake," Mr. Fly broke in passionately. "She couldn't have done it on purpose. She was so happy this morning. Radiant as a bride. She just got mixed up and made a mistake."

"Yes, of course it was a mistake." For a moment Dee's face took on that queer, baffling expression he had noticed before. A shadow of it, rather; gone almost before he recognized it. "She was on top of the world when I saw her too. We were having one of the best times we've ever had until all at once the drinks hit her. If she'd asked you for coffee, I suppose she had that on her mind. Came to enough to turn on the gas, but not to light it, and then forgot what she'd started and flopped back on the couch."

"Exactly. I'm sure that's how it was. Poor girl, poor girl." And indeed it was like Erna. Hospitable as she was, she would undoubtedly have offered him a cup of coffee while they waited for Chad's call. "I don't know why she should lock the door, but—"

"It wasn't even shut when I brought her up," said Dee quickly. "I just closed it behind me, never thinking the snap lock might be on. It so seldom is. Oliver," she added, and reached for the phone. "I should have called him before this. He can meet us at the hospital. I'll go with Erna in the ambulance."

Erna stirred, ever so slightly. Mr. Fly dropped to his knees beside her and prayed.

The ambulance got there just as Dee was hanging up the phone. There was nothing for Mr. Fly to do but stay out of the way while they transferred Erna to the stretcher and wangled it through the door. At the last minute he collected his wits enough to say to Dee, who was preparing to follow them downstairs, "Maybe you'll call me and let me know—? That is, if you don't mind my waiting here in reach of the phone?"

"Of course." The tenseness in her face softened into compassion. She patted his arm. "I'll call you the minute there's anything to tell. Or if you'd rather wait downstairs, I can call you on my phone."

"No, no, I'll stay here. Very kind of you. Thank you, but I'll stay here and—" He made one of his vague, disjointed gestures. "I can air the place out."

"Yes, you do that. That's a good idea. I'll call you here, then. Don't worry, I won't forget."

"I feel she's going to be all right. I just feel it, somehow. Don't you? After all, a young strong woman like Erna, and the gas couldn't have been on very long, probably not even an hour when I—Thank God I found her when I did!" It was a transfiguring thought, a vindication of his faith in fate and her pattern, never ended, only intermittently revealed. This might be why he had been brought to Rushford, that the cross-thread of his life should be the saving of Erna's.

Dee nodded gravely, as if she might be seeing much the same vision. "Yes," she said, "except for you, she wouldn't have had a chance. Strange, isn't it, so strange the way things work out ..."

She went down the stairs, straight-backed and proud.

He left the door to the hall open, to make the most of the breeze that blew through from the windows; already the smell of gas was fading. In the living room the only reminder of the crisis was Erna's slippers, which lay rather pathetically beside the couch, as if she had just kicked them off. He noticed, with astonishment, that it was only seven forty. Was it possible that a mere twenty minutes had passed since he tried the door and found it locked? Why, Chad's call was not a lost cause, after all! Mr. Fly, when he elected to wait here instead of beside Dee's phone, had been reacting automatically; if he had stopped to think he would have said that Chad's "about seven thirty" was long gone by.

Nothing of the sort. Even as he was thinking it, the phone rang. Chad sounded nervous: "Are you free to talk? I've been getting the busy signal for the last ten minutes. What's going on up there?"

Mr. Fly told him, with uncharacteristic brevity.

"Oh God," said Chad, and then came silence, grim and prolonged.

"Chad? Are you still there? Whatever you may think, I personally feel that there's every reason to hope. After all, Erna's a strong, healthy girl. And with everything to live for. That counts, too, you know. There are absolutely no grounds for supposing she would do such a thing intentionally—"

"Suicide, you mean? Erna? No, of course not. Did Dee—She's holding up all right?"

"Wonderful. Not that I'd expect Dee to lose her head, no matter what the emergency. But all the same, a true test of character. Believe me, Chad, she was nothing short of superb."

"Oh yes, I believe you," said Chad, but so sadly, so sadly that Mr. Fly's heart misgave him. "How come Erna and she were boozing it up together? After the fight they had yesterday, I shouldn't think they'd be speaking to each other."

"Oh, but that's all been smoothed over," Mr. Fly explained eagerly. "Again I give Dee full credit. It couldn't have been easy for her, but she took the first step toward conciliation. Not only accepted Erna's apology, but admitted that she too had been at fault. They're friends again. I assure you, no hard feelings on either side."

"I see," said Chad.

"Something else, if I may take the liberty. When I talked to her earlier today, Dee asked about you, Chad. I got the distinct impression that any overtures you may care to make would be welcome. I'm not suggesting anything, of course. I'm simply giving you my impression. It's up to you."

"I see," said Chad again.

"She'll be calling me about Erna. If you want me to—"

"No! For God's sake, don't tell her you've talked to me!"

"What I was about to say," said Mr. Fly with dignity, "was that if you want me to call you back after I hear from her I'll be glad to do so."

"I don't know where I'll be," said Chad. "Thanks, anyway." And with that he hung up.

SEVENTEEN

The nurse came out smiling. Tidings of great joy. "Nothing to worry about," she told Oliver, who had sprung from his chair, quivering like a fiddle string. "She can go home tomorrow. Probably won't even have a hangover, now that we've pumped her out. Well, maybe a little one, from the gas. But she didn't get enough of it to do her any real harm. Go on in, she's asking for you."

He didn't need any urging. Off he went, white with relief.

"Thank God," said Peggy Bascomb emotionally. She was there to dispense moral support. That was what she had said when Dee called her to explain—for she had been due at the Bascombs' this evening; Mr. Fly had caught her just in time. "I'll be right with you," Peggy had said. "At least I can give you a little moral support."

And it really was a kind of moral support to have Peggy there; it kept Dee on her mettle. She might have lapsed into carelessness with only Oliver, who was too distraught to notice what went on. No such margin for error with Peggy: she would have spotted the slightest false note, the smallest unguarded gesture. Not only that, but she gave Dee her cues. Now, for example, was clearly the moment for a convulsive clutch in response to Peggy's extended hand, an echo of her Thank God, if possible a rush of relieved tears ...

Dee settled for a sharply indrawn breath and an eloquent closing of her eyes. She had never been an easy weeper. Then, as Peggy seemed on the point of guiding her down the corridor toward Erna's room, she said, "I must call Mr. Fly first. Poor soul, he was so worried. I promised I'd let him know the first thing."

He gushed with joy and gratitude. "Home tomorrow, you say? She's all right, then, we caught her in time, nothing to worry about ... Wonderful, that's wonderful. You're sure there's nothing I can do for you? Anything at all, I'd be delighted ... Maybe I'll see you later then, after you get home, if you're not too ... Meanwhile, give Erna my best regards. And thank you, my dear, thank you for calling me. I can't tell you how much I appreciate your taking the trouble ..."

"No trouble at all," said Dee, truthfully. It was the only thing that held her together, this concentration on the minutiae, this deliberate ignoring of the woods for the trees. She had inched her way myopically and safely through the last two hours; if she risked a broad, sweeping view of tonight's happenings she might not survive them. Might freeze in her tracks, or, stricken with vertigo, might lose her precarious footing and plunge to disaster.

Meanwhile, Mr. Fly burbled on in happy innocence. The Fly in her ointment, she thought, and again she had to restrain the impulse to laugh. It didn't make any sense, but that was how he affected her—no resentment or vindictiveness, only a kind of helpless amusement at the idea of being undone by someone as absurd and pathetic and muddleheaded as Mr. Fly.

But the laughter was something else that must be saved for later. At the moment what faced her was the visit to Erna's bedside, which Peggy obviously expected of her and which therefore could not be ducked. Well then, get it over with.

What was she afraid of? That Erna would turn on her, wild-eyed and accusing? Even if she did—and the chances were all against it—no one would take her seriously. The babbling of semi-delirium. No, the dread that gripped Dee was irrational, and all the more powerful for being so; deep-rooted and primitive. She had felt it earlier, up in the apartment, at the prospect of walking into the living room where Erna lay unconscious. Now, as then, she mastered it.

Never mind that her legs were trembling as she stepped out of the phone booth and joined Peggy. They got her there. And down the corridor. And into Erna's room.

It helped that she looked so unlike herself. There was hardly any color, even in her lips; above her high cheekbones her eyes were not merely deep-set, they were sunken now, and smudgy-looking. Under the sheet, which was pulled up to her chin, her body seemed strangely flat and unsubstantial. A ghost of Erna, with Oliver hovering over her, not unlike a ghost himself.

"Hi, Erna," said Peggy heartily. Always there with the cue.

"Hello, dear. How are you?" chirped Dee.

"Hi." Erna's response came after quite a long pause, and from what seemed a long distance. A ghost of her usually over-loud voice. But there was recognition in her smudged eyes. They were fastened on Dee, who had a sudden, shivery recollection of Erna's last words to her: "You've got no call to hate me." Was she getting ready to say something like that now? Was that a sneer on her face, or a lopsided smile? There. Her mouth was working, shaping itself for the message, whatever it was, that was on its way. Slow but sure; nothing, nothing could stop it. "Dee." The same faraway voice, after the same disproportionate effort. "Dee, you sure do make a mean Manhattan."

It must be funny, because Peggy and Oliver were both laughing, quoting it as people do a child's bright saying. "How about that? You sure do make a mean Manhattan.'"

So after a moment Dee laughed too. And she said, "I'm terribly sorry, Erna—"

"It wasn't your fault," Oliver hurried to assure her. "She knows it was the gas. You mustn't be upset about it, Dorothea."

"Gas," Erna echoed laboriously. "Only joking."

So much for Dee's fears. And for Erna's flashes of lucidity. Whatever had sparked them, liquor or intuition, they were extinguished now, forgotten, lost in the blur that, for Erna, obscured everything except the Manhattans. Amid such general confusion, the fact that she did not remember turning on the gas would have no special significance. Why should it? Why should she distrust Dee, who had, after all, helped to save her?

Oh, it was funny, all right. No one but Dee knew how funny. Or ever would know; wrecked though her plan was, it remained her secret. She could be thankful for that. She was thankful. But at the same time frustration boiled up in her, a surge of rage and contempt that Erna should be lying here, as gullible and stupid and alive as ever. Typical of her—typical—to reduce what had happened tonight to the level of a family joke.

If only it could be done without planning! To be able to dispense with subtlety, throw caution to the winds, strike out in forthright, soul-satisfying violence, regardless of the consequences ...

Insanity. Dee slammed the door of her mind on it. The trees, not the woods. The safe, meaningless minutiae.

"I just talked to Mr. Fly on the phone," she said. "He was delighted to hear you're okay. Sent you his best." The lopsided smile—not a sneer at all—reappeared on Erna's face. A few more minutes of good cheer and inanities, and the ordeal was over; Peggy and Dee said their goodnights.

"Oliver?" Dee asked from the door.

"I'll stick around a while," he said. He was holding Erna's hand. "Unless you want me to drive you home—"

But there was no need for that, of course. Peggy had driven to the hospital; Dee could ride home with her. It was what Peggy expected—how peculiar, if Dee were to announce that she preferred to walk, really, how peculiar—and that made it mandatory. Even now Dee could not afford the unexpected. And the ride home was not quite the end, either. Surely Peggy would think it strange, not to be invited in for a nightcap? Yes. Surely.

"A nightcap? Dee dear, you must be bushed. Wouldn't you rather I just toddled on home and let you fall into bed? You don't have to be polite with me. Of course if you really want me to—"

"Really," Dee assured her, with a sinking heart. "Please, you'll be doing me a favor."

Mr. Fly had left a note for her on the hall table, informing her—in his headlong, breathless-looking handwriting—that he could be reached, if need be, at the Self-Culture Club meeting; that he looked forward to seeing her at her early convenience; and that he was faithfully hers.

"Poor old boy," she said. "What a state he was in about Erna! I will admit, he scared the wits out of me, galloping down the stairs like that. I couldn't make head or tail of what he was saying at first. But if it hadn't been for Mr. Fly ..."

Peggy nodded solemnly. "It would have been too late, by the time Ollie got home. Gives you the shivers to think about it, doesn't it?"

But no amount of shivers could get her off the subject; the next half hour—which, in its quiet way, was the worst of the evening for Dee—was devoted to a rehashing of Erna's close call, in exhaustive and exhausting detail. Plus all its ramifications: Erna's personality, with special emphasis on what Peggy referred to as her drinking problem; her history as a misfit resident of Rushford; her inadequacies, so apparent to everyone except Oliver ("She must be good in bed," said Peggy); and, inevitably, yesterday's quarrel between her and Dee.

Rather tricky, this last bit, but Dee was prepared for it. She ought to be, since it was her own doing that Peggy knew of the quarrel at all. If telling her had been a mistake, she had no one to blame but herself.

"We patched it up," she said. They were sitting in the "brown study" with their brandies, Dee in one of the big chairs, and across from her on the sofa, Peggy, bright-eyed, sharp-nosed, eternally vigilant. "I was the one that took the initiative, but I think she was just as anxious as I was to make it up. She certainly didn't hold back when I asked her down for a drink."

"It's more than I would have done. Asking her, I mean. Whatever it was she said to you yesterday about Chad, it got to you. You looked like you'd been put through the wringer. I'm not sure I could be all that forgiving."

"I wouldn't be with everybody, either. But Erna ..." She swirled her brandy pensively. "After all, she is part of the family. All the family I've got, Oliver and Erna. And they're leaving. I suppose that was part of it—somehow I couldn't bear the idea of letting her go, after all these years, without at least making the gesture. And I knew it was up to me, I knew how timid she'd feel about taking the first step, no matter how much she might want to."

"But if she really hates you, the way you said—"

"I was still pretty shaken up when I said that. Now I'm not so sure. She resents me, all right, and in a way I can see why. But hate's probably too strong a word. Just because she blew up and said some things she didn't really mean—Well, so does everybody, once in a while. So did I. You can't ever un-say the things you shouldn't have said, of course, but at least you can say you're sorry. That's how it was with Erna and me. Apologies all around, and a mutual agreement to let bygones be bygones."

"Drinks all around too," said Peggy, with a reminiscent grin. "Don't forget the mean Manhattans."

"I'm not likely to." Dee smiled back at her: the tricky bit was safely past. And in the process of getting past it, she had felt the first faint stirrings of another plan. Or anyway, the germ of one that was planted in yesterday's talk with Peggy, and that might grow and flourish. Erna could be dangerous, Peggy had said. If she was really around the bend she could be dangerous. To Dee, for instance; and if Dee in defending herself ... Later. It was something else that must wait until later.

Now she went on, in a tone of gentle thoughtfulness, "She was nervous to begin with, I suppose that's why the drinks hit her the way they did. They honestly weren't that strong. And then she'd obviously had a beer or two in advance. Maybe more, I wouldn't know."

"She could have been swilling away all afternoon," Peggy contributed. "It's been known to happen."

"Well, anyway. She seemed in fairly good shape at first—nervous, as I say, but that was natural under the circumstances—and then all at once, whammo, absolutely stoned. I thought she was going to pass out before I got her upstairs. If I'd had any idea she was going to come to and—Well, of course it never entered my head or I wouldn't have left her alone."

"Of course not. Why should it? Look here, Dee, you're not getting any silly notions about blaming yourself, are you?" Peggy got out of her chair and crossed the room, to peer sternly into Dee's face. "You've got better sense than that, I hope." And she launched into quite a little speech about what a good sister-in-law Dee was, how long-suffering and sympathetic and generous; what a sterling character in general. It was heart-warming, proof positive that Dee had managed to pluck a sort of triumph out of tonight's defeat. The others—Mr. Fly, Oliver, Erna herself—offered little or no challenge. But Peggy, dear old acid-test Peggy ...

They had been here before, she thought as they kissed each other goodnight and she closed the door behind Peggy. What she felt now was what she had felt the night it started, the night of the dinner party and her first little lie. The same elation—I pulled it off, I convinced even Peggy—and the same bone-deep apprehension, almost as if she had foreseen how far it was going to bring her, that harmless little face-saving lie.

So far, so far. Yet not far enough. For the essence of tonight was failure; no amount of fringe successes could change the fact that Erna was not dead but alive, as much of a menace as ever.

And Dee was so mortally tired. That was the difference between now and the first night. She had felt equal, then, to whatever lay ahead. Oh yes, she could handle it, she was the independent, self-reliant Dee Morris all her friends took her to be. Maybe a little too independent to be lucky in love: the men she had chosen, either deliberately or by chance, had so often been the weak ones, the broken reeds. It was not an unusual pattern for her sort of woman.

Except that now, slumping against the door jamb, she did not feel like any sort of woman. It was as if the public-image Dee, so real and solid even to herself, had been stripped away like a cardboard mask, exposing the lonely lost child who had been there all these years. Cowering there behind her false shelter, longing for a hand to hold on to, as Erna was no doubt clinging to Oliver's at this very moment; yearning for someone else to make the decisions and shoulder the responsibility.

Yet the one hand that might have been her mainstay—Chad's—she had struck aside, refusing, out of a perverse kind of pride, to admit her need of it. Pride? Or fear? Something about Chad had scared her, right from the start; maybe it was her recognition that here, at last, was a man not only strong enough for her to lean on, but perceptive enough to see beyond the cardboard mask. Too perceptive. Dangerous. Unforgivable. He saw too much, knew too much, more than she could bear. But what a cruel paradox it was, that the very qualities that drew her to him should force her to push him away!

All right. A cruel paradox. She pulled her head up and straightened her back. Chad was gone, lost, as permanently out of her life as if he had in fact been on the plane that crashed. She might as well get used to the idea, and along with it, to the loneliness that, for an unguarded moment, had all but engulfed her. Because that was how it was going to be, world without end, amen. Now, more than ever before, she had no one to depend on but herself. No one even to confide in, let alone look to for comfort or help. The line she had crossed tonight put her forever out of touch with most of her fellow human beings.

As for the self-pitying lost child business, that was so much nonsense, the result of nervous strain and fatigue. She was no child, she was a woman who knew what she must do, but not yet how; and the sooner she quit feeling sorry for herself and knuckled down to her problem the sooner she would find the answer.

She crossed the living room—was it possible that only a few hours had passed since Erna sat here spouting her maudlin sisterly advice?—and went on into the study to clear away the brandy glasses and ash trays and turn off the lights. Back through the living room and into the kitchen; it gave her an ugly little jolt to see the bottle of sleeping capsules still there beside the sink, instead of in the bathroom medicine cabinet where it belonged. How could she have forgotten to put it away? How would she have explained, if someone had noticed and wondered what it was doing out here?

She had the bottle in her hand when she heard a sound behind her. She turned, and saw Chad standing in the doorway to the pantry.

EIGHTEEN

Her heart gave a leap of incredulous, incredible joy.

Then her mind, which had simply stopped functioning for the first instant, whirred back into action. Mirage. Hallucination. She must be even tireder than she had realized, even closer to the ragged edge. It would pass, of course. Only a momentary aberration.

She closed her eyes. When she opened them again, Chad was a step closer to her than before. The ceiling light fell sharply on his Indian-black hair and bony face. He looked anxious, not sure whether to smile or not.

"I'm sorry if I scared you," he said, and his thin, strong hand made a tentative movement in her direction. Left to itself, her hand would have rushed to meet his, as her heart had leapt at sight of him. But logic, not impulse, ruled her now. Her mind, as if to make up for that lost instant, buzzed with warnings, questions, suspicions. How much did he know? It did not seem possible that mere chance had brought him here tonight, of all nights; yet she could not be certain, even about that. She risked pitfalls, whichever way she moved.

Scared; oh yes, he scared her, now more than ever before. Trembling, she braced herself against the sink and faced him. He waited, watching to see which pitfall it would be. All right, then, so be it.

"Chad," she whispered. "Chad? I thought you were dead ..."

"Don't," he said. His head jerked a little sideways, as if in a spasm of physical pain. "We can skip all that, Dee. Whatever you thought for a while—and maybe you did believe it, maybe you did—you found out yesterday I wasn't dead. I know what happened yesterday. Tonight, too. That's why I came. Because I—"

"How do you know? Who told you?" But she already knew: the Fly in her ointment. And still there was no resentment, only this helpless amusement, indulgent, even rather affectionate. "All right, why did you come? I'd be interested in knowing what your idea was, sneaking into my house, spying on me, jumping out at me. You might at least have called me first."

"I was afraid you'd just hang up on me. And I didn't want anyone else in Rushford to see me, not when you've told them all I'm dead. That's why I left my car outside of town and walked in. Sneaked in, if you want to call it that. It was for your sake."

"Thank you very much. I suppose it was for my sake, too, that you broke in and hid in the pantry—"

"The back door was open," he said mildly. "I figured I'd better stay out of sight till Peggy left." After a pause he went on, in a different, urgent tone. "And I had to see you, Dee. Don't you understand? I have to say it again, what I said that day I left, when you slapped me. I know you don't want to hear it, but—Damn it, I have to talk to you! You have to listen to me!"

"I'm listening," she said. She discovered that she was still holding the bottle of sleeping capsules, and set it down on the drain board. He had already seen it, anyway. He followed, without comment, as she led the way into the living room. They sat, as so often before, in the easy chairs, one on either side of the fireplace. Indeed, it was like a parody of old times, with Chad lighting two cigarettes and handing one to her; except that he did not lean back, smiling. Well. Neither did she.

"I'm listening," she reminded him at last.

"All right. In the first place—" He stopped, stricken by another spasm of inner misery, suddenly bereft of the power of speech. The look he turned on her was the stammerer's look, of hopeless struggle and entreaty.

"In the first place," she said, "how long have you been here?"

Apparently the question startled him back into normalcy. His answer was prompt, if ambiguous. "Not long enough. I was halfway here when I got the word about Erna. But I wish now I'd gotten here this morning. I wish to God I'd called you weeks ago. I wanted to, Dee, that's not what stopped me. It was just that I was so sure there was no use trying. But maybe if I had—"

"I don't think so," she said. "Anyway, it's too late now."

"No! It isn't! Not even now. Because nobody knows but me, and I'm not going to—"

"And Erna. And Mr. Fly."

"I'm not talking about the way you lied. Who cares about that? It's what happened tonight. What almost happened tonight. I could hear you and Peggy from the pantry, that's how I know it didn't quite happen, thank God, Erna's going to be all right."

"Yes, isn't it lucky." Why was she stalling like this? She knew it was futile. Chad was not like the others. He was the only one who knew.

"Listen." He clutched his head in despair. "Do you realize how lucky? For you, I mean, as well as Erna? Do you think I don't know you tried to kill her?"

"So that's it," she said. "That's why you came. To accuse me of murder. Do you expect anybody to believe you?"

"I'm not even going to tell anybody. It didn't happen. She didn't die. So it's not too late, Dee, I'll help you if you'll only face the truth—"

"Look who's talking about facing the truth. And about helping me." She laughed scornfully. "None of this would have happened if it hadn't been for you. You said a minute ago, who cares about the lies? Well, I'll tell you who cares. I do. And it was on account of you that I told them. You call it helping me, turning me into a liar, accusing me of murder?"

"Are you denying it?" He leaned toward her, forcing her to look into his face; it was so tense and somber that she felt an incongruous stab of pity for him. "You can't, Dee. Not to me. Everybody else, but not me. It was the sleeping pills, wasn't it? You doped her drink and then when you got her upstairs you turned on the gas. It wasn't an accident. I can't prove it, I don't even want to. If I did, I'd be talking to Ollie, Erna, the police—anybody but you. Surely you see there's no need to deny it to me?"

"I had to do it," she whispered. "She—" He had drawn it out of her. She must stop looking at him. Must. Couldn't. The only way was to cover her own eyes with her hands. A childish gesture, but it broke the spell. She heard her voice going on, clear, assured, decisive. "She'll tell everybody that I lied about you, and why. Because you walked out on me. It's all I've got left, my pride, I won't let her make a laughingstock of me. Destroy me. I had to do it. There's no other way of stopping her."

"But Dee—"

"I'm not denying it to you. I'm not ducking the truth. What more do you want?"

She heard him sigh. But she kept her eyes fixed on her hands, which were clenched in her lap now. Chad used to admire her hands; she rather admired them herself. Shapely but capable. The silver bracelet he had given her gleamed on her left wrist, comforting and wide, an amulet. Was he looking at it too? Remembering?

He said wearily, "I want you to stop believing your own lies. You really do, don't you? You really convince yourself."

She clenched her hands tighter. Into her mind there flashed the memory of a rainy afternoon, herself in a fever of impatience to get home for Chad's call, fidgeting with her car keys while Peggy chattered on ... But he couldn't know about that! Nobody, not even Chad, could possibly know.

"You had to do it, all right, but—Look, Dee. It's been two weeks or more since Erna found out I'm alive. Where do you get the idea she's so hell-bent on spreading the word? If she was going to do it, she would have, long before now. Certainly she wouldn't have kept still, after the row you had yesterday. But she hasn't told anybody, not even Ollie. Doesn't that prove—"

"Pure chance, that's all it proves. She told me, didn't she? Well, then. It's just a question of time, the right circumstances, the extra drink. She'll tell, all right. She's been looking for a way to get at me ever since she came to Rushford. She's always hated me."

"You've always hated her, you mean. The other way round." Erna's phrase, her words, in that weird moment of lucidity and shared terror. Dee shivered, as she had shivered then. And she shrank back in her chair: Chad was standing in front of her now, bending over her, hemming her in.

"That's why you tried to kill her, why you might even try again, if you don't pull out of here. Don't you see you've got to? You need help, Dee, you can't go on like this. I can't let you do it. Don't shake your head. It's not impossible, you can break loose. Now. Tonight. I'll take you to New York, I'll see that you get help. Please, Dee. Please."

"Help? What kind of help?" He did not answer. She stared at his feet in their dusty brown shoes and cried, "I just want you to leave me alone, that's all. Just go away and leave me alone!"

"Sure, leave you alone with your damn rationalizations," he said savagely. "Leave you alone to dream up phoney reasons for everything you do or ever have done, yes, and to believe them yourself, anything rather than face the truth … Well, I won't do it, not till I've made one last try, and this time I'm not leaving till I've said it all. You're going to listen to me whether you like it or not. Look at me," he added, and he put his hand under her chin and pulled her head up roughly.

It surprised her to see how much grief there was in his face; the anger she had expected. She waited, unprotesting, in a kind of unearthly, eye-of-the-storm calm. Only, when he began to talk, she sensed the sound of impending violence—memory? reality?—the far-off purr that would build to a roar but still would not drown out his words, never, never.

"Your pride. You had to do it to save your pride. It was the only way you could keep Erna from telling everybody in town the humiliating truth about you and me. Never mind that she's told nobody so far. She might, she might. According to you, she would, and then there you would be, a figure of shame, a laughingstock. Okay. What about Mr. Fly? He knew it too, he could have let it out too. In fact, he did tell Erna. Yet he wasn't the one you worried about. You didn't feel you had to shut him up. No. Just Erna. Seems a little strange, doesn't it?"

The purr was closer now, louder, a sort of amplified, steady thrum. Not yet a roar; that would come later. She remembered its different degrees from the other time when he had said what she could not bear to hear, she could predict its rising course. So it must be in her head, not real except to her, inextricably interlocked with what Chad was going to say. Was going to say again. Was saying.

"It's not, though. Not strange at all. Because that's not why you tried to kill Erna. The real reason has nothing to do with what she knew about me. You did it for the same reason you hate her, because she's got what you want and can't have, what you can't even admit you want. Ollie."

Here it came, the stuttering motorcycle crescendo. But there was no protection from Chad's quiet voice.

"He's the only one you've ever been in love with. All these years you've kept it buried, deep, deep, hidden it from everybody—Ollie, Erna, yourself, me too, at first. It's stayed there, underground, at the root of your whole life. Of course you hate Erna. You hated her before you ever saw her—for marrying Ollie and taking him away from Rushford. You couldn't let go of him, any more than you could admit how you really felt about him. When you eloped with that impossible kid, whoever he was, it was your way of getting even, of working yourself into a nervous breakdown so Ollie'd have to come back. Even though he brought Erna with him, you had him here, where you wanted him. And the only way to keep him from leaving you now was to kill Erna."

"No," she whispered.

"Yes. With her dead, he'd stay here, you'd have him to yourself. It's true, Dee, you know it is. Look at the men you've been involved with—always the wrong ones, you made sure of it, you picked them on purpose. They had to be beyond the pale, like Ollie. Only then I came along, and—Dee, Dee, it almost worked, you almost loved me. I know it's too late for that now, but I can still do something for you. I can see to it that you get the help you've got to have ..."

"Help?" she repeated, as she had before. "You call it help. Lock me up in an institution. Turn me over to the psychiatrists." She saw them converging on her, cold-eyed as vultures, bent on stripping her bare, picking her very bones clean, leaving nothing unexposed, nothing. "That's what you mean, isn't it? You think I'm—not crazy, oh no, nobody's crazy any more—but sick. You think I'm sick."

"Of course I do! But that doesn't mean you can't be cured, with the proper treatment. You need professional help, a doctor, maybe a hospital—"

"Stop it! No!" The roar in her head was merciless, terrible, beyond endurance. She wrenched free of him and sprang up, screaming. He stumbled backward against the mantelpiece, and suddenly the poker was in her hand and she was lunging at him, lashing, battering the words out of his mouth, the sight out of his eyes, the knowingness out of his head ...

And after the rip of violence, the hush. She stood over him listening to nothing but her own ragged breathing, feeling nothing but the drumbeat of her heart.

Presently there was another sound, a diffident tap at the door. Perhaps she had been waiting for it; she felt no alarm, no hesitancy about answering it. She was still holding the poker when she opened the door to Mr. Fly, home from his Self-Culture Club meeting, brief case in hand, hair every which way as always, tentative smile in place.

"I hope I'm not intruding—" The smile remained, a forgotten leftover, while his faded, innocent eyes, leaping from her to what lay beyond her, in front of the fireplace, widened in comic horror.

And now at last there was no need to hold back. Laughter surged up in her—huge, raging, towering breakers of laughter. She sagged against the wall and let it come crashing out.

THE END

Jean Potts Bibliography
(1910-1999)

Mystery Novels:

Go, Lovely Rose (1954; winner Best First Novel Edgar Award)

Death of a Stray Cat (1955; reprinted in omnibus as Dark Destination, 1955)

The Diehard (1956)

The Man With the Cane (1957)

Lightning Strikes Twice (1958; reprinted in the UK as Blood Will Tell, 1959)

Home Is the Prisoner (1960)

The Evil Wish (1962; finalist Best Novel Edgar Award)

The Only Good Secretary (1965)

The Footsteps on the Stairs (1966)

The Trash Stealer (1968)

The Little Lie (1968)

An Affair of the Heart (1970)

The Troublemaker (1972)

My Brother's Killer (1975)

Mainstream Novel:

Someone to Remember (1943)

Short Stories:

The Lady Afraid (*Woman's Home Companion*, Feb 1942)

The Other Woman (*Collier's*, Aug 24, 1946)

Restless Redhead (*Liberty*, Feb 1948)

The Box of Apples (*McCall's*, March 1949)

A Family Affair (*McCall's*, Nov 1949)

The Bracelet (*McCall's*, Dec 1951)

The Heart Must See (*McCall's*, Apr 1952)

The Engagement Ring (*Thrilling Love*, Oct 1952)

Let's Start All Over Again (*American Magazine*, Apr 1953)

The Girl He Didn't Marry (*Woman's Day*, Jan 1954)

A Long Day's Journey (*Cosmopolitan*, July 1954)

The Ideal Gift (*Family Circle*, Oct 1956)

The Withered Heart (*Ellery Queen's Mystery Magazine*, Feb 1957)

Murderer # 2 (*Alfred Hitchcock's Mystery Magazine*, Jan 1961)

Just Like Jessica (*Redbook*, Feb 1963)

The Only Good Secretary (*Cosmopolitan*, July 1965)

The Inner Voices (*Ellery Queen's Mystery Magazine*, Apr 1966)

In the Absence of Proof (*Ellery Queen's Mystery Magazine*, July 1985)

Two on the Isle (*Ellery Queen's Mystery Magazine*, Jan 1987)

The Lady Macbeth Case (*Ellery Queen's Mystery Magazine*, Nov 1990)

www.ingramcontent.com/pod-product-compliance
Lightning Source LLC
Chambersburg PA
CBHW070936190726
48292CB00004B/1206